MY KIND
OF
MONSTER

A DARK ROMANCE

BY
LILITH ROMAN

Lilith ♡ Roman.

Lilith Roman Books

My Kind of Monster
First Edition | June 2021

Editing & Proofreading by Mackenzie Letson www.nicegirlnaughtyedits.com
Formatting & Cover Design by Lilith Roman
Photographs from Pixabay.com and DepositPhotos.com

ISBN 978-1-7394803-9-4 (Paperback Edition)
ISBN 978-1-9168889-1-3 (eBook Edition)

To find out more about the author please visit lilithromanauthor.com

AUTHOR'S NOTE

Dear reader,

Thank you for choosing my debut, My Kind of Monster as your next read. I hope you enjoy the ride on this lonely mountain! Happy Reading!

xx,
Lilith

CONTENT WARNINGS

Due to recent publishing guidelines, the list couldn't be included here, however I would never want to put a reader in an uncomfortable situation. This dark romance is a work of fiction, and it contains violent and sensitive situations which could be triggering for some.
Please go to https://lilithromanauthor.com/lilith/books/warnings/ for a full list.

MY KIND OF

Monster

LILITH ROMAN

To the woman currently demolishing the walls built around her
sinful soul by a society that deemed her wrong.
You were bred from fire... it's time
to let the flames burn.

Great things are done when men and mountains meet.
WILLIAM BLAKE

CHAPTER 1

HIM

There's solace here amongst the towering pine trees, at the top of the mountain peak that dominates what seems like the entire world. A sea of white surrounds me and other textures are only visible when the sharp wind ruffles the feathers of the pine trees, scattering more snow to the ground.

In the far distance, the other peaks loom, giants ruling over their lands. As I admire them, savoring the sound of silence, I taste a heaviness infusing the air. The world's gone silent. As if a predator looms and all creatures hide. A calm before a shattering storm.

Interesting...

I breathe in the heavy air and it fuels me, the cold burning my lungs.

There's nothing around this time of year. The birds are hidden, the animals are hibernating or sheltered, and the crickets are long gone.

There is nothing. Nothing but me.

This mountain is my sanctuary, my escape from this cruel fucking world simmering in its own filth. I bought this entire mountain, this peak, when I fucked off the world and left everything behind.

And as my old life ended and my new one began, in the calm of the peak, in the middle of this beautiful wild world, I both found and lost myself. It's a fucking Greek tragedy, a beautiful one, nonetheless.

It's still early, but I can see the sun hiding behind the mountains. The winter is harsh, the days are short, and dusk is my favorite thing to enjoy on this mountain. It's the only time of day I stop everything I'm doing, go out on the first-floor terrace and soak it all in.

There's nothing more satisfying than this view of the sun dying every day at dusk.

And as the heavy air predicted... I hear it.

My solace is broken by a blood curdling scream deep into the woods. That sound beckons me to follow; the fear in it is like a fucking siren's song, and the pain vibrating through the soundwaves is even fucking better.

This here is one of the reasons I had to leave it all behind. Nothing makes me harder than the blood curdling scream of a woman dominated by fear.

"Jesus Christ..."

I wait, my fists tense, fighting the urge to jump the fuck off the terrace, chase that delicious scream through the woods and find the scared woman. It takes everything in me not to succumb to my urges—the darkness embedded so fucking deep inside of me that you can see the demons in my eyes.

If you get close enough to look or are unfortunate enough...

The last strands of the echo her screaming left behind are absorbed by another loud shriek.

Pain and terror; I feel them seeping into my bones, wrapping around my fucking soul, a shiver rushing from the bottom of my spine up to the back of my neck. It awakens something in me, memories I couldn't taste anymore, emotions too far out of my reach.

The pain-filled scream sounds more defeated this time around—she's getting tired. I lick my lips and flex every muscle in my body as I try to hold myself back.

"Fuck!"

I have two options here... I either chase my cravings through those fucking woods and succumb to the demons lurking inside of me or I push everything back inside and choose to save that pitiful woman from the harsh winter cold and whatever made her scream like that.

Fuck it!

I find myself running through the house, down the stairs and out the front door before my decision made it to my inner monologue. I run towards the scream that's still echoing through the woods, without knowing what I'll do when I get there. I dodge through the trees that I know like the back of my damn hand, jump over the dips and mounds and feel my blood getting hotter, my dick getting harder, and a big fucking grin settling on my lips.

Fuck, how I love the chase!

God help this pitiful woman that stumbled onto my mountain. I haven't had a woman in a while since no one can come here this time of year unless they're on foot and have provisions for days. No one comes here anyway, unless they want to have their fucking legs broken or I have invited them myself. And I haven't invited a woman here since the winter started.

So how did this one end up in this predicament?

HER

I am stumbling with every step I take, struggling to run through the thick snow that touches the middle of my naked thighs, and the adrenaline pumping through me is my only layer of protection against the freezing cold. It's useless, all useless. I cannot see what is under the snow, I cannot see where the next step takes me. I could fall through a hole in the ground, I could step in a bear trap, but it does not matter.

Not now.

I have to push forward, run for my fucking life, because even if I fall to my death in these woods, it will be a whole lot better than what I am running from.

I think I have lost him. I hope I have. I run faster than my own legs can hold me, aiming to go down the mountain, but somehow, I still seem to be going up. I can hear him behind me, hear the screeching sound his boots make on the thick snow, but I don't dare to turn around to check how close he is. I keep running.

As the woods grow darker with every minute that passes, my nakedness and the high snow are not the only challenges

I face anymore. The sun keeps dying down, and I am left with no light source. The moonlight can't penetrate the snow-covered crowns of the old pine trees.

When darkness will take over, there will be nothing left. Only me and my worst fucking nightmare.

Many times lately, I've debated how I ended up in this predicament.

Was it my fault?

Did I do this to myself?

All the conclusions that one could reach, I have reached as well, but I have not yet settled on one. Depending on what he does to me, my decision changes and I realize all options might be true.

I was a desperate idiot, and he is a goddamn monster.

HIM

I'm deep in the woods now. The darkness has descended, and the world around me is completely quiet, except for her steps digging desperately into the snow.

If I want the benefit of surprise, I can't turn on the small flashlight currently sitting in my jeans pocket. I stop, stand near an old thick tree and I listen. I can hear her.

Light fumbling footsteps coming my way.

Ragged breaths as she slows down, losing strength.

How she stumbles and falls, more than once, but she picks herself back up and keeps going. Desperation clouds her breaths, but I can't help but smile at her perseverance.

Further back, deeper into the forest, I can hear another set of footfalls. Heavy. Strong. Determined. Now the screaming makes sense. He's coming for her; his steps light but deliberate, making sure that she can't tell where he is. He's chasing her calmly, without breaking a fucking sweat, because he knows there's nowhere for her to run. All he needs to do is follow the trail she's leaving in the thick snow.

My blood boils hotter thinking of this asshole being on

my fucking mountain.

I hear her coming closer and closer and without even realizing, she stops by a tree right behind me. My eyes have adjusted to the darkness, and I can almost see her. Not everything, but enough to know her position and when she starts moving again.

She darts away from the tree with newfound strength, pushing herself harder, but I'm right there. One arm circling her waist, lifting her from the ground, the other straight on her fucking mouth, trapping any sound that threatens to come out.

"Don't scream or I swear to the fucking gods, you'll wish *he* caught you, not me," I whisper, my breathing brushing her ear.

She shakes uncontrollably, she can't help it; I know she's both scared to death and freezing fucking cold. And she's completely naked.

Why the fuck is she naked?!

She feels soft against me, her body curvy, her bones covered by a soft layer of flesh, perfect for kneading under my rough hands. I hold her against me until her body calms, until her pulse slows enough for her to process what is happening.

As I press her harder into me, I feel her muscles relax. Maybe it's my body heat that's making her react like this. Maybe it's the lack of choice. I drop her back on her feet, still holding her against me.

My arm is around her waist and my palm pressed hard on her side, itching to fucking slide down her soft body, because her flesh feels so goddamn good under my touch.

And it does. I can't help myself.

More importantly, I don't want to.

This situation right here is my own personal dirty heaven. The chase, the vulnerability, the lack of consent. All screaming at me in songs of filth and desire.

I slide my hand across to her middle, then down over her belly button, stopping when the tips of my fingers only just touch the curls of her mound. Nothing better than unshaved, natural fucking pussy.

I groan at the touch, and every single muscle in her body, one by one, tenses against me. There's a tremor in her flesh as she attempts to pull away from me, but her head falls back—the tiniest, slightest movement that one would have missed.

I didn't.

She's a tiny thing, maybe a foot or more shorter than me and as my fingers reach her curls, I lean forward, my warm breath brushing the top of her ear. Suddenly, as my dick twitches against her back, she's shaking for a whole other reason.

She ran away from a monster only to fall between the tentacles of a much bigger one.

Oh, little siren, if only your screams didn't reach my ears... If only...

I'm aware that I'm a caveman right now.

I'm aware that in the real world, away from this mountain, you don't do things like this.

I'm aware of what normal human behavior is.

I'm aware I'm not supposed to get hard when a woman screams in fear or touch her the way I'm touching this one right now.

I'm perfectly damn fucking aware.

But we're not in the real world, not now, not ever again. Here, on this mountain, is my world.

The thump of heavy footsteps interrupts my train of thought, and I stop before I can reach her core. Pulling the woman up against me, my arm circling her belly once again, I try to assess how far away the bastard is.

His steps are muffled, but I still think he might be far enough away that he won't see us in the dark if we start moving now.

I spot a fallen leafy branch a few feet away and let go of the woman. I drop my hand from her mouth and she stumbles on her trembling legs. It doesn't take long to see that she's not going anywhere. She'll be lucky if she doesn't lose toes and fingers to frostbite or die of fucking hypothermia soon, if she decides to go on her own.

"Walk on my path. When I back up, you back up. Don't stray or he'll find you," I whisper in her ear. "Unless you want to run away from me as well. If you do, you better make sure I will never... ever... find you."

It makes no fucking difference to me if she does run, because if she does, I will find her. That asshole trailing her doesn't know the mountain as well as I do, no one does. I can kill him here without any trouble, then claim her as my prize either way.

Yet, I like to give my prey a sense of security before I rip it away.

I've never done it without prior agreement though. As much as I've wanted to force my dick in unwilling pussy, I'm not that fucking stupid. It was always a game, always one of my own creation—a game to fuel and sate my filthy non-consensual desires.

A game that would hold the demons in line and keep the monster hidden.

But this here, this is not a game. And if I kill that motherfucker, no one will hear his screams... or hers. No one.

She appears to be smart enough to know that.

HER

I stumble, unsteady on my feet. The cold has reached so deep into my bones that my body is failing me. I do not have much fight left in me, and I am holding on to whatever is still there to fuel my next breath.

Who the hell is he?

He's clearly big, big enough to lift me off the ground like I was nothing.

And warm, he is so goddamn warm.

Fear almost paralyzed me when I felt the air shift behind me. But when he lifted me with one arm and pulled me into his strong body, I damn near screamed with joy. He was so warm, and it took everything in me not to grind against him so I could absorb it all. Everything!

At that moment, I couldn't care less who he was as long as he kept me there, pinned against that warm body that saved mine from freezing. The rough hand covering my mouth smelled intoxicating, of cedarwood and musk, and with his arm circled around my middle, he held me tight. Possessive. Secure.

Then he realized I am naked. His hand traveled down

my belly, touching the wild curls covering my mound, and a mix of fear and disturbing arousal shot through me. My body ached from the tightness of my muscles and my chest hurt from the freezing breath I forcefully caught before my betraying body gave me away.

Nothing made me feel like a goddamn whore more than that one single moment.

Nothing.

After everything I have been through, one would have thought that cock was the furthest damn thing from my mind. I ran from one monster and ended up in the arms of another.

But that's the thing when you are like me, when the demons have crawled deep enough into your body and mind that nothing can get them out. You take pleasure from this.

Pleasure from the sickest moments.

Pleasure from the darkest corners of the human mind.

Pleasure from pain.

Unfortunately, the captor that I escaped did not give a shit about pleasure, even though he used that premises to lure me in. No matter how depraved I am, no matter how much of a whore I feel like right now, he never gave me this feeling. All I had was pain.

Searing fucking pain.

I watch the stranger as he leans over a fallen branch and it clicks. He wants to cover our tracks.

I am not going to argue with that. No matter where he takes me, there is no way it is worse than the dungeon I ran away from. No damn way.

I have made my decision. I will comply for now, even if he did just threaten me. Because in a new place, I can start from zero and find ways to escape. In my old one... I've exhausted all options.

No matter what... This is my only chance.

CHAPTER 2

HIM

I grab the branch and swoosh it around over the snow, bringing as much down as I can to cover the path I made. It doesn't matter if it's not leveled, in this darkness he won't notice the difference, not with all the dips and mounds of the rough terrain.

And snow starts falling again.

I don't need to look back to know that she's right behind me. Taking frail, careful steps, following the path I made in the snow when I came for her.

She's not running though. *Why isn't she running?* I know I warned her not to, but still. Any woman in her right mind would have the good sense to at least try after what I said to her.

We walk back, careful not to make too much noise through the woods, but when I fail to hear the footsteps of her chaser, I stop and so does she. We stand still and wait. He probably reached the tree where I found her, realizing there's no path anymore.

Suddenly a frail little hand touches mine and startles me. She's pushing something into my hand, and I realize it's a rock. I turn and look at her, at her very features for the first time.

Even in this darkness, I can see a faint spark. There's something hidden there. Something I can't quite place. Sorrow? Pain? Unfulfilled desires? Maybe all of them, maybe none. The darkness might be making me see things.

Either way, there's something there and I feel a powerful sense of possessiveness over it.

Fuck...

Mentally shaking myself, I grab the rock and throw it in the distance, listening as it hits a tree. The heavy footsteps hurry in that direction and we quietly carry on with our task, covering the path that leads to my house.

It takes much longer to get back than it took me to get to her, but we have to cover our tracks properly. When the woman loses her footing behind me several times, I realize she's not going to last much longer. I turn back and haul her over my shoulder with little protest on her part. She feels frozen under my touch as I hold her around her thighs and her frail arms try to grab onto my waist from behind.

By the time we reach the house, I bring her down into my arms, but she's completely still. She might be dead for all I know.

I climb the steps to the porch and hurry inside, straight to the living area. I lay the woman down in front of the lit fireplace, on the thick sheepskin, and from the sofa that sits before it, I grab the fur blanket and cover her with it.

But not before I get a good look at her.

She's not as frail as I thought, but as frightened and cold as she is, she might as well be.

Round hips and ass, nice big tits, beautiful legs and soft plump belly, are all wrapped in a deliciously curvy figure. I turn her on her side, facing the fireplace and I grunt when I notice the scars, old and new, some fresh, some soft, some deep, all over her body. It almost feels like sacrilege, marking this beautiful flesh permanently. I don't linger though, there will be time for that later.

I notice her feet, fresh blood covering them.

After I wrap her in the blanket, I bring over a couple of wet cloths and the antiseptic cream from the downstairs bathroom. As I clean her feet, I note the battering they took as she ran through the forest. It will take a little while, but they will heal, the snow offered her some protection from the rough ground.

Still, why is she fucking naked?

I plant myself on the sofa, push my boots off and drop my feet on the coffee table, sighing in anticipation to the long fucking night ahead.

I had other plans for her when I heard the banshee-like screams. When I got a good look at her lush, soft body, my dick got even harder, but then... I had to see her scars. I had to see her fucking battered body and my plans did a 180 on me—my dick will have to wait.

At least for tonight.

But my ardent desire to rip that motherfucker's head off with my bare hands is growing. I will find him. And he will fucking pay.

Yet, I wonder if she realizes that she ran from one monster just to end up in the clutches of a different one. I wonder...

HER

Pain, so much pain...

He is right there, at the edge of the dungeon that he calls my room, watching me as I metaphorically lick the wounds that he inflicted on me. And there, in his clutches, I see the branding iron and I'm both afraid and confused.

He watches me watch him, and even in the darkness, I can see that sleazy smile plastered all over his disgusting face.

I push myself further back until I hit the wet, cold wall behind me, and I wonder what his plan is. There's no fire here, if there was, it wouldn't have been so damn cold and humid all the time.

The strands of terror sear their way through my body all over again as he stalks toward me, playing with the branding iron, rotating it around in his hand, that stupid grin showing his menacing teeth.

"I know what you're thinking, little bird... but the lack of a fire won't stop me from using this here." He gestures to the branding iron. "I will leave my fucking mark on you. I will use it until it's imprinted on your skin by sheer fucking force, through cuts and bruises."

And I believe him, oh fuck, how I believe him...

"I know that's what you like, that's what you crave. I can see it in your eyes, little bird, you crave the pain."

But I don't. Not like this... not like this...

The terror grows, the adrenaline spikes, I start shaking uncontrollably at the terrifying prospect of what's to come and I scream... oh, how I fucking scream.

HIM

"Wake up! Wake the fuck up, woman! You're having a nightmare! It's okay, you're safe!"

And that there is the first lie I'll tell this woman. She's not safe, not by a fucking long-shot. On this mountain, there's no escape for her. Even if I wanted to give her the chance.

I shake her awake with more force than is necessary. She's sweaty from the nightmare she just had, shaking like a fucking leaf in a storm, and every muscle in her body is so tight, I'm surprised her bones aren't breaking with the sheer force of the tension.

Her eyes dart open, and for a split second I see the beauty in them before she looks down in fear.

Christ, she's gorgeous!

She never looks at me long enough, though. It bothers me because there's something there, something of interest, something that I want, and I need to see what it is.

I see the fidgeting and I follow her train of thought through all the possibilities she's thinking of, right up to the point she realizes I am not the same man that she escaped from.

I can tell she wants to look around, to see where she is, but she doesn't dare move, not even her eyes.

Should I throw her a bone? Let her relax before she realizes that meeting me might not necessarily be better than the situation she came from? She might have escaped him, but she's in the fucking belly of the beast right now. I am the kraken and this little siren landed right between my tentacles.

"You're okay." I finally make my choice and throw her a metaphoric bone. "Stay there in front of the fire, you're still cold. You need to warm up." I get up from my knees and head to the kitchen. I press the button on the kettle and get a cup from a top cabinet before I turn around to look at her.

She's sitting now, clutching the fur blanket for dear life against her chest, like it's her fucking soul and she's holding on to it. She's watching me, but not directly. Her eyes so wide, so tense and still, like she's calculating her chances, wondering how bad of a situation she ended up in. Wondering if she should take a shot and dart out the door now or take advantage of the fire and pick the right time later.

But she still doesn't move.

I turn my back to her, grinning like an idiot, just to see what choice she makes. I'm not a fool, I know she heard my threat when I caught her in my arms in the woods, but it doesn't matter. Her fate is pretty much sealed. There's no escape, not unless I want to create it.

As I drop a teabag in the cup, I hear her shifting suddenly, running towards the hallway opposite the fireplace, where the front door is visible from her position. She runs like her fucking life depends on it, even with her battered feet, but it's futile. Even if she's stronger and warmer now, it takes me only a few steps to reach her and grab her petite body in my arms as she kicks and screams like a banshee.

Oh, but how that sound fuels me, how it throws kindling

on the fire and the flames burn higher. How I want to pin her against the wall, rip that blanket away from her body, lift her to just the right height and shove my cock inside of her. In one thrust. To the fucking hilt.

She has no fucking clue what that sound does to me.

I put one hand on her mouth as I press her curvy, soft body to my own.

"Maybe I need to remind you that whoever you were running from might still be out there looking for you. I have a feeling he's not very happy that you escaped, and it will be a looonnng time until he actually gives up. Am I right, little siren?"

Her kicking turns into shoving, trying to push herself away from my body and her screams have now died down to grunts. It's not panic anymore, no, this is all her. This is her strength coming back, her survival instincts reminding her of who she used to be.

No matter. I like her better like this anyway—strong and unyielding. My dick grows even harder when the mindless fear mixes with the primal instinct, because the fight in them is even more appealing.

I love it when they scream though. I love the fucking sharp melody ripping from their throats. It fuels the fire burning around the demons lurking through my mind. She will scream for me, that delightful siren's song, soon enough. But for now, I want her to keep her mouth shut until that motherfucker leaves my mountain.

I need to hear her story, find out who he is... who she is. I'll get him either way, but what she tells me might make my job easier.

Before the long winter is finished, before any road access to this mountain is cleared, he's going to be six feet fucking under.

HER

He is holding me in his arms again. One hand on my mouth and the other one pressing me into his body. Fortunately, this time around the blanket is covering my nakedness, but it does not stop me from feeling his hard cock pressed against my ass.

Why? Why is he hard all the damn time? And why the hell is my body reacting to it?

I kick and shift and I fight to get out of his arms, but he's too strong and my wiggling seems to go in his favor since I can feel his cock pulsing against my body.

That feeling is sending a current through me and I kick harder to get out of his strong grip, fighting with my own filthy mind more than I am fighting him. I'm terrified, because I know for a fact that no good can come from my terrible cravings. My recent captivity proved it.

He did not save me; I have just been captured all over again.

"Where are you going to go, little siren?" he whispers, and his warm breath tickles my ear. "All naked and bruised, damaged inside and out. Where are you going to go?"

Where am I going to go?

On this frozen mountain, among the pines, all alone. No one cares, there's no one out there to look for me, no one missing me. Even if there was, he is right, I am damaged... no one would care either way.

He drops me to the floor and I go straight down on my knees, scrambling to gather the blanket around my body. I sit there waiting for the punishment that I am sure will come. I expect it now, after so long enduring it, my senses are on high alert.

But the violence never comes. All I feel are the vibrations of his footsteps on the wooden floor, walking away from me.

I turn my head and watch him go back to the kitchen.

He is making tea. What a perfectly mundane task.

Perfectly illusory.

He turns and does not even glance at me as he walks back to the sofa. Like he could not care less that I'm kneeling on the floor, like I am nothing... and I am... I am nothing. Adrien almost branded it on my skin.

I watch him as he sets the tea on the coffee table, and I can't help but pause and observe the man that captured me. He is tall, so much taller than I and built like a damn brick shithouse. He has wide shoulders and a wide chest, I can see it even through the thick red checked shirt. The jeans he is wearing are hugging his nice ass and thick thighs, even if they are a loose fit. He looks like a man built by the fucking gods, like he could kill with one hand while drinking his tea with the other.

Perfectly illusory.

I don't get the chance to check out his features before he sits on the sofa with his back to me. I'm not even sure I want to look, especially not in his eyes.

There is something about him, something dark that

makes me shiver from the inside out. And I fear that if I look in his eyes, I might see it.

"Come, little siren. The tea is for you."

His deep, raspy voice startles me. It vibrates low in his chest with an intensity that makes me wonder what I would feel if he shouted at me. Would I piss myself from fear? Would I run or would I sit here like a good girl? Would I challenge him for more?

What the fuck is wrong with me?! Have I learned nothing?

Finally, I get up and slowly walk to him, around the sofa, on the other side of the coffee table. I kneel, still covered in the blanket, in front of the fireplace, facing him. But I don't dare to look up.

"Drink." His tone is deeper now, commanding.

I'm scared to drink. Too many times before there was something in my drink, something to make me more... compliant.

"I said, drink!"

I jump at the commanding tone of his voice. I feel the vibrations go straight to my core and the command makes me scramble to the coffee table in an instant. Grabbing the mug of hot tea, I scurry back in front of the fireplace, before I take my first sip.

"Good girl."

It's disturbing, but I like the praise. I like how it makes me feel. There was no praise before, nothing at all, no matter how much I tried to comply. All I got in return was pain, so much pain.

I feel his eyes on me, so intensely watching my every move, and I try to suppress the need to look up, to look at him. I'm too scared, I do not want to know what he looks like. I do not want his features to match his warm, deep voice. I do not want to like it.

Most of all, I do not want to look into his eyes.

No matter what the tongue speaks, no matter how the body moves, the eyes will always tell the truth. I never fail to see the monster lurking behind them.

Too bad the last time I saw the monster, it was too late.

I drink from the mug of tea and it's surprisingly good. Chamomile sweetened with honey. It's delicious. I cannot taste anything foreign in it, no hidden substance.

"Drink, then lay down and go to sleep. It's still the middle of the night."

I look around me, eyes low on the floor. I am still in the living area, where am I supposed to sleep?

"Here?" I whisper. My voice comes out surprisingly rough, like I have not spoken in weeks.

"Yes. In front of the fire. You need the warmth."

I look behind me at the fireplace and I suppose this would not be the worst thing. My last dungeon felt like a cave, cold and damp stone walls surrounding me. This dungeon is different, warm and cozy. Rather idyllic.

But it is still a dungeon. I must not forget—it is still a dungeon.

HIM

I look at her, really look at her, even though she's cowering away from me. She hasn't looked up once, she doesn't dare to meet my eyes and I can't help but wonder why. Is it submission? Or is it fear?

But even if I haven't seen her eyes yet, I still know that she's beautiful. Dirty and cold, battered and bruised, but beautiful. She has round, high cheeks, pale skin, beautifully defined lips and dark brown hair, almost black, matted from the cold and snow. She looks... innocent, but her response to my touch in the woods tells me she's anything but.

Now, every little sound makes her twitch. The ticking of the wall clock, the wind outside the windows, even if I take a deeper breath. What happened to her? What did that motherfucker do to transform her into this meek little girl? Or has she always been this way? Somehow, I doubt that.

I find myself angry and I can't quite understand why. I doubt I'm better than that man, I doubt I'm gentler, but somehow I feel a pull to her that makes me want to avenge her.

"What happened to you?"

She twitches yet again.

I wait, but she says nothing. She looks like she's pondering the question, but it's not cryptic, no underlying fucking messages. It's a simple goddamn question.

"Little siren, tell me what happened to you." My tone of voice gets more demanding, but she doesn't seem to have any intention to open her pretty little mouth.

Fuck this!

I get up and in two long strides I'm right in front of her. She drops the empty mug and scrambles backwards, shifting fast from the sheepskin to the rough wooden floor, all clumsy and scared, until she hits the wall, the blanket now long gone.

She pulls her knees to her chest, shaking violently, and as I watch her with an annoyance that I can't suppress, I know one thing for certain—I'm gonna rip that motherfucker's head off with my bare hands.

HER

I hate myself. I hate myself for being this frail, terrified version of the person I used to be.

I used to feed on this. Feed on the fear that made my blood boil with need and desire, but that monster turned me into this—a shadow of my former self.

I got used to staying silent, afraid that if I said even a hushed, little word my nightmare would grow bigger, the torture would grow stronger, and I would finally give up.

I want to tell him. I do. Every fiber of my being is screaming at me to open my damn mouth and tell him everything.

But I'm petrified. And he is not my goddamn hero.

My twisted little mind has rationalized that if I do tell him, one monster will inspire the other with innovative ideas.

I know that I have not looked in his eyes. Yet somehow, I do not know how exactly, I feel like the man in front of me is a different kind of monster all together.

He drops to his knees in front of me and there's nowhere for me to run anymore. I'm cornered, backed up into a wall, and all I can do is shake with fear.

But he pulls the blanket off the floor and covers me with it. I follow his hands as he slowly tucks the blanket close to my body. Then, one rough hand comes closer and closer to my face and I still, a shallow breath getting trapped in my lungs, my muscles tense. He brushes my matted hair away from my face and that delicate, kind gesture shocks me. Before I can stop myself, my gaze shoots up, straight to his eyes.

I'm frozen.

Time stops.

The earth stops spinning.

The world becomes silent.

I am caught in the dark gaze of the man kneeling in front of me and all I can see is the deep blue sea.

I feel like I'm drowning.

I know in every fiber of my being that I am right. This man is a different monster all together. Terrifying, ruthless, demanding, unapologetic, and so goddamn beautiful it hurts my broken soul. My body is suddenly covered in goosebumps and I can feel them settle straight into my core.

Then I see them... in his eyes, his demons calling for mine.

My kind of monster.

CHAPTER 3

HIM

Jesus Christ!

She finally looks into my eyes and I am completely unprepared for what I see in hers.

Now, in the flickering light of the fireplace, I see so much more than I saw in the darkness of the woods.

Too much, too fucking much!

I see pain, desperation, dread, and a fear that crawls so deep beneath my skin that a million blades can't cut it free. But deep below the surface, beyond the recent events that shaped her current state, I see her beauty, her strength, her raw sexuality, but most of all, I know that I see demons that mirror mine.

I would have fallen on my fucking knees if I wasn't already here.

I want to ask her a million goddamn questions.

I want to demand she tells me what happened to her.

I want to shake her until her feelings of dread dissipate.

I want to grab her hair, pull her fucking head back and sink into her fucking mouth.

Above all, I feel a need to gather her into my arms and hold her until the shaking stops so she can breathe again.

And that need right there is all kinds of fucked up. An unfamiliar kind of fucked up.

I rip myself from her intrusive gaze, get up and settle back on the sofa. Yet, what I really want to do is leave. I want to go outside and run. Run the fuck away from here, from her, from this day. Because I know, deep in my bones, I know that this is the first day of the rest of my goddamn life.

But I don't run.

I can't.

She's not going to drive me out of my own home, out of the life I built for myself. No goddamn way. She will not change anything. I will fight my way out of this.

She will not change me.

"Sleep," I tell her. My voice rougher than it needs to be, but I can't help it. I'm mad, mad at her for no other reason but that beautifully broken look in her eyes.

Her image will forever be imprinted in my mind. Her beautiful, big almond shaped eyes, slightly curved upwards in the outer corners, giving her this hauntingly exotic look. They are a bright green, so light they almost look hollow. The deep brown of her long, wild hair and thick eyebrows emphasizes the contrasting color of her eyes. With her small, slightly upturned nose, high cheekbones, square jaw, and defined lips, she has this old-world look about her, reminding me of women from the black and white movies that I used to watch as a kid.

I've never been dramatic, I've never been starry eyed, but she makes me feel like my world has begun crashing down. It's an unsettling feeling, and I'm not sure how to deal with it. I know it's not her fault, it's mine. If only I wouldn't have had the fucking desire to be a hero.

Was that my desire though? Was it a hero that I wanted to be, or a hunter? After looking into her eyes, I'm not sure anymore.

I suddenly feel like I'm the one being hunted.

HER

The look in his eyes shifts and suddenly I feel like I have done something wrong. Yet, I am not sure how I reached this conclusion. It's a feeling, because his eyes don't actually look different at all. They feel devoid of emotion, yet filled with too many. They look empty, yet haunted. They make me feel scolded and soothed all at the same time.

And as if that was not confusing enough, he all but ran away from me, when in fact, I should have been the one doing the running. What is he afraid of?

No. It's not fear. A man like him has never felt real fear.

Real fear is not spawned by the anticipation of pain. Real fear is the anticipation of death. The long, harrowing moments before you realize there is no escape and you accept your fate, welcoming the peace that death brings.

This man right here *is* fear.

His deep, dark blue eyes make me think of the unknown dangers lurking in the depths of the ocean.

His wild and wavy dark blond hair, long enough that it touches the base of his neck, looks like he's been running his hands through it far too much. Thin crow's feet around his eyes tell me that he is definitely in his prime, and what is potentially a strong, square jaw hides under a thick, long beard, framing delicious not-too-thin lips.

He does not belong here. I don't mean on this mountain, but in this world. He looks like a child of the Old Norse gods and he belongs in Asgard.

He is not watching me anymore. He is miles away now, and I don't exist again.

I finally get up from the floor, holding the blanket tight to my naked, sore body and walk back in front of the fire. Staring at the flames, following their mesmerizing dance, I wonder what it is about a roaring fire. There's solace, silence, peace, and at the same time, a cruel, painful finality that can consume everything in its path.

I stand there for a few moments, but a soft touch startles me and I jump. I turn to find his back already turned to me as he walks away, and a pillow laid on the sheepskin that covers the floor.

When did he get up from the sofa? When did he leave the room? How long have I been standing here?

I reluctantly lie down, facing the fire, and I fight the sleep that beckons me to follow, because I know lowering my guard around him is a stupid thing to do.

Yet, I have no choice. The dreams swallow me anyway.

HIM

Fuck, I'm in a shitty mood. I twisted and turned on the sofa, I was hot most of the night because of the fire, and I took most of my clothes off. Yet, of course, trying to rest on the sofa was still uncomfortable. Not to mention that I couldn't sleep in case the little siren decided to run again.

She didn't though. She looks like she hasn't had a decent night's sleep in far too long, because she's completely dead to the world now.

Maybe she hasn't slept properly in days. Or weeks? Or... months?!

She's lying on her right side facing me, both hands stuck under the pillow, unaware that the fur blanket has moved down her body, just about covering her belly. Her folded arms, unfortunately for her, don't manage to cover her delicious, full pear-shaped tits.

Fuck, how I want to play with them, knead them in my big hands. Pinch those fucking nipples, bite her porcelain flesh and lick the fucking blood slipping out of it.

In the calm of the morning, she looks ethereal, like

prey that doesn't know it's prey just yet. It fuels me with an anticipation that I can't explain, like my soul knows something I don't.

Before I realize what I'm doing, I'm already on my feet, morning wood on full fucking display under the thin cotton of my boxer briefs.

As if she feels the danger coming, the woman wakes up and goes straight into survival mode. Untangling her legs from the blanket, she jumps to her feet, bright green eyes gazing at me in fear before she runs away. The blanket lays crumpled on the floor, and I feel the corner of my mouth twitch.

Since I'm blocking the way to the front door, she runs through the kitchen and goes for the first potential escape. Her instincts are on point as she turns towards the door that leads to the garage, but there is absolutely nowhere for her to hide from me, no matter where she goes.

I wonder what made her run. Was it my attention on her? Was it just my presence? Or was it my hardening dick aimed right at her?

I stalk after her, but I don't bother to run. My steps are determined, but my stride is calm, every step fueling my muscles with fire, and fuck, how sweetly it burns.

For a split second, I catch my reflection in the kitchen window and there's a great big fucking smile on my face that I have not seen in a long time, maybe ever.

I don't know what's going to happen.

I don't know what she will do, but one thing is for certain—I am the hunter, she is the prey, and this is not a game with rules priorly planned. This is finally the real fucking deal, and my blood boils with sweet anticipation.

HER

Bursting through the door, I almost stumble down a couple of steps and find myself in a large garage. I frantically look around for a way out, knowing that the beautiful behemoth is right behind me.

I do not know if I have any chance of escape. I am on his territory now, but it does not matter. Fueled with new strength due to his care for me that is so unfamiliar, I know that this time around I will fight until my body fails me. I will run until I can't take it anymore, and I will scream until my lungs heave.

I will not submit, not ever again.

I see a small door on the side of the garage and run as fast as I can, but my efforts hinder when I step on something sharp.

"Shit!" I scream, but I don't stop to see what it was. I keep going, pushing through the sharp pain in my foot and quickly get to the door.

I burst through it and the cold hits me like a punch in my damn gut. For a moment, because of the cozy fireplace,

I forgot that I am butt naked and outside, it is the middle of winter.

Running through the untouched snow straight downhill, towards the thick trees, I hear him further back behind me. I know for a fact that he can catch me with ease. He's fitter, bigger, stronger, faster, and I don't know if I'm smart enough to escape him.

I reach the trees and I feel it, a deep sense of freedom within their shadow. Déjà vu hits me like a slap to the face as I realize that I was in the same situation last night. It was a different time of day and a different monster, but I still feel like I'm caught in a disturbed loop.

How did my life come to this?

I dodge trees, jump over big stones, my feet burning from the friction with the cold snow. Yet, I feed on the pain and use it as fuel to take me further. There's pain in my side as well, a familiar pain, and even though the snow has only touched my feet, my side feels wet.

I don't dwell, for some reason I know I need to run. Strangely though, I'm not sure where this flight instinct came from, I felt a different kind of danger when I opened my eyes. One that has nothing to do with the fear I've been feeling over the last few months, and my body feels charged.

I don't look back. I don't know how long I have been running or how close he is to me, but I don't dare to find out. At this moment in time, I'm free. I feel like I can do this, I feel like I have a shot.

This sense of victory is short lived... Of course, it is.

Suddenly, something solid hits me from behind so hard that it knocks the air straight out of me. Screaming involuntarily, I stumble forward and fall on the thick snow.

It all happens in slow motion, somehow.

My arms aren't fast enough to protect my head from

the fall. My breath catches in my lungs. The heavy pressure pushes me deeper into the snow that grazes my naked body. A solid arm slides under my head way too fast, protecting me from the fall.

Ironic really. He's protecting his prey.

I try to push myself up, but he's too heavy. I try to drag myself forward, but again, he's solid. His strong arm that protected me from the fall is right beneath me, and on impulse, I sink my teeth into it as hard as I can. His blood trickles and a flame sparks inside of me. The sweet, rich taste fills my mouth, and it feels like fuel for my soul, charging me with a power I thought had long left my body. I can feel it, seeping from my body to my soul and with every shiver spreading under my skin... I feel alive.

He growls, startled by the pain and lifts himself for a second, just enough for me to drag myself forward from under him. But I'm too slow and he's too fast. With one hand, he grabs one of my feet and drags me back, scraping my body on the thick snow, my breasts burning as I kick back and scream as hard as my lungs can take it. I try to pull myself forward again but to no avail.

He's back on top of me and my demons roar, filling me with a sense of victory. A victory I do not want anymore... at least I did not think I wanted...

His weight is on my lower body, one hand splayed next to my head and as I feel the other wrapping in my hair, he pulls it so fast that it gives me whiplash. My head is bent so far backwards that my neck hurts, my hair is wrapped in his fist and his hot breath is on that sensitive spot, right behind my ear.

My body stills, yet the shivers that run through it are loud. I am not sure what my next move should be, because there is something lurking behind the fear that dominates me now. As I feel his hard cock twitching against my ass and my screwed up, betraying body twitching in response, I realize what lurks behind that fear.

Run, you idiot! Run!

I yell at myself, urging my body to do something, anything else than get wet at the feel of the beautiful, wild behemoth pinning me down. At the burning sensation he leaves on my scalp as he holds my hair in his strong hand. At the sheer power he has over me.

As if reading my mind, he pushes his cotton covered cock harder between my ass cheeks and as the rocks beneath me dig into my flesh, I scream. I scream hard, pain and lust mixing together in this fucked up concoction that fuels parts of my body that I thought to be long gone.

Yet he pushes harder, grabbing my hip with his free hand, his fingers digging in hard, holding me in place.

"That's it, little siren, sing for me." His low, rough voice sends shockwaves throughout my body, just as his cock grinds between my ass cheeks and his fingers bruise my flesh.

I feel pain on my front as I am pushed harder into the forest floor, pain as he bruises my hip, pain as he forcefully pulls my hair, bending my neck backwards. Yet, pleasure floods every single fiber of my being.

And I scream! Oh, how I fucking scream.

My flesh betrays me in ways I cannot control. My mind wanders and memories of the person I used to be come back to me. I almost remember who I was, the dark woman chasing the ride of her life. Searching for monsters that could rule her, for demons that could fight her own.

I shiver as those memories flood my mind.

Suddenly, he sinks his teeth into my shoulder, and I scream harder as I feel the hot trickling of blood running down. His hand lets go of my hip, and the next thing I know, his dick is no longer grinding between my ass cheeks, but his hand is.

Without warning, he pushes something between my folds, straight inside my pussy. I moan and scream at the same time as I feel, what seems like two thick fingers, stretching me. He's pushing violently in and out of my core, stroking nerves I did not even know I had, filling me with feral sensations I did not know I could feel.

My ass instinctively lifts off the ground and I curse my betraying body again. Screams and moans that leave my throat meld together as I all but grind myself on him, his fingers fucking my pussy so hard I think I'm going to break in half and the world will explode into chaos.

He pulls my hair harder, forcing me to lift on my elbows and the pain mixes with the sick, dirty pleasure that he's giving me. This here is true danger, he is ripping my body away from my mind—the one that knows that it has to flee from the one that craves to stay.

I feel like a goddamn whore!

Because I want it... Because I like it.

HIM

I'm straddling her thighs now, two fingers pushing hard inside her tight, wet cunt and god fucking damnit, she looks beautiful. Naked and so fucking hot, I swear there's steam rising from the snow beneath her. Her hair is wrapped around my fist, her head bent back uncomfortably, and her screams and moans mix together into the most beautiful song I've ever heard.

I watch the blood sliding out of the bite mark she left on my skin, and I'd be mad if she wouldn't have moaned when it touched her tongue. Funny how the body betrays the mind, how her brain is clearly screaming at her to flee, but her body is digging its heels into the ground to keep her in place. Then I watch the thin strands of blood trickle down her shoulder where I bit her, and I want to lick it off then give her a taste. I want to mix her blood with mine in her pretty fucking mouth.

So I do.

I lean over, swipe my tongue over the bite mark, then force her head to the side so she can face me. Her bright green eyes are a shade darker, and I can see the conflict

49

within her. Her demons are dancing, but the woman is cowering away scared.

She's fucking beautiful. Just like that, with fear painted all over her face and lust seeping out of her eyes. *Fucking beautiful!*

I force my bloodied tongue into her mouth and kiss her so violently I probably split her bottom lip open. She fights me with everything she has. She's pushing me out of her mouth with her tongue, trying to force it closed, screaming into it, fighting with me in a game of pain and lust. Yet, she doesn't realize that she's pushing herself against me at the same time, her body closer, her mouth harder onto mine.

As I force a third finger inside her tight, dripping cunt, she screams into my mouth and I smile. She clenches around my fingers so tight, I swear she's cutting off the circulation. If she wasn't so conflicted, she would be close to riding them by now.

"That's it, little siren, sing me a song..." I speak against her mouth. Like she's suddenly jolted awake by my voice, she sinks her teeth into my bottom lip, and in a moment of weakness on my part, she manages to drag herself forwards, away from my grip. I catch her leg, but she's slippery from the snow and I lose it as she lifts herself up and starts to run again.

As I get up, ready to stretch this game and run after her, I look down for a split second. On the right, where the side of her abdomen would have been pressed on the ground, the snow is soaked in crimson.

She's bleeding.

Suddenly, I'm running after her for a whole different reason. It's not a game anymore, and I'm not entirely sure why I care. I reach her faster than before, wrap my arms around her body and lift her off the ground, turning us towards the house as she kicks and screams with all her might.

She kicks me in the shins, in the knees, and just about everywhere she can reach, but I don't care. She's a tiny fucking thing, not thin, but tiny, she's barely skimming the surface.

"Stop it, woman! You're fucking bleeding!" I rasp at her.

"Of course, I'm bleeding, you goddamn idiot! You bit me!" This is the first time I hear her voice, not her screaming, not her whispering, her actual voice. It's like a fucking melody when she talks, soft and warm. Her voice is sweet, but low, and I swear it sounds like she sings when she yells at me.

She's quite literally a fucking siren, calling for me.

After all these years...

"No, not your shoulder, your belly, your side." As I say that, she stills in my arms and attempts to look down. I follow her gaze and see crimson drops in the snow beneath her.

I put her down and wrap a hand around the back of her neck, holding her so she doesn't bolt again. I turn her around and there it is. On the side of her abdomen, just under her ribs, there's a piercing wound, but there's nothing in it. No branch that maybe pierced her skin when I pushed her on the ground, it's not a knife wound either. It looks like a new wound that didn't have a chance to fully close before the healing process started.

She uses her hand to wipe the blood to get a better look, but doesn't seem surprised by it.

"It will heal eventually," she states like a simple matter of fact.

I frown as I look into her eyes, and the calm, nonchalant tone of her voice bothers me more than it should. Like this is nothing special; she brushes it off like it happens all the time.

And then it hits me. It did happen, I don't know for how long, but it did. For a moment, I forgot all the old and new scars dusted over her body. For a moment, I forgot about that son of a bitch chasing her on *my* mountain.

For a moment, I forgot why the siren sang the first time I heard her.

I haul her over my shoulder as she kicks and screams again, but I don't give a fuck. I need answers. I need to know where to find that motherfucker and kill him.

But first, I need to check her over and patch her up. As I watch thin strands of blood where her feet hit the ground, I make a mental note to check them as well when we get back.

I'm honestly surprised and strangely content by the power within her. She ran like her life depended on it through these woods, she braved the cold, she braved the landscape, even the rough ground full of twigs, rocks, and fuck knows what else. She kicked and screamed and didn't give up for a fucking second.

Until I sank my fingers into her seemingly unwilling pussy.

I felt her surrender the moment my fingers touched her core, and I knew, I fucking knew that the demons I saw in her eyes last night were cheering me on.

She's mine! She's fucking mine!

Whether she wants it or not.

CHAPTER 4

HER

I am so damn confused. He saves me, he threatens me, he chases me, he all but rapes me, and now he stopped it all so he can tend to my wounds?!

I am upside down, draped on his shoulder like some sort of hunting trophy and I wonder how worthless my life has become. When did I become an object, everyone's plaything?

After escaping one screwed up man, I was not expecting to land in the arms of a delusional one that keeps calling me "siren".

What the hell is that about?

Even though I hate to admit that deep down I am not

hating if he is implying that I have the same effect on him that sirens had on sailors, but I most definitely do not want that. I do not want to catch his attention, to be noticed... I just want to leave.

I do... don't I?

Flashbacks of when he pinned me on the ground run through my mind and my naked body warms instantly. He awakens something in me... something I thought was long lost, beaten down by the son of a bitch that held me prisoner for too long.

This beast of a man forced himself on me, and my demons gasped. Pinned me down, and my demons shivered. Then bit into my flesh and shoved his tongue, laced with my blood, into my mouth... and my demons sang.

I do not quite understand what is happening to me. It was pain that chased my soul away... and a different kind of pain seems to be calling it back.

Yet, it was not the same... right? He was giving me pleasure even before he finger fucked me so close to sweet oblivion that I'm kind of disappointed I ran before I came. The way his body connected with mine, the look in his deep blue eyes, his grip on me; it was all different. He devoured me like I was his last meal and he had to indulge to the point he licked the damn plate.

I should have let him lick the plate.

It most definitely is not the same as it was with Adrien. Somehow it feels worse.

There's menace in his eyes and my body is not the only one in danger. This monster feels familiar in a way I can't explain. The danger I'm in now is different, completely unpredictable, and my soul is already shattered, my heart fractured.

I fear that this time around... I won't survive.

* * *

He walks me back into the warm living area of the cabin and I'm dizzy from being upside down... or is it because I'm bleeding? This time around he takes me up the stairs to the first floor, where I see more hardwood floors and paneled walls, thick wool rugs, and a few doors along a corridor. We walk through one and he sets me down.

I stumble back and hit the cold toilet, but he steadies me, his big hands on my shoulders.

Dark navy walls, almost black, surround me. I lift my eyes to my right, and I admire the natural wood vanity, over the counter stone sink and the simple, thin, brass-rimmed mirror above it. *The mountain man has taste, interesting.* Thick, fluffy towels sit on various shelves on the wall to my right, and I fail to remember the last time something similar touched my skin. The door is on the wall opposite me and I wonder if I should run, but as my sore feet sink deeper into the thick bath mat, I think against it.

This bathroom feels rugged, masculine and rustic, yet modern and so cozy. I can't help but admire it.

I turn to the left, and I'm not sure what hits me when the incredible view assaults me. Potentially the biggest, deepest bathtub I've ever seen sits in front of the most beautiful view and I am convinced nothing will ever top this. The window covers the entire wall and that gorgeous view of the snow-covered mountains and the valleys that run between them is framed by two old pines. Like a giant painting masterpiece, a living one.

It's surreal, ethereal... it's addictive.

I cannot help but wonder, does this big, burly man enjoy soaking in a bubble bath? I almost smirk, but it never reaches my features.

I sit on the toilet and do everything in my power to rip my gaze from that view. I'm watching him as he leans over the bathtub and turns the faucets on. I could actually escape right now, get up and run, he wouldn't be able to catch me in time. But where? Where would I go and how exactly would I get there? In my current state, I won't get far before hypothermia hits. Plus, last night in the woods, I decided to come with him myself. I need to stay; I need to be smart about this—find the right time.

And that bathtub looks so inviting... I haven't taken a proper bath in months, and I haven't actually soaked in a body of water for all that time. I need a damn bath.

Adrien did not allow such luxuries. I got a bucket of lukewarm water and a rag, or at most, a shower under a hose and somehow, it was still my fault I was not clean enough for him.

That one treats his women well, for sure. I mentally roll my eyes at the thought. Yes... he fooled me though. I am the picture-perfect example of what not to do on the internet. They should put me on one of those posters made by the police to warn idiots, gullible and vulnerable people. Idiots like me apparently.

HIM

I turn around and watch her. She's lost in thought, sitting meekly on the toilet, clutching her hands between her legs. All naked and bruised, broken inside and out.

The fire that I saw in her only minutes ago is gone. The frail woman I found yesterday in the woods is back.

I'm not sure what I think of her. I like her frail, vulnerable and broken. Yet, when she fights back, when she kicks and screams, when she bites me... that's when I see her true self, that's the woman I want to hunt.

I look at her and notice that, as she predicted, her wound has stopped bleeding. I don't like it, the fact that she knew from experience.

She should *not* know how long it takes for her body to stop bleeding.

She should *not* know how fast her body heals.

She should *not* know what torture feels like.

At least not *that* type of torture.

I sigh, gather her in my arms, hold her tight as she tries to push back and set her in the bathtub which is now half full. I can feel her body melt under the hot water, her muscles relaxing instantly, exhaling a heavy breath I didn't realize she was holding in.

"You'll start bleeding again, when the water soaks up your wound," I tell her, but she doesn't respond. She barely nods. I don't like this, it's not that she's too compliant, I like them submissive in certain situations... well in most. However, now I feel like she couldn't give a shit about what I say, and it pisses me off.

She closes her eyes as the water level rises and her body slides down into the steamy water. I realize that she's so short, she might actually go completely under if she's not careful. I put my palm on her chest to keep her up and her eyes dart open, her body tenses.

I hold her still and my gaze fixes onto hers. I feel her muscles relaxing under my touch—she seems to understand.

The water turns dirty fast, and I notice how she looks at it. Embarrassment coats her high cheeks and for some reason I don't want her to feel that way. I turn the faucets on again, while draining the water at the same time, just enough to get as much of the dirty water out as possible.

It's not her fault she's dirty, beaten, and neglected. *Shit!*

"Are you hungry? Or thirsty?"

Her eyes shoot up at me. What a fucking idiot I am... of course she's compliant, she hasn't eaten or drank anything since that cup of tea last night.

I grab one of the glasses I keep on the side of the sink, fill it with water and give it to her. She drinks it so fast that I'm surprised she didn't spill a drop. She looks at it, and I see the question running through her mind. I wait for her to ask, but she doesn't.

I grab the glass and refill it before handing it back. She downs this one as well.

This should make me happy. She's drinking, she's feeling better, but I'm not. I'm not happy because I know she's not asking me for another drink because that motherfucker taught her that she's not fucking worthy enough to ask for anything or maybe she got punished for doing so.

She sees the fury in my features, and she freezes again. She holds my gaze, completely still, calculating her next move. But I don't give her time to think too much. I grab the glass and refill it yet again.

"You need to tell me. Who is he?"

She sighs, and I see the embarrassment on her face.

"I don't know..."

"Are you sure?"

"I thought I did... we met online. His name is Adrien. That is all I know, and I am not sure if even that is real."

"Where does he live?" I'm finally getting some information out of her. "Do you remember where you ran from when I found you?"

"You mean when you captured me?" For a split second she throws me a defiant look, and I grin.

She's not wrong, but then again, what was she going to do anyway? The town is miles away down the mountain. She would have either broken her legs, died, or got caught by that motherfucker.

"Yes, when I captured you." I make sure to hold her gaze as I say it. I'm not fucking playing around here. She's mine. And if that scares her and she wants to run, all the better. She would just give me the sweet opportunity to finish what I started in the woods earlier.

She sighs, takes a deep breath and sinks all the way underwater, soaking her filthy hair. The water goes dark again, and I get angrier.

I repeat the previous step—turn faucet on—drain

bathtub—refill.

Yet, even in that dirty water, her dark hair moves softly around her features and flashes of noir movies run through my mind.

"I am not sure," she says, as she comes back up, brushing the wet hair away from her face. "I thought I was going down the mountain when I ran, but somehow I still ended up going up. It was so dark, and I ran for a long time." Her voice is still meek, but so damn warm and melodic.

"How long?" I think I know what she's talking about. Parts of these woods create a strange optical illusion, it's something usually seen on roads in the mountains. When you look forwards it appears that you're walking downhill, it's only when you look back that you realize that you've been climbing the whole time.

"It's not like I have a damn watch on me!" she says with indignation.

There she is... slowly peeking through the fog.

I grin at her defiant answer, but my head is bowed, she can't see it.

"I don't know... I could barely see the moon, it looked like it shifted as I neared the time you caught me. Maybe an hour? He made a mistake when he locked the dungeon, and he didn't realize I was gone, so I had a bit of a head start."

"Dungeon?!" What the fuck is she talking about?

"Yes... where he kept me. Maybe it was a cellar... I don't know, it certainly felt like a dungeon..." Her voice breaks, and that stirs something inside me. Goddamn it, I don't fucking like this, being bothered by all of this! It's strange, unfamiliar... unnatural.

This was not my goddamn intention with her! But then again, I'm a dark, sick motherfucker and while a dungeon sounds fucking appetizing, I wouldn't use it to hold a woman hostage.

"For how long?" My voice is getting lower, rougher, my tone more urgent.

"Well... what month is it?"

Jesus Christ... she didn't just ask me that... *"November."*

She lifts her head and looks at me with a little hope in her eyes. "I thought it was later, I thought maybe Christmas had passed already."

You got to be fucking kidding me. Christmas?! That's what she cares about?

"I met him in April... April Fools' to be exact..."

"April Fools'..." I repeat, and I see my disgust reflected in her eyes. She knows she fucked up, she knows I see the same thing she thinks of herself; however, this is not her fucking fault. He was the wolf, and she was the fucking lamb. He was already out hunting, she just happened to be the willing, naive prey.

April... That means that six and a half months have passed since she's been kidnapped. Six and a half fucking months of...

"What did he do to you?"

Her eyes grow wide, and I can see the slight tremble of her body causing small ripples in the bath water. She wraps her arms around herself, suddenly aware of her nakedness. She gathers her knees closer, holding herself together, like she's afraid that she will physically break apart.

"Did he..." I trail off. I need more, I need to know and I'm unsure why I do. Yet, I feel like the knowledge will be fuel for my rage and I crave the rage this motherfucker deserves.

"Did he rape you?"

The water bursts in dozens of ripples. Finally her eyes turn to mine.

"The rape was the least of my worries..." her eyes go blank. "The only thing I'm truly thankful for is that my contraception worked... "

Jesus Christ, I didn't even think of that. She could have...

"But then again, he did ask me about that even before we met." A disturbing laugh leaves her throat. "It's funny really, he has this thing, he never goes bareback, even when..." she says, taking a deep breath, "even when he... he always ended up putting a condom on. Like I was the dirtiest goddamn thing out there. I never thought I would ever be so thankful for condoms..."

I must admit that is strange. I'm all for it, protection and all, but I must admit, a rapist wearing a condom is quite unheard of.

"Although..." She pauses, and her brows furrow. "He might have had some sort of OCD, I don't know... he wore gloves a lot, not all the time. Yet, when he didn't, he was quite careful not to touch me. Not with his hands at least..." She sighs, and as I watch her, I can see her gaze traveling somewhere else.

Just on cue, I see a streak of crimson saturating the bath water. She's bleeding again, she sees it too, but she doesn't talk. I can see it in her eyes, this willing conversation is over. She's closed herself off, protecting whatever is left... like a split personality.

HEB

This is too much... I do not want to say more.

He's acting like he wants to protect me, avenge me, but that's ridiculous because I know, I know what lurks behind the shadows of his eyes. I can see the demons, and no matter how loud he is calling onto mine, I cannot fucking answer!

He had no scruples when he chased me through the woods. He is a hunter and I am his prey. There are many ways of catching prey—luring it with kindness is just one of them.

I'm bleeding again... I thought this wound would have been closed by now, but I guess that's what happens when you get stabbed with a fire poker. I forgot that it hurt. Is that even possible? Apparently it is, or maybe it just melded with the other pains I'm feeling right now.

I look at the bath water and now it's pink, slowly getting darker. I might actually need stitches... but then, if I wait long enough, with enough pressure, eventually it will stop bleeding. It always does.

He startles me again, putting his hand in the water and pulling the cord for the third time, draining most of it before filling it again. I appreciate the silence.

He hands me a bottle—shampoo. I squirt enough in my hands and lather my hair. I'm about to sink underwater to rinse, but I feel strong hands grabbing me under my armpits, lifting me out of the water before I can protest.

"The water's dirty," he tells me in that low, rough voice of his.

I have no other choice but hold on to him. He turns me to another bit of the bathroom that somehow I failed to see before. On the right-hand side of the bathtub, behind a wall maybe eight feet long, lies a view that might actually top the one of the bathtub. The shower. It's tucked away in this intimate, dark space, only to feel like you're showering out there in the open with another massive floor to ceiling window.

He drops me on my sore feet, and I just stand there, taking in this beautiful image that should not exist. I'm not sure how long I've been trapped by it because I didn't even realize he turned the shower on. It feels like rain. Summer rain.

Something is happening.

I can feel it. The air has changed. It's heavier, charged somehow.

I dare to turn and he's naked behind me, joining me in the shower. I look at him, in his eyes again, and I see it.

An awakening.

I can't explain it and I don't want to, but I feel it in my bones. My body bursts into goosebumps instantly, and a shiver raises havoc through my spine, spreading fast throughout my whole body.

I feel like I'm going to hyperventilate. I take a deep breath, break eye contact and turn my back to him. Closing my eyes, I lean my head back and let the shower hit my face and for a few moments I allow my mind to take me back to my last vacation. Last summer, when on a hike, I accidentally found this amazing waterfall. I ended up stripping and bathing in it for over an hour, in the middle of the woods, just me and the chirping birds, the rustling of leaves, and the warm sunshine. It was an incredible day.

My daydream is broken by his fingers running through my hair. What the... is he rinsing it? I still, because this feels like something... it feels good, and I'm afraid that if I move, I'll ruin it. Yet, I have to ruin it, I have to, this is not real, it's manipulation. It always is.

"Wash yourself." His tone is hard, giving me an order as he hands me another bottle—shower gel.

I'm confused because I have not washed my hair yet, but I hand him the shampoo either way. I pour some shower gel in my hand and place the bottle on the built-in shelves.

I feel his big, strong hands massage my scalp slowly, and I have to stop myself from moaning, from leaning into that touch. I have to remind myself who he is... Only when he starts rinsing the shampoo out of my hair do I realize that I've just been standing there, in a trance, and I scurry to wash myself.

He leans over, pushing me forward slightly, grabbing the shower gel from the shelf. His body, just for a moment, was pressed into mine and the skin he touched feels electrified, tiny currents running through me, and my nipples are instantly hard. My damn body betraying me again.

I hear the squirt of the shower gel, his palms rubbing together and then the magnetic power of his touch is on me. Instinctively, my back arches, my body moves forward, but he stops me. One hand on my stomach, holding me in place as he rubs my back.

This feels like the longest shower of my life and I both wish to stay and run.

His hands move down my lower back and my instincts are

screaming at me to run. Not necessarily because I'm in danger, but because I cannot trust myself. His hand holding me with such gentleness and power feels like a subtle domination that only I could possibly understand, and it scares the living daylights out of me.

I grab the hand holding me in place and attempt to pull it off me as I push my body forwards, away from him. No use, he's strong, but I try again. I pull on his hand with more force, twist my body away from his, but in the next second my face and body are pressed on the cold window and I cannot help but shiver with dread and heat at my predicament.

If we weren't in the middle of the woods, on a mountain peak, people could see me. Naked. Pressed against a window. Looking down at them.

The hand that was holding me by the stomach is now pressed between my shoulder blades, holding me still. All I can hear is his heavy breathing, and all I can feel is his body heat and his other hand sliding down on my naked ass.

I begin to struggle against his hold, but when his hand slides between my ass cheeks, reaching that puckered hole, I stop dead in my tracks. He moves it up and down, seemingly cleaning me, when in fact, I am feeling dirtier then when he started. The hand on my back pushes me harder onto the window, and the other one slides further down...

Shit! My cheek is pressed against the glass, my warm breath steaming it, and from the corner of my eye all I can see is his chest. His strong, wide chest, rising and falling in deep, controlled breaths.

His big hand reaches my pussy, and the steam disappears from the window. I can still feel the slippery soap on his hand as he rubs back and forth. He splits me open and washes between my lips and I know for a fact that the soap is not the reason why his fingers glide with such ease. He does not enter me though... no... he is playing with my mind.

He moves away, and I hear the squirt of the shower gel again. I keep hoping that this shower will end, but it does not, and I just want to scream! My body hurts from the tension, and my mind just feels exhausted. I move to step away from the window.

"No!" Christ, his voice sends a deep chill through my body while warming it up at the same time. He terrifies and excites me all at once. He is like a damn tsunami—you have to run away, but you are fascinated by the colossal natural disaster.

And this is exactly what he is—a natural disaster, and I know that he will catch me, hurt me, destroy me, and leave the heartbroken aftermath behind.

His hands are now on my legs, going up and down, washing me.

He nears my pussy again and I can't help myself.

"I'm clean now, I'm done," I finally say with a shaky voice.

The next second his arms circle me, one grabbing my throat and the other cupping my slippery pussy from the front. My heart is in my throat, my breathing strained.

"I decide when we're done." And that was it. Short and to the point, and I have no other words in response. I'm shaking like a leaf, trapped in a shower with a man twice my size, holding my pussy in one hand and my life in the other.

How the hell am I escaping this?

HIM

Christ, if it wasn't for the blood still dripping down her side, I would have fucked her into oblivion by now. I can feel her cunt dripping into my hand, she's so fucking wet and the shower has nothing to do with this.

Not that the blood is freaking me out or putting me off, fuck no. There's something so primal about being battered, bruised and bleeding. However, I don't like this because I didn't inflict the wound. I don't know how deep it is, I'm not in control of this situation and she's fucking hurt. It's not just some kinky primal shit, this is the result of torture.

She's terrified, shaking in my arms, her body rigid in anticipation, making my dick so hard I could probably slam my way through this fucking tiled wall.

I don't think she understands yet that her fear is fueling me. My demons are dancing in anticipation of what's to come. If it wasn't for the bleeding—the fact that it reminded me of that motherfucker playing around on my mountain—I would have chased her through those woods, slammed her against a tree, and forced my dick so far up her pussy, she would have screamed for days.

I squeeze her harder, and she's silently gasping for air. I don't press on her trachea, no, I just squeeze the sides of her throat, slowly restricting her air flow, and I swear I can feel her pussy pulsating in my hand.

I wanna fuck her so bad my balls actually hurt. She's so soft and plump against me, so fucking perfect to play with, to squeeze and mold against my palm, my paddle, my ropes.

I can't fucking help myself, and I slip two fingers in her pussy as far as they will go, and her hands instantly grab the arm holding her throat.

At this point, I'm not sure if she wants to escape or just hold on for dear life.

I don't care either way, she feels so fucking good, she could do either. And I pump my fingers in her pussy as she claws at my arm and wiggles so hard against my body, it's hard to keep her still. I squeeze her throat a little harder and her pussy squeezes my fingers in response, so tight I swear it's cutting off my circulation.

I can't fucking help myself, and I grind my dick against her back, imagining what it would feel like to slip into her. Not that slipping in would actually work. She's deliciously tight, getting my fat dick in her might actually be a struggle.

My body trembles at the glorious prospect of having to force my dick into her. Oh, how it fucking trembles!

I can feel her in my arms, around my fingers, pulsating more and more. The fucking siren's gonna come. After everything she's been through, she's gonna fucking come around the fingers of a strange man that trapped her in his house, his shower.

Oh, hell no, not yet, the games are just beginning, and I have a feeling she might know how to play.

I bite her neck in the same spot I bit her in the woods just as I pump a third finger inside her tight pussy. Then I pull out, releasing her throat at the same time and take a step back.

She falls to her knees on the floor in front of that glorious view, and I don't know if it's fear or disappointment that brought her down. She looks fucking gorgeous either way.

Tilting my head to the side, I watch her. I wonder if she's that easy to break or if she's just pretending, unable to admit to herself that she's enjoying this.

Interesting.

CHAPTER 5

HIM

I step out of the shower and wipe myself with a bath towel, before wrapping it around my hips. I grab another towel and for a moment, I just stop to look at her.

She's there, on her knees, hands wrapped around her body, closed within herself. It's like her soul has left her body, shattered into hundreds of pieces, floating somewhere around this mountain, trying to stick itself back together without any sort of glue. She's broken, I can see it in her eyes, in her body language, in her rare and sudden sparks. Pieces of her soul are slowly finding their way back, but it's not enough and she's still missing the glue.

I lay the large bath towel over her shoulders and lift her from her underarms. This time around she doesn't flinch and it bothers me. I sit her on the countertop next to the sink, towel laying loosely over her shoulders. Putting my hand on her throat, I lift her chin, forcing her to look at me and my whole-body shudders when I look into her eyes. They're cold, so fucking cold, it's a disturbing, unfamiliar feeling. I can see her demons lurking in the shadows and I know, I don't know how, but I do, that if she was whole, this woman would be capable of great things.

Dark things.

Terrible things.

But definitely great.

"I need to look at the bleeding." Her eyes soften, like she suddenly remembered that she was hurt.

Letting go of her throat, I open the cabinet under the sink, looking around for the first aid kit I forgot somewhere in here. I can feel her gaze following my every move. I must be confusing the shit out of her.

Good.

It means that she'll never know what fucking hits her, never anticipate my next move. I want to play with her, taunt and tease her. I want to haunt her soul, then help put it back together only so I can break her apart again, time and time again, until she knows that I'm the only one capable of doing that.

Until she knows that there's no one else but me.

I rub my eyes and eyebrows, yet it doesn't help me figure out why exactly I want all those things. I never did before.

Why her?

HER

This is when I see him properly, and I try not to get distracted by his strong, naked body covered only by a towel wrapped low on his hips, or by the obvious hard-on.

Full black and gray sleeve tattoos are wrapped around his arms with so many different swirls and patterns that look almost tribal, old symbols reminding me of Norse art from my old art books from University. There is something on his back as well... a woman, maybe an old girlfriend; she looks wild, savage, ruthless, her hair flowing in every direction, wrapping slightly over his shoulders. I cannot see her features from this angle though, I can't understand her purpose.

I also don't understand mine...

I feel abandoned. Still reeling in from the fight happening within myself. My demons are dancing on heathen songs composed by the sheer arousal this man ripped out of me. But my mind is fighting with every breath I take, throwing warning signs at me in wave after wave, getting me to see how much danger I'm in.

I have not asked for it, I have not implied I wanted it, and somehow, I still feel like a whore for receiving it. I have been used so much in the last few months, in so many different ways, that I do not truly believe my body is mine anymore.

I do not want to like it, to feel it like I do. I do not want to feel the wetness dripping down my inner thighs. How can I control myself when this man uses me like a damn doll and my flesh betrays me?!

My throat still hurts; I can still feel his fingers around it. I can feel how my pussy clenched when he squeezed, I can feel the fire burning so deep in my core, seeping through my pussy every time his grip tightened. I can still feel the pressure in my head getting stronger, my gaze hazy. I can still hear the demons singing, and I'm not sure if they were mine or his. I could barely take a breath... and I smile. I fucking smile.

When he stole the nearing orgasm from me, I fell on the floor, mourning the loss of everything he gave me and everything he took away. I wanted his hand around my throat and his fingers in my pussy. I wanted him to carry on, I wanted my life to end in that fucked up beautiful moment, because it was perfect. A moment I chased for far too long.

I know he plans on patching me up, but why? We both know he is not keeping me. Is it just so I am more able, stronger, harder to catch when he will eventually give me that false sense of freedom and I will run?

He is playing with me. He's building a complex, an intriguing and utterly filthy trap and if I am not careful, I will fall right into it, even if I am fully aware of its existence.

It's like a twisted, fucked up game of survival. One that I am struggling not to play.

I clutch the ends of the towel with both hands and wrap it around myself. Hot steam clouds the bathroom yet I am getting chills.

"No. Open it up." His voice is stern.

I look up at him, then down and to the side and let go of the towel. I got used to my nakedness in the last few months, but around him it's starting to feel different.

"Straighten up and lean back," he orders me like it's second nature and I am compelled to follow blindly.

I lean back, resting my shoulders on the mirror behind me and look down at the poker hole in my abdomen, slowly spilling blood over my light skin. It is a calm, steady flow—nothing life threatening, I do not think. It is quite mesmerizing. Reaching over, I catch the flow and watch this essence of life running slowly down my fingers, eventually staining my palm and hand. Before I can stop myself, I lick one finger, enjoying the steely taste on my tongue. I always did love the taste of blood, there is something deeply primal about it.

I look up and the mountain man is frozen, watching me with feral eyes that bring promises of death and destruction. I shiver and he suddenly moves towards me, but I stop him, my bloody hand staining his strong chest, holding him away.

He stops and looks down at it. I cannot move. *Why did I do that?* He grabs my wrist and pulls my hand to his mouth, jerking me forwards. His eyes find mine again, that ocean blue pinning me in place as he brings my middle finger to his mouth, slowly sucking it, and I can see the flame in his eyes the moment my blood touches his tongue. Every single one of my muscles contracts at the same time, keeping me from moaning as my pussy clenches so hard it spreads instant goosebumps over my body.

He carries on licking my hand clean without breaking eye contact, and I do not know what to do with myself. I do not know what he is doing to me. This is primal, this is raw... this is me.

He drops my hand and pushes me back until my shoulders

hit the mirror and I can breathe again, my muscles relaxing one by one.

"Now stay still," he orders like nothing happened, like my blood is not currently staining his tongue.

He cleans the wound, and I do my best not to wince when the alcohol hits my flesh. I watch him as he threads a needle and I tense. *Fuck...* I look at him just as he lifts his gaze to mine. He does not say anything, he does not need to. I prepare myself.

He comes close, between my spread legs, with my pussy on full display, but he keeps his gaze away, fully focused on the task at hand. I cannot stop but distract myself with the hard, thick body pressed between my thighs—strong, built like a Viking god by blood, sweat, and tears. His body proves to be a good distraction from the needle sliding in and out of my flesh, because he finishes in no time and steps back, his gaze lingering between my spread thighs.

I close them quickly and wrap the towel around myself, suddenly very aware of my nakedness. I am not giving him any reasons to touch me again. I do not miss the flicker of a grin on his lips though.

"Follow me." Everything he says is an order. Cold and calculated.

I do as he says, jumping off the counter and follow him down the corridor. We walk past a couple of doors and when we finally walk through one, his scent hits me like a slap in the face. Musk, cedarwood, and something else... something I cannot quite put my finger on. *His bedroom.* I follow him in, stopping when he does. The curtains are closed, but I catch glimpses of the manly lack of decor. Every piece of furniture, rustic, yet polished, perfectly fits the environment. The bed is a work of art though. Utterly beautiful with a complex wood carving in the headboard—an image that looks like something ripped out of pagan books, framed by four posters fixed straight to the ceiling. Impressive, absolutely impressive. The lack of decor does not seem to affect this room at all, as there is cozy fur everywhere—on the end of the bed, on the floor, on the large armchair sitting by the closed curtains. I would have trouble leaving this space if it was mine.

"Put this on."

He startles me. I look at him as he hands me what looks like his boxers, a t-shirt, and a hoodie. I take them from him with hesitation, turn to the bed and lay them there. They look unfamiliar. Clothes... They have not touched my body in so long. How will it feel? After so long...

"What did he do to you?" his warm, deep voice asks softly, almost whispering.

HIM

"Everything," she replies to me as she watches the clothes laid on the bed like they're foreign objects.

Fuck.

"I don't know what that means, little siren. Tell me... what did he do to you?" I approach her, and she tenses. She can feel me, my body heat close to her naked skin. "What did I just stitch up, how did he do that?"

"Cast iron fire poker," she answers in such a calm matter-of-fact tone.

What the fuck? Cast iron what?!

I'm seething. My breathing heavy, my body tense. I wanna rip his motherfucking heart out through his goddamn throat!

"Fire poker?!" I rasp. She tenses and scrambles to grab the t-shirt, quickly pulling it over her plump frame, covering all the scars on her body.

I'm not angry at her. I'm just angry. I'm fucking fuming, not only because of that fucking bastard, but because I appear to care for some goddamn reason which pisses me off even more. I don't want to fucking care, but that motherfucker is not the same monster I am.

He's the kind that needs to die.

"Get dressed!" She pulls the boxers on and then the hoodie. Everything is so big on her and she seems to enjoy it, wrapping her arms around herself, pulling everything closer to her body. She looks positively adorable, drowning in a hoodie that reaches her knees. I'm a big man and she's barely half a human.

I give her a pair of socks that are far too big for her and tell her to follow me downstairs. It's past mid-morning... I need to eat.

* * *

An hour later I'm sated, bacon and eggs in my belly and she ate better than I expected. She even moaned when the coffee touched her tongue, it was delicious... not the coffee.

"He fed you well?" I ask her. I need more information. There is this powerful desire inside me that wants to know everything, everything she's been through.

She sighs. "Yes. Nutritious, not tasty. He said that he needed to take care of me, keep me healthy..." she trails off, looking out the window, to the blanket of snow covering the mountain. "He only did it to make sure I healed, to make sure I would survive... unlike the last ones."

"The last ones? What the fuck are you talking about?"

Her gaze is fixed, still looking out the window. "I was the third. The first two are buried somewhere in his garden. One of the first things he made me do after he got me was make me dig one up and look at her. Look at what she became and what would become of me if..."

I'm still, clutching the wood countertop, feeling it creak beneath my grip. *If what?!*

"Then I had to cover her with the dirt and bury her all over again..."

I grit my teeth, it's hard to keep calm.

"How... how did you end up with him?"

Her gaze shifts, looking down at the hands she's now fiddling with in her lap.

"I was looking for something, someone... we talked for a long time, I thought he was what I was looking for. He did an excellent job of pretending he was..."

"What were you looking for?" I watch as her cheeks go red. First drop of color that I've seen on her skin, and it looks good on that gorgeous alabaster. I wonder how the aftermath of my spanking... or my paddle... or my belt... would look on that beautiful skin?

I shake my head and refocus.

"It is not important anymore..." she answers. "I do not know where he held me... I do not know where he is, but he is definitely not close to your cabin."

"He couldn't be close, I own this peak, this is my land. Unless he's at the base of the mountain, maybe on the other side where I rarely go. There are some old cabins around, but the territory is vast. I know the people living around me though, none of them are named Adrien."

"Own the peak?" she asks meekly.

"Yeah." I brush off the worry I hear in her voice. "I know what area of the woods you were referring to, where the hill looks like it's going downhill, it's a start."

"I'm sorry." She drops her eyes to the empty cup she's holding between both hands.

"I'll talk to someone. I'll see what they know. Did he look like he lived there for a long time?"

"I do not know... all I saw was the dungeon... even the garden, I saw it at night, one spotlight aimed at the grave.

Everything else was dark. When I ran out of the dungeon, I went straight for the treeline for cover. I did not see anything else around." She's trying, she is actually trying, but if she doesn't know the area, the mountains, it's impossible to give me directions.

"What's your name?"

She lifts her gaze from the empty cup and looks at me, still and analytical. There's an internal debate going on, and I can see the wheels spinning.

She could just lie to me right now, yet somehow I feel like she won't.

"Suki, my name is Suki..." She looks at me like she told me the biggest secret she's ever held, like she entrusts me with this terrible burden. Almost like she needs to make sure someone does, someone knows her name and she won't disappear into the abyss.

But her name, it goes in through my ears, gliding through my mind, wrapping itself around it, knotting so hard that I know there's no fucking way I will ever pry it out.

"Suki..." I whisper. It spills gently from my tongue and I wanna lick it back in, unwilling to let it go. "Japanese?"

"Yes, my dad was a history buff. Loved the Japanese culture..."

I nod. "I'm Nik... Niklas."

"Niklas," she whispers gently and, *fuck*, if my name on her lips isn't the sweetest damn sound I've ever heard.

I look at her, sitting there on the chair like it's the most natural thing in the world for her to be in my kitchen, dressed in my clothes. I don't know what to do with her, I don't know where to put her because in my house, in this house, no woman has ever had a place.

Not to mention that my intentions for this one are definitely not domestic.

Most definitely not domestic.

"Please, let me go." Almost like she read my mind, she speaks in that small voice again.

"No." I don't hesitate for a second and I know why. This woman sitting in my chair is not the same one I ran after in the woods and I will not let her go until she shows herself to me. I can't even explain to myself why, but there's something about her, there's something hidden there and I need to find out what it is.

"Please," she whispers. It's like there's no power in her voice anymore, no power inside of her to make her fight for her life, for a future. She's on the brink of giving up and I can't have that. Not now, not when I'm so determined to hear the siren's song again.

"None of us are leaving this mountain until spring comes." We could technically hike, but it would take days and it's not safe. There is another solution, but I don't intend to tell her that yet.

Her eyes dart up and her back straightens at those words.

"Spring?!" Life's being bled back into her eyes at the realization that she will be trapped, here, with me, for months. I like it. There's apprehension, uncertainty, and whole lot of fear in that bright green gaze.

"I cannot stay that long, there are people worrying about me. I have to leave." And there it is, the first lie she's telling me. Funny how she only thought about these people now. I can't help it, so I start laughing.

She gives me a disapproving grin, merged with slight panic. I don't have time for this though.

"Come." I start walking up the steps. "There's nowhere for you to go outside, the temperature is in the negatives now, you'll die of hypothermia halfway down the mountain. If you don't get eaten by wolves that is." I turn my head to watch her reaction and as expected, her eyes went wide. Was it the cold or the wolves that got to her? Somehow I think it's the cold, there's a passion in her that would make her fight the wolves to death. If only she would remember how to bring that passion back to the surface.

I carry on up the stairs and enter the guest bedroom closest to my master.

"You can stay here." I don't want to linger. I don't want to be nice, even though there's some unnatural craving inside of me that wills me to be with her.

Suki... Goddamn it, her name... her eyes... fuck!

I walk out of there, leaving her in, and closing the door behind me.

FUCK!

CHAPTER 6

SUKI

S pring," I whisper.

I am doomed. It is November and I am supposed to stay with him until Spring?! Somehow I have a feeling I will not survive it. Physically, mentally, I will not survive it.

I know that slowly I see glimpses of my old self come out to the surface, but it does not matter. It's not like I was the strongest person in the world before. I need to find a way. Be compliant, do what he wants me to do, make him think I am accepting my fate. I need to do it all so I can plan my escape. There is no way it is truly impossible.

I walk to the window to look outside and the view assaults

me yet again.

We are high, so damn high on this mountain and all I can see is the light blue sky, other mountain peaks surrounding us in the far distance and tall frozen pines peeking through the thick snow. There is an eerie calm in this breathtaking view. A gentle swoosh of the pines, the sparse white clouds moving gently in the sky and the odd bird gliding above the trees. It is snowing, big fluffy snowflakes layering on the top of the trees and I cannot move. I cannot detach myself from this.

I need to get out!

Suddenly I feel hot, so goddamn hot, I just want to be there, touched by those floating snowflakes, buried by the sheer beauty of this view. If I wasn't a prisoner in this house, I would want to stay. For this, this view. This world. His world...

I lied to him before. There is no one waiting for me, no one looking. My family is dead. There are no friends to talk about, barely acquaintances I accidentally meet once in a while in the corner shop. I own my apartment, so there isn't even a landlord to report me missing and my neighbors could not give less shits in that dump. No one misses me. No one even knows I am gone.

I could die right now and the world would still be the same, there would be no loss, no dent made, no Suki-shaped hole in anyone's existence.

And here, on this peak, among the snowy pine trees, it would not matter. No one makes a dent here. No one misses you anyway if you live here and then disappear. Here, we are all equals. We are the invaders of this beautiful, eerie scenario and it does not matter whether we stay or leave. We are privileged just to experience it.

* * *

The air is heavy, my skin feels charged with a tantalizing electricity that threatens to burn through. I open my eyes and he is there, standing before me, a few feet away from the bed, his dark blue eyes completely expressionless, cold and unyielding. I cannot move, pinned with just his gaze, making me feel like I'm lost in the deep blue sea and his eyes are the only thing keeping me alive, while drowning me at the same time.

My skin bursts in goosebumps and I shiver, only just slightly, but I know he notices. He knows I am affected, yet I do not quite understand how. There is an internal battle within me, one that I do not fully grasp, because I know for a fact that my body betrays me, my flesh weak and traitorous, and my mind is battling the demons who are calling for his.

They are getting louder.

Screw it.

"Can I help you?" I ask with newfound courage. The cold gaze breaks for a split second, I would have missed it if I blinked, but he does not break the connection. I feel the chill in eyes traveling in-between us, piercing mine and inserting itself under my skin. It is eerie, that gaze can freeze you from the inside out and I feel like that is exactly what he is doing to me. Controlling me.

"There's dinner ready downstairs." The annoyance in his expression is so subtle, I am not even entirely sure if I am imagining it. He turns and leaves the room, leaving me with far too many questions on my tongue. One lingers.

Dinner?!

I turn my gaze to the right, looking out the window I discover that the bright blue sky is gone and the light of the moon is the only thing keeping it from turning black. But the stars...sweet Mary mother of God, *the stars*!

I move the blanket and walk towards the window. For

the second time today this view hits me in the gut with an unimaginable force. I can see them all, all the stars, defined constellations, so bright and unobstructed by the intrusive, rude light pollution of the cities. This here is straight up magic. The night does not even look right, all this snow makes me feel like I am in some low contrast, black and white silent movie, bright but muted, dark, but too light for the night.

The wind picks up, the snow dances in waves through the air. There is something disturbingly beautiful about the scene unfolding before my eyes, secrets hidden in the forest, threatening to break out through the trees, under the bright moonlight that makes the snow sparkle.

I have to force myself to break away from this image, yet I need to imprint it in my mind, behind my eyes, forever, because if my future plan will work... I am not going to enjoy it for long.

NIKLAS

I watched her all night. Watched her as she walked downstairs, her beautiful legs gliding down the wooden steps. I watched her as she tried so fucking hard not to look into my eyes. I watched her as she shivered when I accidentally touched her fingers when I handed her the fork. I watched her as she licked the steak juices off the sharp knife and my dick shot up, ready for action. I watched her lips as she formed shy words. I watched every single move she made tonight and came to no rational conclusion.

Spring. What the fuck am I supposed to do until spring with her? She's not my fucking guest, how the hell am I supposed to act?!

While she was sleeping the day away, I called Connor in town, the sheriff with questionable morals, the bastard that brought me here, the only person that ever understood why I needed to be here. I asked him to do some digging, find out if there's anyone new in the area, however I didn't give him too many details about my situation. Why? I'm not sure. Maybe because he's a cop and I'm technically keeping an abused woman hostage in my home? Maybe because I'm not sure what's going to happen and it would be best no one even knew she was ever here?

Either way, he doesn't need to know more than the fact that there was someone on my mountain and everyone knows not to come here.

"I don't think his house was in the middle of the woods." She startles me out of my train of thought. I look at her, head turned towards the window. "I had a dream and it reminded me of something, something from months ago. The dungeon had this small window, up high, but I managed to reach it once, managed to look through and there were no trees in my field of view, maybe on the far sides, but I could see the moon clearly. No obstructions. He boarded it after that..."

I turn my gaze to the roaring fire and contemplate what she said. Maybe he lives somewhere at the edge of the forest or maybe in a clearing. Either way, it would have to be secluded for him to do what he's been doing.

"This... dungeon..." For some reason I spit the word out in disgust. "What did it look like?" My eyes still on the fire. Somehow I felt like I had enough of looking at her tonight and I need to keep my dick in check. It seems like every time I catch her gaze, my fucking dick roars to life.

"Stone. Big old stones and wet. The humidity was ridiculous. It felt like an old dungeon, or an old cellar, deep underground. To be honest... it felt and smelled like a cave."

Old. Interesting.

"Why do you want to find out so badly?"

That particular question makes me turn around and look at her. I debate my answer for a split second.

"He came on my mountain. No one comes on my mountain."

There is slight disappointment in her eyes. Why? Did she

think I'm doing it to fucking avenge her? I'm not her goddamn boyfriend to defend her fucking honor! I'm not the nice guy she probably now believes I am.

Goddamn it!

What am I doing here?! I wanna kill that motherfucker, but not because he hurt her, but because he's doing this on my fucking territory. He dared cross the boundaries, which means he has no clue who I am and he needs to fucking find out.

This is the only reason, the only fucking reason.

I'm going hunting!

"Go to bed!"

SUKI

I watch him as he heads for the door, his normally cool and intense exterior faltering just enough for me to notice, but not enough for it to matter. He turns the top lock, then unlocks the bottom one with a key he took out of his jeans pocket.

Ok...

Then it hit me. He is leaving.

"You are... you are leaving me here, alone?"

He stops just before he opens the door, turning his head slightly to barely glance at me from the corner of his eye, then pulls it open. A strong gust of wind blows so hard into the night, bringing inside thick fresh snow and the man before it looks like a goddamn model with his hair and clothes blowing in the wind.

"Where the fuck would you go?" he asks casually before pulling the door behind him.

I somehow missed the raging snowstorm happening outside. He is right, he could leave every window and door unlocked, he could leave them all wide open, it would not matter, I would not go far at all.

Which begs the question, where was he going, in the dark, in the middle of a snowstorm?

* * *

I wake up startled, shifting suddenly in a sitting position, alerted by the distant noise. Frantically looking around, I realize I fell asleep on the sofa and I am all alone this time around.

I'm not sure what is going on with me. A couple of days have passed and I have struggled to keep myself awake for most of them. Like my body is finally able to rest and it is taking advantage of every single opportunity it gets. Yet, there is no point in denying this—it's this house as well, it relaxes me, I feel strangely safe and protected under its warm shadow. The wood, the fur, the roaring fire and the view that makes me wish I could build my own place on one of these peaks. Somehow, it is better fitted for me than any other place I have ever lived in. However, I technically do not live here.

This place will be hard to part with.

A muffled noise distracts me and I jump off the sofa, walking slowly through the darkened kitchen, trying to figure out where the sound is coming from.

Garage...

I walk slowly towards the kitchen door that leads into the garage and crack it open. I lean in and I see the beautiful Viking, beating the shit out of a large boxing bag hung from a thick beam in the ceiling. I'm still, watching his fast fluid movements, strangely fluid for a man of his size and weight. His back is to me, yet I still find myself pinned in place, unable to rip my gaze away.

Away from his damp back, glistening with sweat in the dim garage light.

Away from the thick muscles, one by one flexing with every punch he throws at the boxing bag.

Away from the wide, round shoulders and tight biceps.

Away from his forearms... the sinew, the thin strands dancing under his skin with every flex.

I watch his movements, each punch, each ragged breath, the beads of sweat flowing down his taut back, following their descent down to the sweats hanging low on his hips.

His movements look strained, heavy thuds, weighed by too many thoughts going through his head, punches so powerful that it makes the beam above creak dangerously. There is a raw, primal power in this man, in his body, like he was baptized in the tears of his enemies.

Suddenly, I realize I am about to be the former.

Lost in thought, I missed the fact that he turned around, facing me. My gaze shoots up and catches his. He is heaving, his breaths deep, heavy, every muscle in his body tense to a breaking point. Both his hands are fisted, mouth ajar, head tilted downward slightly, just enough to shoot me the most menacing look I have ever felt on my skin.

Suddenly, I become all too aware that I am alone with him in his house, on this mountain, on his turf. Alone in this world.

He pins me with his dark blue eyes that look black in this dim light, holding my stare, unyielding and terrifying.

I feel like prey.

I feel like a deer in the headlights of an enormous monster truck, watching in slow motion the last moments of my short life, before it will be taken away from me.

His breaths somehow become more intense, his gaze bores into me in a way that strips me naked and flays me alive. His fists flex once and he takes a slow menacing step towards me.

And I run.

I did not even realize that I ran until I was already doing it. I turn on my heels and head for the front door, my fight or flight response pushing my body before my mind even processes what is happening.

I pull the front door open and with bare feet I jump straight into the white freezing night, off the porch, running as fast as I can. I know he is following me, not because I hear him, but because I feel him, his eyes on me. That intense gaze that is somehow always following me is like a touch, a strong electrifying touch and I feel it everywhere. On the back of my neck, between my shoulder blades, on the small of my back, on my ass, my bare legs, making me shiver, making me run faster.

Making me wet.

Making me smile.

I feel the heat pool in my belly, running down between my legs. Feel the adrenaline fuel new life into me, not the old life that I lost after Adrien captured me, no.

This is different.

This is new.

This is exhilarating.

I feel the rush of endorphins and the anticipation of the unyielding force that threatens to collide with me. But I will not give in to him. I cannot give up this electrifying sensation that he builds inside of me, the adrenaline that pumps so fast I swear it is making my legs move quicker.

This, right here, feels like freedom.

Which is ironic, since I am anything but free, at least by normal standards. However, this is my own type of freedom, freedom to be myself and bathe in the deep, raw, filthy sensations that make my blood run hot.

The pure fear that makes me think that any one of these breaths could be my last.

NIKLAS

I'm running after her before my brain registers the movement. I can't help it. When she realized I caught her staring she had this intense look in her eyes, a combination of lust, fear and... challenge. And they sparkled, I swear I could see those demons behind her eyes. There's something there that's making my dick so hard I could fucking drill a hole through a reinforced concrete wall.

One step from me was all it took for her to run, and I could have howled at the moon in victory. I can feel the fear in her, I can smell it in the air, I can feel it on my own skin, like strands of electricity stretching from her, wrapping themselves around me. Out of nowhere, just before her head turned, I caught it—a twitch upwards in the corner of her lips.

This is it.

This is what I've been missing my whole fucking life and what I never thought I would find on this lonely mountain.

So I chase it.

Chase her. Through the house. Out the door into the freezing night. Through the thick snow. I watch her short frame running half naked, down the mountain, between the pine trees.

Her dark hair bounces and flows from side to side with every step forward and every time her feet bounce off the ground, I catch glimpses of her thick ass cheeks under my hoodie that she's wearing. Every step she takes looks stronger than the last. She fits, right here in this unmovable scenery between the old pines. She fits.

And I smile. This is even better than I thought it would be.

She runs hard, never turning her head around to see if I am following, never faltering. It breathes new life into me. I chase my prey with even more determination and unlike the first time I ran after her, this is different. I am not letting her win, I am actually running after her, truly running. I gave her a bit of a head start once she ran out the door, I wanted this, wanted her to believe she had a shot and to be honest, I wanted to give her one.

Why?

I'm curious. Curious if I can push her to come out, out of that fucking shell, break the wall that motherfucker built around her fiery soul.

I'm more determined than ever.

I leap forward, closing the distance between us and my heavy steps in the snow must have distracted her because hers falter. I reach her, circle my arms around that small body and lift her up against me as she kicks and screams.

Oh, how she screams. That fiery siren's song, rubbing every inch of my body until it reaches my dick and calls it into action. The song that makes me squeeze her harder just so I can hear more of it. My left hand goes down, around her hip and my right goes up on her throat, squeezing just enough, tilting her head backward, holding it tight against my right shoulder.

I bury my head in the crook of her neck and take in her smell. Jasmine. There's no perfume, no feminine products in my house, yet she smells like jasmine, like fucking spring in the frosty, winter night.

I drag my tongue from the crook of her neck to that sweet spot behind the ear, clamping my teeth on the soft lobe and she swears at me. Dirty words rasping into the silence of the night and I squeeze the sides of her throat harder. She gasps for air for a few seconds and squirms more against me, making my dick dig deeper into her back.

She's stuck, stuck in my arms, no matter how much she kicks she can't go anywhere, controlling her is actually quite easy. I ease the grip on her throat and she screams bloody murder, her arms going backwards, grabbing the back of my neck and squeezing as hard as she can, clawing at it, futile attempts at distracting me with pain.

A strange sound escapes my lips before I even realize what's happening. I'm laughing. I don't even remember the last time that happened. I forgot what it sounded like.

She stills in my arms and I silence myself. She watches me from the corner of her eye, taken aback by the strange noise that left me.

My dick pulses into the small of her back and I feel her tense harder, not her whole body, just her back, her ass. Almost like she's forcing herself to stay perfectly still, as if in this specific moment it is the most unnatural thing for her to do.

"What now, little siren?" I whisper in her ear in the most menacing voice I can muster.

I watch as her eyes move frantically in every direction, looking for options, any options, anything at all. And then she kicks me, so hard, aimlessly, yet she found my knee, making me flinch just enough for her to claw at my arms to free herself.

I let go and she falls to the ground, unexpectedly slipping on a rock, and goes straight on her hands and knees at my feet.

Isn't that just goddamn beautiful, almost like this forest is rooting for me.

She tries to get up, but I put both arms on her shoulders and push her right back down. I like her here, on her knees, at my feet. My right hand starts moving slowly, enjoying the slight tremble in her body as it glides over her upper back and behind her neck, grabbing her possessively.

I push her forwards and she falls on her belly to the ground. Before she can get up, I drop down on my hands and knees and cage her in. My front to her back, legs on either side of hers, dick pressed hard between her ass cheeks.

"Get the hell off me!" she starts screaming, anger seeping out of her voice.

I stay quiet, holding myself on one arm, and push the other one between her shoulder blades, holding her down.

"I know you're not deaf, get off me!" she yells again.

I grin. I can't fucking help it. Her voice is breaking in the most delicious way, revealing the fire that I knew is still burning inside of her.

Letting go of her back, I give her a small sense of security. She squirms beneath me and slides out fast, attempting to run away. But she fails to understand one important thing—I'm a hunter, and she is prey. And I like playing with my prey before I devour. And I will devour.

She's almost out from underneath me, so I use my free arm to pull her back by her legs and flip her over, before I move swiftly on top of her, between her legs, caging her in yet again. My eyes are at the same level as hers and I can see the panic and fear as she tries with all her might to push me off.

"You get off on this, you sick bastard. Let me go! What the hell is wrong with you?" She carries on yelling expletives at me, yet I don't falter. I bathe in the high pitched tone of her voice, laced with fear and something else I can't quite place.

And then she digs her nails on the crook of my neck, on both sides, knowingly drawing blood.

I'm done.

CHAPTER 7

NIKLAS

My lips find her delicious ones and I push my body so hard onto hers that she exhales a sharp breath and I swallow it. I force my tongue deeper, fighting her own lips, licking every single inch of her. She fights me even now. Fights me with her tongue, like a twisted tug of war, only there's no tugging.

I press harder onto her, grab both of her wrists and catch them in one hand above her head, the other one I wrapping around her small throat. I squeeze a little harder and her hips buck upwards, the thin fabric of my boxers that she is wearing, sticking to my jeans covered dick.

One thing I know for sure: she is dripping fucking wet.

I break the kiss and look at her, into her bright green eyes, shining in the dark of the night. There's fire in them, vengeance and a deep sense of foreboding.

I don't break eye contact and she doesn't either. Her breaths are deep, her breasts pushing upwards and I swear I can feel her pussy twitching. I choke her harder, just as I press my dick into her core and her eyes explode, clamping her mouth shut I can feel it in her throat under my hand—the moan she's trying so hard to suppress.

I move my hands from her throat, pushing it hard on her flesh as I slide it down her body, until I reach that lush hip. I give her a bruising squeeze before I slide it under her, grab her ass and press her into me, painfully grinding my dick onto her pussy, to the point I'm convinced my boxers ripped.

This time around her self-control falters and she moans and bucks, her eyes laced with hate. So much fucking hate and I wonder if it's truly aimed at me... or her betraying body.

Yet I wonder, is she betraying anything at all?

She squirms and kicks again. Refusing to accept her current predicament.

But then something curious happens. She screams, from the top of her lungs she screams, while looking straight into my eyes. My whole body vibrates, charging with the electricity from her voice—the siren screams for me.

She knows. She fucking knows!

This is not fear.

Yet, it's not quite a challenge either. It's an excuse for her to get what she truly desires without accepting or even acknowledging it.

It takes me a second to let go of her arms, grab the hem of the hoodie along with the t-shirt and rip it up her body and over her head. But I hold it there for a few seconds, simply looking at her fantastic naked tits. She tries to squirm, kicking and screaming filthy swears at me, but she can't move, her head and arms trapped under the folded hoodie.

She looks so fucking beautiful, trapped under me, her tits pushing upwards. A fucking invitation, weather she likes it or not. I go for her right nipple and clamp my teeth on it, before swiping my tongue to soothe it. I bite the flesh of her tit and lick again. I move to her left one, and I repeat the assault.

Her screams turn into violent moans and her kicks turn into shivers. Her whole body responds to me in a way her mind can't truly accept.

She's still trapped and blinded by the hoodie, so I let go of her hands and before she can even fucking move, I rip the boxers of her body, exposing that beautiful fucking pussy that I only caught fleeting glimpses of. Before she can pull the hoodie back down I rip it upwards, forcing it over her head.

There she is. Completely fucking naked, on the top of a mountain, in the middle of the eerie forest, with a monster on top of her.

She's so fucking beautiful, lying here in the thick snow, in the freezing cold, all flushed and wet, fighting the conflicting feelings raging inside of her. Believing she is terrified by me, but I think she's more terrified of herself, terrified of what she may find in the depths of these woods.

She can't lie to me, I can see her demons dancing in those fiery green eyes. I know she's found home.

SUKI

My nipples are hard, my pussy is wet, my arms are trapped, held by one of his large hands and I am under him—completely fucking naked.

I want to scream. Not at him, but at myself, at my betraying flesh, at the demons inside of me bathing in this excruciatingly delicious feeling raging havoc inside of me.

He is half naked. His delicious, strong body so close to mine, his taut pecks and thick abs are dusted with hair, his shoulders are so impossibly wide and strong, and his arms somehow look bigger bathed in the moonlight. I force a groan back inside myself and try not to shiver.

I do not want to give him the satisfaction of my arousal.

I return my eyes back to his and kick my legs under and up as hard as I can, trying my best to push him off me. But he barely even twitches.

He covers my pussy with his huge free hand and squeezes so tight I cannot help the pain-filled scream escaping my lips. And just as the pain rips through me, he pushes two thick fingers inside my wet pussy and I scream for a whole different reason.

Somehow he pulls pain out of pleasure and pleasure out of pain, rips the gates of hell to welcome a dark heaven and I fucking embrace it.

I embrace it all.

I embrace all the filthy sensations raging havoc through my body.

I embrace the destruction of my mind and I admire the cracks forming in the thick wall built by the fucker who broke me.

And now... Niklas breaks me in a completely unique way, as he pushes a third thick finger inside of my swollen pussy with a delicious force that threatens to stretch me way too hard.

He looks straight into my eyes with an intense, menacing gaze that promises death and destruction as he starts finger fucking me into oblivion. I buck and I scream underneath him. I feel so much, too fucking much. I feel pain as he stretches me, but the sweet pleasure I take from that pain is so fucking delicious that I know my screams are asking for more.

And goddamn it, he gives it to me.

I should feel cold right now, naked and bruised, lying on the snowy forest floor. But I do not. My flesh is on fire and the snow is keeping my electrified body from burning.

I cannot take it anymore, my body is at the brink of an explosion from the inside out, I am trapped in that intensely dark gaze and it's the most disturbingly delicious thing I have ever felt in my life.

And then... that vibrating rough voice comes out of him.

"Let go."

Two simple words.

Two simple words that set off an uncontrollable chain of events that crack the walls built around the chamber that used to hold my soul.

Two simple words that detonate a bomb inside of me, pleasure exploding through every pore of my body, my pussy is on fire and my lungs are burning with words I cannot form.

So I scream instead.

I scream my orgasm out of me, scream as the pleasure rips through every cell of my body, changing the very fibers of my being.

Then I scream for a completely different reason. One long thick reason.

I don't know when or how it happened, but the behemoth on top of me pushed his thick cock between my folds in one long thrust and I swear I'm seeing stars. His cock is rubbing the walls of my pussy in the middle of my orgasm and I scream because I do not think I can take any more ecstasy.

He pulls out slowly, stretching the vibrations of my orgasm and the thick head of his cock barely reaches my entrance before he thrusts inside of me so hard, I swear I felt the ground shake beneath me.

I'm still riding high, but I cannot catch a break.

He holds himself up on one forearm right next to my head and with the other hand he grabs my throat, holding my head aimed at him, forcing my gaze into his. And he thrusts again and my body breaks into shivers. I cannot stop myself as my hips shift and adjust to take more of him. He picks up the pace, he pulls out slow, but thrusts back in fast and hard, pulling painful pleasure out of me and I scream at every inch of his invasion.

My arms are above me, holding on for dear life to anything beneath me—dried grass, tree roots—anything to keep me grounded to this world, because I do not wish to be taken away, miss this, this beautiful chaos reigning through me.

His pace becomes frantic, his hand around my throat

tighter and I want to gasp for air, but I stop myself. The pressure inside my head grows, the fire builds, the demons dance on music sang by his own and I drown in the fire, I drown in the pleasure, I drown in the pain and I smile.

I am alive.

He thrusts again and again, harder than before and just as he lets go of my throat, I let go as well. I scream my orgasm, just as he grabs my hip and lifts me higher onto his swollen cock that jerks frantically inside of me, spilling his warm cum.

We ride together, ride that orgasm to the ends of this god forsaken world, I scream, he growls and together we become chaos—filthy disturbed chaos.

NIKLAS

This was the single most intense fuck of my entire life.

No, I can't call it a fuck, it was a goddamn sexual awakening. The awakening of the monster that lurked deep in the shadows of my soul, beyond the demons that guarded it.

The siren brought it forward without even realizing it and I'm grateful. Grateful that I got to feel it all—the pain, the pleasure, the inner torture. I ripped it out of her with excruciating thrusts and it was goddamn beautiful. She was a work of fucking art beneath me.

I watch the last shivers of her orgasm fade away, my dick still nestled inside her warm, swollen, tight pussy and she opens her spent eyes, looking lazily into mine. They slowly grow wider and I can see her mind processing the events of the night, pulling her back into the present, back to me.

Her whole body shifts, it grows suddenly cold, her eyes go blank, the spell broken.

I don't linger.

I pull my dick out, get up and pull my jeans back on. I would offer my hand to help her up, but I know she'll refuse me, so instead I go to grab the hoodie that I tossed to the ground.

Half of it is wet, and I suddenly feel an ounce of remorse. I turn to her to find her standing, watching me, uselessly trying to cover herself with her arms.

"It's wet," I say as I hand the hoodie back to her.

She shoots me a look filled with disgust and rips it out of my grip. She's growing bolder—walls that hide her strength are cracking.

I grin.

She shoots me daggers with her eyes, turns on her heels, and walks back to the house with angry, heavy steps, without sparing a glance back to me.

I follow behind her through the woods, and when we reach the house she goes straight upstairs, ignoring the shit out of me. Good. The last thing I fucking need right now is to hash out whatever the fuck just happened outside. I can't deal with it myself. I can't deal with how fucking amazing it felt. How fantastic she felt wrapped around my dick.

Fuck.

It would have been different if I forced it out of her, if she fucking hated it. But she didn't, not one bit. She looked like she hated herself more.

I feel like all the tension I was trying to work out earlier, when she found me punching the boxing bag, is back. But I don't have the damn energy to go through that again.

I extinguish the fireplace, lock the door, and head upstairs.

* * *

BANG

What the fuck?!

I wake up to this loud bang and shoot out of bed, ripping open the door and take three steps at a time as I run downstairs.

I'm raging and worried, and what I don't expect to find is the shortstack of a siren, on her knees on top of the kitchen countertop, in the far too bright kitchen, looking at me with big, scared eyes, holding a pot that she pulled out of the top cabinet.

This is potentially the cutest fucking thing I have witnessed in my kitchen and I already hate myself for even thinking that.

I look at her, still on the countertop, then look down and see a pan that used to reside in that same cabinet. Walking over, I pick it up and set it on the cabinet next to her. I look up and she's staring at me with shocked, bright green eyes. She's wearing my, now dry t-shirt and she looks absolutely fucking delicious in it.

Grabbing the pot from her hands, I set it down as well and slide my hands under her armpits, pulling her down until she's sitting in front of me. Her wide eyes drop down the center of my body before they settle low, and I follow them.

I'm stark fucking naked, sporting morning wood.

Looking up, I catch her lips twitch like she's trying far too hard not to bite them. I grab her ass and pull her forward until my dick settles in between her legs, realizing she's fucking naked under that t-shirt, my dick pressing on her bare pussy.

It feels like fucking home.

I grab the back of her neck with my other hand and pull her face to mine, but the cheeky siren stops me dead in my tracks when her small hand connects with my cheek.

She fucking slapped me.

A deep, menacing growl escapes my throat. I squeeze the back of her neck harder and she plants one hand on my naked chest, pushing me away. I look down at it, then I look at her, cocking my head.

I pull her ass, pushing her pussy harder onto my cock.

She does it again. One sharp slap across my face.

"Fuck this shit."

I pull her face to mine and press my lips so hard onto hers I'm sure it fucking hurts her. It hurts me. I kiss her with a ravenous hunger, forcing my tongue into her mouth, grinding my dick onto her pussy and it's enough to coat it in those warm juices that betray her.

Fuck!

I break the kiss, drop down, hold her hips and bury my face between her sweet legs.

She yelps in shock, and I pull her harder, licking her slit from back to front, sucking her swollen clit, then press my tongue as hard as I can on it, licking it forcefully.

She can't help it, she moans and twitches, then grabs my shoulders and sinks her nails into them. She draws pain, and I fucking love it.

Sinking two fingers inside her pussy, I'm still fucking amazed at how tight and small she is. I lap at her clit, pumping my thick fingers inside of her and she can't sit still, squirming on the kitchen countertop, bathing in the bright sunshine of the day— she's fucking gorgeous. I curl my fingers inside of her, rubbing that delicious sweet spot on the walls of her pussy, before I bite her clit. Her orgasm rips through her like a fucking tornado, she's shaking and...

"Niklas!"

Fuck! My name... on her lips... in this moment... Sweet Mary mother of god!

Before she even reels back in from her orgasm, I sink my dick inside of her in one long, quick stroke and I swear I fucking found heaven when she squeezes me with the shocks of her orgasm.

I don't wait for her to come back to earth. I grab the back of her neck, place my other hand behind her ass on the countertop and fuck her.

Hard and fast, pulling every ounce of pleasure from her as she wraps her fine legs around me, her arms tight around the back of my neck, holding on for dear life.

She's wrapped around me like a fucking gift ribbon, ready to be untied so I can find the delicious surprise inside. She moans and screams with every thrust, each one more powerful than the other because it doesn't feel like enough. I need to get deeper inside of her, so deep that no one can fucking pry me back out, because this is it, this is my own personal oblivion. Sweet fucking oblivion.

I sink my teeth into her shoulder, drawing blood, because I need it. I need the violence, the fight, the sirens song. I need it all from her!

She screams from the bottom of her lungs and sinks her fingernails into my skin, slashing my back before she bites my shoulder so hard, I can't help but roar.

I thrust harder and when I feel her tongue licking the blood she pulled out of me, I come undone, spilling inside her warm pussy, my dick jerking violently inside and then she follows me. Riding these flames together, we burn in chaos.

"Fucking beautiful."

She lifts her head at the sound of those words leaving my mouth, her bright green eyes freezing me, electrifying vibrations running down my back.

Fuck.

CHAPTER 8

NIKLAS

"*A*re you up for a walk today?" I ask her.

The tension between us has shifted, still there, still thick, but different. Although it's hard to ignore the sexual tension building up. The fleeting glances, the hitched breaths when I pass by a bit too close, the stillness when I look at her... fear is one thing, but this... this fear is laced with lust. I can practically see the hate she carries for herself in her eyes, the conflict in her mind. Either way, I thought that at least on my part it would have subsided... it usually does after you fuck someone, right?

Then why do I feel like I merely glanced into the abyss and now sense this burning need to take a leap? Why do I want more?

After I pulled out of her, she sat there for a few seconds, focused on something deep in her mind, her breaths short yet heavy. When her eyes refocused on the present and she found mine, her demons were peeking through, utterly focused on me.

Fascinating.

I gave her another hoodie, boxers, and an old pair of joggers that look absolutely ridiculous on her short frame, but I have nothing else that could even remotely fit her. Either way, she did not protest, she even thanked me... a strange compliance and I'm not entirely sure how I feel about it.

We ate the breakfast that she cooked for us in complete silence. The tension was thick, but the silence comfortable. The glances we exchanged, even the fleeting ones, were electrifying, like we were both thinking the same things and found no reason to open our mouths to voice them. A silent conversation. A debate...

"A walk?" she asks me, slightly confused.

"Yes. I want to see if I can jog your memory. It's still early in the morning, if we start now, we can cover quite a bit of ground and maybe get a bit closer to that motherfucker's location."

"Because he trespassed on your territory." She puts her head down. I know this is a dig at me, but I don't give a fuck right now. The important thing is to catch him.

"You're mistaking me for someone I am not. I'm not that type of monster, but still a monster nonetheless, and I believe we have already established that I enjoy the fight... and I can easily make you comply." I don't blink as I watch her shift from annoyance to fury by the time the last word leaves my mouth.

She shoots me daggers with her eyes, and I swear to the

fucking gods that I can actually feel them piercing my body. My skin prickles. I like it.

"Screw you!" she rasps at me as she pushes her chair back forcefully.

She walks off, but I don't spare her a glance. I don't fucking have time for this. I wipe my mouth with my napkin, grab the dirty dishes and calmly take them to the sink.

I turn around towards the stairs and she's there, on the first step, heaving. I don't stop, I keep walking towards her, watching her body tense, her posture straightening. She waits until the last moment to turn around and walk up the stairs ahead of me. I follow her gorgeous legs as she climbs every step with composure, resisting the urge to touch her as her round hips naturally sway from side to side. If I do... I'm not fucking leaving this house today.

"I don't have shoes," she says, stopping me just before I close my bedroom door behind me. I turn around to see her defiant little face looking at me, holding on to what little pride she managed to pry out the depths of her shattered soul.

"I'll bring you something."

SUKI

"Whose are they?" I ask him as I study the hiking boots that are just one size bigger, clearly another woman's. He shoots me a bored look, like there is no damn way he is going to waste time with this conversation.

Rolling my eyes, I pull them over the thick socks that definitely help with the difference in size. I tie the joggers tighter around my waist and pull the thick jacket over the two layers of sweatshirts I'm wearing. The jacket is clearly not his either, it's probably one or two sizes bigger than my own.

I cringe at the thought of wearing another woman's clothes, a woman familiar to him if she has hiking boots and a casual winter jacket here. Maybe he has a wife. Or maybe he... had a wife... For the love of god, I really hope he doesn't have dead bodies buried behind the house as well.

"You need to move your ass faster and stop rolling your damn eyes, because I swear I will make your ass hurt so bad you won't have a choice but to stay here."

I raise an eyebrow at him, his gaze on me unmoving, menacing, laced with something that one could mistake as playfulness. Somehow his threat did not sound like the punishment he intended it to.

And that right there is the reason why I got in trouble the first time around when that bastard, Adrien, trapped me.

* * *

Half an hour later, we're calmly walking through the woods, him in front of me, making a path in the thick snow. I thought it would be colder, but it is actually quite pleasant outside. The sun is shining, the beautiful rays penetrating the crowns of the pine trees where birds are singing, and there is something quite poetic about this image.

"I'm going to take you where I found you, okay?"

When I do not answer, he turns around to give me a scolding look. I know I am acting like a brat, but I do not care right now. Three days ago this type of behavior would not even cross my mind. Adrien beat my personality out of me a long time ago, but with Niklas... well... he brings it out of me. Pushes me to my damn limits and I do not know whether it is intentional or not.

He punishes, he does. He fucks hard. He draws blood.

However... I fail to see his bad intentions for what they are. Is this some sort of fucked up Stockholm syndrome? Because if it is... I am not entirely sure how I can stop its progression.

"They're my mother's," he sighs.

Huh?!

"The jacket and shoes," he explains without stopping or turning to look at me. I do not know if he thinks that is why I am giving him the silent treatment and he is trying to make good, but the information shocks me.

Obviously, I know he did not just magically land on this planet from freaking Asgard itself, but... thinking of him as an actual human being, someone's son... it is strange.

"Your... mom," I whisper.

"My family comes maybe once or twice a year. Last time they came she left those here... I think she just wanted to make sure I knew she was coming back." There is conflict in the tone of his voice.

I appreciate the explanation, I do, and involuntarily I relax. Was that why I was so tightly wound up? The last thing I need right now is to be bothered by the prospect of him having a girlfriend or wife. No way in hell am I going to care if he does.

"Your family does not live close?" I ask.

He sighs, "No. On the West Coast."

"Oh... "

We walk in silence for quite a while. Suddenly, I want to know more, but I have no clue what to ask. There is an internal battle inside of me that does not actually want to know him, humanize him. I do not want to look at him differently than the monster he wants me to see. Because he is. A ruthless monster that gives no shit about consent. He takes whatever the hell he wants, corrupts, draws blood, wreaks havoc, and then abandons.

Damn it!

"Why did you leave?" I ask, and watch his steps pause for just a fraction of a second.

"Life got too... complicated. Too much work, little reward, there was nothing for me there."

"But there is here?" I frown, and he stops walking. He is slowly turning around, his eyes reaching mine before he is completely facing me and there I am again, a deer in the headlights.

He does not say anything. He just holds my gaze with an intensity that brings cold shivers from the base of my spine to the base of my neck, and I cannot move.

My palms get sweaty, my nipples get hard, and my pussy clenches.

His dark blue eyes grow darker, and he barely puts any effort into looking like a savage, yet he does look like one. I should run, but I know by now that doing that will get me fucked, quite literally, fucked.

Is that a *yes* though? Is there something here for him? Besides the mountain and the material things.

"We're here." He breaks the silence and releases me from the spell he put on me, and I slowly breathe out air that I was unconsciously keeping trapped in my lungs. I cannot do this, not for much longer. The intensity, the fear, the threats, the tension... I need to get the hell down from this mountain. I need to get away from him, otherwise I will not survive this. Physically, mentally, or emotionally—he will destroy me.

I take another deep breath, exhale slowly, and look around. I have absolutely no idea where I am, there are just trees around us, nothing else, no distinctive marker that gives me any clue.

"I think you were running from that direction." He points to a random spot in the woods, ahead of us, and I wonder if he's making this shit up. Everything looks exactly the same in every direction. To the point that if I spin a couple of times and someone covers our tracks, I will have no clue where we came from.

He does not wait for me to say anything. He just turns around and heads in the direction he just pointed at. I have no idea how long we have been walking, but it must be a while, because the sun is high in the sky now and I could use a break. No matter the difference the socks make, the shoes are still a bit too big for me and my already battered feet hurt.

"Niklas..." he stops dead in his tracks, like saying his name has some sort of strange effect on him. He turns slowly. "My feet... Could we stop for just a bit?"

His gaze softens as he looks down at me. There is a broken tree a few feet away from us. He cleans the snow off it and points for me to sit.

"Thank you." Those two words feel strange coming from my mouth. Not because I do not thank people when they do something nice for me, but because in the last few months I have been forced to say them... too many times. Adrien made me thank him for everything he did to me. The beatings, the abuse, the rape...

"Did you live in town?" He breaks my dangerous train of thought.

"What town?" I ask confused.

He frowns. "Bear Creek?"

"I have never heard of it." The truth is that I have absolutely no idea where I am. Considering my surroundings, I have a feeling it is somewhere in the Rockies, but that is where my knowledge ends.

"Where did you live before?" he trails off.

"South Dakota."

There is a slight shift in his expression, his head tilts just a fraction and his gaze grows in intensity.

"You're far away from home, little siren." Those shivers, they come again. Every time he uses those words on me, when he calls me *little siren*, it does something to me. I do not know how to explain it. It's like a filthy chemical reaction, two opposite substances combined in the same beaker, threatening to implode.

"It was not home anyway... just where I lived," I answer him. It's true. Yes, I was born in South Dakota, yes, it was technically home, but it never felt like it. They say that home is where the heart is. For me, home is where my heart was destroyed.

"What happened to you...?" he asks a simple question, but I am not entirely sure which "happening" he is referring to. My home? My family? My life? Adrien? My soul? A lot has happened to me...

I turn my gaze away from him and sigh. Then it hits me... no one has ever asked me that, this simple question. Not even Adrien.

He was interested in facts like if I actually had a family or friends, or people that cared about me. Later I realized that it was because he needed a person that did not have any of those connections to the world. Silly me, thinking he was paying some genuine interest. And even though he was perfectly aware that I was alone in the world, he never ever asked why.

I turn my gaze back to Niklas.

"Everyone died." That was it. A simple, truthful answer to a simple question.

"How?" He holds my gaze. He is not letting me go and I get it. He shared with me. My turn to share with him.

"Killed." Monosyllabic, I know; however, there is no trust between us. How much can I really share?

"By whom?" His head tilts and his gaze narrows.

A noise in the distance saves me from answering that particular question. There is no simple answer for it. We both turn our heads in a fraction of a second, looking around for any sign of life. We are in the middle of the woods on a mountain, there are many wild animals lurking through these parts.

Niklas pulls out the rifle he's been carrying on his shoulder. When we left the house, he pulled it out of the locked gun cabinet in the living room. I looked at him funny, but when he told me about the bears, wolves, and wild cats, I suddenly wished I had one as well.

We look all around us and cannot see a soul. No animals, no people. And even though we are under the crowns of the snowy pines, it is the middle of the day, there is plenty of light in the forest.

"Maybe it was just the trees... snow falling from the branches?" I whisper while still looking around me.

"Maybe," he says as he looks around us through the scope of the rifle. He stops, looking towards the opposite direction from the one we came from and I wonder what he is seeing.

Suddenly, I am freezing. Not because I'm cold, but because I suddenly remember that we are looking for traces of the man that held me captive for months. The man that tortured me. The man that molded me to his insipid, disturbing desires.

"Suki?" he says my name with confusion in his voice, but... he said my name. For the first time. It flowed from his lips, vibrating through his delicious, rough voice and I feel like the walls inside of me are cracking a little bit more. It sounds delicious, like it belongs on his tongue and his tongue only.

"I'm good... I'm good." I do not want to show him how absolutely terrified I am of Adrien. Not because it will expose even more of my weaknesses, but because I do not want to give Adrien anymore of this privilege. No, I am done, I have to be. There is only so much I can handle.

NIKLAS

I'm convinced I saw something through the scope. Somewhere in the distance there was movement, however I'm not entirely sure I want to follow it now. I somehow feel too exposed with Suki here.

I might not be the only one with a rifle, out in these woods. I think tonight is a perfect time to go hunting. Alone.

I turn to Suki and she looks like she's about to bolt. I'm not sure if she's realizing it, but she's shaking and it's not actually quite that cold. She looks scared, not the way I scare her, but... terrified.

"Suki?" Her name escapes my lips, and I feel the need to lick the sound that rolls off my tongue. Almost like that name was meant for my tongue, meant for my throat to vibrate with the sound of each letter.

It pulls her out of her spell.

"I'm good... I'm good." she says in a voice that sounds like she's trying to convince herself more than me.

"I think maybe we should go back now. We got far enough today."

She doesn't question me. She turns quickly on her heels and tries to steady the speed of her pace as she follows the path we made through the snow.

Yup, terrified.

I'm fine with her walking in front of me though. Gives me the opportunity to look around and behind us without freaking her out some more. I keep telling myself that I don't care how scared she is, but I do. *Fuck it, I do.*

Mostly because it's not the same as the fear she has for me. No, she is terrified of that motherfucker, Adrien, and I'm not having any of that.

Some would see this as jealousy, I see it as my fucking territory.

* * *

It takes us less time to get back to the house. Partly because the path through the snow is already made, but mostly because she's been walking so much faster, ready to go back to shelter.

Once inside, I can see her shoulders drop, her breathing relaxes and I'm not sure how I feel about her viewing my house as a safe place.

Her safe place...

I shake my head, close the door behind me and lock it. I go to the fireplace, light a fire and she follows, kneeling in front of it.

I want to turn around. I want to look at her. I want to admire that porcelain skin touched by the warm light of the fire; I want to see the flames reflect in the bright green of her eyes.

But I hold my ground.

We just sit here, both of us on our knees, watching the enthralling dance of the flames. There's solace here, a comfort

I've never experienced before. With anyone...

I exhale, my muscles relax... the monster lurking behind my demons smiles.

Home...

CHAPTER 9

NIKLAS

*M*y mother killed my family," her small voice surprises me and her words shock me. I guess she's not avoiding the conversation after all.

"My father, my stepmother... and my baby brother."

I turn my gaze to her, but don't say anything, she doesn't need me to. She knows I'm listening. Her eyes don't move from the fire, almost like she's having this conversation with the flames.

"It was the middle of the night. I was seventeen and just coming back from a party where I drank quite a bit, so I was in a deep sleep. I thought I was dreaming... I was hearing noises, thuds, voices. I did not realize it was not a dream, not until I heard the baby cry."

She sighs, but her expression doesn't falter. Like all the emotions were already spent, all the tears cried.

"I headed straight to my baby brother's nursery. He was three months old, an adorable thing with golden hair and blue eyes. I have never seen a more beautiful baby in my life. For me... he was hope, a new beginning. And my mother sliced his throat in front of my eyes."

I flinch. I can't help it. I've seen my share of violence. I've seen death, but this, this is different, a crime against purity, killing more than just one person's innocence.

"I ran to my dad and stepmom's bedroom, my dad was stabbed, multiple times, throat cut, but not enough to kill him. Enough for him to bleed out slowly. He was crawling on the floor... trying to get to us. My stepmom had her throat cut in bed and was dead. She came in after me, my mother, she was high as a kite, drunk and absolutely and utterly insane. She laughed at me. She told me that one day I will understand, that one day the demons will sing for me too."

The demons... I wonder if she knows they are there, that I can see them in her eyes.

"I wanted to save my dad, but there was nothing I could do. He was coughing blood, and with the last of his strength, he was waving for me to go, so I kissed him goodbye and ran downstairs. My mother did not follow me, she did not seem like she wanted to kill me. I think she genuinely believed I was like her. Seconds later, she set the house on fire... I think she spilled petrol all over the place while we slept. The flames took no time to spread."

I watch her beautiful, expressionless face gazing at the fire in front of her as she talks about the day that changed her life.

"She wanted to die there, in the flames. She saw them as a purification of her soul. So I stabbed her with her own blade, held by her own hand, and then used it to puncture her throat, in this sweet spot that gives you a slow, excruciating death. It wasn't quite suicide, but for her delusional self, it felt like it. There was no purification of her soul that night."

She killed her own mother...

"The demons did not sing for me, but they danced on heathen songs as I watched her body bleed to death."

Then there was silence. I turn my gaze back to the fire, and everything I think I know burns away in those flames.

This is no meek woman kneeling next to me. The death she caused was no accident, no self-defense. Her demons call onto mine because they are kindred. They crave the same sort of destruction. They crave lust and chaos.

They crave each other.

She is the way she is now, broken, because of Adrien. And Adrien will pay. Not just for being on my mountain, but for breaking her.

I turn my head and look at her. She mirrors me. There's no fear in her eyes, no worry that what she told me will shock me, no great expectation. Just a calm relief.

SUKI

I look in his gorgeous, dark blue eyes and there's no trace of judgment or shock. Just a calm understanding, one that I expected.

I'm not sure what he understands, not sure what he sees in me, but I don't care.

No one knows this, no one knows how I truly killed my mother. I claimed self-defense when the police came and no one questioned me. A neighbor's camera caught her sneaking into our house. There was already a police report against her for domestic violence against her child, her drug abuse was well- known, there was a restraining order... all the evidence pointed towards her.

But now, now he knows as well and I feel... relief. Not because it was a burden I was carrying. Hell no. That feeling I had when I sank that knife into her flesh was potentially the most esoteric experience of my life. Watching the blood pool at her feet, the life leaving her body, her eyes draining of color... I will never experience anything as disturbingly satisfying as that decadent moment.

I am relieved because I was finally able to share it, with pride, and I can see the monster in his eyes, smiling at me, nodding in approval.

My monster.

I smile at him, a small smile, barely reaching my lips.

He smiles back.

This right here is the moment I realize I am trapped. If I will ever leave this world alive, my soul will not come with me. It will forever belong on this mountain, with him.

* * *

I turn my gaze back to the flames. This feels like an unspoken truce between us. No one is running and no one is chasing. Not today, anyway.

We sit in front of the fire in a comfortable silence for a long while, when his deep rugged voice breaks it.

"The man that killed my girlfriend is the first man I ever killed."

First... I do not move or respond. I give him the same courtesy he gave me, but that word... it makes me shiver.

"We were on this backstreet, there wasn't anyone there, it was already dark outside... no cameras. She jumped out of my car, turned to cross the street, and was in the middle of the road when he hit her, then drove off, just... drove off. I ran to her, she was still alive, dying in excruciating pain, her body twisted unnaturally, her right arm was almost completely ripped off her body..."

I turn my head and look at him. His expression is blank, there is no emotion in those eyes, like the story he is telling me is something that happened to someone else... He turns to look at me.

"She was running across the street because I just broke

up with her, after almost six years together. She thought I was going to propose that night..."

Christ...

"She died because of me."

No matter how much I want to believe it was fate or just meant to be this way, it is hard to argue his point... If he wouldn't have broken up with her... she wouldn't have been out of the car, running across the street.

"The police looked for the person that killed her for months. Eventually they told us that there was no evidence, no way to find him."

He holds my gaze, growing in intensity, and I feel a cold chill running up my spine as his eyes darken and the monster reveals itself.

"But I had already found him. Less than a month after he killed her, I found him. I had no intention to tell the police, I just needed to wait for them to stop looking, to close the investigation. I was patient, I waited, studied him, and planned. I gutted him like a pig, spilled his insides at his feet while he was still alive."

I want to be shocked by his words... by this revelation, but somehow I know that I did not expect any less from him.

"He didn't deserve to die, not like that. I knew it was an accident, he cried like a fucking baby the whole time... I knew all of this, but it didn't make any difference. I killed him because he represented my guilt, and that guilt had to perish. He needed to die, so I could escape that gnawing feeling that was eating me up inside, even though I didn't love her anymore, probably never did, it was still my fault she died."

"Did it work?" I sigh because I could not stop myself from interrupting. "Did the guilt go away?"

"Instantly. With every intestine sliding down out of his shredded body, my threads of guilt were dissipating."

His eyes sparkle with unspoken revelations. Something else happened, something he is choosing not to reveal. Not yet anyway.

Killing a person with your own hands does something to you. If you have the right personality, it molds you into something unnaturally beautiful. Maybe it made him more violent; he already mentioned that man was the first.

That was not the effect it had on me, I did not kill again... but my thirst for violence grew considerably. Killing my mother broke a part of me, a cage that contained the real threads of my soul.

I crave blood and violence.

I crave chaos and lust.

I crave an unnatural love.

I crave a destruction of souls.

NIKLAS

The air shifted this morning, yet... after our revelations, it imploded.

We shared secret stories, stories that broke us and then stitched us back together into the people we are today. Stories that were not meant for anyone's ears... But here, on this mountain, among the snowy pine trees, in front of the dancing flames of the fireplace, our demons found each other and their stories had to finally come forth. Because they knew... we knew... no one else would ever understand.

These weren't confessions of our sins. This was a liberation of our souls to the world they belong in.

When I killed that guy, as his guts were slipping on the floor, the threads of guilt were replaced by something else. Something that clawed itself out from the depths of my soul. Something that was always there, lurking deep beneath the surface, behind the evil that danced through my mind.

The monster. He craved blood and a violent lust that threatened to consume me.

I look at her, in those mesmerizing, bright green eyes and

I know one thing for sure—the threat is not there anymore, not because the craving is gone, but because it already broke free, consuming me.

The moment I heard this siren's song, the monster bellowed, but when I first looked into her eyes and saw her demons calling for mine, the craving for violent lust was truly fulfilled.

Like I finally met both my victim and my match, wrapped in this beautiful, decadent, lustful package.

CHAPTER 10

NIKLAS

I'm going back, back into the woods in search of that son of a bitch. I waited all day for this moment, for darkness to fall, because during the night, no one can out-hunt me.

Suki and I spent the rest of the day in an unfamiliar, comfortable silence. It felt like a truce between us, a calm before an all-consuming storm.

We ate, we moved about the house, each of us doing random things without doing anything at all. She was in the guest bedroom when I left and I didn't tell her I was going. I didn't hide it either. I'm not worried about her trying to run away, not after today, not tonight.

But when she will, because I know she will run eventually, I will chase her, chase her to the end of the fucking earth, because the siren's song is addictive and I'm fucking hooked.

* * *

I stop and look around the darkness of the woods. I'm in the same place where we heard something earlier today. I stand here for a few minutes, in the shadow of an old pine with the rifle hanging heavily on my shoulder, a hunting knife in my boot, and my Colt in my holster.

I'm not anticipating killing Adrien tonight, I'm just doing my homework.

I grab my rifle and look around through the night vision scope. *Nothing*. I focus in on the same direction where I'm sure I saw something earlier today. *Nothing*.

I keep walking. I looked at satellite images today, and I saw something that could potentially be the house the asshole is using. I'm not sure though, because even though it's at the edge of the woods, it was still covered by pine trees, so I couldn't exactly tell if it was an old hunting cabin or what. Either way, it's at the edge of my mountain, on my property. If that motherfucker lives there... I have grounds to kill him. If I do it publicly that is. Too bad the edge of my property is so fucking far away. I could have saved time with the snowmobile, but that fucking thing is broken, and I would have made too much noise anyway. The sound travels far too well in these woods.

I walk for a long time, just over two hours, once in a while stopping to look through the night vision scope since it's not just Adrien I'm weary of, but animal predators as well. There are plenty of them on this mountain.

I finally see it, the cabin. I'm probably around a hundred

yards away, yet I can see it's quite small, very old, built on a stone foundation.

This must be the place, with that foundation it's bound to have a stone cellar as well... the dungeon. I get closer, more careful, constantly looking through the scope. Rather than going straight for it, I go to the left until I reach the end of the woods, then I circle back and head right, so I can see from the other angle. There's no light on, no smoke coming from the chimney... maybe this is not the place after all.

A fraction of a second later, I almost stumble. I've been walking through thick snow, making a path, but now, I've stumbled onto a different path. Freshly made. Not mine. I follow it and see that it leads to the cabin. If I had any doubts about this being inhabited, I don't anymore. I go for it. I hide through the shadows until I reach the small building, ducking under the windows, making sure no one can see me.

The thing is, he'll know I was here when he sees my footprints around the cabin, but as long as I won't be seen right now, I don't give a fuck. I walk all around the building, looking through every window, until I reach stone steps that go down beneath it. Against my better judgment, I decide to walk down, only to be greeted by a padlocked, thick metal door. Clearly this is not the original.

This is the type of door you use to keep people in, not out. *This is it...*

I'm sure there's no one in the cabin, but I still can't make noise by trying to break the padlock. Noise travels too well and fast in the quiet of the night. I have to leave it.

But then it hits me...

"If there's no one in... why is there a fresh path through the snow?"

I look back from where I came from, tracing with the scope the path that I did not make. I start walking, following it just as the snow starts to fall. Maybe my footprints will be covered after all.

I follow the path with steady, careful steps, looking through the night vision scope more often. As much as I want to hurry, I have to have the element of surprise. I can't risk him seeing or hearing me before I do him.

At least two hours must have passed when I reach this frozen pond in the middle of the woods, and the realization of where I am hits me like a fucking punch in the gut.

Fuck... Fuck! Fuck!!! The motherfucker is going towards my house!

And I run. I run so fucking hard, I feel my knees burning from the sudden strain, and I swear my goddamn legs are going to give out!

But I have to get to her...

Suki...

SUKI

I wake up in the middle of the night, all sweaty and breathing heavily. I was dreaming again... Sitting up in bed, my mind still hazy, I look around, adjusting my eyes to the darkness.

The house is silent.

I know he left earlier this evening, he did not try to hide it. I debated finding a way to escape, but the debate was short-lived. Not today. This needs to be calculated, the conditions are too harsh and I barely have any clothes. Not today... I'm not willing to acknowledge that the outside conditions are not the only reason why.

The cold hits me hard the moment I get out of bed. The house is warm, but on my damp skin it feels harsh. I tug on a pair of thick socks, the boots he gave me earlier, and pull a thick, knitted sweater over the over-sized t-shirt I'm wearing. It is obviously only over-sized on me, since it is Niklas' t-shirt, as is the sweater that brushes the top of my knees.

Wrapping my arms around my body, I leave the room and head downstairs.

I'm thirsty.

I stand in front of the kitchen window, drinking a glass of water and enjoy the view. Watching how the moonlight is absorbed by the smooth snow, brightening up everything around the cabin. It's beautiful.

There's solace here... among the pine trees.

I take a deep breath, absorbing this moment of calm, beauty, and silence. I catch my reflection in the window, there is a faint smile on my lips. It's hard not to love this. This dark, silent beauty of this scenery, so calm... too calm.

The promise of a storm. I shake the gnawing feeling away.

After a few more moments, I turn around, walking through the darkness of the house and open the door that leads to the garage. I turn on a light that blinds me and look around. I haven't actually been in here before, not without running away from the monster that holds me in this beautiful illusion of comfort. Tools, gardening tools, power tools, just tools, everywhere... on the floor, on the walls, nicely organized, but yes, so many tools. In the middle, there is this huge, black pickup truck. Even I have to admit it looks hot as hell.

I wonder if I could drive this down the mountain. I walk around it and bump into something covered by a tarp. I look down, studying it. It's big, but not too big, it has a familiar shape. I lift the tarp and look in awe. A snowmobile! Surely, this can take me down the mountain. So, we're not as trapped out here as he made it out to be. However, traveling through the thick, high snow could prove quite challenging even on this. I hastily look around, weary that I could get caught studying the very machine that could be my means of escape—my only means of escape. I pull the tarp uncovering most of the vehicle, studying it. There's no key.

Damn it.

Of course it requires a key. It might not even work, maybe

that is why it is covered. *Shit*. I make a mental note of the manufacturer. The key might have that engraved on it, if I ever find one in this house.

I cover the snowmobile and move away, a fresh smile on my face, hope blooming inside of me. It's a strange kind of hope though, more like... thankful for the option, instead of an obsessive need to find the key.

Interesting.

Before I reach the door to head back in the house, I make sure I look around on every wall, just in case there are keys hanging around among the numerous tools, but there's nothing. He would be stupid not to keep them on himself, especially with me here. I sigh and turn off the light before stepping back in the dark kitchen.

My eyes are taking their time to readjust to the darkness. I keep my hands around myself, careful not to bump into anything and walk back to the sink, guided by the light coming from the window. Filling another glass of water, I just stand there, yet again admiring the almost-white sky bleeding snow, the bright moon that bathes everything in a sharp light, the mountain peaks in the distance, the pine trees forming the edge of the forest in front of the cabin. How am I not growing tired of this beauty?

Suddenly, I see something among the trees at the forest's edge. Movement. I lean over the sink, closer to the window. It must be Niklas... coming back. I straighten and focus my eyes.

It takes a second for them to process the terrifying picture developing in front of me and two seconds for my brain to realize the danger I am in.

There is nothing at the edge of the forest. What I'm seeing in the window is not the view from the outside, but the reflection of the inside.

The sinister reflection of Adrien standing but a few feet

behind me, with a triumphant, cruel smile on his sleazy face.

I'm absolutely frozen in place, completely silent, even my heart has gone quiet. He knows though, he knows I see him, his grin is getting larger, the evil in his eyes getting darker.

My skin prickles, my bare legs get cold, my breathing heavier. I clutch the glass in my hand and I swear I can feel it giving up under my grip. I can feel the fear, the absolute terror creeping up from my spine, wrapping itself like massive spider legs, around my body.

I want to scream. I want to bellow and yell. I want to call for Niklas.

The power of this moment hits me like a punch in the gut, knocking the wind right out of me. *Niklas...* I'm not sure when the line between kidnapper and savior blurred.

I think of him and my breathing steadies.

Niklas...

I think of him and my mind gets clearer.

Niklas.

I think of him and my skin gets warmer.

Niklas!

I think of him and I drop the glass in the sink, shattering it.

Niklas!!!

I gently reach in and grab the biggest shard, hiding it behind me as I turn to face my worst fucking nightmare.

"Ntz Ntz Ntz..." Adrien lets out that scolding sound, like he is so disappointed in me. "I've missed you, little bird."

His grin gives me an uneasy sensation, creeping like slime on my skin. I do not move.

"I've been looking for you. Wondering why you ran away from me. I thought we wanted the same thing, you and I. Cut from the same cloth..."

I frown. My view on the world is distorted, but his is

downright paranoid.

"Never," I say, clear disgust reverberating through my voice.

His grin fades, his thick dark brows arch.

"You've been getting comfortable, little bird, too comfortable... with him." His eyes are downright terrifying now, madness exploding out of them. "Maybe I need to remind you who you belong to."

"No." A little bit more fear coming through my voice.

"No?! No, what?! You stupid bitch! No, you haven't been getting cozy?! Fucking him?!" he yells at me, all of a sudden slamming a huge hunting knife, tip first, into the butcher block of the kitchen island.

I jump at the noise, watching as he flexes his big hand around the handle of the knife, his knuckles turning white, veins pulsing hard, the silver blade shining in the moonlight.

"Or no, I don't need to remind you who you belong to?" he continues. "Because I know I do, little bird! I need to fucking remind you, mark your pretty pale skin over and over again so you will always know who the fuck you belong to! Not that you'll end up being fingered in the woods by that asshole ever again!"

He rages and stalks forward, I flinch and clutch the piece of glass in my hand, feeling it sink into my flesh.

Adrien has been watching me... I feel bile rising up my throat. All this time, he's been watching me, watching us. I hold my ground as he stalks toward me, our bodies almost touching, the knife now in his right hand, its thick blade promising to draw blood.

"Which one is it? Huh? What are you saying no to?" he asks, almost whispering.

"Everything." I look straight into his brown eyes.

He clutches the back of my neck with his left hand and

suddenly brings the knife to my throat, the sharp blade resting at the base of it.

I suck in a breath and hold his mad gaze.

"Everything." I repeat louder as I shove the piece of glass in his lower abdomen, next to his pubic bone. His upper body is covered by a thick coat, but on his lower body he's only wearing jeans. Strange choice for this environment, but advantageous to me, nonetheless.

I push in the piece of glass as hard as I can, pushing him away at the same time, while using my other arm to move the knife away from my throat, taking advantage of his momentary distraction. The shard sliced my skin, but the pain feels sweet.

He bellows and yells bloody murder as he clutches his groin.

I run. I run as hard as my feet can take me, straight to the front door, praying to the gods that Niklas didn't lock it. Adrien screams harder behind me, and I hear glass shattering on the floor, before his footsteps move on the wooden planks.

"I'm gonna fucking kill you, you fucking bitch!"

I rip open the door, noticing that it must have been locked before, because the window is now broken. I run down the steps and straight for the forest, suddenly being drowned in a sense of dejá vu.

"But first," Adrien bellows, "I'm gonna catch you and make you dig your own fucking grave, little bird."

I run as fast as I can because I know he will do it; he will make me dig my own grave, and he will fill it with my blood before he even puts me in it.

Yet again, I find myself jumping over the dips and mounds of the snow-covered forest floor, dodging trees and branches, trying hard to see where the hell I am going. However, this time around I am not completely naked, and I have shoes on.

My chances are already higher.

I can hear his heavy footsteps behind me, he is not hunting me like he did that night when I escaped. No. He is chasing me like the terrible beast he is, and he is not hiding behind trees anymore.

My lungs are burning from the cold, my thighs and calves are getting tight from the strain, and I'm running aimlessly through the dark forest. Everything around me looks the same, no hiding spot, no nothing. The only chance I have to veer him off my tracks is if I fall through a damn hole in the ground.

My brain goes on overdrive, tears filling my eyes at the prospect of being caught yet again by him. I have nowhere to go, no matter how fast I run, there's nowhere for me to hide.

When I hear Adrien's heavy steps getting closer, I'm not sure if I have been running for minutes or hours. I feel him behind me. My steps are smaller, slower now, and no matter how much I push myself... I cannot outrun him. I am not giving up, but the terrain is harsh and moving through the high snow is burning me out.

All of a sudden I feel his body heat and I know that I am no match. If I had a weapon I would have had a chance... but just me, on my own...

Fear fills my veins, replacing the blood that keeps me alive, terror covers my skin in millions of little goosebumps, panic fills my throat, and with one deep breath I scream.

I scream from the depths of my lungs as hard and as loud as my throat can take it.

I scream because I know... He will hear me, and he will come.

I did not get to finish that thought before Adrien catches my loose hair in his hand and pulls me back so violently, I stumble backwards, falling back first on the forest floor, the wind snapping right out of me.

He pulls my hair again, and I hear a loud bang before I realize that was the sound of my skull hitting the ground.

Everything goes black.

CHAPTER 11

NIKLAS

I t hits me so hard, like a dropkick splintering my body.

The blood curdling scream from deep in the woods, the same sound that beckoned me to follow only a few days ago, the fear in it... the siren's song devouring the silence.

The difference now is that the pain vibrating through the soundwaves is making me see red, the fury spreading through my body with a force that threatens to shake the fucking earth and split it open.

I can't seem to run fast enough though, because when the silence swallows her screams and the forest goes quiet, I don't know if I'm running in the right direction. I'm still following the same path he made through the woods, but I know this takes me to my house and I have a sickening feeling that they're nowhere near it anymore.

I have no choice though, so I keep running. The rifle hitting my back with every heavy step and leap I take over the occasionally rough terrain of the forest.

I don't know how I ended up at this particular point. I fail to understand what it is about her. I never attach myself to anyone, never create any connections; nothing strong enough to bring this reaction out of me. Yet I react like this for her... for Suki... for the siren I just met.

What is it about her? Why do I feel this burning need to possess her, own her, fuck her...? Save her?

She's not mine, not in the typical way. I don't care for her, I don't want her like a normal man wants a normal woman, because we are neither.

As the silence completely fills the dark woods and I run on the existing path through the thick snow, my mind drifts to the first time I realized what fear did to me. The first time I loathed its effects. I remember it like it was yesterday, that dark winter evening.

* * *

Seventeen years before...

By the time I finished class it was past p.m., and the sun was long gone, the moon high in the sky.

I always cut through the park when I went home, on the twisted paths through the thick trees, lit by the dim old streetlamps. My mother always told me not to walk through there at night, but I was fifteen, of course I wouldn't listen to her. Not necessarily because I was a typical stubborn teenager, no, but because the park was my escape, my quiet time... my solace.

It gave me time to be with myself and I wanted this most of all. I never quite understood why everyone always wanted to talk to me; they all wanted to meet with me, be with me, be around me. And they always talked, so fucking much, they wouldn't shut up. Especially the girls in school.

I've been told by the girls that the guys swarm around me because I'm the star of the football team, the guy all of them want to be. I'm already taller, broader, and stronger than most of them; my Viking genes must have something to do with that. On the other side, the guys told me that the girls always swarm around me because I'm the quiet one. I never give them enough attention, or any at all, so apparently that makes me attractive. I'm not an oblivious bastard, I just don't care to waste my time.

The other reason people fail to leave me alone is my mind. I'm not a fan of the more liberal subjects; however, anything technical—math, physics, chemistry, anything involving numbers really, that's where my skills lie.

What I don't excel at is human interaction, yet that doesn't appear to stop everyone from pissing me off all the time.

My mom talked to me about this. A while back she told me that it's good to have friends, people around me... I always think she says that because she somehow wants me to see how other people act. I overheard her speaking with my father, apparently it has been suggested by my teachers that my social interactions are lacking. They recommended getting me tested for some sort of syndrome I didn't care enough about to remember what it was called.

I couldn't give a shit either way. I just go with it, let them talk, let them swarm around me... I joke with the guys and entertain the girls, even though most of them are mindless fucking bimbos. When I'm finished with them all, I walk through this park and clear my mind. I always take far too long to walk home, drawing out the time until I have to talk to yet more people.

As I walk slowly on the wet path, breathing in the cold winter air, I hear a muffled noise that sounds like someone struggling. I frown but keep to my route. Then I hear shuffling and I try to look around me to see if I can see something.

Nothing. I'm all alone...

"Aaaaaaaaaaahhhhh!!!" A woman screams, loud and screeching!

Like a fucking banshee permeating the frigid air of this silent night and I feel the fear in it. The emotion is so strong it almost knocks me on my fucking knees, traveling through my blood until it reaches my dick with such force it stops me in my tracks.

I look down at myself, wondering why the fuck am I sporting a semi right now.

Then the woman screams again, the banshee screech filling the night and without thinking I walk in its direction. I look around myself several times, but no one else seems to be around. My dick is pulsing in my jeans, my blood is boiling, my pulse is racing, and I swear to the fucking gods, I feel the strain of a smile on my face.

I'm a long way away from the path, hidden behind some thick trees, the light from the path too far away for this area to be lit. I see a man, lying face down on the ground grinding its body against something. My eyes can barely register what's happening, but when they do, I see it.

Rape. Fucking rape.

My dick jolts and I feel like I want to throw up. Bile rises up my throat, burning its way until it reaches the back of my tongue and just as I hear shuffling somewhere behind me, I flee in the opposite direction until I'm a few dozen yards away. I stop and throw up until there's nothing left in my stomach.

Loathing... disgust... confusion... not at what that son of a bitch was doing... no... at my dick springing into fucking action, at my blood rushing through my veins, at the delicious shiver spreading all over my body leaving goosebumps in its trail, at the fucking rush of lust and pleasure that spread all over my body when her fear hit my ears.

I dropped on my knees and stayed there for what felt like hours, processing what had happened.

That was the first time I actually felt someone's emotions, and empathy is not my strong point. I understand my mother loves me; I learned how to read people, I understand the shifts in disposition, the rise in the pulse, the strain of the facial expressions, the way the temperature of the skin changes depending on moods, but actually feeling someone's emotions... no... that night was the first time.

I didn't know how to process it... I could feel it haunting me for days... she was terrified, she was in pain... and I ran...

* * *

Present day

That night haunted me for years. I looked for that rush in every girl I was with, but then I realized that I was gaining a reputation at school. I was the beast that fucked girls until they screamed. Yet no matter what, most of them still came back for more. I'm not sure if it was a challenge for them or if they actually craved what I had to give. I didn't give a shit either way; I fucked them all anyway, searching endlessly for that banshee scream that made me feel.

I never found it... I enjoyed it though, throwing them around, stretching their young pussies with my fingers and my dick. I enjoyed pushing their limits. Further and further, I pushed. And sometimes though... sometimes... I slammed my thick dick into them without any prep and even though they never said anything, I knew it hurt them and I fucking loved it. I loved the yelp they let out from the pain, I fed on it, fed on their nails digging hard into my skin, feeling how their bodies tensed up and their pussies strangled me—it was the closest thing to what I felt that night in the park.

Eventually, I thought it was an anomaly, a horrible dream or a beautiful nightmare that twisted that sound in my head, made me think it meant more than it truly did because nothing I have tried since made me feel the same thing ever again.

Until one night, years later...

Fresh out of University, barely twenty-two years old and as I was going home to my rented apartment after a night out with some friends when the banshee revealed herself to me.

Down a quiet street, through a dark and dirty alleyway, I found her. Trapped against the filthy flesh of a man trying to abuse her. The banshee screamed and screamed, even against his filthy palm and all the memories came flooding back. That pain in the soundwaves, the fear in its wake, the foreboding... it filled me with adrenaline, with pleasure, with pain—I felt it all, felt what she felt, and it made me feel alive, so fucking alive. Yet her voice, there was something about it, something I couldn't quite put my hand on. A song.

My dick came out to play as well, hard as a fucking rock, but this was not its time, no... this was fuel for my soul, like a beautiful, dark self-discovery, my senses blooming, reveling in all the new sensations flooding them.

I went straight for them and with a smile on my fucking face I beat that filthy motherfucker to a pulp until he couldn't get up anymore.

I didn't kill him, no, I just left him mangled and bloodied on the wet concrete, cradling his stomach as he was going in and out of consciousness. He fucking deserved it all, and I turned my back on him with a new purpose embed deep into my soul.

The woman though... in that dark alley, I didn't get a good

look at her, but her hair was wild, long, dark, and thick; it seemed like it was floating around her and those eyes... even in the dark of the night, they shined. There was something about her, but she ran before I could say anything, yet strangely, she stayed until I was done beating that asshole.

That night I found my way into a couple of fetish websites and I searched and searched until I found women willing to play my game.

And I played... for years I played... and it was fun, they fed my hunger, but never enough to be fully sated. I never ever found what I was looking for, what I craved, what my soul needed.

That banshee scream that completed my soul.

SUKI

I feel the pain, traveling like lightning through my body, a psychological one that is threatening to destroy me.

Then I feel the physical pain. My scalp is burning badly, my back, my ass and my legs feel like they are being dragged through hot coals.

I blink a few times only to realize I am actually being dragged by my hair, through the rough terrain of the woods, the snow ironically burning my skin. I wince as I throw my arms backwards, finding the hand dragging me along, and I pull as hard as I can, scratching his skin in the process. That action earns me a painful slap on my right cheek, making the throbbing pain in my head even worse.

I wince and dig my heels into the ground, thankful for the boots I am wearing, and pull on his arm as hard as I can. He stumbles forward, losing his grip and my head hits the ground with a loud thud that makes me see white. At this point, I most likely have a concussion, yet it is still the least of my worries.

"You fucking bitch!"

I see his boots turning fast towards me and I try to scurry backwards, but I do not manage to move far enough before I see his boot coming violently towards me. He kicks me once in the ribs and the pain spreads so quickly through my body that it almost stuns me. I push through it as I urge my body not to falter and I try to get up.

He kicks me again, getting my belly this time, making me instantly nauseous and it makes me stumble. I'm hunched over somewhere in front of him, but I dig my heels in the ground and push myself forward as hard and as fast as I can, slamming my body into his. He grabs onto me and tries to hold his balance as he stumbles backwards, slipping on the icy snow at the same time.

"What the fuck?!" he yells at me as his body slams hard into a tree, and I use the force of a punch in his gut to push myself away from him.

I take a step back and before he regains his wits, I side kick him in the bleeding wound my shattered glass left behind. He bellows in pain, yet those sounds are filled with hate and peril.

"I'm gonna fucking kill you, little bird! I'm gonna burn you, cut you, brand you, then I'm gonna tear your fucking heart out as my dick rips your fucking cunt open!"

I turn to run as those words sink deep beneath my skin, fully aware that they are not empty threats... not at all. I manage to run a few yards before the pain in my ribs knocks the air out of me, but before I can even process what is happening, I feel something hitting my back so hard, I land face first on the ground, my arms barely reaching under me to break my fall.

I try to get up, but in the next second, he flips me over with another kick to my belly and the first thing I see is his black snow boot sitting heavily at the base of my throat. My gaze follows his jeans covered leg, up to his blood-soaked groin, to his heaving chest and straight into his eyes. So dark and evil, I know for sure, if I don't escape now, this is my end. There is no doubt about it, no denying it, this is my end.

He is pushing me down with his foot, constricting my airways as he presses harder and I grab onto it with both hands, panic starting to settle in my gut. There is a sick grin on his face and I recognize it.

So I do the only thing that feels natural at this moment.

I scream.

I scream as hard as I fucking can and before I know it I'm screaming for *him*...

NIKLAS

She's screaming my name... *my* name.

There's so much in that voice, in the way every sound of each letter forms my name. There's pain, desperation, fear, so much fucking fear, but... hidden between the pain-filled lyrics of my siren's song there is hope. I can *feel* it all.

And as my heavy steps hit the ground, I wonder how it's possible for me to feel all that. Before her, in other women, I could feel the fear and only that, but when Suki screams... I feel everything, every single emotion painted in her songs. Every. Single. One.

I was already running fast, but now, if it's even possible, I run even faster, holding the rifle from hitting my back, clutching it so hard, I could fucking bend the metal.

Suddenly, the siren's song stops, and I realize that for the first time in my life I actually feel fear.

Fear for what I'm going to find when I finally get to her.

Fear for what it's going to do to me.

Fear... for my fucking future.

I went off the trail to follow her scream and after what

seemed like hours, I finally caught a new one through the snow. It looks different, it doesn't look like someone walked on this path.

The motherfucker dragged her!

Dropping on one knee with one fluid motion, I grab the rifle, pop the scope against my eye and look ahead as far as I can. There's nothing. I follow the trail with the scope, but there's no one there. I get up and keep going, perfectly aware that I'm out in the open and if that motherfucker has a gun, he could shoot me at any time. I have to take the risk though, I know I have to.

I follow the trail through the silence of the dark woods until it stops. It actually fucking ends, and as I look around and take in the way the snow looks, I can feel my blood boiling, anger seeping through my veins at the realization that the motherfucker did to me exactly what I did to him when I saved Suki. He covered his motherfucking tracks just as I did. I know that the moment I have him in my hands, I will rip him apart, limb from motherfucking limb while he flails in front of me.

There's no time to waste, the forest is too silent, and the loss of her song is felt heavily, even the air is missing it. The night vision of the rifle is the only thing that saves me right now, giving me enough light to try and identify where the snow looks different, where the trail was covered.

I pick up faint marks in this sea of white that look like they could be it, even though they're already covered in fresh snow. I go for it, but with the scope against my eye, I can't run.

Probably around half an hour later, I hear something, a shift through the trees, and I throw myself on the ground just as I hear a loud gunshot and feel a burn in my left arm.

Motherfucker shot me!

Getting up on one knee, I keep as low as possible behind

the thick snow, and I grab the rifle, trying to get a good look through the scope. To the right of the path, in the far distance, I see him, running away.

I aim and shoot, just as he takes a sharp left, narrowly avoiding the bullet.

Son of a bitch.

Aiming for his legs again, I shoot. This time I know that I at least grazed him because he screams for just a second but keeps going. I get on my feet, and just as I'm about to run after him, I hear a weak moan in the opposite direction.

Fuck! Suki...

I have no choice, I follow the moan until I reach her, cursing as I look at her unconscious, frail frame sprawled on the freezing ground. A soft, thin layer of fresh snow covers her body. She has a sweater on and my mother's boots, but her legs are naked.

Dropping on my knees next to her, I look through the scope scanning the area around us. I can't see him anymore. I realize now that the shot he fired was random, he didn't shoot to kill, he shot to slow me down so he could escape.

No matter. I know where the motherfucker lives; I will find him, and he is going to fucking pay.

I gather her cold body into my arms, and she moans again. She sniffs the air in her confused, dazed state and suddenly her small hands grab onto my jacket, trying as hard as she fucking can to bury herself deeper into my body, like she's attempting to make a hole and crawl inside of me. I tense.

When she's satisfied that she's gotten as close as she possibly can, her whole body relaxes; she's soft and comfortable... She fits, in my strong arms, her small delicate hands holding on to me for dear life, her head nestling in the crook of my neck.

She fucking fits! Damn it!

CHAPTER 12

NIKLAS

I look at my broken front door and curse. The cold is already getting in the house, the fire is off.

It's dark, but I have to put her down to turn on the light. I lay her gently on the sheepskin in front of the fireplace, cursing again at the irony of the situation and the fucked up déjà vu.

After I check the damage to the front door, I drape a leftover piece of plywood and cover the hole where a window used to be.

I hurry back to Suki, and I can't help but let out the faintest gasp. That motherfucker did a number on her. The left side of her face is red and slightly swollen, her right temple is bleeding. I look at her bare, soft, pale legs and I turn her gently on her side.

"Fuck!" I'm seething. Her beautiful legs are marked by bloody scrapes and red lines. I know the fucker hit her and dragged her through the fucking snow, but seeing her body like this... I curse violent promises under my breath.

She moans again, the softest sound. I thought she was coming back to reality, but she isn't. She shivers and gathers her body, rolling into a ball on the sheepskin. I take that as a cue and shift to the fireplace so I can build the fire, but halfway through the process I decide it's not enough, and I head upstairs after I cover her cold body with the blanket.

When I come back downstairs, she's in the exact same position, still unconscious, and I scoop up her battered body, carrying her upstairs to the bathroom. The bathtub is halfway full by the time I lay her gently on the floor right next to it, and the steam from the hot water is already calming her shivering body.

I undress myself first, then gently pull off every single item of clothing covering her body, before I finish with the boots.

I can't stop looking at her. So many fucking battle scars from this motherfucker. No matter how many times I see her naked body, I can't seem to get used to the idea. On the contrary, my anger grows, my demons howl in hunger for the savage that did this to her.

I gather her in my arms, step into the bathtub and lay her down, feet first, before sitting behind her and gathering her between my legs, her back against my chest, her head resting on my right shoulder.

"Niklas..." she whispers, and I swear to the fucking gods something shifts in my brain, almost like it's getting rewired, like voice fucking recognition getting used to its user. Those letters flowing from her pretty, pale lips sound like they invented my name themselves, almost like it never really existed before she put those letters together. Fucking surreal.

I take a deep, slow, strained breath, and I feel her shifting in my arms.

"You're okay, Suki. You're okay."

"Niklas?" she finally sounds like she's waking up. I shift a bit so I can see her face. Grabbing a sponge, I start cleaning the blood from her temple as she's slowly coming back to reality.

"Thank you..." she tells me in her tired voice as her sleepy, gorgeous, bright eyes knock down more walls inside of me. She shifts, lies back in the middle of my chest, and I loosen my grip on her body. She slides down until everything but her face is underwater—lying there, in-between my legs, almost floating in this big bathtub, her eyes fixed on the ceiling. I let her be, but I can't take my eyes off her.

She's mesmerizing, like a true fucking siren, her dark hair dancing gently in the water that's turned pink with our blood.

"For a man that wants to hurt me, you seem to be saving me quite a lot."

She's right and isn't that fucking ironic. "For a woman that keeps running from me, you seem to seek me quite a lot." She stiffens in the water at my words. Like she only just realized that she's been calling my name for real, not just in her mind.

I wrap my arm around her ribs, under her boobs again and pull her onto me. She doesn't protest, but she winces in pain and I groan. Only her head is out of the water, the rest of her is safely tucked away in the warmth of the bath.

"What happened?" It wasn't hard to figure it out, but it's my detached way of asking her if she's okay.

She sighs, "He saw us..."

It's not fear that I hear in her voice. It's... annoyance.

"What?!" my tone harsher than I intend.

"In the woods... when you chased me... when you pinned me down and..."

"Fucked you?" I finish for her.

She sighs again, "Then too..."

"Motherfucker..." I mouth. That bastard watched us, all this time he knew where she was, and I was the asshole that couldn't protect her. I'm also the asshole that wasn't supposed to protect her. This is not why I brought her here, she wasn't supposed to be mine to protect...

"What now?" she asks. There's no fear in her voice, no emotion, just a matter of fact type question.

"I will kill him. Your life... He has no claim to it."

"And you do?!" her tone grows stronger.

With a slight grin on my lips, I bring my free hand to her frail throat, cupping the sides and squeezing. My thumb tilts her head to the right and I bend my head, all but touching her ear.

"Yes. When you screamed in that forest for the first time, your demons wailed and mine responded to the call. That was the moment your life became mine, little siren. Do not mistaken my actions for kindness."

I can feel her pulse getting faster under the touch of my palm. She doesn't falter, but her heart betrays her.

"Who hurt you?!" her sassy tone comes forth.

I squeeze her middle closer to my body. I know her bruised body must hurt already, maybe she just needs a slight reminder that it can hurt even more. "What makes you think someone hurt me, little siren?" my tone grows rougher.

"This incessant need for violence... it must have come from somewhere," she says as her body relaxes into my violent touch.

"Some monsters are not made, Suki. Some monsters are born."

SUKI

Yes... some monsters are born. I already know this, don't I?

I have seen the demons in my mother... I see them every time I look in the mirror. No matter how much I do not want this to be true, some people are indeed born evil.

He holds me pressed to his chest, my head tilted to the side and I should squirm, I should fight, but I do not, because yet again, my life is literally in his hands and I feel... free. He takes my free will, he takes my power, he takes my control and gives me pure freedom instead. I cannot make sense of it, but there's a sweet release that I feel deep within my core, release of everything that I am and everything I can become. I feel like anything can happen and I do not even have to bother deciding what.

I smile as his thumb moves slowly up and down my throat, and I just stare out the picture window, admiring the starry sky, the same color as his eyes.

"Suki..."

He says my name in that low vibrating voice, and I sink into every sound that leaves his mouth.

"Why did you kill your mother?"

I knew this question would come eventually. Yes, my mother killed my baby brother, my father, and my stepmother. However, even though I would be justified to kill her in retaliation... she was *my mother*. I was expecting him to catch on, but that does not mean I am ready to strip my soul for him.

"Because she killed my family," I respond in a calm, even tone.

"Suki..." his tone is a warning, his hand squeezing my throat ever so slightly.

"Because she killed my family!" my tone more urgent.

This time he squeezes my throat harder without saying anything else, constricting my airways just enough to convince me.

"Niklas..." He squeezes for a few more seconds and I hear him inhale deeply, his nose buried in my hair. I close my eyes just for a second, allowing myself to enjoy the strange intimacy—his hand on my throat, his nose in my hair, the smile on my face. He releases me and my head falls to the side.

I cannot read him. I do not understand his actions half the time. Almost like he wants something but refuses to admit it to me... or himself. His touch speaks louder than words though, I just need to learn his language.

"My dad... he worked so much to support us, to give us all we needed. He loved her so much... and she, my mother... she shit on everything he did." I sigh... I am not sure if I am getting off this mountain alive anyway, so what difference does it make if I bare my soul to him and puke out the cruelty?

At least this way there will be one person in this world to truly know me... even after I am gone, even if he will be the one to end me.

"I do not remember a time my mother acted like a

mother. She beat those memories out of me, ripped me open and burned it all to the ground. She had a drug problem," I continue, "and not enough money to sustain her cravings. When she was high, the world was okay... when she was coming down... I had to hide. When she was in withdrawal with no way of getting the drugs... there was nowhere for me to run. She beat me, countless times, for years. She told me she would kill me if I told dad... I believed her. I was a child, it all happened before I was even ten years old." I inhale a centering breath.

"She fucked men for drugs... I was in the house most times it happened. One of those times... he wanted more, her old-ass pussy was not enough." I feel Niklas' arm around my ribs tensing. Somehow I know he does not intend to hurt me, he is just... holding me... or onto me. I sink into the feeling...

"Did he...?" he tentatively asks almost in a whisper, unsure if he truly wants the answer.

"No. He got close... but then my mother had this rare moment of clarity and stopped him. It was short lived because after he left without giving her the drugs she needed, she took it out on me. She was so careful every time, she never hit me where dad would see it, but finally, one day he actually caught her. Came home early... saw it all... He never forgave himself, until the day he died, he never forgave himself for what she did to me and the fact that he was blind to it for so many years."

"Did you blame him?"

"Never. He worked so hard for us, he did everything for us. I blamed myself... for years. Blamed myself for not fighting her off me, but then again... I was a child. Even then though, I didn't want dad to suffer, to worry, so I took it all... I knew he loved her... I rationalized my secrecy with keeping the object of his affection close to him."

"When did he remarry?" His questions are barely audible, like he does not know how to ask them and show disinterest at the same time.

"I was fifteen... she killed them almost three years later."

"Then you killed her."

"Yes."

"Good."

Here it is again. That tone in his voice that approves of this, of me, of killing my mother. It sounds like pure evil, vibrating so deep inside of him, like the depths of hell are urging me to embrace the darkness inside of myself.

"How am I less of a monster than she was? After all... I took a life as well." I turn my head to the left and catch his midnight gaze.

"Because you took the right life." He holds my eyes, I cannot blink.

The right life...

"Does that justify what I have done?"

"In this world, Suki, we don't need to justify ourselves. Stop playing by the rules of a world you don't belong to and let the demons roam free. Let them sate their hunger, let them revel in the blood they crave."

His hand is cradling the side of my head, his thumb moving gently on my skin, making me spin out of control. My head is already pounding from Adrien hitting me, but now, it is even worse. I do not know what to make of this, of Niklas. His words bite, they threaten and possess, his hands though, they possess as well... just not in the same way.

I take in his words and turn them over in my head repeatedly. I'm not entirely sure what world I belong to. I always fought too hard to feel like I belonged in the world I was born in. However, I do not know if I belong in his world either.

There is remorse in my soul. Isn't there? I feel like I am floating in limbo, trapped between two worlds, each of them pulling me in their direction for totally distinct reasons.

"Niklas..."

"Yes, Suki."

"What do you want from me?" I hold his gaze as he ponders my question. I need to know. My head is spinning, my heart is stumbling and my body is trembling with the confusion he creates inside of me. His words say something, his body language something else, and the man himself... the man gives me all sorts of mixed feelings, from fear to desire to murderous hunger and lust.

I touch the hand cupping my face and the arm holding my body afloat. Then I run my fingers through his thick wiry beard before cupping his cheek and it is then that I see it. His brooding expression falters, and I swear I can feel his skin softening into my palm. I do not want to miss this, miss that spark in his eyes that only seems to happen because of me.

I see it when he touches me.

I see it when he is about to run after me.

I see it when I scream.

But I'm afraid if I look into his eyes for too long, he will know what I see... and he will somehow end it, hide. I close my eyes, feeling like I would rather stop looking now, rather than never see it again.

"What do you want from me, Niklas?" I ask again, my eyes closed, hand still on his cheek brushing slowly past his temple and to the short hair at the side of his head.

I feel his cock hardening against my back, but he does not move. He does not even twitch.

"I don't know anymore..." My eyes dart open and I am assaulted by his blue gaze. I feel like I'm drowning again, pulled into the depths of an ocean of his own creation, demons welcoming me and the monster, the monster is coming for me.

He doesn't know...

I turn my gaze, looking at our bodies, fitted together like two Tetris pieces in the pink water.

Pink water?

I run a hand over the spot on my head that hurts and I see the blood smeared on it. I know there are at least two cuts on my legs that must have been bleeding and turned the water pink as well.

There is something poetic about this, bathing in the pink water stained by my blood. I would cut myself even more just so I can saturate the color to a more satisfying shade.

I turn my head towards him again, but then I notice his arm.

What the hell?!

I reach over with my hand and touch what looks like a deformed hole on the side of his bicep. He does not even twitch at the contact. He does not even look down to it. He just... watches me.

He's bleeding, quite hard as well, but he does not seem bothered by it at all.

I cannot help it... the blood smears over my hand, the crimson glistening in the soft light of the bathroom. I bring my middle finger to my mouth, spreading his sweet scent before plunging it between my lips, sucking the blood off it.

I hear a muted moan in my ears and the next second his hand is on my throat, tilting my head upwards, before he presses his lips onto mine with a hunger that threatens to devour me. I realize the moan came from me.

My bloody hand grabs onto his arm, the other ones goes into his hair, pulling him and pushing him all at the same time. His sweet blood is on his lips now, and damn, he tastes like maple—sweet, rich, dense... addictive.

His cock grows even bigger, pressing into my back and I arch with the electrifying sensation traveling from my blood-stained lips to my nipples, down my belly, and to my pussy that he just covered with his large hand, squeezing just enough to make me squirm in a delicious pain.

Suddenly, I feel... alive! Ravenous! Like I have been starved for centuries!

I break the kiss, turn around onto my knees with his hand still holding my throat in a possessive grip, and I straddle him. His thick cock rubs on my swollen flesh, moving just enough so he can probe at my entrance. The look he gives me is murderous, and I grin as my body breaks into shivering goosebumps.

I look at his bleeding arm and lean in, licking the blood off slowly just as I impale myself with his thick cock. The growl that escapes his throat vibrates through my body, making my pussy squeeze him even harder. Looking into his eyes, I swallow the crimson maple syrup that is his blood just as I take him all in, painfully to the hilt.

The hand on my throat pulls me in, his lips crashing onto mine, his tongue pushing violently into my mouth. His other hand pushes hard on the small of my back, seemingly wanting to thrust his cock even deeper inside of me, holding me there for as long as possible.

I cannot blame him. I want to mold my body to his, my pussy to his cock. I want him imprinted inside of me so I can never forget this delicious pain that makes me want to explode in screams and disturbing laughter.

We're fucking in a bathtub filled with our diluted blood. How sinisterly poetic.

I force my hips up, against his grip and slam down as hard as I can, water spilling out the bathtub.

He holds me there again, and I feel his cock twitching inside of me, pushing on flesh that I have never felt before, never knew existed.

I force myself up again and slam down hard, water falling in waves onto the tile covered floor. I hear a moan escaping from him, into my mouth that's filled with his tongue, exploring every crevasse.

My hands move on his back, right at the base of his neck, and I rise again. Just as I dig my nails into his flesh, drawing blood, I slam down so hard onto his cock, I swear the flesh of my pussy tears, and I scream into his mouth from the pain and desire that came from it. He growls like a monster, and the hand that was on my back, moves to my hair, pulling hard backwards, bending my throat now held tighter in his grip.

I do not rise again, I just sway my hips, grinding on the cock impaling me. He pulls my head back until I am forced to release his neck and brace myself with my hands behind me, holding onto his legs. He releases my throat and thrusts his hips up, just as he pinches my left nipple, and I cannot help but let out a strained scream.

He thrusts again and pinches the other nipple. He does it again and again and the world around us bursts into chaos.

My banshee screams...

His monstrous growls...

The slapping of our skin underwater...

The water falling in wave after wave onto the bathroom floor...

Delicious chaos. And we sink into it.

All of a sudden, it all happens at once. He releases my hair, pulls me close to his body, shifts his legs under himself, bending forwards and pushing up with a force that must have emptied half the bath water. In a fraction of a second, I find myself lying back on a soaked bathmat that used to be thick and fluffy with a behemoth of a man buried between my spread legs. Face first.

He's lapping at my sore pussy, licking his way inside as I squeeze my thighs around his head. But he does not let me, his rough hands push my spread legs up until they press onto my breasts.

His attack on my pussy drives me crazy, and I find myself holding on to the backs of my knees for dear life. He uses this to his advantage, releases me and plunges his fingers so deep into my core I feel like I could burst into a million orgasms then and there. But I don't, because in the next second he pulls them out and adds yet another finger, stretching and massaging the walls of my pussy, sending shock after shock into my body.

"Fucking beautiful," he whispers as his eyes burn into mine.

His assault continues, and I feel his fingers spreading inside of me, stretching me and I find myself screaming for more before I can stop myself. He doesn't hesitate. I feel the forceful intrusion of yet another finger and I look down, watching four of them sliding in a slow, delicious motion into my stretched pussy and the pleasure I feel makes me want to scream.

So I do.

He pushes in, to the knuckles, picks up the rhythm and finger fucks me so hard and fast, stretching me in a way that promises to split my pussy open, but then the ecstasy takes over and I feel like I could burst into tears.

"You're fucking perfect, Suki, just like this pussy stretched hard around my thick fingers. Fucking perfect..."

"Niklas..." I whisper, my pleading voice asking for something, for more, for everything.

"Fuck." I hear the strained voice just before he stops

the assault, shifts his body, and his cock impales me to hilt, ripping yet another scream from my lungs.

With my legs folded onto my body, he reaches so deep inside of me that I swear my organs rearrange themselves just to accommodate him.

He pulls out in a torturously slow movement, before he thrusts hard. He does this countless times, ripping yelp after yelp from my throat, the torture delicious, yet excruciating at the same time.

"Niklas... I can't..." I cry.

"Look at me, Suki." I did not even realize my eyes were shut. I open them and his eyes are on fire, a ravenous fire at the bottom of the ocean and I find myself swimming towards it.

"Open," he orders as he pushes his index and middle finger into my mouth, coating them with my saliva, before he reaches between us and pushes them hard on my clit.

I cannot help but notice that our bodies are smeared in blood. His blood, mine, who knows. We look like we came from battle and this is our fucking prize.

I moan as my hips attempt to buck upwards. He continues to rub my clit—around it, on top of it, up and down, then in circles, and when he finds that delicious movement that makes my whole body squirm, he holds on to the rhythm and I cannot take it... his thick cock stretching me, his fingers finding just the right spot, his eyes burning into mine...

I come with a force that promises to shake the fucking ground. Wave after wave of pleasure, strangling the cock that thrusts into me with even more force now, pushing me so hard into the soaked floor, I know my back will be covered in bruises tomorrow.

I ride those waves just as he comes hard, spilling fire into my core, his cock jerking violently inside of me, groaning in ecstasy.

I find myself wrapped around his crimson smeared body with every limb. Holding on for dear life as he crashes on top of me, careful not to suffocate me, but his delicious weight is anything but suffocating.

Our ragged breaths are the only thing disturbing the silence of the house.

And I find myself smiling. Yet again.

CHAPTER 13

NIKLAS

I finally gather the strength to pull out of that sweet, tight cunt and she releases me from the clutches of her limbs. Instead of rolling over, I sit back on my knees, before falling back on my ass, leaning against the tub.

She's fucking beautiful. The siren sang her song for me tonight, and she did it... she pulled me into the depths of the ocean so fucking hard that I'm not quite sure what happened to me, but I'm certain I don't want to return to the surface.

Sitting back, I watch her beautiful, soft body lying naked on the wet floor, her eyes covered by one forearm, the other hand pressed on her sternum as it rises and falls with deep, centering breaths. My eyes drift to her spread legs and to my cum spilling slowly out of her beautiful cunt, through her folds, towards her plump ass cheeks. I cock my head, lost in this beautiful picture before me, I could fucking frame it and look at it all day... every single day.

I lean over and slowly run my index finger through her folds and she startles, her swollen flesh far too sensitive right now. I spread my cum on her pussy, then between the curls of her mound, on her lower belly, drawing aimless patterns on her pale, soft skin.

She doesn't protest, she doesn't squirm or move away, she just lies there, and to my surprise, she relaxes under the twisted touch. Her breaths get deeper and slower and it makes me want to ask the same question she asked me... what does *she* want from me?

I know... I know she wants me to let her go. At least that's what she wanted until she took control in the bathtub, fueled by actual bloodthirst. I couldn't move as she impaled herself on me, wiping the memory of any other pussy that's ever touched me. Stunned. Trapped in the primal movements of her eyes taking me all in, trapped by the moans vibrating in that throat that I wanted to constantly feel under my palm, trapped in the delicious silky feeling of her tongue licking the blood seeping out of the bullet wound.

Fuck!

Obviously, what she wants from me is not something I would have had a reason to ask her even three hours ago, but now... after what she just did, I would quite enjoy finding out what the fuck is going on through that twisted mind of hers.

Yes, she's my captive.

Yes, I saved her.

No, I'm not letting her go.

Not yet anyway, not until I get my fill of her, not until

her demons stop singing for me. I'm not making her develop any fucked up Stockholm syndrome, that is not my aim and it's quite obvious that I don't treat her well enough for that anyway. However, my behavior is exactly what she needs, it's what her demons crave.

I turn and reach for the sponge sitting on the edge of the bathtub, rinsing it under the tap, before leaning over and cleaning my cum off her body. She props herself on her elbows and watches me as I wipe her swollen pussy, her curls, then her belly, rinsing the sponge in-between each before leaving it on the edge of the bath. When I look up, there's confusion in her bright green eyes, mixed with emotions I can't quite grasp.

That's something I could never quite understand. I can read people's actions, predict their behavior to the point that words are quite unnecessary. However, handling other people's emotions or trying to understand their origins and impact, feels like I'm forced in solitary confinement with a bomb I need to disarm before it's too late.

It's interesting. Even now, in this silence, in this situation that should be filled by awkward unspoken words, it's anything but. It's comfortable, even with that curious, scrutinizing gaze in her eyes. The unspoken words traveling between us are part of an ethereal conversation that somehow we both understand. We know this meant something, yet neither of us truly knows what.

But it was pivotal.

She breaks the eye contact and shifts, bringing her legs under herself and lifting onto her knees. She comes towards me and my breath gets caught in my throat until she straddles my naked thighs.

I'm once again stunned by the situation and the shift I see in her. She's taking control. Of me, of herself, of the situation.

It should make me uncomfortable, but instead it sparks a curiosity in me that was never there before. It's something of her own creation, a demon she birthed inside of me and that only she controls, probably without even knowing.

I watch as she leans over to the basket sitting on the bathtub and grabs a washcloth that she runs under the tap. She moves to my bicep, wipes the bullet wound and inspects.

"I don't think there's any remnants of the bullet. Clean straight through. You do however need stitches," She says in a soft, faint voice that swirls through my soul.

I look down at my arm. I'm still bleeding, but it's not quite that bad. Looking at her, I inspect her head where the skin was broken, brushing a strand of hair away from her beautiful, pale skin. She needs some closure strips on her temple, her eye is now bruised and a little swollen, and I'm not entirely convinced she doesn't have a concussion.

This is a reminder that I lost control. I do not like losing control.

SUKI

He moves me off his lap before he gets up, and I'm left here kneeling, wondering what just happened. I was simply taking care of him, as he did to me before. I look up, only to find his sinewed arm pointed at me, palm facing up, waiting for me to grab it.

You're overthinking things, Suki.

I take his hand, get up, and for a few seconds we both seem to forget what we are supposed to do—we simply stand here, looking at each other. We are both smeared in blood and in the aftermath of that intense fucking, we just look dirty.

However, no matter what, the sweet maple flavor of his blood will forever be imprinted on my tongue.

I bring my gaze to his dark blue eyes, his head cocked, watching me, studying, yet his expression betrays nothing. There is an emotional emptiness in his eyes that I cannot read, an intensity that I cannot quite describe. It is something specific to him and him alone and it scares me.

Suddenly, his expression shifts, like he is done observing and he reached a conclusion. He turns and heads to the walk-in shower, stopping right at the entrance and turns to me, silent.

For a split second, I thought he wanted me out. Just for a split, irrational second.

I walk over and enter the shower, stopping in front of that magnificent view. It's dark, but the moonlight is still reflecting on the snow that covers the landscape. I take a deep breath through my nose and midway, it hits me so hard I stumble backwards, under the stream of the shower and right into his hard body.

I'm shaking.

"Suki?!" I hear his deep voice vibrating through me as one of his strong arms encircles my chest above my breasts. I clutch it with both hands, holding him tight, pressing it into my body.

"He could..."

"No. It's treated. Same as the window above the bath. We can see, he can't."

I let out the breath I was holding and relax under his touch. I look up at him, so damn grateful for this... He nods, ever so slightly, in acknowledgment.

He lets me go.

A few minutes later I'm sitting, yet again, on the countertop next to the sink as he applies cream to whatever new scrapes and cuts I have on my body. He reapplies on my feet, which have not healed yet, but thankfully they do not hurt. Or maybe I just got used to pain. He inspects my face, tracing my bruises with his calloused fingers and I see something in his gaze. Something that was not there before and I cannot quite figure out what it is. An emotion. I am convinced I am seeing it because it is something new, something he has not learned to hide yet, because he does not know it exists.

It is mine. I see it behind his eyes. A demon that smiles

at me.

I smile back.

He carefully mended the cut on my temple with some closure strips and already gave me some meds for my growing headache. Now I watch his thick fingers threading a surgical needle, aiming it at the bullet hole that pierces his arm. Covering his big hand with mine, I pull the needle away from him, just as I wrap my legs around his body, pulling him towards me so I can see the wound properly. I can feel his gaze following my every move.

He doesn't even wince when I apply more alcohol to the open wound. Not even when I push the needle into his flesh, slowly and carefully stitching one side to the other, before moving to the back of his arm, where the exit hole is.

That intense gaze feels heavy on me. Not on the wound, not on the needle going in and out of his skin, but on me. He does not move, does not wince, does not protest, he simply shifts in whatever direction I push him in for better access, watching me the whole time.

When I finish, he takes away the needle and thread and places it on the other side of the sink, before inspecting my handiwork in the mirror. He turns to me and this time his gaze holds a surprised, questioning look.

"I learned..."

The unspoken heartbreak lingers heavy in the air, and he takes in a deep, charged breath. I learned, I had to. Adrien never did this, take care of me like this stranger does. He did, however, leave a first aid kit in my dungeon.

I learned...

He turns and leaves the bathroom. I sigh and turn to look at the moonlit scenery once again. This. I'm going to miss this.

I sigh again, jumping off the countertop just as he walks back in the bathroom holding another one of his t-shirts. I thank him with a slight smile and pull it over my head after handing him my towel.

We walk out of the bathroom together and stop in the hallway.

"Thank you..." I finally say. It feels surreal. This man saved me and captured me all at the same time. This whole situation is a sick contradiction that would make no sense in any other world but ours. A victim does not thank her kidnapper, but he is the lesser of two evils and no matter how much I want to believe otherwise, Niklas is my kind of evil.

He gives me a slight nod and turns around.

Surreal.

I turn and head to *my* room, climbing under the covers of *my* bed. I'm safe now. Sleep takes me immediately.

NIKLAS

I didn't want to leave her alone, not since I have a feeling she might have a concussion, but she doesn't belong in this room and I need to be here.

I watch my computer screens come alive, all five of them sitting on the large desk of my office. I might have sold my defense technology company, but my skills have been useful for completely opposite purposes.

However, over the years I figured out how to branch out from developing systems that can be used for defense, especially in war zones, to using my tech skills so I can find people that no one is searching for. I created my own programs, my own defenses, my own face recognition software. I developed codes that could destroy their lives in minutes, reduce them to shadows, codes that would quite literally destroy every single mention of them in history.

I've also developed codes that would erase everything from these computers, even from my cloud section hidden in the dark web, like nothing ever happened and no one could ever hold it against me. I have a backup for all my technology, of course I do. No matter what, I will never stop. I will rebuild if it comes to it.

The thrill of the fucking kill will always be mine and no one will ever take that away. Evil howls inside of me when it witnesses those red threads of life leaving my victims' bodies and the monster inside of me roars in fucking victory.

I find the chaos. I harness it. Then I destroy what's left behind.

I know who I am. I'm no fucking assassin, I'm no outlaw. I don't pretend to be some sort of fucking indestructible badass. No. I am destructible. I am perishable. However, my 163 IQ certainly helps me have superiority over the motherfuckers that leave their lives at my feet.

What I am is a killer. Plain and simple. A killer.

I choose my victims well though. Unfortunately, there isn't a shortage of motherfuckers out there that truly deserve to die. My specialty is child molesters, abusers, rapists, and killers—I don't discriminate. Men or women, it means nothing to me. Evil is evil and it's not my kind of evil, so it must be destroyed.

My skills are allowing me access to disturbing corners of the dark web and even though the authorities are monitoring a lot of these places as well, I know that they don't have the skills or the resources to do anything about most of these people. Most of the time I don't want them to anyway. I want them all to myself. I want to carve their fucking hearts out and sink my teeth into them while they take their last breaths, watching me.

I can't help but smile. Funny how Suki has an affinity for blood as well.

When I heard her in the woods, when she sang that delicious siren song for the first time, this is not what I imagined. This is not where I thought I would be.

A switch was flipped inside of me, and I'm not sure where I stand anymore. I still have the debilitating urge to destroy her fucking soul and claim it as mine. Only... she seems to be relinquishing to me the few slithers left of her soul anyway, but she's not surrendering it. No. She's giving me access to it. To enjoy it, play with it, rip and sew it back together, all while reveling in the pleasure and pain I bestow on her.

I wanted to give her only pain, because before her I was never interested in anything more. With all the women before her, I never gave a fuck enough to focus on the pleasure pain could bring, they drew the pleasure themselves, but I never offered it. But with Suki... I'm definitely fucking offering it.

Her demons demand pleasure from me, challenge me, threaten me in ways I don't think she even realizes. Her actions scream "no", but her eyes, her eyes burn with an indescribable fire and her demons dominate with an immovable force, challenging me for more. She's forcing her mind to scream "no" as well and it creates this delicious combination of opposite forces fighting for a goal I'm not sure she's conscious of. Two parts of her opposing a third that's more powerful than the others.

No matter how much she tries to oppose, her flesh betrays her. With every touch, every push and pull, every violent finger fucking, it yields, and her body language changes. I wonder when her mind will yield as well.

I realize I've been grinning like an idiot and too much time has passed since I've been standing in the middle of my office, thinking of the fucking vixen staying in my spare bedroom.

Funny. It's all so fucking funny, and I can't help the deeply satisfying feeling settling in my core.

I power up my system and get to work. I need to find everything there is to know about Adrien and get an update from the sheriff.

CHAPTER 14

SUKI

I wake up from the deepest, most calm and safest sleep I have experienced since April, since I was captured. Come to think of it... since long before that. Bright sunlight is streaming in and the air feels light, peaceful.

After last night, after what happened in the bathtub, what I did... I know that the change is permanent. I felt it afterward, but not like I feel it now. It's almost like last night's sleep solidified what my mind barely knew then. A confirmation. This is permanent, his mark on my soul, the demon I created in his. No matter what will happen in the future, no matter where I will be, this will never change. And I fear it, I fear the meaning of this, because it's a destruction of hearts and souls and I don't know if mine can absorb anymore chaos.

I turn on my back, my palms flat against the soft cotton sheets. I squeeze them lightly in my fists, and take a deep breath, slowly shutting my eyes as the air reaches deeper into my lungs. I hold it in. The rush is coming. The pressure building. My lungs are pulsing. My heart is speeding up. And there... in the darkness, I see them. Always clearer than those glimpses I catch in the mirror. The demons come out one by one.

I feel this change in them as well. Their familiar, uncontrollable, chaotic movements long gone. What I see now is pure contempt, satisfaction, control... power. It scares me, it is like they know something I do not.

I feel the warmth. I feel the fire that brought the demons forth long ago... back when the dreams were my only escape. The dreams that started it all. The fire is brighter now, it burns hotter, but the flames are calm, like in the dead of the night, devoid of wind, they burn silently. I wonder if it is because they do not need to crave the danger anymore.

No, it's because it got its first taste. The hunger is sated... for now, and no one else will ever taste the same.

I exhale the deathly breath I was holding in, clutching the soft sheets in my fists, panting heavily. When I turn my head towards the window, my body instantly relaxes. This... this view... No matter how many times I open my eyes and see it, no matter how much time I spend absorbing every tree, every crevasse, every mountain... it's not enough and it cannot just become... normal.

This guest bedroom window is, as the bathroom, at the back of the house and the landscape is only slightly different from what you see at the front. Here, all the lines seem sharper, the mountain peaks higher, and the incline down the mountain steeper. It's wild... well and truly wild. No road, no access, no nothing. Walking in that direction means certain death for whoever doesn't know this mountain. Maybe even for those that do.

My breaths are calm now... my hands relaxed, my body is sinking into the comfortable mattress, and I realize that if I don't get up now, I'll end up drifting away again. I need it, I do... but my stomach needs food as well.

I throw the covers off my body and sit up on the bed facing that calm view, pushing myself to peel my eyes off it. I like this room, cozy and calm, dominated by neutral, soft colors and minimal furniture—a double bed close to the window, a dresser by the door and a mirror, armchair, and wardrobe opposite the bed, all made from light ash wood to fit the soft neutral theme.

He left more clothes for me as I was sleeping.

A rollercoaster, this is what this experience feels like—a rollercoaster. Demons dominate everything he is, the monster lurks in the shadows of his soul, yet sometimes he is... different, and what happened last night, the new emotion, the demon that smiled at me, tells me he is only different with me. It scares me that I want to believe that.

I grab the neatly folded pile of clothes from the dresser—a hoodie, t-shirt, boxers, socks, and a pair of joggers that could potentially cover my whole body head to toe. I decide to risk it and wear everything but the joggers, since the hoodie reaches my knees anyway.

The house is silent. There is no sound coming from his bedroom or the bathroom I walked by before that, so I step carefully down the stairs as I head to the kitchen, since I'm not sure if by any chance he is still sleeping.

This silence, this beautiful peace and quiet, this warm house filled with wood and furs, this mountain... it spreads shivers from my toes, traveling up my body, to the base of my neck and I burst into goosebumps. But when I think of the man that owns it all... I shiver for a whole different reason altogether.

Shaking myself mentally, I turn my attention to the French press to make some coffee before I pull out some ingredients for breakfast. It's funny really. This is something I never thought that I would miss—cooking. So many months with no access to a kitchen and here I am, doing this perfectly mundane task of cooking pancakes, bacon, and eggs... I cannot quite believe how satisfying this feels.

Twenty minutes later, breakfast is cooked and this damn house smells like home. Not like my apartment back in South Dakota... no, it smells like home. If Niklas doesn't scare me enough, this... this does. I shake the thought away, because I know how heartbreakingly impossible this is. Purely suicidal thoughts.

After I split the food between two plates and put his in the oven to keep it warm, I feel the need to get out of this house for now. Walking out on the snowy porch, I take a deep breath that floods my lungs, and I can't help but moan. It's exhilarating. Fresh, cold... it smells like new beginnings. I sit on the steps of the porch with the plate on my thighs and quietly eat as the sun warms my bare legs. This view is like seeing the visual part of those sound machines some people play to fall asleep.

This is it... the birds fluttering their wings as they fly above the trees, the sounds the branches make as they gently sway in the breeze, the frozen snow falling off them and hitting the ground, running water somewhere far away in the background... even the sun seems to make a sound.

This could almost be too much, after months of being in complete darkness, in a dungeon, underground. It's not... it's just right.

I'm halfway through my breakfast when I feel the intensity of his gaze searing itself onto my skin through the two layers of clothes I'm wearing. I turn my head slightly towards the right, stopping just for a second, just enough so he knows I know he's there, before I continue eating. I know it's Niklas, I felt that searing gaze in the woods when he found me, I felt it when he chased me outside... I felt it in the shower. It seared itself into my mind and my body now recognizes it.

I hear the door open and close, before his enormous figure sits next to me on the steps, casting a large shadow over me and I feel the echo of a shiver running through my body.

"Thank you." I hear his sleepy, thick voice that sounds even rougher than normal. Sometimes I feel that if he would yell loud enough, he could split the blankets of snow from the peaks looming in the far distance and create avalanches.

I turn to him and for the first time since he found me... I smile and it reaches my eyes.

NIKLAS

I'm trapped.

She stopped time. With a smile. She stopped time and now, bathed in my shadow, the sun casts a halo around her and the siren looks... empyreal. I would believe it, I would believe she could have come from heaven if I didn't know what I know of her.

But I can see her now like never before, in the calm of the late morning on this snowy mountain, on my territory, I see her—she fits. Her soft, pale skin belongs with this snow. Her unnaturally light green eyes belong with the trees. Her smile... it belongs with me. I see the smile lines in the skin at the outer edge of her almond shaped eyes, the freckles that dust her nose and fade on her cheeks, the shiny line that defines her Cupid's bow, making her plush lips stand out.

And that soft smile... she could conquer empires with it.

She breaks the spell and carries on eating, yet here I am... still staring at her—her gentle, upturned nose, the curve of her lips, the square jaw, her throat moving as she swallows, its softness under my strong hand...

I shake the image forming in my mind and finally turn to look at the plate of food she made for me—crispy, streaky bacon, two fried eggs that smell of butter, and four pancakes.

"You like it here." She turns at my words. "The view... the mountain." I gesture towards it.

She smiles and nods, turning her gaze back at it all, and I follow suite.

"My mother was not surprised I chose to move here. She laughed and said I came back to my roots, where I belong."

I feel her gaze on me. I'm not even sure why I'm still talking, why I'm sharing this.

"My parents moved here from Sweden just before I came along. My last name is Bergman... it quite literally means *mountain man.*"

She chuckles and something breaks inside of me. Music to my fucked up soul...

Somehow it feels like home... not this house, not this mountain, but this moment... this whole morning.

For the first time in a long time, I slept in. Too bad it's because I stayed up far too late looking up information about Adrien. When I opened my eyes and the snow greeted me as always this time of year, it felt different. The snow shining under the sunlight, the snowflakes sparkling, the birds flying above the trees, singing their songs, everything felt charged with a life force that didn't seem to exist until this day started.

Every breath I took in felt different, and it had nothing to do with the delicious, faint smells that assaulted me, clearly coming from the kitchen. The air feels light, my soul calm. The next breath I took filled me with the smell of bacon, butter, and coffee, and my mouth watered instantly. I turned towards the bedroom door, looking at it in disbelief, expecting to wake up at any moment. I didn't. I was awake. And Suki was in the kitchen... cooking.

I turned on my back and laid there, under the soft comforter, trying to make sense of how it all came to this.

She was supposed to be the object of my darkest desires.

She was supposed to be the one I finally got to destroy.

She was supposed to be the one where all bets were off, and I could finally succumb to needs I was never able to properly fulfill in my old life.

And she is... she fucking is... but not like I ever thought. She's willing, but not like the others. Never like the others. This is not a silly, kinky challenge for her. It's not a desire. It's not a sexual craving.

This is hunger! Heart wrenching, soul debilitating starvation. A need that ruled her mind and body since the moment she started to exist. This is her soul demanding a darkness only I can give her.

She needs to burn and I will happily set her on fire.

There I was... in my bedroom, my flesh broken by a bullet I took for her, my dick hard thinking of the blood she took from me, and the smell of her cooking making me grunt in satisfaction.

Fucking surreal.

No matter how much I wish this wouldn't have happened this way... it did. It shook me to my fucking core and brought me to my knees, and there's no fucking way I'm walking away from it.

I should have been more eager to go downstairs, perhaps worried that she will attempt to run away from this house... from me. I wasn't. If I am to pursue this, I need to know I'm not chasing shadows, phantasms.

When I finally walked downstairs, the scene caught me by surprise, even if I was expecting it. The maple syrup was waiting by the stove, the coffee in the French press, and she was bathed in the sunlight, sitting casually on the steps of my porch... that's the surprise I was not expecting... how she fit. Now I sit here, eating the breakfast she prepared for me, drinking the coffee she brewed, with her by my side, her body covered in my clothes.

Surreal... surreal was the only word that could describe this perfectly mundane image, only it was not mundane at all. I know that with the right look in my eyes she would run and she would know I will follow.

But as I look down at her bare legs and see the healed scars—a cut on her right calf, another one under her left knee, above as well, smaller ones following some sort of pattern on her left thigh... and then on her right one, peeking from under my long hoodie, a deep scar...

Before my brain realizes what my body is doing, the now empty plate is on the porch floor and I'm lifting the hoodie to get a clearer look.

Her skin breaks into goosebumps instantly, and I can see her muscles contracting, but her body is still, like she's anticipating an attack. As I realize what the scar is, my eyes dart to hers and she's gone... her mind no longer here.

"Suki...?"

SUKI

It's been four, maybe five days, I do not know, but it feels like I have been here with Niklas for an eternity. This terrifying sense of belonging is looming inside me, and I try my best to push it back every time it moves closer to the surface.

When he lifts the hoodie from my thigh, uncovering one of my ugliest scars, I realize that I have not thought about them since he brought me here. Maybe it is because of the trauma, maybe I am clinging onto this new reality, trying to erase my old one... Maybe it is the terrifying sense of belonging that distracted me, but when Niklas acknowledges it, it all hits me at once... just like that branding iron did months ago.

I hoped the memory would fade... but it burns just as hot as it did that day...

I cried... I cried for weeks...

I cried when he stripped me naked and took every piece of fabric away from me...

I cried when he tied me up for the first time and hit the back of my body with a belt almost a hundred times...

I cried when he left me there... bleeding and tied up...

until the next day...

I cried when he tied me up for days and made me sit in my own filth...

I cried the first time his filthy dick ripped through my unwilling core...

I cried the first time his dick made me throw up as it hit the back of my throat...

And then I stopped crying... No matter what he did, my mind went somewhere far, far away like the victims you read about, developing a split personality to cope with their abuse. I never understood the science behind that until those moments. I wasn't quite at that point, my emotional side was, but my body felt every lash, every blow, every thrust inside of me. Unfortunately, the lack of tears proved to be a mistake because, as I found out later, that's what he craved... my tears...

One day, as I saw him come into the room where my dungeon was, my mind was already traveling to that place where it was safer. However, he had something new up his sleeve and nothing could have prepared me for it.

In that darkness, I never saw it before—the old stone fireplace in the corner of the room, outside my dungeon. He lit it and with its warmth radiating through the cold stone dungeon, he managed to pull me out from the place I hid inside my mind.

I thought he was doing something nice for once... I thought... it doesn't matter, I thought wrong. Because I missed something else as I was distracted by the warmth I have not felt in weeks, I missed the branding iron he held in his hand... I missed how he warmed it up in the flames of the fireplace... I missed how he stalked towards the door to my dungeon...

The key in the lock pulled me out of the warm place I was enjoying. The hot red end of the branding iron made me throw up instantly.

That was the first time I found out that what he wanted from me above all else were tears of pure, unhinged pain... he got them that day... and every day since.

I blink and I realize I am not in the dungeon anymore. I also realize my voice is raw.

Have I spoken all those words out loud?

I am shaking and Niklas' large hands are holding my upper arms, holding me together in a moment I think I could quite literally fall apart limb by limb.

"Suki..." his voice is laced with pain and a new fury. The fire in his eyes burns hotter than ever before and it fuels mine. My demons howl in response, singing heathen songs and dancing around the fire.

Slow tears run down my cheeks, and I am not even sure why I am crying. Is it pain? Is it trauma? Is it... relief?

"Suki..." he says my name again, his voice stronger, laced with an emotion I cannot quite understand, but its impact is strong... and I break.

I cry... I cry so hard I feel the wooden floor shaking under me. I hear the birds flying away from the trees. I feel my mind trembling with the aftershocks of an earthquake no one could have predicted. The next second he pulls me to his chest, and I feel like I could suffocate from his huge body encircling me. I am completely surrounded by him and I hold on for dear life, my small hands clutching the sides of his body as my tears soak his t-shirt.

And I cry.

I cry for the pain I have been through. I cry for my broken soul. I cry for the stupid girl I was when Adrien caught me. I cry in relief that I will never, ever be in that situation again— in the arms of this stranger... I know that for sure.

And when the tears are finally gone, here on this porch,

wrapped tight by the man that gave me what I needed without even asking, I make a vow.

Adrien's beating heart will be mine, and I will burn it as he watches.

The crying stops, and as Niklas pulls away from my body I take a breath that reaches deeper and deeper as he moves further away from me, still clutching my upper arms. And when that breath fills my lungs completely and my eyes close, I swear... I can feel them, every single shard, every piece of my soul that was scattered around this mountain, being melded back together by the fire burning stronger inside me.

I am not my old self anymore. No, I am starting to become something else, something else entirely.

And when I open my eyes to find Niklas staring at me, his strained and confused gaze shifts instantly. It turns evil, monstrous, satisfied—and he smiles.

He fucking smiles. And it is beautiful.

CHAPTER 15

NIKLAS

Understanding emotions was always something foreign to me. I could never quite figure them out, could never pinpoint what they were or what they meant, what repercussions they could have or what brought them forth. Body language though, that was different. I could read a person like a fucking book. This always helped me in my professional career, it was the only way I could connect to people, but at a personal level... I never cared much to connect outside my own family. Even with my one and only girlfriend... no matter what I did, that relationship was dominated by logic and doomed to fail from the beginning.

Once in a while, I remember the overheard discussion my parents had about my teacher's suggestion to get me tested. So many things make sense, I made the connections myself, yet it doesn't matter. I am who I am, and it all forged me into the person I became. I revel in it. I could not give a fuck whether there's a diagnosis tied to me or not, because my lack of emotion towards certain situations was exactly what I needed, especially in business. I was ruthless and it brought me to where I am today.

Sounds and touch are the senses that truly make sense to me. I'm sensitive to them, to the point of pain when it comes to sound; however, it's probably the only way for me to actually feel emotion, not just to know it exists, but actually feel someone else's emotion.

Touch was what always helped me when it came to women. I had trouble reading them, their actual words, so I always followed their body. The temperature under my palm, the softness of the flesh, the pulse of fear, the pulse of arousal or anticipation. How the skin grows cold when the pulse increases due to fear... how arousal makes it soft and hot.

Now, with Suki, as I listened to the story she didn't even realize she was speaking out loud, as she cried tears of mourning and relief into my chest, as I hold her upper arms in my big hands and watch as her soul is getting pieced back together, I realize she's different. She always was.

I can understand the various sentiments in her story, I can taste the emotion that spills out of her tear ducts, I can read the earth-shattering emotion that burns in her eyes right now— Vindictive Hunger.

My demons howl.

My monster roars.

I smile.

For the first time ever, I can see emotions, I can see them

in her and she... she is doomed because of it. There is no escape for her now. Not after she birthed this in me, the ability to feel her emotions, to taste them, to be hungry for them.

My perpetual attraction to screams has always been because I could feel the pain in them, I could feel the emotion traveling through their bodies. Sounds in general, the sensitivity I have towards them is all tied to the fact that the emotions vibrate through them. I can see the undulation of the soundwaves and pinpoint their roughness, softness... everything that makes them what they are.

And touch... the pulse... the warmth... the combination of both, I can feel the moment before they begin to tremble, either from fear or desire or both at the same time.

I fed on these senses, on sound and touch, fed on them because they were the only things that could ever make me understand, that could make me feel them. And I craved the screams because I couldn't feel any other way, never by simply looking at them.

But this moment here... this has been the first time I have ever seen it, actually seen it. The way her pupils dilated, how the bright green turned a shade deeper, the broken look in her eyes, the pain in them was screaming at me and that's when it happened... her emotions became part of me. And when she transitioned from pain to vengeance, the green of her eyes sparkled with golden flakes from the fire inside of her, her skin looked tighter, her breaths calmed and became deeper, and she screamed in hunger from inside me. I could feel it all, traveling through her until it reached me, clutched my fucking soul and squeezed tight until I burst open for her.

Is that the meaning of it all? Have I never been able to understand emotions because I couldn't feel them myself? Beyond anger or indifference, I never felt anything else. But Suki... Suki bled her emotions onto me and they fucking melded together in our fire.

I could feel her pain and only one desire flooded me—annihilation.

I could feel her strength, and it makes me want to fucking kiss her until her lips are swollen and bruised and now...

I can feel her determination, and I want to follow her into battle.

SUKI

Time stops yet again, and here I am, trapped in that ocean-blue gaze with the mid-morning sun kissing my skin. Even the birds stopped singing. The river stopped flowing. The trees are moving without making a sound.

And suddenly they all do. All at once. Invading my senses, charging me with their potent wilderness. My gaze breaks from his, and it travels to his wild, dirty blond hair swept on the right side of his head, exposing the buzz cut on the left side, to his thick brows that shade his fearless eyes, his strong straight nose, then to that long, thick, wiry beard that makes my fingers itch to run through it.

I want to touch him, his face, I want to run my fingers through his hair, trace his eyebrows with my thumbs, down around his eyes, around his cheeks. I want to hold his beard-covered jaw in my small hands, but I don't... it means too much. I can see it in his eyes, there is understanding in them, a sense of camaraderie, but his need to capture and conquer is still there and I am still very much its target.

I might feel determined and ready to take on Adrien, but

this man right here, Niklas... he's a whole different kind of monster and there will be nothing left of me if he truly catches me. He will protect my soul, I know he will, but he will break me—my restraints, my barriers, my walls, my rules—he will break my goddamn heart without even thinking of it, without intention. He will rip it out of my chest with his bare hands and devour it in front of me, piece by piece, until it is all gone and there will be no chance for it to be restored by any other man but him. He still very much terrifies me.

I can feel it already, the battle he is having with my mind. It is a game of his own creation, one that I have been playing too, but only he knows the rules.

One of his hands drops from my upper arms and covers the healed mark of the branding iron, holding my thigh, squeezing ever so slightly. The heat from his palm is searing a different kind of fire on my skin. It feels like he wants to brand me himself, burning away the painful memories of my former captor.

How will my new one brand me?

"What do you want from me, Niklas?" I whisper, but I know he hears me. I feel the almost unnoticeable twitch in his palm on my thigh, I see his pupils shrinking.

"At this moment, I want to make sure you don't confuse me with something I am not and never will be."

I cock my head and watch him. What could he possibly be talking about?

"And that is?" I ask.

"Soft." He doesn't waste a breath.

"Nice." He pierces my eyes with his.

"Good." That last word holds weight.

I watch his deep breaths pushing his chest forward, exhaling steam with each one. I watch the permanent ridges of his forehead getting deeper with a frown. I look at the darkness in his eyes and I feel like I'm falling. Again.

With barely a splash, I dropped in the deep ocean, gliding down, my last breath burning my lungs, but I do not let it out. I harness its power and let myself sink deeper into this blue abyss, every shred of control falling like pieces of a puzzle behind me. And when that breath cannot fuel me anymore, when the pain is too unbearable, I get pulled out of the abyss only to stare at that monster again. The one that lives inside of him, the one that smiles at me time and time again. His demons stand behind him like warriors ready to follow him into battle.

How could I ever believe he is anything but this monster. Yet monsters do not need to do monstrous things constantly to prove what they are.

And Niklas doesn't either.

This is what scares me the most, his terrifying ability to play with my mind, that sliver of me that has helped me to survive everything, that sliver that keeps me whole. He plays with it and it is never by intention on his part, not at all. It is his nature, the nature of the beast, the nature of the monster that wants to play with its prey. He scares me, then he soothes me, he hurts me, then he pleasures me—making my mind spin out of control. I want to learn the rules of the game, because I want to know what is real and what is not.

Is the way he takes care of me real? Do I want to know if it is? And if it is, indeed... what does it mean?

I quickly shut out all those ideas, push them from my mind, because inevitably, I will start playing a game of my own. This cannot happen. I need to leave. I need to break free of this place before my mind splits into shards and anything left will be an empty shell. I need to leave to protect my newly mended soul and my frail heart.

As I think those words, I hear my demons wail in protest,

hitting the walls of my mind and soul—fighting, pleading, but I cannot listen to them, I cannot trust them. Last time I did, I ended up with Adrien...

But you did not see his eyes until it was too late... I hear them speak in unison inside my head. Sometimes I wonder if I have schizophrenia or if that is just my subconscious talking and I just give it too much power.

Whatever it is, it's right, I did not.

I look back into Niklas' eyes only to realize that I have been in my head for too long, and he has been waiting patiently... quietly. He is always so quiet... like his mind needs all its resources to plot and design tortuous plans. He prefers the sound of silence most of all.

"Monsters do not need to do monstrous things constantly to prove what they are," I repeat my thoughts to him and watch his expression flicker with an emotion I cannot place. "Nevertheless... that does not make them less of a monster."

I sigh as his gaze deepens, almost like there was something in my words that he did not quite agree with.

"I know who you are, Niklas. I can see them in your eyes, all of them. It is a constant reminder of chaos and destruction. My destruction," I continue. My words surprise me, because I do not know what this will do to me, what impact they will have. Acknowledging his demons, letting him know I know, but he strips me bare, and since knowledge is power, this is the power I am holding onto. I want him to know I see him, and he could never hide what he is from me.

His gaze shifts suddenly, and I feel the need to shift with it, backwards, away from him, but his hands move to my waist in a split second, gripping hard, pulling me back to him.

Those eyes hold promises of chaos and now I know what my words did to him—they brought it all out in the open, tearing down the walls holding them in line. There is nothing holding him back now.

What have I done?

He holds me in place, his fingers digging into my flesh, my hands falling back on the wooden floor as I lean back. His body, kneeling on the step between my open thighs, straightens to the point that I feel like death itself is looming over me.

It dawns on me that, until now, his body took a soothing, less threatening stance. He made himself small in front of me to help me feel better, to allow me to come back down to earth. I did exactly what he just warned me about—I saw him as something he is not without realizing. Now, his wide torso, his broad shoulders, and his thick, strong arms speak a totally different language, one laced in chaos and destruction. I both fear it and crave it and I do not know which is worse.

Then he speaks, and I can feel the vibrations that rip out of his throat, that travel down his shoulders, through his arms and straight into my flesh. I shiver. "Little siren..." his tone is murderous, doused in maple-syrup-tasting blood. "I believe you missed one crucial thing..."

I feel like he wants me to ask what, but he continues either way.

"I see you, little siren."

I shiver as his fingers bruise my waist.

"I know who you are Suki... I can see them in your eyes as well."

Now I am scared. Truly terrified, because he is right, I did miss that. I did not think he could, but then... our demons howl together, how could I have missed that he could read me just as I him?!

That means... he knows.

"I can see them right now, trying to fight an unspoken decision you made." His head moves from side to side, his gaze switching between each of my eyes. I shut them involuntarily and one hand flies from under my hoodie to my throat, gripping possessively.

"I can see what you crave. I can see what your soul looks like now, tainted in blood and lust. I can hear the heathen song your demons dance to..."

I feel his breath getting closer, his tongue swipes along my jaw slowly, then moves to the edge of my ear and finally behind it, leaving a trail of fire on my skin.

"And I can sing it too..." he whispers.

My eyes dart open, and I know he sees fear in them, because his grin is yelling the words at me.

"And they willingly dance to my melody, because, Suki, this is what they crave, what you crave."

He knows...

"Sometimes Suki, sometimes the hunt is unnecessary. Sometimes you don't even need to set the traps. Sometimes... prey wants to be prey."

He has me. He knows he does and knows that I know too. Suddenly, I learn a rule to his game. *Never underestimate your opponent's knowledge.* Always assume he knows everything you do... maybe even more.

I squirm under his painful grip, moving my hands that hold me steady and claw at his covered forearms. There is a faint spark in his eyes, and his hold loosens momentarily, enough for me to get out and scramble to my feet. I know the woods will not aid me, not in the daylight with the whole scenery bathed in sunlight. So I run inside the house, through the kitchen, grabbing the biggest knife I see and run up the stairs to the first room that I can reach.

I do not hear him behind me, and I shut the door slowly, looking around frantically until I see the chair with some clothes draped over it. I push them down and prop it under the door handle. I am not entirely sure what this does, but everyone seems to do it in movies and it seems to work. It might have been a bad idea, but then again, I am not sure what my options are. I cannot run through the woods again, not now, not dressed like this and I am hoping by the time he comes upstairs and finds me, he will be calmer, more rational. But then my demons laugh, and I know they know I crave the complete opposite.

I'm shaking, watching the door, taking careful steps backwards. I hear his footsteps on the other side, I hear him trying a door, but it's not this one. I breathe out.

Then another door and my heart sinks. It's not this one. I breathe out.

Then one more, and I hold my breath, expecting him to try this one next, but he does not, and I wonder why. The next step backwards makes me hit something cold, and I quickly turn, almost dropping the knife from my hand at the marvel.

Big glass windows and doors, floor to ceiling, cover an entire wall. They lead to a terrace aimed at the most marvelous view I have seen, better than any from all the other windows in the house. Maybe not better than the view from the bathtub, but equally as beautiful. Bathed in sunshine, the peaks of the mountains, the trees, everything sparkles, full of life and joy. Birds are flying everywhere, and I'm lost in wonder at what kind of birds are awake this time of year. The pines are looming proudly, the sun rays dancing through the landscape and it almost makes me cry, the sheer beauty of it all, right here on his doorstep.

The beauty of this image resembles a hallucination, my gaze travels through the valleys in the distance, dips and mounds, so crisp and saturated... I lose myself.

My spine turns cold. I feel him... the electric jolt traveling up and down my body wherever his gaze hits. I see his

reflection in the window now, standing behind me and I react, but he is so much quicker. One hand traps the one I hold the knife in, the other circles my throat and presses me into his body.

He bends over as the hand that holds my throat pulls me up, until his breath tickles my ear and my neck threatens to snap from the sheer force. Holding me there, at breaking point, I see his grin reflecting in the window that separates us from that beautiful, wild scenery and I realize that it all fits—his violence, my chaos, my frail throat in his big hand, the knife in mine... somehow it all fits.

Sometimes prey wants to be prey... *his words echo in my head.*

Chapter 16

SUKI

He forces my arm to bend until the face of the knife is pressed on my belly and he holds it there, pulling me away from the window. My legs want to protest, but he keeps me in a hold that forces me to move along with him, otherwise the edge of the knife could slice through the fabric that keeps it away from my skin.

He walks me through the room that is clearly his bedroom, yet it looks completely different bathed in all this light. I catch glimpses of warm tones, terracotta and wheat, but they disappear too fast as we walk into the ensuite bathroom. A tall cabinet is moved away from the wall and I'm shocked to see an open hidden door behind it—this is how he came in the bedroom.

As we walk through it and he closes the door behind us, the darkness that meets me weaves threads of fear through my mind.

"I need you to see Suki, to feel... I need you to know."

"Why?"

He doesn't respond... I do not think he knows the answer.

I hear a flick then a dim light floods the black-walled room and I do not know if I want to scream, run, melt, or just stand there hoping he will forget I am here.

My gaze travels to my left and I note a door that most likely leads to the corridor and next to it, hanging below a shelf are various playthings—ropes, two wooden paddles, two canes, belts, nothing fancy or of great variety, but one does not need many props to achieve the desired effect and I fear his methods will be effective enough... enough for me to desire more.

He moves again, my body being led forward by his, towards the opposite wall that holds something beautiful, something great, something that scares me and intrigues me all at once—a St. Andrews cross.

The wall to my right is covered in soft black curtains, and I know they block the same view that you can see from his bedroom, since it's on the same side of the house. I cannot help but wonder how this black room would look against that bright white scenery, the contrast of it is intriguing. The grip on my throat tightens and he spins me around, before he pushes me against the cross. He presses his large body into mine, our hands clutching the knife between us, and my mind drifts to that blade against our naked flesh instead, pressed between our bodies... nicking our skin at the same time... A shiver runs through me.

I may have been wrong the night he saved me—I feel more like a whore now than I ever did in those woods, because the hunter caught the prey and even dominated by fear, prey wants to be prey.

His gaze penetrates mine, whatever softness resided there is long gone now, replaced by a coldness that can freeze bones... and the prey whimpers.

He squeezes my fist hard, and when he lets go, the need to soothe my hand makes me drop the knife to the floor beneath us. The hilt brushes my foot when it falls and I think the edge of the blade touches him, because there is a sudden slight hitch in his breath, even if his stance does not falter.

Releasing my throat, he brings his hands to the hem of my hoodie and the t-shirt underneath as I fight for some sense of control, pointlessly holding onto it. He does not look impressed, his gaze stern as he forces the hems up, roughly grazing my arms until he rips them over my head, pressing his body onto mine to hold me in place.

He looks down between us as he gently pulls away, and I could have sworn I heard a low growl when his eyes landed on my breasts. I shake myself mentally... must have imagined it because his eyes hold the same stern, emotionless expression.

"Do not fucking move." The sheer force of his voice pins me in place. He promises pain devoid of pleasure and that is a side of it I would never want to experience again.

So, I do not fucking move.

He squats down in front of me, pulling out what look like rectangle shaped shelves from the base of the cross. Cocking his head, he looks me up and down, before he refits them on the cross a foot above ground and then it dawns on me—foot supports... so we can be eye to eye.

Shit.

Grabbing my waist, he lifts me off the ground before I even

realize what is happening and instinctively my feet search for those little shelves. The corner of his lips quirk ever so slightly, victory flashing on his features for a split second. *No, I will not give him the satisfaction!* I slam my hands on his strong chest and push as hard as I can, but he leans forward, pinning me against the warm wood, my arms trapped between us. He pulls one out, and I realize he has me exactly where he needs me... like he anticipated my reaction.

Will he anticipate all of them?

He slowly and deliberately ties ropes around each wrist, my arms spread in a V above me. He takes his time, twisting beautiful knots around them as I try and fail to break my body free, his erection growing against my belly the more I fidget.

He steps back, and I struggle for balance as I almost fall forwards, the restraints digging into my flesh. With a fresh rope in hand, he comes to me and loops it over my shoulders, knotting it in the middle of my chest, from the sternum down my torso just above the belly button, the ropes wrapping around my ribs, holding me secured in place on the cross.

I catch his gaze on me, and I do not know what I want anymore. No matter how much my demons scream in victory over the potential of fulfillment of long coveted, depraved desires, the fear over my current predicament is real. He is, after all, a stranger, even if our demons appear to be familiar. He is unpredictable and anything... absolutely anything could happen right now. I am no longer a deer in the headlights... I am sprawled over the hood of the fucking car and my life is seconds away from ending.

I close my eyes and two lone tears run down my cheeks. I'm startled when I feel his hot breath on my cheeks and his tongue gently licking the tears off. Can he taste it? Can he taste my fear? Worst of all... can he taste my lust?

Mere minutes later, the boxers I was wearing are cut off

my body and my thighs and ankles are tied to the cross as well, holding me in place. It is strange how liberating this feels, standing, yet not holding myself up. I look beyond Niklas and I notice that the entire wall across from me, where the door we came through stands, is covered with mirrors and I force myself to recognize the person staring back at me.

Naked, spread-eagle on a St. Andrews cross, ropes digging into her plump flesh, her eyes laced with fear and hunger.

I watch him turn his head, looking at the same person I see in the mirror.

"Fucking beautiful," he whispers, and my core tightens. My pussy twitches and I look at myself again. Trapped. My control is stripped, and I have nothing to protect me from the incoming storm.

He comes to me and places his hands on my thighs, squeezing until my breath hitches in slight pain. He moves to my waist, squeezing, fingers digging into my flesh and by the time his palms slide over my ribs it feels like fire spreading over my skin. His hands cover my breasts, sinking into my flesh, creating this delicious pressure inside my chest, before he pinches my nipples between his fingers until I internally scream in pain... my mouth open, yet no sounds form.

His brows twitch ever so slightly, and he does not soothe the hurt... no... he leaves my nipples aching as one hand slides over my chest, grabbing my throat, constricting the airflow, while the other settles at the back of my head, fisting my hair.

"You're awfully quiet, little siren. It doesn't suit you." He grins for a split second, showing me a devious side of him that I have failed to see before.

Turning his attention to the wall that holds the few instruments he owns, he picks the smaller wooden paddle and my skin instantly explodes in goosebumps. He comes back way too fast and with no warning whatsoever, he hits the inside of my left thigh with the paddle. The sound was louder than the hit, yet I instinctively wince. He repeats the action on my right thigh and this time my pussy twitches along with the flesh of my leg.

Shit.

The paddle hits me again in the same spots and it burns this time, the shock traveling through my body faster than before, the pain barely, just barely, reaching my mind.

I wince, and he growls.

He hits me again on my hips and the pain is different, my pussy does not respond, but my mind does—I feel a crack.

He moves higher, smacking the paddle against the flesh of my breast, below the armpit and I wince, my breath hitching, a strange pain filling my mind. Each slapping sound, each burning sensation, each slither of pain builds up and before I can stop it, the pain splits in two—one grips my pussy until it drips down my thighs, and the other grips my mind, splitting it open.

Pain!

It floods me with the force of a raging storm. This is what I craved—pain, chaos, and destruction—and when that paddle hits the soft, damp flesh of my pussy... I scream. I snap my mouth shut since my screams are what he wants yet holding them in hurts me.

He slaps the paddle on my pussy harder, and it instantly tightens in pain, yet when I relax it... the pleasure releases, dripping down my thighs and tears fill my eyes as a muffled scream threatens to escape my closed lips.

There is a strange burn against my wrists and ankles from the struggle, a soft burn that feels like hot velvet against my skin and I revel in it. I want to run, I need to, far away from him because he knows I cannot take this. He knows I do not want to give him what he needs, yet he also knows it hurts me not to... because it is what I crave as well.

He grabs my throat in his hand, gripping tightly to the point that I can barely breathe in.

"Look at me!" his tone low, threatening.

I'm sinking into his eyes, stripped of self-control. I cannot grab onto anything to bring myself to the surface, but when the paddle hits my pussy one more time, I'm suddenly flying out of the abyss, and when I hit the surface, I scream. Pain, pleasure, desire, anger—it all seeps out of the raw sound ravaging my constricted throat. His warm hand suddenly covers my pussy, soothing the hurt as one finger glides between my drenched folds, spreading my wetness on my pulsing clit, and I shiver as moans that I cannot stop escape from my lips.

He is giving me everything I craved when I thought I found it with Adrien. He is forcing me to release my goddamn mind and soul and revel in chaos. The chaos I crave, the chaos I need for my soul to thrive.

I stop myself, yet again refusing to give him anymore of what he wants and denying myself what I need. There is a fierce battle happening inside of me, because if I release my mind and soul, he will catch them and control them. He can control my body, but my mind is mine and my soul, I only just pieced it back together—I cannot entrust to another again.

He grunts and lets go of me. I'm startled and surprised, but then I see him lean down and when he stands in front of me again, he holds the big knife I dropped on the floor. I watch his eyes shine with victory as fear seeps from my pores. Yet some of that fear melts to intrigue because one thing I know for sure—he will not kill me.

He brings the knife to my throat, touching my skin ever so slightly with the cold blade.

"You will have to be very, very still for me, little siren."

I look into his eyes, seeking something, anything, some sort of reassurance, and I am not even sure how I see it, but I do. My muscles instantly relax.

The corner of his lip twitches slightly and the blade moves, around my throat, the tip barely scraping the skin, up until it reaches my earlobe and I urge the shivers away as the blade leaves a cold trail of excitement behind it.

It travels down my throat, tracing my clavicles until it reaches the hollow point between them. Then it goes down, between my breasts, and I cannot help but close my eyes. I do not want to see anything, I want to feel, I want to revel in the excitement. He scrapes the flesh under my breast and moves up, around it, and the sensations are electric. Lust melded with fear and the loss of control, my breath hitches and before I can stop myself, I shiver and the blade nicks my breast. The faintest, softest moan escapes my lips, my eyes open lazily and his are fixed on me... dark, deep, and raw. And then... he carves.

This... this is it.

I squeeze my eyes shut when rough fingers press suddenly on my already sensitive clit and a stinging cold sensation mars the skin that covers my ribs just under my breast. My breath hitches, his is steady, and even though I don't see him, the heat of his gaze warms the coldness the tip of the knife leaves behind. The pressure on my clit increases as the tip of the blade carves unknown patterns on my skin, releasing an invisible pressure that lives under it and even though he puts an unerasable mark on me, I feel... free.

With more pressure on my clit... more stinging on my flesh... lust floods my body and crimson floods my vision... the same shade as the one trickling down my ribs right now. He carves me slowly, the blade moving in the same rhythm as his fingers on my clit—one drawing pain, the other pushing pleasure. I should care about what he is imprinting on my skin, but I do not. Amongst the painful scars that mar my flesh, this one feels beautiful.

I hear him exhale as he pulls the blade away, and the sting feels like it belongs. His tongue replaces the blade, but I do not open my eyes. He lingers a little longer than is probably necessary, tasting the sweetness of my blood as the blade comes between my breasts again and I moan low in my throat.

The danger posed by this knife is pure ecstasy and I cannot stop myself from sinking into the sensations. The blade travels down until it reaches my mound and when he takes it away, suddenly I freeze, and my eyes dart open.

I look at him, but he is looking down, at the face of the knife aimed at my pussy. I close my eyes again just as I feel the cold blade pressed to my clit. The moan that escapes my throat now is strained, strained with pain from the inability to move, because the sensation is too much, the danger, the fear, the ecstasy—tears build up at the backs of my eyes.

Then he takes it away, and I breathe out frantically, my eyes searching for his, for the strange calm and reassurance he brings me. He centers me and I am both relieved and hungry for more.

I watch him swiftly flip the knife in his hand, the thick hilt aimed at me.

"I must say, little siren, I was not expecting you to like this quite as much."

My breathing is still erratic and there is not much I can do to calm it down. I look at my breast and I see a thin drop of blood coming out of a small, shallow cut, half an inch long at most. So different from what Adrien ever did to me, so delicate. Pleasure was never the purpose of his actions, and no matter my dubious consent in this situation, Niklas' eyes tell me a different story altogether. If I did not know any better, I would think that most of this is for me... not him.

"I wonder what else you will like..." his words bring me back to the present as he kneels in front of me. He allows me to see his hand before it disappears between my spread legs. His palm open to me, dangling the knife by its blade between his index and middle finger, handle aimed at my pussy, coming closer and closer.

He looks into my eyes and this time I do not need him to tell me not to move.

He touches the handle to my opening, and I feel my world splintering, the crack in my walls getting larger, electric shocks spreading goosebumps over my skin, my breath hitched in my throat, my nipples so hard he could probably finish me by just touching them. My whole body is a storm, a silent, electric storm that ravages everything in its sight and when he pushes the handle of that knife inside of me, the sheer sensation sends me to a world I have never seen before. A world full of lust, desire, and fulfilled fantasies. A world I have been searching for my whole life.

He pulls the hilt out, then slowly pushes it back in until I can feel his warm palm against my pussy. When he pulls back out, I swear I feel like I could come from the sheer idea that he is fucking me with a knife. He goes back in again and again and again, in deliberate movements that ensure my safety, yet the idea that he could cut me is disturbingly erotic. My head falls back against the wood and my eyes fly to the mirror, watching myself get fucked by the knife that was meant to protect me from him.

I feel the walls of my core squeeze the hilt of that blade as it glistens in the mirror, disappearing again and again inside of me and I am so close, so close to coming undone from the sheer erotic image of myself in this predicament.

Yet as fast as it started is exactly how it finishes. He pulls the knife out of me, my orgasm dissipating with it, and it takes everything in me not to scream in protest. I hear the blade hit the floor as he throws it to the side, and I watch him rise to his feet, we are at eye level now, yet somehow he is still towering over me.

He growls, he actually growls and that exquisite fear returns in my bones. My eyes go wide and his hand grabs my throat just as his other hand flies straight between my legs.

"Sing for me, little siren," he all but whispers.

Dissatisfied by my silence, his fingers rip through my pussy straight up to the knuckles, hurting the flesh of my lips. He thrusts in an out violently and the wet sounds my pussy makes fuel me with lust and I moan in a broken whisper. I do not want to sing for him, because this is what he craves, what he needs, and I need to stand my ground. If he pushes me, I am pushing back. But then I feel his fingers spreading inside of me, stretching my walls, drawing pleasure out of my core before one more finger slides in and my body burst into flames.

My moan breaks the barrier of my lips and fills the heavy air around us. My pussy clenches in response to the delicious stretching and my eyes water with the pain his knuckles leave on my lips.

Through this decadent torture, every time I feel the pressure in my head becoming too much or my lungs screaming for air, he loosens his grip on my throat, and I wonder how he knows that it is the right time to pull me away from the edge.

His fingers spread me again, my pussy stretching too hard. My eyes go wide, and I feel a faint burn against my perineum, but he fucks me harder, deeper, somehow distracting me from the burn and I cannot hold it in anymore. The pleasure is too much and I moan, I moan with a strained cry leaving my lips as his thumb catches my clit and pushes hard, moving in a rhythm that makes the chaos explode inside my body. The storm is not silent anymore as I scream and it bursts through my core as I come undone on his thick fingers.

The thrusts turn slow and demanding, pulling more of me through my pussy, milking me dry.

I finally focus on his eyes and I freeze.

He is not done.

This is his game, and I shiver because I am about to learn another rule.

My pussy is wet, tender yet relaxed from the orgasm that still echoes through me and then I feel him... a fourth finger pushes inside of me, stretching me to the point of burning and I cannot stop the words that leave my mouth.

"Please... no, please... stop."

Then he does something, hooks his fingers and moves in a way that touches something inside of me that spreads fire through my body and I tremble so hard, I swear he touched the pleasure center of my brain. I moan and he grins again.

"Are you sure, little siren?"

No. I am not sure, yet I am about to say *yes* when his fingers begin thrusting in and out, my body attempting to arch against its restraints. I cannot take it, the pleasure and the pain combine too well, right there between my legs, deep into my gaping pussy. I feel everything I never knew I needed as he pushes pain inside of me and pulls pleasure out.

I lost control over my body, but he took it and harnessed it, wrapped it tight with a fucking bow and gave it back to me as a present laced in lust, chaos, and desire.

Panting hard, I look at myself in the mirror, at his large body in front of me, his right arm moving frantically as he finger-fucks me raw. I look spent, broken and undone, yet more like myself than I ever have before.

In this dark room, tied to a St. Andrews cross, as I watch in the mirror how he releases my throat from his grip and sinks his teeth into it... I break.

My pussy spasms uncontrollably with my second orgasm, hurting from his four fingers stretching me, and I cry in pain laced with that sort of pleasure that you can only imagine, but never think you could ever feel. A pleasure that can only be birthed by filthy acts, and as I watch myself fall apart, my head falls onto his shoulder and I wonder... what else can make me feel this type of ecstasy?

I feel him tugging at some of the ropes that hold my body tied to the cross and my arms fall limp over his shoulders. It takes seconds for him to undo the others, almost like he pulled on a magic string that unravels them all.

He carries me to his bedroom and lays me on the bed. I watch as he rips the clothes off his body and the sight of him instantly wakes me. He is a marvel. Heaving breaths pump his thick chest dusted with hair, his shoulders wide and strong, his fists clenched, pumping blood through the veins strained over flexed muscles, his legs strong and thick. *Goddamn gorgeous*. Then his cock. Oh... his goddamn cock, long and thick, veins strained under the thin skin leading to the thick head glistening with pre-cum.

My eyes travel back to his and ice and fire spread instantly through my body, both at the same time. Don't ever assume the monster has finished his torturous game. He will bleed you dry and when he is done, he'll fill you up with your own blood, only to bleed you again.

CHAPTER 17

NIKLAS

As she catches my eyes, hers go from exhausted to fully awake in a split second. She scrambles back on the bed, but I grab her legs and pull her back towards me as I kneel, sliding my thighs under hers. I lean over and in one swift move she doesn't anticipate, I wrap one hand around her throat and the other goes to her pussy, fingers sunk deep. She's both shocked and scared, yet I catch her trying to look down at herself. I circle my hand to the back of her neck and lift her slightly and use my thighs to push her hips up, bending her back just enough for her to get a clear view of how fucking gorgeous her pussy looks stretched around my fingers.

I never knew how much pleasure I could give myself by doing this, watching a woman break apart for me, push their limits until they can't take it anymore. But Suki, Suki is different, she craves more and more, and she doesn't even know it until it happens. I just push her limits a little bit more each time and her protests falter when the ecstasy hits.

I can tell by the lustful look in her eyes as I stretch her pussy so hard it could split open, that she never knew she liked this. And she didn't like it, not until I hit the right spot inside of her and she forced her mind to let go. She's different and she has no fucking idea how much she scares me. Probably as much as I scare her.

The wet noises her pussy makes are so fucking delicious and even like this, even as I try to stretch her to the limit, her pussy is still fighting to be as tight as it can. She starts moaning, no longer able to hold herself back as she's been trying so fucking hard to do since she ran up the stairs.

I need her. I need to hear her. I need to break her. I need the siren to sing, and I fear what I'll do just to hear that song again. I slow my movements, my fingers go in and out of her slowly, deliberately, and I know a devious grin hits my lips, just as I aim my thumb at her entrance as well.

Fisting has always been a craving of mine, one I have only managed to sate once. I never knew how much I wanted to do it again until now, until the fear in her eyes grew to the point that the siren finally came back to me.

But she suddenly claws at my forearms and she screams bloody murder, the sirens song that drives me wild. She sings it so beautifully, and I feel my dick threatening to come right here, right now, without even touching her. I've been hard since I hit her pussy with the paddle, but now, now I think I could fuck her through the goddamn bed.

I pull out my fingers, squeeze my dick in my hand to calm

it down just a bit, and in one long, deep thrust I push inside her to the hilt.

She screams again, but this time there's little pain in those soundwaves, so I fuck her so hard the bed is creaking violently. Her arms fly to the headboard as she braces herself against it, her eyes closed, pleasure painted all over her face as she yelps at every thrust.

Without warning, I pull out and spin her around, lift her ass up and wrap her hair around my fist, pulling as she bends her back and rests on her forearms. Then I fuck her raw, grunting with every thrust as she screams at the same time. I drill into her like my fucking life depends on it, with deep strokes that I swear are touching her goddamn soul.

I slap her ass and the siren sings songs of lust and pain, her pussy strangling my dick, even after I stretched her. It's like my fingers weren't even in there. We do this violent dance until the siren's song ends on a high note and she comes so hard around my cock that I see stars behind my fucking eyes. I spill inside of her, my dick jerking violently as she claws at the sheets, whispering filthy words, her body shaking with an orgasm that vibrates straight through me.

The siren's song ends, but it cracked walls inside of me, walls that were built not only for the safety of my soul, but for the safety of everyone around me. They're cracked now... pieces crumbling to the ground... I craved the siren's song, I just didn't know what it would do to me.

I pull out of her sore pussy slowly and watch my cum slide out of her.

"Fucking beautiful."

Her thighs shake and she collapses on the bed. I can't help but smile. I broke her and she broke me. What a fucked up fairy tale.

I force myself to get off the bed and bring a wet washcloth

from the bathroom along with the antiseptic cream. Spreading her legs with no protest on her part, I wipe her carefully until she's perfectly clean, then I apply some cream on the soft lines I carved on her skin They belong there... I go to the bathroom one more time and run the cloth under icy water, lie on the bed next to her and pull her to me until her head rests on my arm.

"Lift your legs and put them over my thigh."

Her eyes open lazily, and she slowly brings her legs over my thigh, wiggling to get comfortable. I press the cold washcloth on her pussy and her eyes dart open as she winces, but I quickly wrap my arms around her small body and hold her in place until the hiss turns into a low moan and her body relaxes again.

"The cold... it feels good," she whispers.

I know we technically just woke up, but after something like this, what I've just done to her, it's bound to drain every ounce of energy from her body. She rode high on adrenaline, fear and pleasure, and now she is completely spent. I am as well, the control needed to do what I did without losing myself... it's harder than it looks. But it was fucking worth it.

She needed to know this, needed to know that no matter what, the monster's always there. No matter if I treat her nicely or not, the monster will never go away and it will always demand more. And after what I just did to her, I know one thing for sure, she's more than satisfied that he's not going anywhere.

I watch her drift away, wrapped tightly in my arms, her beautiful pale skin covered in a thin layer of sweat glistening in the sunlight, and the siren looks ethereal. Her eyes close, her breathing slows down, and her body relaxes completely. I look at her beautiful features for the first time when she's like this. Her thick arched eyebrows, her dense brown lashes, the curve of her cheekbones, the naturally contoured lips, and the defined square jaw, she's beautiful in such a special way. A different kind of beauty, old-world, the kind that rarely exists anymore and you only see it in old paintings from the end of the 1800's.

I take a deep breath, close my eyes and pull her closer. As I feel myself drifting away into the darkness, it dawns on me that this is the first time I've ever done this with a woman in this house... the first time in a long time I just held a woman...

I squeeze her harder and sink into the darkness.

SUKI

Nothing could have prepared me for this, not even the desires I had since I was a teenager, since those dreams took over my life and presented my needs in vivid detail. Details I could not understand at the time, but that haunted me later until I cracked. I gave in only to find myself in the arms of a monster that destroyed my body, broke my soul, and almost split my mind.

The dreams...

I open my eyes suddenly, finding myself wrapped in a cocoon made of Niklas' limbs. The fine dusting of hair from his naked pecs tickling my right cheek, and I cannot stop myself from rubbing my cheek gently against his chest.

So warm...

Our legs are tangled, his right arm holding me tight against his body and at this moment there is nothing possessive about his touch. There is comfort... safety... fear... fear of loss.

Is it mine or his?

They flood my mind again—the dreams. They stopped

the moment he brought me here, in his house. They stopped when I saw the demons in his eyes.

The fear is mine...

"Mmm?" I hear his questioning moan and tilt my head as best as I can to look up at him.

Have I been thinking out loud again?

His eyes are moving gently and when he opens them, he squeezes my body until I let out a strained breath. Like a child squeezes a kitten because he does not know when it is too much.

I look into his sleepy eyes as he gazes into mine silently and his demons calm me, they tell me what I need to know... My dreams stopped because they came true.

I understand why he did what he did this morning and as much as my conscience rejected it, I knew what it meant. My mind reveled in it, my heart burned with happiness, my soul sang and my body... my body welcomed it all.

He needed to bare part of his soul to me, force me to see it in a way that would make me fear him. He needed to show me his cravings, the relentless need for control and power, for drawing pain and even blood, my blood. But the fear... he needs it like I need to be hunted.

It wasn't about some BDSM play. No. It was about hunger. A hunger he feels that I need to sate as well; I just never expected to be so ravenous.

I cannot explain it, I probably will never be able to, but he understands my demons, he knows what I crave. My body sings and he learned the song, almost like he knew it before it even played. When he touches me it feels like he is reading Morse code on my skin.

He does not talk much, but he feels, I can tell by the way his eyes move slowly and gently all over my features, I could tell by his calm breathing when he paddled my pussy, when he finger fucked me until I felt like I could split open in pain and burst into flames of desire at the same time... when the knife touched my skin.

He might be a monster, but he is my kind of monster. He is the one that haunted my dreams for so long. He draws fear out of my soul, but I crave this fear. I crave the destruction of my soul that his monstrous, unfaltering gaze promises.

I fight him because it is my nature, it is what I crave, what my soul desires and he knows it. However, now that I have it... now that I know what it means... now that I know how all these cravings feel when they are sated... this relinquishing of power and control... Do I want it?

Do I risk my soul to sate this eternal desire?

I pull my gaze away from his and bury my head between his thick pecs, closing my eyes and forcing my mind to feel anything else. It is not easy, not when just days ago I was running away from another monster through these woods, only to end up running from a different one now.

ding ding

My body jolts at the sound. I feel Niklas sighing ever so slightly before he releases me from his strong yet comforting hold and turns around.

A phone... of course...

After months trapped underground, it is interesting how I almost forgot about all these... comforts. I think about it, the phone, calling for help, but who would I call? And do I really wish to be saved anymore?

He picks it up and reads something before he gets up, sitting on the bed. He looks at me, contemplating something for a couple of seconds before he swipes the screen and lifts the phone to his ear. He does not break our gaze, and I just lie here, covered in the thick duvet, watching him.

"Morning," he answers.

There is silence for a few seconds.

"I don't give a fuck."

Silence, but his gaze darkens.

"You don't need to know what happens next, stop asking the fucking questions if you can't know the answers."

I am curious about his conversation, of course I am; however, he is still watching me, and I feel like I am intruding. Turning on my belly, I clutch the pillow under my head and turn my gaze to the large floor to ceiling windows that overlook the terrace and the gorgeous view.

The sun is higher in the sky and the beauty of this landscape takes my breath away. As I take a slow deep breath, I feel a smile touching my eyes and the thick duvet slowly sliding off my body. I twitch ever so slightly, but I feel my skin prickle with anticipation.

I do not shift and I keep my eyes on the view.

"If you want to help in any way, you're going to have to accept whatever happens next." I hear him say as I feel his calloused hand slide down my naked spine, barely touching it, but burning through me either way.

"If I tell you, you will involve your fucking department and there's no way I can allow that." His fingers reach my ass, and the movement slows as he brings his fingers in between my cheeks, almost coming to a stop at that tight entrance. Almost.

I am not sure what he is doing to me, but this moment here feels like it is much more than every other moment we have shared together. Everything else was animalistic hunger, a relentless devouring of souls. This... this feels like a tempered indulgence and my body softens, sinking deeper into the comfortable bed that feels like such a luxury after my time in the dungeon.

"A woman..." I flinch at the word, just as his fingers sinks in between my folds, inside of me and I clutch the pillow harder, squeezing the walls of my pussy around the intrusion.

He huffs at whatever the other person is saying on the other line, and I cannot help but think that it might be some sort of law enforcement, since he mentioned a "department" earlier. He is talking about me... just as his fingers move deep, but slowly inside of me, drawing out pleasure in a sweet, torturous way and I realize my hips are moving on the slow rhythm of his thrusts.

"It's not my story to tell... "I flinch at his words and his fingers reach deeper inside of me. I'm getting wet, so wet that I feel it in between my thighs. His fingers fuck me so slow, I think I am moving my hips more than he is moving his fingers.

There is something so intimate and vulnerable about this image right here. The beautiful view, waking up after a violent discovery, our comfortable nakedness on these wheat-colored sheets, basking in the noon sun... too vulnerable. Fear floods my body, a strange kind of subtle fear that hums its way through me. I want to run for vastly different reasons now.

Yet I do not move at all. This... his slow, deliberate, almost gentle touch has me trapped, filling me with an unknown need. I have to know how this ends.

"Yes. All you need to know right now is that he deserves everything that could potentially come his way." His fingers curl inside of me, hitting my G-spot with a pressure that makes my hips buck upwards, my ass up in the air. I bury my head in the pillow that I am now clutching in my arms, just as a moan threatens to escape my lips.

His fingers continue their slow, delicious assault, rubbing my G-spot hard and slow, his thumb now on my slippery clit, and I feel my orgasm at the edge of my nerves, close, but not close enough.

"Seriously? Yeah, that would be great, just... don't ask

questions you don't want answers to."

His fingers move faster, my clit is on fire, I am biting the pillow as my pussy drips all over my inner thighs, and I am holding a scream back, my chest threatening to explode. I feel him shift on the bed, but I do not dare move, the orgasm just at the edge.

"I'll find out and let you know."

He rubs harder and I find my hips pushing against his hand and at this point I could not care less what their conversation was about because this feels too good for anything else to matter. I have been deprived of pleasure for months and now, now I am like a beast devouring every last drop that comes my way. I am hungry, ravenous, and he feeds me.

The orgasm builds up, the nerves of my spine lighting up one by one from the base of my neck, faster and faster down my back, until it reaches my pussy and I explode, red stars filling my vision, and I moan into the pillow without even realizing that the conversation ended or that his fingers are not inside me anymore.

The next second, his cock pushes at my entrance and I welcome it. It slips in through my drenched folds, straight to hilt, as I'm still riding that orgasm. Throwing my head back, hair flying everywhere around me, I prop myself on my elbows and I arch my back as my pussy squeezes every last drop of this pleasure.

He stays there, completely still, his cock buried deep inside of me as I am reeling back. With each pulse of my pussy his cock twitches inside of me and my hips roll onto him, up and down, then in slow circles until he rests his front to my back, on his elbows on either side of me, caging me in.

It feels like he is covering me, protecting me when I am at my most vulnerable, unknowingly stripping my soul... bare naked.

My hips move against him slowly, impaling myself, and I feed on the delicious feel of his cock getting harder and thicker inside of me, twitching slightly every time I push against him, my hips rolling slowly when I reach the hilt.

I repeat the delicious torture while he does not move a muscle, rolling my hips more and more. His cock dances inside of me and I feel like he is touching every nerve in my body through this one spot inside of me.

I throw my head to the side, my hair falling on my right shoulder and onto the pillow, yet I do not look at him. I tease him by pulling my hips away, the very tip of his cock the only thing inside of me and I squeeze the walls of my pussy just as I take in a little bit more of him, before I pull away again.

Suddenly his weight is heavier on top of me, just as his right hand catches my hair and holds me still. His hips move, the tip of his cock slides a little further, his breath on my ear, his tongue on my lobe, swiping against it. His teeth catch it, and his cock slides further. His teeth sink a little deeper, my hips push into him, his cock pushes into me, the hand in my hair grips tighter, and the heat in my belly burns hotter.

He pulls out slowly, then in a sudden thrust his cock impales me, before he pulls out again. He carries on this torturous dance while his tongue swipes on my ear, behind it, down my neck, leaving electrifying sensations in its trail. My back arches, my hands clutch the pillow, his hand pulls my hair, bending my neck a little further, my eyes close, his cock rubs my G-spot as his hips keep rolling over and over and over again, jerking in, then slowly pulling out. This torturous dance fills the air with my moans and his low growls until we sing louder and harder and explode on a decadent high note. We finish almost simultaneously around each other, his cock buried inside of me to the hilt, my hips pushing hard into him as he holds me under the delicious weight of his massive body.

He crashes on top of me for a few seconds before rolling to my right, pulling me along with him, his cock still buried inside my body, spooning me. We catch our breath, my eyes stuck on the peaceful view, a massive contrast to the heart I am urging not to shatter under the weight of him.

This was different. This... was a sweet indulgence, this was a whole other level of intimacy and I feel him differently, his touch on my skin, on my soul... He is leaving permanent marks on them and there is no way I can handle that, not now... not after everything that's happened, no matter how much I wish I could take it all.

His cock comes out of me and the weight of him disappears from the bed.

"Shower?" I hear him behind me.

I decide against refusing him since I can feel what's sliding out of me, so I run behind him to the bathroom as his cum runs hot on my inner thighs. I stop in front of the mirror and gaze at the carved flesh of my rib and... I smile. A good memory mars my skin... yet its words are foreign—*ditt monster* —Swedish maybe?

The gorgeous view assaults me yet again, this whole house creating this addiction inside of me. An addiction to this delicious environment, an addiction I will not be able to shake off for a long time... if ever.

And as if the damn view was not enough, facing it now is this man that looks like he was built by the blood, sweat, and tears of his victims. His muscles showing their intentions before the body even moves, one by one flexing like a little dance.

This is when I finally see it properly for the first time, in the light of day, the bust of the woman tattooed on his back. The image of her is haunting. Black and gray, her head tilted slightly upwards, her eyes looking straight at me, terrified and terrifying all at the same time and she is screaming, her mouth wide open, almost unnaturally so. Her hair is wild, flying all over his back wrapping over his shoulders, the beauty and horror of this image is surreal. The level of detail, the contrast of the ink, the sheer talent of this creation makes me feel like my soul can hear her scream.

It is all surreal—the image of this hauntingly dark tattoo against the beauty of the snow-covered landscape outside the window. It does something to me, this contrast...

It marks my soul, a permanent brand that I will carry with me forever, because it feels real...

CHAPTER 18

NIKLAS

"Who was that... on the phone?" she asks as we're both finishing the potato wedges and chicken I made. She kept quiet for a while, pondering whether she should ask me or not.

I could quite literally see the question on the soft wrinkles of her forehead as she was debating the best course of action. It almost made me laugh a couple of times.

"Connor. He's the sheriff down in Bear Creek." I could tell her more, but then again, maybe I should only give her the information she asks for, rather than everything I know. Her eyes go wide for a split second, just enough for me to notice, but not long enough for me to catch it if I would have blinked. I wonder what's going through her head now, I wonder if she's thinking of finding a way to contact him and turn me in.

"Was it about me?" She's beating around the bush. I can almost hear her heart beating faster, her eyes a little brighter at the prospect of someone helping her. But Connor won't help her...

"Yes." My answer earns me a scowl. She wants more, but I'm giving her answers to her questions, it's not my fault she's asking the wrong ones.

I turn my gaze to the plate and take my last bite of food before I grab it and get up to rinse it in the sink.

"He doesn't know about me, does he? He only knows about Adrien." I hear her shuffle behind me.

I sigh as I think of what lies ahead. I don't want Connor involved in this, mainly because I never involve anyone in any of this, but Connor could have his uses in this situation. However, his involvement could complicate things with Suki, with her presence here... more and more I feel like she needs to be here, as controlling and fucked up as that is... she belongs.

She belongs to this mountain.

She belongs in this world.

She belongs to me.

I put the plate in the dishwasher and turn to her, crossing my arms and lean against the countertop.

"I called him a few days ago to see if he knows of anyone being on my mountain, or in its vicinity. Anyone new to the area. However, you... he just found out about you." I watch her features as she contemplates the information and I'm not sure what to think of her emotions.

Sometimes, I look at her and I feel feral with need, the need to have her, own her and make her mine. Trap her here on this mountain until there's no conceivable way she will ever want to leave. Other times, I look at the glimpses of serenity in her eyes and I know for a fact that she knows she belongs. Yet those moments are rare, only slight twitches in her gaze.

I know she wants me, no matter how much I force my touch on her, she craves the force, she craves the fear and even though fighting is her game, she takes it all willingly. She wants exactly what I have to give her. When she screams in fear, she screams for more. She pushes me away and pulls me to her all at the same time.

All she needs is right here, in front of her, and I can see an internal battle going on inside of her, but I don't know which part of her is winning and that thought scares the fuck out of me...

She's the only person in this world that makes me feel like I have something to lose and the worst part is that she's the one that can make me lose it.

"What happened the other night, when he came?" She asks me, pulling me out of my disturbing thoughts. I spend the next few minutes telling her about my walk through the woods, the cabin at the edge of the mountain and coming back for her.

"You heard me..." It's more of a statement than a question.

"I did." I take a few steps towards her seat.

"Both times..." Her eyes soften as she looks at me, and there's unshed tears behind them, filled with a strange emotion I can't understand.

"Both times." I walk around the table.

"You came for me..." There's a slight tremble in her shoulders and I think I understand... I came for her... someone came for her.

I move right behind her seat, put one hand on her shoulder and the other one on her chest, pressing it until I can feel her heart beating through me.

"I came for you," I say as her body leans into me slightly, her shoulders relaxing.

Maybe a minute passes before either of us moves. We're both pondering, both of us having unspoken words with our own demons. I know what conclusion mine has come to... I wonder what hers has decided.

I move away and go to make another coffee. I know I'm going to fucking need it, I have a lot of shit to sort through today and most of them are my thoughts. I hear her by the sink, but I don't turn around. She's not done asking questions, I know she's not, and I can't blame her, she barely found out anything.

Her cup slides in front of me and I just look at it. It's a small thing, but even in this insignificant gesture I can see her confidence is there, no longer the meek woman curled up in the corner of my living room. I turn to look at her and find her gaze aiming straight at me. She doesn't shift, move away, or drop it.

That's it, little siren, meekness doesn't suit you, this right here, this confidence... this looks good on you.

"Are you going to involve the police in this?" Suki asks.

"What do you mean? In what?"

"Adrien. I know you have plans... I do not know what they are, but I know you have plans. Otherwise you would not have gone scouting his location."

I watch her for just a second as I ponder what I should say...

"If Connor's going to be involved, and it's a big *if*, he won't be involved as police. He can be trusted."

"Can you?" she asks bluntly, and I don't hesitate.

"No."

She turns to leave, but I stop her and pull her back by

her hand.

"But when it comes to your safety and Adrien, you don't need to worry about trusting me. The motherfucker is going to pay, no matter what you think of me."

I'm only holding her wrist, yet her body is completely stuck to mine, her head bent back hard so she can look at me, since she's a foot shorter. My other hand goes to the hair flowing down her back and I wrap some of it around my fist, holding her there, her eyes stuck to mine.

"I can't trust myself around you, which means that you shouldn't either, but Adrien... he's a whole different story. Do you understand this, Suki?"

I see her gaze moving between each of my eyes, her brows furrowed just enough to form a little crease between her eyebrows, like she's trying to see the lies in my eyes. She's trying to figure me out, but no matter how our demons sing to each other, no matter how hard she looks, my eyes can't convince her to trust me. She's alone in assimilating the information in front of her and making the decision.

"Yes..." she finally speaks, and her eyes are not on mine anymore... she's looking lower. My other hand goes to the base of her throat, laying it possessively around it. I feel her pulse speeding up under my palm, her breathing a little bit faster, and her body shivering lightly like a low humming, vibrating through mine.

So I do the only thing that I truly crave right now. I lean over and touch my lips to hers. I savor her, indulge in her softness, barely grazing her lips. I kiss her with an unnatural gentleness and I feel her melt into me, her body relaxing under my touch, her lips parting slightly, playing this gentle game with mine.

Her hands are on my chest and I'm not even sure she realizes how hard she's clutching my sweater in her fists, holding me to her, our lips gently pressing into one another, brushing side to side, nipping her lower lip before my tongue opens her up for me.

This is different... just like it was when we woke up for the second time today. She looked so serene, laying naked on her belly, in my bed, clutching my pillow as she was quietly contemplating the view. She looked soft against the cream sheets, even her scars looked beautiful bathed in the midday sun. It was different compared to what we did in the morning. What I did to her... I had to... I needed to...

Now... I'm different...

She's different...

We're different...

I swipe my tongue inside her mouth as she explores mine and this fucking moment makes me feel like I'm finally home.

Where do we go from here?

SUKI

He smells of musk and cedarwood and tastes like sin, sweet goddamn sin. I am clutching his sweater as he holds me by my hair exactly where he wants me and exactly where I do not want to be, but where I feel I need to stay.

This kiss feels like a silent conversation, each swipe of our tongues, a word, each brush of our lips, the end of a sentence. There is so much possession in his touch, one hand in my hair holding me still, the other on the base of my throat, yet this kiss... this has nothing to do with my body... no...

This is a possession of my newly mended soul... my fractured mind... my frail heart... This is the worst kind of possession, the one I will never be able to escape, the one that will trap me here, the one that will devour me alive and spit me out a mangled mess that could never be restored to its previous form.

Yet I cannot seem to be able to let go of him.

The slow, torturous, and delicious kiss keeps going for what seems like hours and I definitely understand now. He cannot trust himself around me just as I cannot trust myself around him.

He cannot stop touching me, and I crave it. He cannot stop brushing his lips against mine, just as I cannot stop enjoying it. And for some damn reason, he cannot keep his hands off me... and I cannot seem to stop reveling in the delicious feel of his grip around my throat.

My guard keeps going down, sinking into the damn ground and it is getting too slippery. I am losing my grasp on it and cannot seem to be able to lift it back up.

How does one stop themselves when the captivity becomes enjoyable? How does one distinguish illusion from reality? How does one convince themselves that they are still prey?

The kiss stops, but he still holds me tight in the same position, his lips only just touching mine. His chest rises and falls with deep, slow breaths and mine seems to be matching his as my body tries to compose itself.

He finally lets go of me, yet my body cannot seem to be able to move. We are standing here, in this beautiful kitchen furnished with natural wood cabinets and white granite countertops, on these warm wooden floors, just staring at each other.

I have to admit it. This man looks like a ruthless god; he is beautiful yet rough, with his wild wavy hair and bushy long beard. He is quite well-groomed without it being too much, and I wonder how come he cares. He lives on a mountain alone after all. Why bother?

No, I cannot do this. I cannot keep falling because I will be too far gone and will not have the strength to lift myself back up. He has this effect on me, emanating this energy that pulls me in and keeps me close, making me soft and compliant.

Suddenly, I feel like I have no air. He is too close, and this open space is not big enough for the two of us. I take a couple of steps back as my hand glides on the edge of the countertop and my eyes hold his. I stop and catch the slight shift in his gaze. For a split second he looked confused, and I am trying hard to figure out what he could be thinking, but this damn man is so hard to read.

His head cocks slightly to the left and even though his expression remains devoid of any feeling or emotion, I feel like I'm being passed through a CT scan. It is uncomfortable, intrusive, and even though I know he cannot read minds, I cannot help but feel like it would not be such a stretch for him.

I try to read his expression, but there are no words there for me to read. His look is passive, but stern, strong, dominant, already holding the answers to questions he did not even need to ask. I know for a fact that he is not even trying to scare the shit out of me. Or anyone that finds themselves at the receiving end of this glare for that matter. No. This is all him, this is natural, this is in his blood, and I find it difficult to hold my ground.

I do not know what he wants from me. Last time I asked, he said that he doesn't know anymore, and I am not entirely sure what to take from that. Am I still prey? I feel like I am hunted, about to be eaten alive, but maybe not killed. I have to escape; I need to escape. If only I could stop thinking of him catching me and all the filthy things he could do when he does.

All of a sudden, he turns around and continues with his task like nothing ever happened. I shake my head, physically shake it and look around me to find everything the same. Everything in the same place as it was ten minutes ago and it feels wrong, because I am not... I am not the same... and I know for a fact that he isn't either.

He fills my cup of coffee and slides it my way on the countertop, closing the distance between us in two long steps.

I am forcing myself not to step back, but that is exactly what I wish to do. The proximity to him is painful and addictive and I cannot afford the drug.

Yet he does not stop, and suddenly I feel like I can breathe again. With his own coffee cup in hand he walks around me and goes upstairs.

"What the hell...?" I whisper to myself, confused. I stand there, braced against the white granite countertop and breathe. I know, I know I have to leave, but how? There is a snowmobile in the garage that may or may not work, yet that does not mean that it even has enough gas to take me down the mountain. Also... how long is the trip down the mountain?

I know nothing. I have no idea where I am, I have no idea where I need to go, and I am also half fucking naked! I am trapped. I am fucking trapped on a mountain in the dead of winter with a man that threatens not only my body, but my sanity too. This is a whole other level of destruction, completely opposite from what Adrien put me through, and I cannot deal with it. I am not ready for it.

I feel like I could drop on my knees right here, right now and just bellow from the depths of my lungs because I no longer feel like my life is mine. I do not know what to do, where to go, and all I want is freedom. I want my life back; I want to feel like no one owns me anymore...

But how can I be free when all I crave is to be trapped in the strong grip of this sadistic Viking?

My elbows crash on the countertop and my head falls in my hands, tears spilling on the white shiny surface. I am fighting myself as much as I am fighting Niklas and Adrien... I am fighting my needs as much as I am fighting theirs. Yet how can I not? How can I possibly trust my instincts after what I have been through?

For six months I talked to Adrien online. Six long months

where he gained my trust, learned everything about me and he did not even have to try too hard, because I just fell for every ounce of bullshit he spit at me. I craved the darkness, I craved the fear, I craved the pain, all wrapped up in a bow of pleasure—he promised me all of it. Six months he made me crave it, promised me a world of pain and pleasure, promised me to make my dreams come true.

Not some sweet metaphorical notion, no. My actual dreams, the ones I had since I was little girl, the ones that haunted my whole life... How can I trust my instincts when he managed to shit on them?

I wipe my eyes, run my hands through my hair and after a few deep breaths in through the nose, out through the mouth, like my PE teacher taught me, I feel better. Logic must prevail. I am still in the game, I just do not know all the rules yet. Most importantly, I do not know him yet. I will not have a chance to win the game if I do not get to know my opponent.

* * *

Maybe half an hour has passed, my coffee cup is empty, but Niklas has not come back down yet. The days are so much shorter in the winter and from looking outside, I can tell the sun is getting tired, yet the view is even more beautiful.

I look at the boarded-up door and suddenly bile rises in my throat. It is impressive how my current situation, Niklas in particular, manages to erase Adrien from my mind in a way that makes me forget that he is still searching for me, watching me.

He could quite literally be watching me right now.

I jump from the sofa faster that I thought my body could manage, and I stare to the door almost expecting Adrien to burst through it. Or catch his reflection in the window again.

Goosebumps creep their way up my body and terror crawls on my skin.

I am sprinting up the stairs before I even realize what my body is doing and when I reach the landing, I am not sure where I want to go. I know which door leads to my room, yet that is not the one I am staring at right now.

How come, even after I rationalized with myself that being around him is bad for my soul, I still find myself looking for his protection? How come my instinct is to look for the safety I know he can provide?

CHAPTER 19

SUKI

I have been standing here for at least a minute and I cannot help but feel a little ridiculous. Not because I am afraid Adrien might be watching—that fear is more than rational, but because I am debating if I should be in the same room with the only person that can protect me from him right now.

Of course I can. I have to be alive in order for me to escape, and if Adrien gets his hands on me again, there is no way I'm leaving this mountain—not alive anyway.

I press the handle to Niklas' room, but as I cautiously enter, I realize that he is most definitely not in here. I turn back confused and close the door behind me. Looking around the long hallway, I note a door to my right that is most likely his... playroom? Kinky room? Torture chamber? None of that fits what he did to me in there... it was much more, so much more and so much better.

No, he is most definitely not in there, not alone. I walk towards the only door I have not gone through yet and press the handle, but midway through my grip shakes as I realize I should have knocked first.

Shit, I should have knocked!

"Umm... Niklas?" I call before the door opens fully.

"Is that your backwards way of knocking?" I hear his calm, condescending voice behind the door.

Shit. Well... he did not tell me to go away, so...

I open the door fully and take in the image in front of me. This room is probably the smallest one of all the ones upstairs, such a contrast to all the others with its black walls and deep red themed prints on the walls. On the wall to my left, there is a cozy looking black fabric sofa, the wall opposite me has a row of windows, most of them covered with almost black roller blinds, and tall wood tripod floor lamps sit in the corners. To the right, facing the sofa, sits a massive wood desk, simple, almost mid-century style, filled with four large screens and a laptop I don't quite recognize. He sits behind the desk, his chair turned towards me, and he looks menacing.

I have invaded his space, but I cannot back up now. Stepping into the room, I close the door behind me and pretend I do not feel his murderous gaze on me as I look around.

My eyes fall on the three prints framed on the wall behind him—trees, woods, or maybe a park, a wild woman and a dark alley. Their colors have been altered, bathed in a crimson hue, and I am wondering if these prints are intentional or if they are just art he found online.

I keep ignoring the intense gaze that is burning a hole through me, turn around and take a seat on the sofa, getting comfortable before he can tell me to leave. I finally look at him, and his chair is turned to face me, his forearms resting on the desk, watching me through the intentional gap between two screens.

"Please, come in. Take a seat." He gestures sarcastically from the door to the sofa, but I can see a slight curve in the corner of his mouth.

"Thank you." I match his sarcastic tone with a sweet smile on my face. Crossing my legs on the sofa, I rub them together to get warmed up, cursing myself for not bringing the blanket with me from downstairs.

He sighs, then continues typing away. Several minutes pass and I'm getting colder. I cuddle in the corner of the sofa, bring my knees to my chest and cover them with the hoodie that is too large for my body anyway. I see him watching me in the corner of his eye, trying but failing to ignore my presence in his space.

He is concentrating now, tapping too many words per minute on his mechanical keyboard that makes a nostalgic noise ripped out of the late '90s. I do not know whether it is the cold or restlessness, but I have to get up. Walking up to the only window where the blinds are open, I am assaulted by yet another magnificent view. These windows are on the side of the house and the landscape feels new to me... for some reason this makes me angry.

This world, the solitude... these views alone are reason enough for me to be convinced that this is where I belong, that I need to stay, and it is infuriating.

I do not need reasons to stay! That list is getting too long now. I need more reasons to leave!

But how can I leave when that son of a bitch is still out

there?

"What are we doing about Adrien, Niklas?" I turn and watch him as he types away. He completely ignores me. I take a couple of steps towards him, flexing my fists, trying to control my temper.

"Niklas, seriously, we need to talk about Adrien!" my tone is laced with annoyance, yet all he does is take a deep breath, his gaze focused on one of the screens.

I close the distance between us and slam my fist on the desk, everything on it rattling at the impact. "For the love of god, stop fucking ignoring me!"

In the next second he turns, one hand is on the small of my back pulling me, while the other hand is on my throat, guiding me roughly until I am laid on his lap like a disobedient child waiting for a spanking.

"What the hell?! Niklas let me go!" I scream at him as he lays one forearm on my back, holding me down, typing on his laptop with the other.

"Shhh." He shushed me! He goddamn shushed me!

"Are you kidding me?! Let me go!" I grab onto the legs of the chair and force my body to rise, but his weight on my back is making my efforts futile.

"Suki, I will mark your fucking ass in crimson if you don't keep your mouth shut and let me finish this."

My body stills, and I curse my betraying flesh because there is fire in his voice, promises of pleasure laced with pain, and I wonder if he would keep them.

"Please..." I whisper. Yet I am not sure if I am asking for him to let me go or make good on his promise. I want to say more, to clarify, explain myself before he does the one thing I desperately want him to do, just to find out how it feels.

But my time is up.

NIKLAS

She is absolutely infuriating. Not only does she casually invite herself into my office, but she makes herself comfortable and then demands my attention when I'm clearly in the middle of something.

On top of it all, she decides to be rude and slam her tiny fist on my desk like she damn well owns the place. Yes, I might have been rude by not answering her question, but I have no need to be polite when she can clearly see I'm busy. I make the fucking rules here, and I fear I may be growing soft with her!

I follow the trail of goosebumps that burst all over her bare legs as that one delicious pleading word leaves her lips and fuck, how I wanted her to give an excuse. She's not sure what she's asking for, but she doesn't appear to be squirming to get out of my grip anymore, her body is still and completely tense in anticipation.

I lift the fabric that covers her body, pull down yet another pair of my underwear from her ass and before she can protest further, I slap her right ass cheek so hard her whole body jerks. She yelps at the impact.

A red handprint appears on her flesh.

"Fucking beautiful," I whisper and smile.

I slap the other cheek harder and she curses at me, but I give her two more before I open my mouth.

"Excuse me?!" I ask. "I told you to keep that pretty mouth of yours shut until I finished what I was doing."

My palm meets her ass twice more, this time on that sensitive part where it meets her thighs and I know the impact will be felt in her core as well. She's clamping her mouth shut, pushing back the sounds of her pleasure. I'm not being gentle here, I'm not practicing any safe BDSM, this shit is not about that. I give her two more and she finally cries out, but pain is not the only sound I hear.

I want to fuck her, god how I want to fuck her right now, but damn it, I can't. I have work to do, and I can't constantly submit to this little siren! She makes me mad and I can't fucking keep my hands off her.

I stop myself after two more hard slaps, resting my hand on her right ass cheek, kneading it as I attempt to compose myself. I know she can take what I give her, harness it and turn it into pleasure. She wants it as much as I want to give it to her, yet she fights it, she fights her nature and I can't figure out why.

But then again, how can I blame her when I'm fighting myself as well? I thought I needed to be myself with her... it turns out my demons sing a different tune around the little siren.

Fuck.

I sigh, pull the underwear back up, lift her off my body, holding her hips so she doesn't stumble. She's standing on my right, her hands gripping my forearm and the look of pain, lust, and confusion painted on her face is amusing. She looks like she doesn't know if she should yell that I spanked her, complain that I didn't finish the job, or just walk away before she gets in any deeper. Yet she doesn't do any of it, she just watches me, her brows furrowing, her look analytical. I feel like I'm trapped under a spotlight and a whole crowd is watching me.

"Sit." I pat my jeans-covered thigh. She doesn't move, and I feel my eyes rolling to the back of my fucking head, so I pull her until she's reluctantly sitting in my lap.

The moment she sees the photo blown up on one of my screens, her body jerks backwards, her back stuck to my front and her hands clutch the edge of the desk. I circle one arm around her waist and it seems to relax her.

"Sorry..." she mumbles. "I just wasn't expecting... you found him." I slide the chair until we're as close as we can get to the desk and more importantly, the keyboard, and she's gone. Looking at every screen, reading all the information I found, her curiosity relaxing her body.

"Son of a bitch... Adrien Long, born April 1st 1981... I was a goddamn birthday present for him?!" The disdain in her voice is palpable, but she carries on reading the information I dug up. "Wait, he was caught before on suspicion of kidnapping?!" Her pretty little head whips around to look into my eyes, her long brown hair flipping over her shoulder.

"Apparently so, they couldn't prove it though." She turns back to the screens and absorbs all the information on it. Adrien Long, born in Long Island, New York, to an unknown father and an abusive whore of a mother who pimped him out to strangers for drug money. He was in the system before he hit thirteen years old and due to his troubled upbringing, he was the opposite of what he is now. Quiet, reserved, a punching bag for all the bigger kids. I could have potentially felt sorry for him if I didn't know that under that mask lurks a monster.

"How did you find all of this, Niklas? This is... sealed information, not even the police would be able to unseal this unless they went through fifteen different bureaucratic channels, since Adrien was a minor at the time."

"I have my ways." She turns to me and holds my gaze. She's demanding an answer and I have a *what the hell* moment making the decision for me. "I used to do this for a living, I owned a tech company and we specialized in defense technology. I'm good at this, finding people, information..."

"Obviously you are, but wouldn't a defense company deal with bigger fish?"

"They do."

She knows I murdered the motherfucker that killed my ex, she heard me when I said he was my *first*, she's seen the monster lurking in the shadows of my mind. Yet, I can't help but wonder what she will think of me when she will hear the truth, when she will find out who I really am... what my demons urge me to do. I hesitate because I don't want to push her away... she fucking belongs.

"I don't." I pause to see her reaction, but she doesn't move or blink. "A long time ago my mother told me that I'm different than the other boys in school. She told me that she never intended to point it out, she wanted me to grow up without actively knowing that I'm different. But after discussing it with my father, she decided I needed to acknowledge it and embrace it. She noticed my lack of emotion... my trouble understanding what others around me felt in certain situations... my lack of empathy. Like when my grandmother died and everyone was crying around me, yet I seemed to be the only one that understood that it had to happen, and it was better she died when she did before becoming a fucking vegetable." Suki sits in my lap, green eyes watching me, patiently waiting for more.

"She said my teachers recommended a formal assessment by a doctor, but she refused. She said that she knew what diagnosis they would give me and that meds would be the answer. But I was who I was, and she never wanted to change that; however, she also felt like me acknowledging the differences between other people and I would allow me to understand them, form better connections, learn."

I can see the wheels in Suki's mind spinning. She's intelligent enough to make the connections, the spectrum is large, but the milder side of it is common enough.

"So you do not know if it could have been something else entirely."

"No." I know what she's referring to. Lack of empathy... yes, that is definitely characteristic to a certain type of person and she's afraid to say the word—psychopath. "It didn't matter, I functioned perfectly fine. I went to University, all went well, I was excelling in all the technical subjects and that is when the idea of my company started forming. What happened after is totally different story. I was twenty-two when I killed for the first time, not long after Uni and it felt like a burst of energy that had been dying to come out my whole life, always there... always hiding, always craving..."

Suki watches me with wide eyes but doesn't move. There's something in her gaze, something I can't quite place...

"When his guts spilled on the floor, and the room filled with his pain, I felt it. I recognized the emotions, his fear, the defeat, the sadness, and it fueled me. The sight of his blood on the floor was like fucking gasoline and I had a big smile on my face when I watched his eyes go from showing his excruciating pain to lifeless orbs as his soul left his body."

"Something was born inside of me that day, this burning desire for more blood, something I unconsciously suppressed my whole life and I could have never gone back even if I wanted to. The next one I killed was a child molester. I split his dick open as he watched, I fed him his balls, and the satisfaction I felt as he died was unmatchable. Until the next one I killed, a woman this time, stupid fucking whore that killed her own child. She died with her womb hanging out of her body."

Suki flinched on my lap, and I felt her legs trying to get closer to each other, cringing at the vivid picture I painted for her.

"I couldn't give a fuck who I kill, Suki, but I prefer to choose the ones who deserve it, the ones that slip through the cracks."

"How many?" she asks, and I know she fears the answer.

"I don't know. I don't keep track. I've slowed down since I moved here."

"Five, ten, fifteen? You must know a ballpark. How many?" Suki's tone is more urgent, and I'm not sure why a number is so important to her.

"Maybe around thirty. I don't keep track, nor do I revisit their files."

She takes a deep breath, her lips parted, her heart beating hard in the silence of the office.

"You're a murderer," she whispers.

"So are you, little siren." I hold her stare and challenge her.

"It only happened once."

"And you've craved to do it again since. I see your demons, Suki, they sing the same old song as mine. Listen to it. Harness it. Accept it."

She shakes her head violently. I'm trying to understand her adamant rejection of her nature. Why?

"What are you afraid of?"

She stares at me, various emotions twisting the expression in her eyes, but she doesn't answer.

"So, you use your skills to research these people." She changes the subject, urging me with her eyes to move on. Fine I'll play... for now.

Sighing, I finally answer. "I do. I need to make sure all bases are touched, that I cover my tracks, and if it's too complicated or risky, I leave it for the authorities to solve. Maybe I'll throw them a bone. I need this, my soul fucking needs this, but I don't need the complications that may arise, so I don't throw myself in situations that are too fucking complicated."

"Like what?"

"Loving wife. Big families. Too many people that care. I've done it before, I've managed it, orchestrated some twisted situations where they left their families and ran away to the Dominican for a new life or some shit like that, but it's too much work and I can't be bothered."

"And... you have no regrets, no remorse?" she asks like she's looking for reassurance, not an actual answer.

"None."

Her eyes go down from mine before she turns around and looks at the photo of the man that put her through hell for the last six months of her life.

"None..." she whispers.

SUKI

I look at the brown eyes staring back at me from the screen and I am not sure what I am feeling. Shock that Niklas found him, and this could be all over soon, or fear, because I am sitting on the lap of a serial killer? Is he a serial killer? Or an assassin? Or just a murderer?

No matter what his brand is, he kills for pleasure and I am not sure if it is fear or jealousy that I am feeling. There is a pressure in my chest, in this hollow place below my sternum, a pressure that I started feeling after I killed my mother, behind the walls I built and whatever is on the other side is fighting to get out.

"What is the next step?" I ask.

"I need to make sure that no one misses him. I have more research to do and then... plan." Niklas replies, and I am left wondering if I wish to be part of the plan or not.

"What can I do?"

"Nothing."

My head whips back, and my torso turns as much as his arm around my waist allows it. "I am the reason this is happening. I am the reason why you have been... forced into this situation. I need to do something."

"Suki," he sighs. "This is my battle as well. Yes, you're the reason this is happening, but no, I have not been forced into this situation. You fail to see that I could have simply ignored your screams. I could have ignored your pleas for help the second time around. I could have even handed you willingly back to him. I could have made other choices. Yet I did not. I chose this and I made my decision even before he shot me."

My eyes move to the bandaged bullet wound on his arm, and I shake my head gently. "I need to do something."

I feel his fingers under my chin, forcing it up, and my eyes go to his.

"When the time is right, you will." His blue eyes pierce mine, and I believe him. When the time is right... I will.

* * *

A couple of hours have passed now. I am lying on the sofa with a book in hand and if an outsider saw this picture, they would think it was sweet. Him working, and her keeping him silent company. A nice couple. Yet when you look closer, he is researching his next victim, plotting their demise, and she is the confused captive reading the works of Thomas Harris on his sofa, because she is too afraid to be alone in the rest of the house.

Perfectly illusory.

"Connor's coming in about a week or so. He asked for a list of things you need." His warm voice startles me out of the cannibalistic universe I had submerged myself in.

I turn my head and look at him. The desk is dark, no longer lit by the light of the screens, everything is turned off and I wonder for how long now. When did he finish? For how long has he been watching me? I feel heat rushing to my cheeks, and I quickly drop the open book over my nose, attempting to cover it before he sees it.

Confusion strikes me. I could leave with Connor, I could leave this house, I could leave Niklas, yet... he is asking me about what Connor could bring me... here. There is no implication that he is going to bring me things so I can leave comfortably. No.

I am still a prisoner, and he has no intention to give me my freedom. I blink several times to keep the tears that prickle behind my eyes at bay. *That* he certainly did not miss. He cocks his head to the side, and I can see the scrutiny in his eyes.

"He won't cross me, Suki. Connor will not take you away from here, not without me telling him to. On my mountain, his law has no impact."

"Why... why keep me here? In some ways you are no better than Adrien. I am your prisoner, even if the dungeon you keep me in is comfortable." My patience thins, the book now thrown on the sofa. No longer relaxed, I am sitting, rasping at him, spitting out emotions that I cannot hold in anymore. "Why?! What the hell could you possibly gain from this?!"

I watch his slow, deliberate movements, as he gets up from the chair. His muscles straining one by one, from his thighs covered by thin gray sweats, to his torso and arms dressed in a black V-neck t-shirt. For a second I tense, believing that once again he is coming for me, yet he does not. He walks casually towards the door, and as he grips the handle, he turns his head just enough to see me from the corner of his eye.

"You." And just like that, he opens the door and leaves.

That is not the answer I expected. It is short and heavy with meanings that pierce my soul. *He gains me.* How am I supposed to interpret that? Me to kill? Me to hurt? Me to fuck? *Me...*

CHAPTER 20

SUKI

I sat on the barstool of the kitchen island as he cooked a delicious smelling pasta dish. One cannot help but marvel at the beautiful Viking behemoth moving effortlessly through his kitchen as he cooks potentially one of the best Arrabiata that has ever touched my tongue.

I chose not to dwell on that one simple word he spoke earlier. *Me*. I had more important things to think about now, and ignorance is bliss sometimes.

We ate as he summarized to me what he found out about Adrien. One of his more disturbing finds were the multiple conversations he had online with various women, I being one of them.

"Did you read any of it?" I ask the dreaded question.

His eyes lift to mine, but his head is still aimed at his plate. "Yes."

I take a deep breath and wonder why I even asked this question. I should have known he would read it... see my gullible stupidity plastered all over those words.

"I didn't realize it was you until a couple of days into the conversation," he pauses as he takes another bite, "and then I stopped... Miss Knoxx."

Of course! I am definitely an idiot, he had no way of knowing that it was me, I wrote under my username. And he stopped... he stopped reading when he realized it was me. But he knows my full name now... I wonder what else he knows. I am certain now, certain that I am riding a damn rollercoaster through the rapids because the twists and turns he puts me through are making me dizzy and giving me whiplash.

He is a bad man with good intentions? Does that sound about right? No. What does then? Because I feel like he cannot make up his own damn mind. He wants to hurt me, he wants me to fear him, yet he protects me, defends me... and even shows me respect at times.

I know better than to let my guard down and accept it. He was, is, and will remain a means to an end and the end is my freedom. This is simply attraction, unbelievably electric, goddamn sizzling lust. That is it. Just lust.

I must not fall, not again, not after last time.

I must not fall.

I swallow and let out the breath I have been holding in.

"How many others?" I finally ask.

"Seventeen."

My head whips up, shock clouds my eyes, yet he is looking at his plate, unfazed by this.

"Seventeen?! Including me?"

"Missing before you. He was constantly seeking for a new victim, even when he already had one, almost like they weren't the right ones. Yet after he got you... the discussions were much more sparse... casual."

My appetite is gone, but when I drop the fork on the plate I notice it is pretty much empty anyway. Damn, he makes tasty food. I lean back onto the barstool, running my hands through my long hair.

"How long has he been doing this?" I ask.

"About ten years, more or less. Not here, though. He disappeared from the radar and went off the grid about two years ago. I think he has been on my mountain for the last year. Yet, I don't think he stayed here constantly. I think he's been coming and going and most likely lives off the grid somewhere on one of these mountains."

I watch him finish his food and gather the plates. I feel like I should be nice and clean them since he's the one that cooked, but I cannot seem to focus.

"He had you the longest... the ones before you, the ones you saw..." I know he's referring to the buried ones, "he had them between two weeks and two months. I think you were his favorite."

I look into his eyes as he says that, and I do not miss the sparkle as he said that word. Am I his favorite too?

"What about the others, don't they have families? Friends looking for them?" I urge myself not to dwell.

"No. He had a type—women with no connections, no families, reclusive, isolated, no social lives," he says as he cleans up after us.

I feel his words like they are leaving my own mouth— they taste bitter. I am one of those sad women with no life. I guess it is practical... uncomplicated, as Niklas explained.

"Yes, I heard recently that it is the preferred type of victim." I can't keep the sarcasm at bay.

He is bent over, putting plates in the dishwasher and the muscles of his back tense, one by one like a domino that predicts doom. He does not get up though, finishing the task at hand, and I feel the little hairs on the back of my neck stand and my body stills. When he is done putting the dishwasher on, he turns to me, his movements too fluid for a man his size, and I feel like an antelope in the Savannah. I see the cheetah. The cheetah sees me. I freeze, hoping its belly is full.

His palms rest on the kitchen island across from me, spread wide as he leans into them, holding my gaze.

"Is that what you think I do? Is that what you think I am, little siren?"

I swallow the lump in my throat, and I swear it echoes through the space.

"You took me... You kill people..." my voice is shaky.

"I kill people because I need the *blood lust* and fulfilling it *calms* me. I kill people because their *fear* is the only emotion I was able to feel for years, the only food that satisfies this gnawing hunger. I kill people because it's the only thing that *makes sense* in this world. *Death* is the only thing that makes sense," he speaks slowly, accentuating all the right words, and with every sentence he seems to get closer to me, towering higher, even though he has not moved at all.

"I took you, Suki, because like a siren you sang your song and lured me in. I took you because your song is the sound I searched for, for over a decade. I hold you because for the first time ever, fear is not the only emotion I can see and feel. I keep you because you... you are the only person that makes me feel human. I keep you because you are not whole yet."

My lungs hurt, and I realize I have been holding my breath. His eyes... his eyes bore into me and I see a fleeting emotion, something that I do not think he knows exists and his words weigh heavily, so heavily on me. Tears fill my eyes, and I cannot explain why I feel the need to cry. His words carry sadness, and I realize that is the emotion I saw. Sadness.

I must not fall.

I must not sink in the ocean of his eyes.

This is just lust.

He straightens and leaves the room abruptly. I hear the bathroom door close and suddenly I can move again. Wiping the tears that filled my eyes, but did not fall, I actually ponder our conversation from earlier today, in his office.

Human.

His attachment to me... it is not just lust, it is not just a psychotic attraction, it is... heartbreak.

Emotions.

He is never going to let me go. Not when he believes I am unique to him. I will never be free again. Yet my twisted mind can rationalize it. My twisted soul feels for him. My twisted heart breaks and wants to hold on to him.

Do I need my freedom when the man that holds me is the only person that understands me?

Do I need my freedom when he is the only soul that would never judge me?

Do I need my freedom when he is the only one that gives me everything I ever needed and all the things I never knew I wanted?

NIKLAS

Human.

I never truly understood it until now. Her insult that I am just like Adrien woke my defensive nature and the anger seeped through, bringing out revelations along with it.

Human.

She's my undoing and I could never unleash all that I am onto her. I am beginning to understand I was never going to do it anyway... I was just blindly following a path I thought I needed to take. I could never truly hurt her because she makes me feel... feel human.

My body leans into my palms laid on the white sink, and I look at myself in the mirror.

Breath in. Breath out. Breath in. Breath out.

"Human."

Is that what I want? Is that how I want to feel? Is that who I want to be?

"Fuck."

I mentally shake myself and splash some water on my face before going back into the living room.

She's sitting on the sofa, wrapped in the fur blanket she was so emotionally attached to the first night she came here, and I can't help but admire how far she's come in a short amount of time. In the last few days, she's been on an emotional rollercoaster, mending her broken mind and soul and even though the effects of her captivity can still be seen, her strength is certainly returning to her. I don't know who she was before Adrien, but I can see who she's becoming.

The little siren is evolving, but she's holding back on me, on herself.

Just as her mother before me, I see the demons in her eyes. I saw the sparkle when she told me about the day she killed her mother. I saw the sparkle when she licked my bleeding bullet wound. I saw the sparkle when she stopped crying and promised herself vengeance.

There's something buried deep inside her soul, something she wrapped up tightly long ago, and I can fucking taste it sometimes. I need to see it, I need to feel it, I need to pry her open and break her apart until it comes out. I need her to accept it, because it's part of her, no matter how disturbing, no matter how painful, I need her to be herself.

Is it selfish of me?

Maybe it is, but I don't give a fuck. I need to see who she really is and then show it to her, because... maybe then... there will be a chance.

Maybe then she will realize where she belongs...

I walk towards the sofa, and I see a slight but sudden change in her stance. There's so much hidden in that pretty little head of hers and sometimes I wish I could just crack her open to find out what it is, before I put her back together.

Sometimes I truly feel like a psychopath.

"Tell me, what do you need Connor to bring you?" I take out my phone to write a note.

"Umm... I don't know... What kind of things can I ask for?" She genuinely looks concerned that she could be too much trouble.

"Anything. Clothes, toiletries, whatever you need."

"I don't understand... how is he bringing everything? I thought no one can come up here?"

"Helicopter. He used to be a pilot in the Army and he's pretty good at flying one. He was coming anyway, bringing me a couple of parts for my broken snowmobile."

I see her eyes flicker, and I wonder if she already thought of leaving this mountain on that snowmobile. Considering her fleeting disappointment that I could have missed if I blinked, I'm sure she did.

"Oh, okay. That's good. Could I...?" She reaches towards my phone, and I hand it to her. I realize that she hasn't held a phone in months as I watch her slow movements over the touchscreen.

I busy myself in the kitchen, making some tea for us while she makes that list. As I wait for the tea to brew, I lean against the counter, watching her as she finds her way around a phone again. There's some signal here, so if she would try to call or text someone, she would be able to. This right here is an interesting test.

Will she attempt to contact someone? She wouldn't be able to hide it from me though. Who would she contact anyway? I'm not sure if it's wishful thinking on my part, but I don't think she'll make any attempt to contact anyone. I can see a conflict building in those beautiful eyes of hers. Every time we talk, something grows in there.

When I bring the tea, she hands me back the phone, but I don't look at the list, I just put the phone in my pocket. She looks surprised like maybe she thought I would check it first. I smile to myself because I like this, keeping her on her toes, confusing the hell out of her. The problem is that I seem to be confusing myself as well.

She does something to me, something that I'm only just starting to understand, but to actually accept it... that's the tricky part. I've never been this person, the one I am with her. I've put on facades, yes. I've shown people the person they needed me to be—in business, with my parents, during school or university. I learned. Yet with Suki... with her there's no I.

The monster is out and it purrs at the thought of her.

She compares her captivity here with the one she faced with Adrien, and I feel insulted. Yes, logic dictates that she is not wrong to do so, but she must see that things are different. There is no way she can't see that I am different. Even the man she met in the woods all those days ago is a different version of myself. She's the reason why.

Unless something is stopping her from seeing me... a different version of herself.

She's running away from her own demons, and I'm holding her captive so I can pry her fucking soul open and make her face it. Maybe she anticipates this. Maybe this makes her want to run faster.

I'm sitting on the sofa, on the opposite end of where she sits. I get comfortable, left arm on the backrest, the tea in my right hand, and I can't help but study her. Her beautiful eyes, tilted upwards in the outer corners, her small upturned nose, that bone structure that reminds me of the soft women from black and white movies.

And she studies me right back. I wonder what she sees when she looks at me. I feel slightly uncomfortable. I've been watched my whole life, mostly because I was the quiet one, often mistaken for broody by girls, then women. I'm used to people watching me... but Suki... Suki's eyes bore into me, their scrutiny runs deep under my skin and sometimes I feel like she communicates with my demons when her eyes fixate on mine. Almost like she can see beyond it all.

Maybe she can.

"So tell me," I need to break this, the quiet assessment, "what do you do for work?"

She takes a few seconds to reply, seemingly taken aback by the question. But I need to see beyond the beauty, beyond the siren song, I need to see her.

"I used to be an interior designer."

"Used to be?"

"Well... I've been on a long unintentional sabbatical for the last six months." She rolls her eyes, and I feel a strong need to tie her to the St. Andrews Cross all over again.

"Do you still want to be an interior designer?"

She sighs, "Yes. I love interiors; planning a home is not as easy as people might think. Style is not enough to make a home. It's a relative concept. What feels like home to you, will most likely not feel the same for someone else." I swear her skin seems more luminous and her back is straighter as she talks about this. She didn't even need to tell me she loves interior design, I can quite literally see it painted on her body.

"But you're not a massive fan of people, how did you manage this career?"

"Online. I'm not a conventional interior designer, mainly because, well, you said it, I don't like people. I just like their homes. They send me plans, videos etc., we talk a little bit, I send them sketches, renderings, mood boards, furniture suggestions."

Sketches... interesting. She draws.

"And this works? People actually trust the process when you're not actually going into their homes?"

"Yes. Believe it or not, not everyone wants a conventional

interior designer, not to mention that I cover a side of the market that is much more accessible, cheaper. It works. Well... it worked."

"It will still work, especially since you can do it wherever you are... your office is pretty much your computer." I tell her, wondering if she gets the allusion I'm making. She could work in a different town, in a different state... even on a mountain.

Fuck. I have no business having thoughts like that after I've known this girl for just a few days!

Yet, I can't seem to help myself. A lifetime... a lifetime has passed since that first scream broke my soul open, a lifetime since the second one pried the demons out... and she... well she made the monster want her. And fuck... I want her, I want every single bit of her. I want her beautiful voice, I want her unnaturally bright eyes, I want her long hair wrapped around my fist, I want the pulse of her throat under my hand, I want the taste of her blood on my lips, I want to pry open her mind, not just to find out what she's hiding from me, from herself, but I want it so I can learn every detail about her.

I want her... I can't let her go...

She's my banshee, and I am her monster.

CHAPTER 21

SUKI

My computer.

I sit here, on the opposite side of the sofa, curled up under the blanket he wrapped me in the first night he brought me here, pondering his implication.

I have to admit that being able to do my job in this setting could be highly inspirational. I have never lived in a place as beautiful as this. The landscape, the forest, the wildlife... the views. And this beautiful damn house.

This house...

"Who designed this place?" I ask him.

"The house was already here, just in a different form.

I hired an architect and contractor, but it was done to my specifications."

Knowing what I know about him, I can imagine he is an architect's worst nightmare.

"So... the theme of it, the material and fabric choices... the bathroom, was that you or the architect?"

"I'm no architect or designer, I can't take full credit. However the initial ideas were all me. I knew exactly what I wanted; it needed to be simple most of all, casual, cozy without being too rustic, but rustic enough that it fits in this environment. Plus... it needed to focus on the views."

The views. Damn these addictive views. He focused on them alright, the bathroom is something out of a dream. Being able to take a bath or a shower and face these valleys created by the looming mountains is absolutely incredible. Then his bedroom... it is simply perfect.

"Well... you certainly achieved it." I agree.

"How long have you been doing this? Interior design," he asks me.

This sudden interest in me, in what I do, it feels like he pulled the rug out from under my feet and I am caught off guard, on the floor, wondering what the fuck is happening.

Why the questions? Why the interest?

Yes, I know we already shared... intimate details about ourselves, secrets that no other souls know... but this is different, this is a different kind of interest.

"It has been just over six years now. I started working online when I was in the last year of University, since we were supposed to do a work experience year anyway."

"Where did you go to University?" he asks and his curiosity intrigues me now.

"San Francisco."

His eyes go wide for a fraction of a second, his body

twitches ever so slightly, and I think it is time for me to ask some questions now.

"What is it?"

"Nothing... when did you go to University?" His stance changes and I feel like he is hiding something.

"Ten years ago actually. I finished it five years ago and moved back to South Dakota about three years back."

"Fuck..."

"What the hell, I cannot do this Niklas, I am sick of doing this. You need to talk to me!"

"I'm from San Francisco, Suki. I was born there, I lived there... until about two and a half years ago."

I sit there, on his sofa, in his cabin, drinking his tea, thinking about this strange connection. It is barely even a connection, really. Let's face it, San Francisco is huge, there is no chance we ever ran into each other, ever saw each other... ever been in the same vicinity. Yet... it is a connection, a thin one, but it exists.

"Why San Francisco?" he asks me.

"I don't know. I got accepted to a few Universities. San Francisco was a nice change of scenery, busy without being too crazy, studies were a bit more liberal... it felt right."

"Was it right?"

"Nothing has been right since the night I killed my mother. Nothing has ever been truly right... not since the dreams came..."

I should not have said that. I should not have said that. Why is it that every time this crazy man talks to me I feel compelled to spit it all out? Why is it that he creates this intrigue inside of me? Why is it that I enjoy answering his questions? Am I that desperate for attention? So desperate for the interaction? Or is it the fact that it is him asking the questions that intrigues me?

He does not look or act like the kind of man that pays any interest in other human beings. Not because he is a dick, but because knowing someone else's life would not benefit him in any way. He would not be there long enough for the information to matter. He is quiet, brooding, cold...

And he makes me want to talk because he seems to want to talk to me... I feel like I do not want to miss the opportunity.

"Dreams?"

And there it is.

Oh... what the hell... "Since I was a little girl I have had these dreams... I say these dreams, it is one dream, in a different form... every night."

His eyebrows scrunch as he weighs the words.

"Every night... nightmares?" he asks.

"They used to be... not anymore."

He studies me, studies every single syllable that leaves my mouth, and I half expect him to press, just like he always seems to do, even when we are not talking.

"What was not right?" The question throws me off.

"Anything but the job. People, atmosphere, food, location, apartment... nothing was right. I cannot explain it, I just did not feel like I belonged."

He nods, and I see the understanding in his features. It is unmissable. Yet he knows where he belongs, he found it, he found his place in the world, he even found his morbid calling.

"Why did you move out of San Francisco?" My turn now.

He takes a deep breath, his thick chest straining against the sweater and I am sure he is debating how much to reveal, yet again.

"It wasn't right. It never was."

Interesting. Another thin connection tying us together.

"That's it?" I need to push him back.

"Things we're becoming risky."

"In what sense? Were your murderous extracurricular activities becoming too dangerous?" I swear, I would have more success with a pair of pliers, torturing him.

"No. Women became too risky."

Well that, I certainly did not expect.

"I can either keep asking you question after question, or you could just give me the story Niklas."

He sighs and rolls his eyes, and it is probably the most relaxed and comfortable I have ever seen him.

"You know I told you I owned a company. It was a big, high profile company. Because we worked in Defense Technology, we also worked with high profile customers. This meant that my extracurricular activities with women had to be so tightly wrapped in a fucking bow that no one could ever find out. I needed to have a certain reputation and my tastes in sex are anything but conventional."

"Well, I'll be damned... I could not have guessed that," I say sarcastically with my hand on my mouth and big shocked eyes.

In this brief moment, my heart stops beating. His smile. A genuinely amused smile behind his bushy beard, at the brink of laughter—I did that. I made him smile, even if it was just for a couple of seconds.

Shit.

I do not need this. I do not need to see him like this. I do not need to see his humanity. I do not even need to see his monstrous personality. Because they all pull me closer and I need to be anywhere but.

"I had contracts; mainly because everything I needed had to be discussed prior, roughly planned, safe word, limits, scene, comforts, etc."

Well that sounds nothing like the man I know... safe words? Limits? All he seems to do is chase me into uncomfortable situations, test my limits, and make me feel in danger... nothing safe about it. This is why he left... that was not what he craved. This... me, is what he craves. And he still has not found my limits.

"However, when you have the money I had, there will always be at least one woman trying to sell her story, information about me and my... pleasures, to the press or my customers. I was done fighting with them just so I could have something that just wasn't fucking worth it, something that barely sated my hunger. And I was tired." He inhales slowly, and I only see his calm exhale, I do not hear it though. "I needed to find the place where I belonged."

I nod because I am not sure what to say in this moment. I understand him. More than I want to admit. And I envy him.

"And you moved here two and a half years ago?"

He nods. "Bought it around three years ago, the whole peak... I needed to be alone. Renovated it for the most part of a year, when it wasn't snowed in and moved in after about six months."

"What about your parents... how do they feel about you being so far from them?"

He gets up from the sofa and I frown.

"I think it's time for bed, little siren."

I start laughing because this is absolutely ridiculous, he cannot tell me when it is time for bed. But my laugh is interrupted by an annoying yawn that just proves his point, and I am even more annoyed now. My body betraying me in front of him, as always. I swear I have no control around him, my body just listens to all his cues.

"Come on, it's late." He shows me the clock on the phone he pulled out from his pocket and I believe him now. I did not realize how long we spent in his office or how late we ate.

I get up and look at him in pure disbelief. Why exactly

does he care about how late it is? Maybe he is just trying to avoid the questions, but I yawn again and realize that I could quite happily go to bed. I walk up the stairs behind him and before he can say anything I head into the bathroom and lock the door behind me. I am pretty damn sure he is currently in the corridor staring at this beautiful wooden door, wondering what the hell just happened.

I brush my teeth. Wash my face. Take a quick shower. And when I go out of the bathroom, the corridor is empty. I feel a slight disappointment settle within me, but I brush it off as fast as I feel it. I walk quickly towards my bedroom and close the door behind me, leaning against it.

I do not want to want to be in his bedroom. And I cannot have him take me there... because I will not be able to say no.

I finally peel myself off the door, change into one of his t-shirts that smell like him, and crawl into the bed. This whole situation feels unreal... so goddamn unreal, because at this particular moment in time, the craziest thing is going through my mind.

I did not say goodnight to him... and I feel bad.

I lay on my back, staring at the ceiling that looks gray in the moonlight and I cannot help but wonder... what the hell is wrong with me?

NIKLAS

She didn't even say goodnight to me. I don't know what I expected though. Half an hour talk and then suddenly she would be all sweet and compliant? I don't know... she's holding back on me though... and I need to hear more about her dreams.

I've never heard of that before, having the same dream over and over again for years. Is that normal? What do I even know about normal?!

And I want to see what she draws... I need to feed her soul and one way to do it is to feed her passion. A passion she hasn't been able to fuel since Adrien got her.

After I'm done in the bathroom and back in my bedroom, I pull out the phone and have a brief look over the list she wrote. Nothing crazy: clothes, a couple of toiletries and feminine stuff, and that is pretty much it. I add a few things in there and copy it all in a text for Connor. Hopefully he'll be able to get everything.

As I lay here, staring at the view outside my window, I can't help but wonder if she'll ever realize that this is where she belongs. I see it, why can't she?

I close my eyes and all I see is the green-eyed banshee that flipped my life over and threw it into fucking oblivion... nothing will ever be the same again.

* * *

Darkness... a change of smell... a shallow movement...

I open my eyes, but it's too dark, yet in a fraction of a second I have the intruder pinned by the throat under me. I take a deep breath and the scent of jasmine clues me in. Her small, smooth throat pulses under my palm, and her hands are holding onto the arm that's pinning her down.

"Fuck, Suki!" I get off her and lie back in bed, on my side, trying to look at her. But I'm barely conscious and the room is dark. "Is everything okay?"

"I could not sleep... I... I'm sorry... I... I thought I could be alone."

I breathe easy. I honestly thought she would have trouble. Ever since that motherfucker stepped foot in my house when she was here alone, she has had trouble... like yesterday when she couldn't be in the rest of the house on her own, even though I was just in a different room.

"It's okay." I cover her with the duvet and try to pull her closer to me, but she resists. I don't have time for this. I wrap my arm around her plump body and pull her towards me, holding her there until she starts relaxing.

"Goodnight, Suki."

I hear her exhaling a breath she seemed to have been holding for a while and with that her body relaxes further. Fuck, I wish I could hear what's happening in that beautiful brain of hers.

"Goodnight, Niklas."

* * *

I open my eyes, facing the windows, and the sunshine is so strong I feel the need to hide under the covers. I'm half expecting Suki to be downstairs again, but the delicate arm wrapped around my waist from behind says otherwise.

Her breathing is calm and soft. I hear a noise that could be mistaken for purring, but it's the slightest, softest snore I have heard in my entire life, and I know for a fact that she's still sleeping. I know I take her on a fucking rollercoaster ride every single day and most of it is intentional, some of it is not, mainly because my decision about her is not completely made. But... she learned the rules of my game and she's now playing it in her favor, because I feel like I'm losing.

I feel like I'm the one being played... At this point I'm not sure if it's involuntary or intentional.

Am I ever going to get tired of this view? I watch as the sunlight hits the tops of the trees that run down the mountain towards the valleys, and I wonder when I started liking the sunrise more than the sunset... Was it when I started waking up with her in this house?

I put my hand over hers and I feel her warm body shift behind me. She's pressed onto me, making me the little spoon, even though with her ridiculously short frame, her head barely reaches above the middle of my back. But she's spooning me... my ass in her lap and she wiggles, wrapping herself around me even more.

I could get used to this. I really could. Even though I would have never thought I could be the type... interesting.

I squeeze her hand a little harder and her whole body tenses in an instant. She's awake. She attempts to pull her hand away, but there's no way I'm allowing it. I hold it there.

"Good morning." I want to make sure she knows I'm

awake, and I'm pushing her to accept that she was the one seeking me.

"Umm... good morning..." her voice sounds a little rougher in the morning, and I like that I'm noticing this.

I shake myself mentally, baffled at the fact that it is me having these thoughts. It's hard to believe, I'm not entirely sure who this person is to be honest...

"I did not mean to..." she starts speaking again, "to..."

"Go in the other room without saying goodnight?" I interrupt.

"Umm... I..."

"Or coming into my bedroom anyway?" I interrupt again.

"I..." she tries again.

"Or spooning me during the night?" I do it again, and it's getting hard to keep the laughter in. I'm not even sure what I find funny, I have no idea, but I can't stop myself. My chest starts vibrating and my cheeks feel like they're on fire.

"You bastard!" She catches on, and I feel her small free hand slapping the back of my head.

It takes me a second to use the arm wrapped around me to pull her over as I turn on my back and she lands on top of me. She tries to brace herself, but it was too fast and she's here, the real Suki, looking at me in sleepy shock since she didn't get a chance to put her guard up yet. Messy hair falling in front of her and on my chest, big, beautiful eyes looking into mine, her gorgeous, soft body laid on top of me. I can't help myself, and I just start laughing as I hold her here, my arms wrapped around her.

"So? What didn't you mean to do, little siren?" I finally ask as she slaps my chest again.

She lets out a loud breath, and her lips almost pout before she quickly realizes what she was doing and straightens her face.

"You are being a dick. I was trying to be nice..."

I wanna smack her ass so hard right now, but I'm staying away.

"I did not mean any of it..." she finally speaks.

I stop laughing.

"Then why are you here, Suki?" I don't blink as my face straightens and I watch her eyes go completely still.

Maybe it's time to change the rules of the game.

"I was..." she sighs again. "Since Adrien... since he came here..." she's mumbling, and I'm losing my patience. It's not like I don't know what she wants to say, but I want her to fucking admit it.

"Suki..." my tone holds warning.

"I am scared, okay?! I am scared... I don't know if he is just going to show up out of nowhere."

I shake my head. Was that so hard?

"Even if he is, I'm not going anywhere. Not without taking you with me. And if I'm here, he's not getting you. He's not touching a hair on your body, Suki, never again." As I say those words to her, my arms around her squeeze her body tighter to mine involuntarily.

She nods, her head shaking.

"So, that's it then... you were just afraid to be in that bedroom alone." I speak as I start releasing my grip on her.

"Yes, that is it." She nods.

Okay, then. Time to change the rules of the game.

I gently slide her body off me, laying her on the bed.

"I'm going to take a shower and then we'll have breakfast." I don't stop or turn my head as I hear her meek *Okay* behind me. I just leave the room.

Chapter 22

SUKI

He was still in the bedroom by the time I left the bathroom and came downstairs. After he abruptly, but in a strangely polite way, left the room to take a shower earlier, I shook my confused brain and decided to do the same in the other bathroom.

Now, as I am pulling out breakfast ingredients from the fridge, I cannot help but think about the subtle, yet sudden shift in his behavior. As he held me there on top of him and I spoke those last words, I saw the monster in his eyes—he promised war as he slowly retreated. A different kind of war, because I felt the need to follow.

I am most definitely overthinking this. I shake my head for the fifth time this morning alone... I'm going to give myself whiplash. I hear his footsteps as he walks downstairs, but I carry on with making breakfast for us.

Making breakfast... for us...

"What is it?!" I hear his confused voice behind me and slowly turn around, holding the broken shell of an egg in both hands.

"Is this Stockholm? Niklas... is this what Stockholm syndrome feels like?"

"What the hell are you talking about?!" He cocks one eyebrow as he rubs the back of his head with one arm, in that pure manly way that would look even hotter if he was half naked, his thick, imperfect abs on full display.

"I am making breakfast for *us*. Voluntarily! Like I have accepted my fate, my goddamn captivity, Niklas!" my tone grows urgent, angry, and I wonder what the hell broke in me all of a sudden. Yet again I am making breakfast for *us*, like it is the most normal and natural damn thing in the world. Like we are a goddamn couple, not hunter and prey.

He shakes his head and sits on one of the barstools. "Do you want me to make breakfast?" For some reason his words make me angrier.

"Goddamn it, Niklas!" Now we really sound like a couple. Having a ridiculous fight about who is making breakfast. I cannot deal with this, this is too normal... too natural. I cannot have this, damn it! This normality that promises a future that I cannot possibly think about.

I turn back to the bowl that holds one lonely egg and just stare at it.

Breathe in. Breathe out. Breathe in. Breathe...

And I feel him behind me even before I feel his arms on my shoulders.

"Go. Sit down." I hear him say.

I do not wait for another word and I go straight outside on the porch. I let out the longest breath as I take in the calming view. It settles me instantly, and that bothers me. Running my hands through my hair, I try to let it all go, but I am not sure what bothers me more.

Is it Niklas' domesticated behavior?

Is it mine?

Is it the fact that this environment feels perfect?

Or that none of it feels wrong?

Get it together Suki, get it the hell together, otherwise you will never leave. I will always feel like I had no choice, I will hate myself for it, I will hate him for it. *Focus...*

After a few slow, deep breaths I am finally calm.

With every day that passes, my fear grows and unfortunately it is an internal one. I am afraid of myself more and more because he brings out the worst in me, yet he is showing me it is not the worst at all. Here lies a monster, not his, but mine and no one has seen it before... not even me. Yet I felt him stir twice and that brought forth a thirst in me, a thirst that I never, ever, want to sate.

One could argue that I have been unmoved by everything Niklas has told me... he is a murderer, a cold-blooded killer with a need for blood. He is not opportunistic, he is methodical, he is not hasty, he plans, he does not do it because he has to, he does it because his soul needs to. Yet I did not bat an eye lid... on the contrary, his story was what stirred my monster the second time.

And that scares the living hell out of me.

It awakens an unnatural craving, a depraved thirst, a horrific hunger inside of me, one that I have kept buried deep my whole life, ignoring its existence. If I stay here, with him, I will sate it and then what kind of person would I be? I cannot turn into him...

I never thought it possible, finding something I was searching for my entire life in the same place that threatens to unearth something I have been burying for the same amount of time. I want to run and stay all at the same time. How could I possibly decide which is the best choice?

I have been standing here, in the freezing cold dressed in nothing but a hoodie and a pair of boxers, and I am not entirely sure how much time has passed, but the harsh winter finally hits me. When I open the boarded-up door and step inside, the smell of pancakes and bacon assaults me. All those months Adrien fed me tasteless, strictly nutritional food, a lot of the time forcing me to eat so I would be strong enough for his games. I never realized how much I missed simply smelling good, tasty food.

I sit at the kitchen island and watch him as he finishes cooking. The ruthless Viking that threatens to destroy me... moving seamlessly through the kitchen.

Perfectly illusory.

* * *

"I'm going to have to fix the front door. I have spare glass panels in the workshop, I just need to take measurements and take the door apart," he tells me as we finish drinking our coffees on the sofa, watching the flames of the fireplace in the mid-morning light.

"You keep spare glass?"

"Yeah. Always. In these temperatures you never know when a window could crack. Plus you could just have an accident and there's no way of going to town and ordering glass panels."

Okay, I must admit, that makes sense. Living in the city

you do not really think of things like this. You always have access to anything, not matter how much snow has fallen. Here, you have to work hard for your creature comforts. And I cannot help but think how much more satisfying this is. I feel like I should offer my help with this task, but I keep my mouth shut, even if that window was broken by Adrien in order to get to me.

It is not my fault Niklas decided to capture me and bring me here. Or is it called saving?

I catch him watching me, and I wonder if he wants me to offer my help, but I do not have time to dwell on it before he shifts and goes upstairs. I turn to the dancing flames of the fireplace and I wonder... what are the next steps? I know he gathered all the information he needs in order to safely dispose of Adrien, but... is it really going to happen?

I never thought of myself as a coward, as a scared little woman, but Adrien turned me into this pathetic version of myself. A version I do not even recognize and even though Niklas has made my demons sing again, every time I think of Adrien, I feel my skin slowly breaking into cold sweats. That pathetic version of myself has not left my body just yet. It is simply hidden behind a veil... and I cannot seem to break her out and fucking kill her.

I need to kill her. I need to dispose of her. I need to move forward.

How can I though? How can I when he is still out there? Not out in the world... but out on this mountain. He could be behind the line of trees outside this house right now. He could be watching me. How can I stay here when the thought of him makes the marks he left on my skin burn?

My soul is conflicted. I want to run away from and after him all at the same time. I want to break him like he broke me. I want to show him who I really am when my guard is not down. But the wounds are too fresh, my soul barely mended, my heart still frail.

I hear Niklas' confident steps coming down the stairs, but I do not turn to look at him. Sure enough, he ignores me and I hear the same steps moving away before the door that leads to the garage slams closed.

I breathe easier when he leaves the room, and I am still not sure why. He has this talent, this unintended talent to make my breath hitch in my lungs. I feel him when he enters a room even when I am not looking. I feel the air around him touching me before I even feel his body. I hear his heartbeat from across the room, and I am not sure if it is because it's always so quiet here... or maybe his heart beats harder when he is around me.

No.

I must not fall... this is still a dungeon. I am not free. No matter how much I wish I would be.

Still here... but free.

NIKLAS

Most of the day I stayed away from her, keeping busy with various tasks that needed doing around the house, including taking apart that front door and fixing the window. Since I brought her here, I've been ignoring all the shit that needs doing around the house, from maintaining the heating system, making sure the pipes don't freeze, to the outstanding projects that need finishing, like insulating that damn workshop.

I desperately wanted to go for a run, but I couldn't risk leaving her alone again. Not when I know that motherfucker is watching my goddamn house. If I didn't care about this plot of land and had access to some damn land mines, I would have booby trapped this whole fucking place... but then again, getting my hands around his throat is going to be so much more satisfying than watching his guts fly through the air. So instead of running, I resorted to working out in the garage again.

I kept checking on her though, once in a while going inside the house, making sure she's okay, safe. Yet I didn't linger. I changed the rules of my game, but she is still playing one of her own making, hiding behind it, pretending she hates everything about her current predicament. We both know that's bullshit, I just need her to admit it to me... to herself most of all.

I brushed past her a few times, spoke only when it was necessary, and gave her attention without giving her too much.

If she figures out the game or not, I know the outcome will be the same—she will either become increasingly annoyed or she will fall for it. Either way, the prize will be claimed and the winner will not be me.

The day went by faster than I thought it would and by the time we went to bed, *my bed*, she already looked a bit suspicious, but tried her best to keep a straight face. I had a lifetime of observing people and reading facial cues, there was no way I wouldn't notice that.

"Goodnight, Suki." I keep my tone soft as I watch her turn around to face me. We're both on our sides and the moon bathes her in a soft blue light that makes her look like a surreal scene from a cyberpunk photo.

"Goodnight, Niklas."

It dawns on me that she's the only person in my life that calls me by my full first name. The way her sweet voice hits every vowel and consonant makes me feel like she should remain the only person to ever speak it.

I hold her gaze for a few more moments and roll away. The last thing I heard before falling asleep was a soft sigh.

* * *

"Niklas?" I hear her soft knock on the workshop door as she slowly pushes it open. "Can I come in?" It's already been a few days of me politely ignoring her and slowly I see her pulling herself closer.

I debate for a few seconds if she should come in, not because I don't want her in here, but because this means she will have further insight into me, while I can't seem to gain more into her.

"Yes," I sigh and shake my head.

She opens the door and as her eyes move around the room from left to right, they're getting wider and wider, and by the time they find me she's trying hard to pretend she's thinking of anything else. The monster has talent. Funny... I know.

"You... you did all this?" She closes the door behind her without looking back, her eyes stuck to mine.

I nod and she steps further in, walking towards me, her gaze is everywhere but, inspecting the space.

"Here, I made some tea. Thought you could use some." I notice she's carrying a steaming cup, and I grab it from her before she drops it since she's looking anywhere but in my direction.

As she turns her head to the left, I hear a small gasp and follow a shiver running through her body before she goes completely still, a sharp breath caught in her lungs. I follow her gaze and find the object of her surprise—the banshee. The same one tattooed on my back, only this one is carved into a large piece of oak and is hung on the wall.

"Her..."

That's all she says. She's so still, like someone pressed pause on a remote control, but her eyes... fuck, her damn eyes are filled with emotions I can't understand. Her mouth is slightly open and I swear to the gods she looks like she's about to burst as I watch another shiver slightly shaking her body.

She turns to me and I see them in her eyes—the demons, they're all watching me, and I feel caught off guard.

What the fuck?!

I look at the carving—the lips—I turn to Suki, my brows

furrow. I look at the carving again—the high cheeks, upturned nose, square jaw—I turn to Suki. *No...*

I look into her eyes again and the demons are still there, in the same position, unmoving. A shiver runs down my spine, and I can't understand what's happening.

"Who is she?" she finally speaks.

"The banshee..."

She breaks eye contact, turns back to the carving and suddenly I feel like I can breathe again. I turn as well.

"She's part of you." As she says that I know she doesn't mean that she's tattooed on my skin.

"Always..."

"But the banshee doesn't scream out of fear." She turns and her eye contact bores into me with an intensity that gives me goosebumps.

"Neither do you. Not anymore." Her eyes go wide.

"I thought... I thought it is fear you crave. I thought that's why..." she mumbles.

"I can taste fear, Suki. I can taste it in the sound waves and it's fuel for my fucked up soul. *Your* fear though... it's layered. You're not scared of me, Suki..."

"Am I not?" Her gaze stills—anger, fear, confusion, all assaulting her at once.

"You wish you were..." She's heaving, mainly because she knows I'm right.

Sighing, she rubs her eyes with her palms, before running her hands through her thick hair.

"When did they start? These... cravings."

I can't help myself, and I laugh. By the look in her eyes, I can tell she doesn't know whether she wants to be annoyed or just plain confused at my reaction.

"These... cravings... when I was about fifteen." I tell her the story about the woman in the park as she finds a seat on a wooden bench and listens to it. Her body fidgets as the story evolves. I can tell some parts make her uncomfortable and some make her flush. *Interesting.*

"So you've been... doing this since then?"

"No... I was around twenty-two when I finally understood the games I needed to play."

"Who is she then? Is she the woman from the park?" she asks again.

I look at the wooden carving, the carving that I now can only see as Suki...

"No... she's my trigger, she's the reason why I finally understood what I needed. She's a woman from an alley..."

Suki turns her head to me, her brows furrowed in confusion, her body a bit tenser than before.

"Alley?"

For a man that had trouble speaking to people his whole life, I sure as fuck can't shut up when this little siren asks me questions. She's playing me like a fucking violin, and I'm trying to understand why talking to her comes naturally.

I tell her how it happened about ten years ago... how I finally heard the banshee scream again, how, like a siren she involuntarily called me to her. I tell her about the alley, what I found there, and with every word I speak her body shifts, her arms now wrapped around herself.

"There was something about her, something I wasn't able to find since... not until..." I trail off. Not until Suki... but this is not the moment to reveal this. "She ran before I had the chance to talk to her... but only when I was done beating that motherfucker. She stayed for that whole bloody, violent scene and to this day I wonder why. To this day I wonder if she wanted to make sure he wasn't able to come after her or maybe she enjoyed the show, the retribution... the bloodshed."

I watch her throat move almost in slow motion as she

swallows a lump, her arms wrapped around her body, her eyes blinking rapidly. She parts her lips to speak, but ragged breaths are all that's coming out.

What the fuck?!

I want to go to her, but I'm afraid to break this spell, mainly because I feel like I'm miles closer to breaking her. My comfort is the last thing I should give her right now.

"It was the show... the retribution..." Her gaze looks deep into mine, her voice breaking and I see her demons. There's fire, strong fucking fire. Recognition. "...the bloodshed." Tears fill her bright green eyes as she looks back at me... *shiny eyes... like... hers.* I turn my gaze back to the carving for a split moment.

A fraction of a second. That's all it took for me to walk to her and kneel in front of the bench she's sitting on. I can't speak though... I can't. There's no possible way I could say the right thing at this moment. I grab her face into my hands and look at her. She grabs my wrists. My ragged breaths connect with hers. I wipe her tears with my thumbs. She squeezes me with her small hands.

I don't know what this is.

I don't know what my soul feels.

I don't know if it's shattering or breaking open.

I don't know what this means...

I'm not one to believe in fate, but then what the fuck is this?! What the fuck brought her on my doorstep after all these years? What are the motherfucking chances?!

My soul hurts.

"I saw them that night." She swallows hard, her breaths catching in her lungs, unshed tears pooling in her eyes. "The demons in your eyes... I saw them that night. It was the only thing of you I saw..."

"Suki..." her little face in my big hands looks so fragile right now. She's not upset, her unshed tears are not about that... she's overwhelmed... she's confused... she's everything that I am in this moment.

"I ran because of the demons... for a second I thought they would follow me..."

"For a second I thought so too... but it wasn't the right thing to do."

"I didn't know it was you... I should have known..." She tries to shake her head, but she's trapped in my hands.

"It was so dark, Suki, I didn't know it was you either... there was no way." I let go of her, but she still clutches my wrists as I lay my forearms on her lap.

We sit in silence for a couple of minutes. How does one come to terms with such a revelation? How does one process the fact that she was the one that caused this chain reaction inside me, the one that broke open all these cravings? The one to bring out the monster.

"What do you mean it wasn't the right thing to do?" she asks.

"You were attacked, assaulted. No matter how hard my dick was, that was fucked up, I couldn't have come after you. And the adrenaline, the fear in your voice... the reason why I was there, I was in a strange trance caused by it all, by... you," I sigh... this is harder than I thought, and there's this overwhelming pressure in my chest, something I can't quite process and for some reason my body feels fragile.

She shakes her head, tears dropping on her plump cheeks, her eyes even greener amongst the red of pooling emotions.

"I was not attacked... I mean, I was, but..." she sighs, shaking her head again.

I frown because I know I saw the opposite in that alley.

"That night I decided to give in... for the first in my life, I decided to give in, give it a try, fulfill those dreams..."

"What dreams, Suki?"

She lets go of my wrists, and I sit on my heels in front of her, my palms around her thighs as she gathers her thoughts.

"I do not know when they started, but they are the first thing I remember from when I was a child. Not my mother, not my father, not playing in my room, not my friends... I was a toddler, yet my first conscious memory is of me running... running away from a monster. I am terrified, screaming, but as I turn to look for him... I am smiling."

The tears are flowing hard now. She swallows her breaths and I swear I can see her demons wailing in her eyes. This... the cravings I only caught glimpses of, these were not sexual kinks of hers, no, these were so much more.

"I had that dream every single night." she sighs, and my eyes go wide. "Every. Single. Night. Until..." she trials off.

Until when?! Until what?!

"The dreams evolved. Even though they followed the same plot line, the action was not always the same, but the fear was bone crippling at times. And the monster... the monster felt different. I got used to it. Years passed, and the dream became part of me, until I finally understood that it did not become anything—it was me, an extension of myself. I expected it now, craved it, feared it, and reveled in it..." She shakes her head yet again, looking at the banshee... at... herself.

"After so many years, I got used to it and it did not feel the same anymore. The dream did not stop, but it did not affect me in any way. It did not sate my hunger, settle my cravings... it did not feed my demons. It just was not enough and because of that, it became a haunting. The monster haunted me... taunted me..."

She takes a deep breath, looks into my eyes and suddenly I feel too much, I feel it all, and I find myself breathing on the same strained rhythm as her.

"After all that happened with my family, after leaving

my home and going to University, I felt numb. A strange emotionless state, yet at the same time, I was overwhelmed by feelings. Over time, as I grew, the dreams matured with me and they turned into these blood boiling sexual cravings... not like some BDSM prey kink, my body was not the only one involved. It was an insatiable desire my soul needed. I craved the chase, the fear, but most of all... I craved a monster. "

She wipes her face with her palms and I help her, gently swiping my thumbs under her eyes. Her gaze follows me as my thumb goes in my mouth, her salty tears staining my tongue and hunger painting her face. That night she craved a monster as well... and she found it.

"I arranged that," she continues, "I found a random stranger in a bar, and somehow I knew he was a depraved bastard. I knew he wasn't into this kink; however, I saw the danger in his eyes. His demons did not sing with mine, but he scared me, he scared me enough to know that if I said no to him, he would become a monster. And maybe... just maybe... it would fuel my cravings enough for the dreams to stop being hauntings."

"Shit, Suki..."

"I did not think... he was strong, I was stupid. It got out of hand. It helped though... it helped me. Because the monster I found that night was you, not him. It was always you hunting me in my dreams ever since..."

Short breaths fill her lungs, and suddenly the world around us goes quiet... our breaths the only noise pollution. This was a confession... one that I feel so deep in my soul that my monster roars in victory. I didn't see it before, there was no way, but my demons did, and my monster came out the day I found her because he recognized her. To say that this is surreal is simply not enough.

"You're my banshee, Suki... the siren that sang the only

song that ever fueled my soul... I searched for that melody ever since and it took a few years for me to understand that the song wasn't what I was looking for, it was your voice... No one was able to sing it the same."

We found each other that night, we found exactly what we were craving, but somehow, I don't think either of us were in the right place in our lives to do it right. I don't think it was the right time for us to truly meet. That night was a discovery, a revelation and for me... acceptance. Acceptance of something that disgusted me all those years before. Something I didn't understand...

"I don't know..." she starts speaking, but I stop her. I don't want to hear doubts, rejections, nothing. I grab her upper arms and bring her on my lap, her legs straddling me, her short frame reaching just under my chin. I wrap my arms around her, one on the small of her back, one at the nape of her neck and I hold her to me, my face buried in her hair that smells so different than mine, even though she uses my shampoo. She slowly relaxes, and her whole body molds to mine, her arms and legs wrapping around me.

I hold her there, tight against me, and I realize that it's not for her comfort, but for mine.

I need this. My soul is not shattering, it's breaking open and I don't know how to deal with it. I don't know how to catch everything that's spilling out because this is unfamiliar territory. Too fucking unfamiliar and I need her. I fucking need her!

She's my fucking banshee. I bled for her; I branded my skin with her beautiful scream... she's mine.

"Niklas...?"

"Yes."

"What did you carve on my skin?"

I smile. "Your monster."

CHAPTER 23

SUKI

I hold on to him for dear life, he is grounding my soul right now.

Your monster...

How... how is it possible for this to have happened... he is *my* monster. All those years ago, all those nights I did not want to go to sleep because I knew that he was only a dream, that he was not real and never would be again. And all the other nights when I forced myself to go to sleep because I needed to feel him again, feel him behind me, feel the fear traveling through my bones, the scream in my lungs, and the wetness between my thighs.

He was mine long before I found myself in his woods... he

was mine, my monster.

I squeeze him tighter in my arms as I hear him take a big whiff of my hair. He is holding me so tight and I am not sure if it is for my benefit or his. But this... this here is pure affection. I am not wrong, I am not seeing things, I am not fooling myself. We have a connection that was built individually, separately for so many years and now... now the strands of our past and present are grabbing onto each other like invisible tentacles, pulling us closer and closer together.

We do not know each other, but our souls... our demons do.

Is this enough? Is this enough for me to stay? Will he tire of me eventually?

As my palms press harder onto his back, it suddenly dawns on me.

"Your tattoo," I speak against his strong chest.

He rubs his fingers against the back of my neck and it takes everything in me not to start groaning at the involuntary massage. As I roll my head back, his fingers keep the rhythm.

"What about it?"

"It's... it is me. You have me..."

"Tattooed on my back." His ocean blue eyes pull me into their depths, yet my heart feels like it is catching fire.

His lips crash onto mine, pressing painfully as he holds me tight and inhales slowly, deeply, like I am his life essence, and my heart cannot bare it. It bursts in a silent explosion that spreads like wildfire through me, ravaging everything in sight until it reaches my mind and I cannot take it, cannot keep it in... contain it.

I break the kiss, look at him, my lips parted, my breaths short, and I sink. I sink into his blue eyes because at this moment they are the only thing that can extinguish this explosion. He is right there, sinking with me, and I am not sure how I am certain of this. I do not know where we go from here. There aren't enough words to surmise what this means, this invisible connection that spans over years.

We swim back to the surface, together, and the mind clears. It is just us now. Looking into each other's eyes. Our features expressionless. The sound of silence, calming. There are emotions in his eyes and I am not sure if he knows this.

I tilt my head to the left, and he mimics me. I quirk the corner of my lip up and so does he. And when his demons rise and his gaze turns dark, so does mine.

I feel a shift in the universe, and I know that he feels it too. As cliché as it sounds, this feels like the first day of the rest of our lives. Chapter one in an unwritten story. The prologue started that warm night in a dark San Francisco alley and ended last night. And if that was the prologue... what is the main story going to bring?

He presses his hands on my back and neck, pulling me back into his body and I do not resist. Holding me in his strong arms, my body surrenders and I feel like I could happily fall asleep. Deep inside, I know he needs this as much as I do, I feel it in the rhythm of his heartbeat, the flow of his blood pulsing through his veins. He needs this.

"Suki..."

"Yes."

"Do you still have those dreams?"

"No."

"When did they stop?" he asks, but his voice is laced with an unfamiliar insecurity.

"The same night you brought me here."

There is silence as a slow breath escapes his lungs.

"But you had a nightmare that night. I woke you up, if you remember."

He is right. The beautiful dreams I had of him all these

years have been replaced by nightmares of Adrien. Almost like a chapter of my life ended, because the quest was finished. The object of my desires was found, and my mind was cleared to think of everything else that haunts me. And Adrien haunts me in the most disturbing of ways.

"I did... about Adrien. It seems that once my recurring dream ended, my mind opened up to normal human processes. Nightmares."

His hands wrap around my forearms and they push me away from his body, holding me far enough away so that he can look into my eyes.

"You are mine, Suki. I am your fucking monster and your only nightmare. He has no goddamn place in your mind and no right to haunt your dreams. I will break him, Suki, break him apart bone by motherfucking bone. I will reach through his fucking throat, pull his heart out and gift it to you. This..." he points between us. "This is it for me. I need you to understand it. I will kill for you. I will burn this world to the ground if it means that you will be safe. I will decimate it if that's what will make you happy."

My skin breaks into billions of microscopic electric shocks as I process every sentence that left those delicious lips. He would do this for me? He would bring hell on this forsaken world because it would please me?

"Niklas... I..."

"Always," he interrupts.

Always.

"You will never let me go, will you?" I ask.

"Never... I let you go once, Suki. I'm not sure which gods I have to thank for dropping you into my fucking lap, but I'm' happy to give them a human sacrifice for it."

"What if I run?"

"I will scout the ends of the earth. I will break through

mountains. I will drain the oceans if it means finding you. I might not be able to stop you from running, Suki, but that hunger that's going to ravage your soul, will. I told you before—stop playing by the rules of a world you don't belong in—succumb to who you are. This is not about giving in, this is about embracing. Your soul belongs here with me, it always did and it will forever... how will you survive if you run and it stays here? What will your life become?"

I cannot help but feel like I am being emotionally blackmailed while his rational train of thought ravages through me.

"I am not sure what you want from me, Niklas. What are you asking for? Because I do not think I can give it to you."

He shakes his head, but his gaze never leaves my eyes. "I don't want you to give me anything. There's darkness inside you, Suki. A beautiful, decadent, darkness that needs to break free, yet here you are, keeping it caged because the world you believe you belong to frowns upon it." There is menace in his eyes, and his tongue is laced with subtle evil. It scares me, because what I have inside myself is not darkness, it's a sickness.

A sickness that broke my mother apart. A sickness that turned her into the depraved junkie worthless piece of shit that bled out under my blade. A sickness that tainted and burned my childhood to the ground.

I cannot give in. I cannot become my mother.

I look down, because I don't want him to see the fear and shame in my eyes. No matter how much my demons will torture me for this, I cannot give in and become her.

I see his hand reach for me and his fingers pinch my chin, bringing my head up. He doesn't push me though. Instead, he kisses me with an unnatural softness for the brute he is... his beard and mustache tickle my skin and a soft moan escapes my lips. I feel his quirk upwards, and he shocks me when a chuckle escapes his throat.

What the hell? He almost never laughs. I slap his chest because these heavy moments need this, we need to bring some light into this atmosphere charged by unbelievable revelations.

"What?! You bastard!" I pretend to be annoyed as I move my lips away from his and look into his eyes.

He chuckles harder, and I slap at his hard chest again.

"Hey! Stop that before I flip you over my knee, woman!" There's amusement behind his menacing tone and it makes me smile.

I think about it for a second... last time he did that, he left me needy and wet. I definitely would not mind him finishing the job. Yet somehow it does not feel like the right time.

"Then tell me why you are chuckling like an old man under your mustache?!"

"Old man?! Oh, you silly little siren!" his tone is devious, and the smile on his face is dangerous as his big hands squeeze my ass cheeks to the point I hiss from the pain and grab onto his shoulders to steady myself. "I'm barely four years older than you."

"Are you? Oh... could have fooled me." I tease, and he slaps one of my ass cheeks so hard my whole body jerks forward on his lap. My hands go around his neck and my eyes fixate on his.

I can taste the intensity of this moment on my tongue. Like crimson spreading through my mouth... our lives intertwined in a dark way that we are just beginning to understand. The laughter feels like an acknowledgment... a full-stop for two separate stories.

I am not sure if it was truly the prologue. It could have been part one... or the last chapter before the end.

NIKLAS

Sliding my hands under her ass, I lift her off me, getting up from my heels so I can set her on her feet. I'm kneeling in front of her, my hands on her round hips, hers on my shoulders.

I curse myself for not recognizing her, but then again, how could I? That alley was so fucking dark, all I could see were shapes and her bright fucking eyes that shined even in that darkness. This connection... this... I can't help it, how can I not believe in fate when it hits me in the gut like this? She's mine, my banshee, my siren, my awakening... she helped bring forth all that I am, she cracked the fucking walls and the monster broke through for her and her alone.

Nothing, not even the games I played in school, in Uni, with my ex, nothing helped and now I understand why. I understand why it's her.

She wasn't just my siren, she wasn't just the one that gave me the taste of fear that I needed, she was the catalyst to the violence that I craved. I bled for her that night. I almost killed because of and for her. I pushed that sack of shit to the brink of death as she watched in delight.

She isn't just my siren. She's my fucking demon queen.

I finally get up, but my eyes are still following hers.

"What have you been doing inside?" I finally turn from her and return to my latest wood carving project. There's a tension in the air, but then again, after this revelation, there is no other way. Laughing helped though.

"Reading. There is not much to do around here."

"There's always something to do around here," I say, laughing. "Unfortunately, you don't have the right clothes for everything that should be done."

"What do you mean? What is there to do?" She's inquisitive, sounding genuinely interested.

"It's a house in the dead of winter, there's a lot to do. Even if it's bringing in supplies, like meats and cans from the cold storage, chopping wood, maintaining the heating system."

"I do not mind helping Niklas... it will make me feel a little bit better..."

Her body language shifts, her muscles tense ever so slightly, and I have a feeling she's thinking about her current situation again. About being trapped here, on this mountain... with me. After what we've just found out about ourselves, I can't help but feel a little bit... actually, I don't know what I feel. Mainly because... I've never quite felt like this before.

I step back to put some distance between us, turning my head to the side, looking at nothing in particular. My brows furrow as I'm trying to pinpoint what the fuck is happening inside me right now. I know this situation is different, I know I told her I don't want to let her go... I know I have done or told her things that would scare the living shit out of a normal woman. But Suki is not a normal woman, and this is not a normal situation. And what we share... this connection that unbeknownst to us, spread over years, means something.

For fuck's sake, this means something! It has to mean

something to her as well... not just me!

Is this how it feels to be hurt by someone?

I'm not asking her what she means by wanting to feel a bit better. I don't want to acknowledge it and fuel that fucking idea. "There's not much you can do, unfortunately, we don't have appropriate clothes for you just yet. After Connor comes though, you can help me as much as you want."

Her stance shifts. She relaxes, yet I swear I can see the wheels spinning in her head. She's a cunning little siren. I know she is. No matter what, I need to make sure I don't underestimate her, for her sake more than mine. She seems to have a knack at putting herself in dangerous situations with men, no fucking way I'm letting her get into another one.

I know for a fact that if she leaves this place, her cravings will lead her to seek danger again, there is no way she can stay away from it. Wouldn't it be better if her cravings could be met right here... by me?

"Connor, yes. Okay. Can I sit here with you?" I cock my head as I watch her gently sit on the bench. "I brought my book." She shows it me.

"Sure. There's a couple of furs in that corner." I point to a basket. "Lay them on the bench, get comfortable."

She nods and does as suggested, only she spots the fire and makes a little nest in front of the fireplace. I carry on carving the baroque inspired piece that I was working on when she came in.

Every few minutes, my eyes are stolen by her, curled in front of the fire, wrapped in animal furs, reading her book. This is quite an image, something I could and most definitely want to get used to. Like everything else involving her, it fits.

This thought lives rent free in my head now and nothing can pry it out. She fits in my world, and I can fucking guarantee that she knows this, no matter how much she will fight and deny it.

She fucking fits.

"So, did you kill all these animals I'm lying on?" she interrupts my train of thought, and I realize I was still staring at her.

"Most of them. Some I bought when I moved here. Down in Bear Creek, they hold all sorts of markets when spring comes. When I moved here, there was much I had to learn. Skinning, drying, and preparing hides was not something I knew. So some of them are the work of locals."

"That is nice. Markets..." she trails off, lost in thought. "How big is Bear Creek?"

"Small, real small. Maybe a couple of thousand people. Barely a town."

"Oh, wow, that is small. Doesn't it feel strange... you can be invisible in the big city, but here, here everyone can know your business. What if someone finds out..."

"About me?" I can't help but laugh. "No. I take my business elsewhere. And if... business comes up in town, I pass it on to Connor."

"So, what do the people of Bear Creek think of the big bad wolf that bought the peak?" It's her turn to grin now, and I like the curves it creates on her pretty fucking face.

"Exactly what I want them to think. I'm good to them. I invest in the town. I engage enough. Yet, if you come on my mountain with bad fucking intentions, you will leave with your tires slashed and two broken legs. I made sure they understood I came here for the privacy."

She laughs, "You can't be serious! Did you actually do it?! Break someone's legs?"

I don't laugh, though. I cock my head to the left and hold her gaze without blinking. I feel the slight grin in my lips hitting my eyes as well. She stops laughing. He mouth slightly open. Her eyes grow wide.

"Holy shit, you did." She shakes her head. "Why did I even question it. I think for a second there I forgot who I was talking to."

"It was three of them, actually."

Her mouth falls open. "At the same time?!"

"No. One came. Then the other two to... avenge him." I can't help but laugh at the memory. "They wanted to play with the new guy in town... wanted to rob me as well." I shake my head with a big fucking smile on my face.

"Oooh... and you took them all. Of course you did..."

"What was I supposed to do, Suki, roll over and show them my belly?! Fuck, no. The only reason one of them isn't dead is because I actually want to live here... for the rest of my life. And as assholes go, those ones are apparently well-known in this town."

"So, where are they now?"

"Connor put them in jail. I think they might be out, I'm not sure. They learned a lesson anyway. No one has come here with bad intentions or uninvited since."

"No one?"

I'm confused.

"Yeah... what do you mean?"

"Not even... late night guests?"

I'm certainly smiling for a different reason now.

"There have been some slip ups... but even they learned that they should never step foot here uninvited." I lick my lips, my eyes fixed on her. I catch the blush on her plump cheeks, the way her lips tense, but most of all, the flicker of dark promises in her eyes. Her stance shifts, and I'm not sure if I'm looking in the eyes of jealousy... or revenge.

"Mhm." That's the only sound leaving her body, not even her mouth. Oh, if this little siren would accept her fate even hell would weep. I can see the fire that burns within her, I can see the demons coaxing her, begging for her to let go and if she would, it would be quite a fucking show.

"Connor is the only one that tends to come uninvited. Nothing can fucking stop him though." I can't help but roll my eyes. That son of a bitch will be the death of me someday. Mostly because there's a big chance I'm gonna accidentally shoot him.

I turn my attention back to the wood carving sitting on the table in front of me.

"Is he like you?"

"No one's like me, Suki." I look up and I catch how a subtle shiver travels through her body.

"I don't mean... ufff... does he kill or you know... He knows of you, Niklas, he can't be all that fucking innocent!" Her slightly exasperated tone and attitude takes me by surprise.

"I don't know, Connor is... a good man. Yet... there's something about him."

"You think he's hiding something?"

"No... at least not like we are." Yes, I fucking said *we* and it startled her. We're hiding murder from the world, a delicious depravity, a taste for blood, cravings that normal people pay for. "I don't think even he knows what he's hiding. However, no person can hold themselves hidden forever. Sooner or later who we are comes forth. We just need the right catalyst."

My eyes bore into hers as I speak those words and she catches my intention, yet chooses to ignore it.

"I can't wait to meet him." There's sarcasm in her voice and she's not even trying to hide it.

"You'll like him. You two might have a lot in common." Two can play this fucking sarcastic game.

Two more seconds I hold her gaze, then, yet again, bring my attention back to the carving sitting in front of me.

CHAPTER 24

SUKI

I woke up as Niklas was tucking me into his bed under the soft covers.

"Shhh... sleep."

I want to protest, I need to brush my teeth, but it is warm and comfortable and the sheets smell like him. I inhale the smell until it hits my soul and the darkness falls heavy on me as I clutch the duvet to my chest.

"Adrien, no! For the love of God, please, I beg you... no..."

He brought the whip again. I watch him as he slices the air around me with it repeatedly. He loves this, he fucking loves this because he knows I dance around the room, pissing myself in fear when he cuts the air too close to me.

He whipped me once and my back still bears the scars, the pain still burnished in my skin even now, so long after it has healed.

"Little bird, I like to see you dance. I like to see that fear in your eyes, because I know you're curious about this. About the pain that could paint your skin."

I shake my head, tears falling freely over my cheeks, my arms wrapped around myself, hiding my breasts, protecting the sensitive flesh from an accidental slice of the whip. He walks to me and grabs my chin with the other hand, bringing my head to him. Holding me there, he trails the cold leather of the whip on my side, on my ribs, down on my waist, on my hip, bringing it between my crossed legs.

"On your knees, little bird." The crack of the whip in the air brings me down instantly. I'm facing his crotch and somehow, the noise of the zipper being pulled drowns the menacing sound of the whip slicing the air.

Bile rises in my throat, yet I know there's only one thing I can do to distract him from this delusional thought that the type of pain he gives me is the one I need.

"That's it, little bird, show me how much you appreciate what I do for you."

His disgusting cock in my throat does nothing to push the bile back. The whip cracks, his dick slams to the back of my throat gagging me, and his slimy grunt makes it harder to keep the bile down as his cock is slowly sliding out. The whip cracks again, his dick slams harder into the back of my throat, and the vomit is harder to keep at bay. The whip cracks again, his cock slams again, the slimy grunt gets louder, the vomit bursts all over his cock, his abdomen, his clothes, my breasts.

I fall on all fours as he spews out swears at me.

"You ungrateful fucking bitch! This is how you treat me? After giving you everything you desired?!"

I throw up again, and when I hear the whip slicing the air, I know that the next thing being sliced is my skin. A split second was not enough to prepare myself for the pain. I jump and move away as fast as I can, my back to him.

I have nowhere to go, but I aim to shift constantly so he cannot catch me with the whip.

"Aaaaaaarghhh!" The scream that rips through my throat leaves me raw, my body flaming, my muscles tense, struggling to cope with the shock that hit me with full force.

I look down at the thin leather wrapped around my leg, streaks of blood painting my skin. I cannot move, afraid that I will make it worse. All I can do is look down and stay still, however when I hear his disturbing laugh behind me, bile rises up my throat again, a strained breath invades my lungs, and I fight hard to hold the tears in.

And then he pulls. He pulls so fucking hard I'm convinced the leather hit muscle, but my face hits the stone floor before I can process more.

"Suki!!! Wake up, you're okay, wake up!"

Somewhere in the distance a deliciously rough, warm voice fills the air, reaching closer and closer to me.

"Suki! Wake up, little siren."

Little siren... Niklas!

My eyes open, and my body jerks into a sitting position. I rip the sheets off me and my hands go straight for my scarred leg, rubbing up and down. Even now, after all this time, I can still feel the whip in my flesh...

"Hey, hey, it's okay! Look at me!"

His voice centers me. My eyes close, I breathe in and out a bit slower, and suddenly his rough hand is on my leg and my whole body scoots up on the bed until my back hits the headboard.

"Suki, it's me!"

I know. I fucking know it's him! Yet my brain is having

trouble adjusting.

My eyes finally find his and that image is potentially the best distraction, the best drop back into reality. Lying on his side, propped on his forearm, his strong abs dusted with short hair on full display, his wide shoulders strained by this situation, all bathed in the cool moonlight. He is the most beautiful man I have ever seen, and it is not easy admitting to myself that I wanted him since the first moment I laid eyes on him... Even then, when my feet bled after running through his woods, away from Adrien. Even then, I felt this disturbing attraction between us.

How could I not fight it, though? How could I not fight him? This is not normal! Nothing about this is fucking normal. I am not supposed to be attracted to another man two seconds after I escaped a six-month long capture! If anyone would look down on this, on this bat-shit crazy dynamic between us, they would think I am certifiable.

Yet... it feels so goddamn right; it makes me want to cry.

It is chemistry. There is no other way I can explain the intensity with which this instant attraction ripped through me... pure chemistry. Since the moment his hand touched my skin in those woods.

Apparently, even before that, in the alley where all I saw was a spark in his eyes and the shape of his body beating the shit out of the sleazy man that wanted to shove his cock inside of me.

Shit.

Niklas touches my bare leg again, slowly brushing over the scar that spirals all around it, from the top of my thigh to about two thirds down my calf. I am watching his hand, but I feel him watching me. As it glides from my knee, up my thigh, I feel my core tightening, but he stops, right below my pussy. The only thing touching it is the heat emanating from his skin and a shiver runs straight to my damn nipples.

The next thing I know, he squeezes my thigh hard and in one swift move he pulls me to him, somehow flipping me on my side, spooning me. One arm slides under my head, the other one around my waist, my back flush to his naked chest, my ass in his lap. I cannot help but be a bit disappointed that he did not go further.

I lie there for a few minutes, watching the stars through the huge windows, moving ever so slightly in the night sky. I appreciate this—the silence. He knows, he acknowledges the pain, yet he knows this is not the time to talk about it. Sometimes he pushes me too hard, yet in the right moments he holds back.

"You're safe..." is the last thing he whispers in my ear before the darkness takes over again.

* * *

Two days have passed since our revelation. Two days, and I am not sure how many before that since he touched me. Properly touched me, and I cannot fucking believe I am angry about this. I thought I was his damn siren! I thought he craved this, this fucking need that haunts us both. The need for lust and chaos!

Yet, he has been calm, so damn calm that it puts me on edge. Even this morning, I planted my ass in his lap just before he woke up. Morning glory poked me, and I pretended to be asleep as I moved ever so slightly, rubbing it between my ass cheeks.

No matter how much I tried to resist, this man is sin embodied and fuck, I miss being a sinner.

And then, the son of a bitch pulled away from me. He did not exactly reject me, no, he just turned on his back and pulled me to him, my head resting on that sweet spot where the shoulder meets the chest. I would not have been that bothered, but I feel like he's been playing with me. Always touching me in a way that feels sexual, yet it never leads to anything, paying me attention just enough to make me feel good, but not enough to make me feel satisfied. He keeps me at this level where I am always goddamn craving him.

I would be lying if I said that what he's doing is bringing this out of me. No, it is simply revealing it.

"Motherfucker!" He changed the rules of the game!

I jump off the sofa and head straight to the front door, walking barefoot through the cold snow, and the sun hits my skin just right as my long strides take me straight to Niklas' workshop. I am halfway there when it dawns on me that maybe he simply lost interest in me, but I am not backing down now.

"You son of a bitch!" I storm through, oblivious to the fact that his first instinct was to grab the biggest chisel he had closest to him and aim it straight at me.

"Jesus Christ, woman! I could have fucking killed you." He shakes his head and drops it on the table.

"This is why you are fucking keeping me here Niklas? So you can play with me? Play goddamn games because you are bored and you feel the need to be entertained?"

"What the fuck you talking about?" he speaks so calmly, and it takes everything in me not to grab the first thing I see and haul it at his beautiful damn head.

"Don't you dare pretend you do not know what I am talking about. I am not playing your game, Niklas. Stay the fuck away from me!" I turn on my heels, storm out and slam the door behind me.

I'm in the kitchen when I realize what a mistake that was. I stupidly thought that because a few days have passed, he was not a threat anymore. I laugh at myself as my body is lifted off the ground and slammed ass first onto the island countertop. *Stupid little girl,* I think as he rips every piece of fabric that covers my body, scratching my skin with the harsh, violent movements.

When the last rags fall to the floor, my lungs are charged, my breathing deep and heavy and my pussy hot and tight.

I missed this.

I fucking missed this, the beast in front of me, the violence he brings, the pleasure he gives. I craved it like the most delicious, mind splitting drug. I craved it all.

He is heaving. His shoulders lift every time he takes a breath, he holds me pinned with a ravenous gaze and I feel like I am about to be devoured. Before another thought can cross my mind, he does exactly that. He devours me.

He drops down and I do not get a chance to see if he is kneeling or squatting or what the hell is going on before he digs his fingers into my thighs and pulls them apart so harshly, my whole body jerks forward to the edge of the countertop. My naked feet quickly brace themselves on his shoulders and my body falls back on my elbows.

I'm split open and exposed to him, and as I look down all I can see is pure hunger in his eyes. His gaze lingers over every fold of my pussy, and I involuntarily squeeze its walls, my whole body visibly shivering in response. A moan escapes my throat, and the next second his tongue assaults me.

I cannot call it any other way. He eats me out like I am his last meal, his tongue swiping up and down, circling, penetrating in a frenzy that makes me mad. He sucks my clit and I see stars behind my eyes. He sucks my lips, he sucks every fold, pushing and pulling, but when his tongue reaches inside of me and he circles it around pressing hard on the wall, I know that I will gladly lay myself on silver platter for him. I will put a fucking apple in my mouth if it means that I will be the only meal he has for the rest of his damn life.

My body jerks violently when he suddenly bites down on my clit. I look at him, my eyes and mouth wide open, body still, a scream trapped in my throat. He watches me, a devious smile on his face, eyes promising pleasure, the teeth holding onto my sensitive, swollen clit giving pain. The world around us falls silent, the earth stops spinning, and I feel like he is the one responsible for it. We are completely still, and his eyes seem to be weighing down his options—bite harder or let go?

There is a spark in my pussy, a drop slides down through my folds and as if on cue, his teeth bite harder and the world explodes in a mash-up of sounds I cannot process. My body falls back, his tongue laps at my clit violently and I feel my soul leaving my body when his fingers forcefully enter me, curling straight up to that sensitive spot. It must work like a goddamn self-destruct button because the orgasm ripping through my body takes me by surprise. I am shaking, my pussy tightening around his fingers so hard I can actually feel the curves of his knuckles.

I do not notice when he gets up or when he puts his rough hand around my throat, but when his fingers slide out of my twitching pussy, I am back. His eyes bore into mine as he licks his fingers, then he shuts them for a second like he is savoring the sweetest dessert. He does not linger though. His hand squeezes the sides of my throat harder and when those wet fingers touch my lips, my mouth falls open with my tongue out, and he pushes them inside until he reaches the back of my throat. I slide my tongue between his fingers, dragging it slowly, tasting myself on him and I cannot help but moan.

He pulls me by the throat towards him, and my legs wrap around his waist just as his lips crash down onto mine, swallowing every noise that comes out of my mouth. Before I can take another breath, his cock rips through me, straight to the hilt and the screech that leaves my throat drowns into his.

He holds me there, by the throat, squeezing harder every time he slams himself deeper into my core, stealing life from me. His other hand wraps around my body, fingers digging into the flesh of my ass, holding me in place on the kitchen countertop.

He thrusts again and again, his grip bruising me, his eyes gleaming with a satisfaction that fills my body with fear and anticipation. I can feel how close I am getting to the moment my life could begin leaving my body. My eyes close as I take in every powerful thrust that makes my pussy feel raw.

"Eyes," he orders, and I comply instantly.

My face contorts with the strain of pleasure, my eyes feeling the pain of the pressure inside my head. I open my mouth in a powerful silent scream, my belly hot with a fire that doesn't burn close enough to my core to allow my release.

His hand releases the flesh of my ass and damn it if I don't feel delicious bruises forming instantly. He dips two fingers into my mouth, pushing down on my tongue, holding me in place as my hands grip the edge of the countertop, holding myself from sliding backwards.

His assault on my body picks up pace, slamming himself faster inside of me, the slapping of damp skin echoing through the room, his breaths ragged, mine non-existent.

It all happens at once—he pulls the fingers out of my mouth and pushes them onto my clit, rubbing in that rhythm he learned gets me off as he chokes me harder and finally his cock pulls out the invisible thread of the fire that burned a little too far out of reach.

"Scream for me." His gaze burning with lust and chaos.

And with the last breath I held in my dying lungs, I scream. The fire burning my pussy to the fucking ground, melting it onto his cock as he draws it on himself and comes violently inside of me. As I'm riding the orgasm, I scream like the banshee painted on his back and even though he's not choking me anymore, the feeling lingers and it fuels me like no other.

His grip moves to the back of my neck, the other hand pressed on the middle of my back, pulling me flush to his body, my head resting on the base of his throat and with every breath, his woodsy scent fills my soul.

Yet again, this is different. Not only lust or possessiveness, but an unspoken vow.

And I embrace it.

Chapter 25

NIKLAS

G ame fucking over, little siren.

Even though I'm not technically done yet. I waited for days to see when she would crack, when she would finally admit to herself that it isn't just me wanting her.

I haul her naked body over my shoulder and walk upstairs, through *our* bedroom and straight to the room that holds the few, but more than satisfactory toys, and lay her on the high bench face down. It's the only other piece of furniture in this fairly small room, apart from the St. Andrews cross, and both of them I built myself.

This was modeled after the classic spanking benches,

wood and soft leather, only I customized it to fit my needs—my height, specifically. Suki tries to scramble off it, but I press one hand on the small of her back to keep her in place.

"Niklas, what..."

"Lie down, little siren. You challenged and got your wish."

"I did not..."

Her protest is interrupted by my palm smacking her right ass cheek, a deep gasp fills her lungs and her hands wrap around the wooden handles, below the bench. Her dangling legs look for comfort and when her knees find the purposely built supports, at the same height as the handles, I can't help but admire the glorious fucking view.

Her head and torso are the only bits of her splayed on the bench, wide enough for the width of her body, without allowing space for the shoulders. The bottom edge of the bench hits her hipbone, giving her enough support there to keep her in place, and her legs are spread wide, her knees resting on comfy supports. She's on full fucking display as I watch my cum slowly dripping out of her gorgeous pussy, red and swollen from the abuse it got on the kitchen counter.

"Don't move, little siren."

I walk out to the bathroom and come back with wet wipes. She twitches when the cold wipe touches her sensitive cunt, yet she can't suppress the moan escaping her lips. I take care of her, clean her up, and when she's nice and relaxed, when her guard is down, I smack her swollen pussy with my hand, and I can taste the pain and surprise in the yelp that paints her lips.

Fuck!

I could come from that. Jesus Christ. My dick is not yet ready for round two, but if I stare any longer at her in this position, it's not going to take me long. This image in front of me, her beautiful body, worn out, yet capable to take more. The sweetest cunt I've ever fucking tasted and that's so responsive under my touch. Her beautiful mind patiently waiting for the pleasure she knows will come. She's perfect. Absolutely fucking perfect and I'm not entirely sure why the gods dropped her in my lap. What the fuck did I do to deserve her?

Walking around the bench, admiring how beautifully she fits on it, I stop at the opposite end. Her head is right at the edge of the bench, her chin resting on it and I can see her eyes growing wide, quite literally facing my cock for the first time.

And when she disobeys and moves, it all happens too fast and I can't do anything to stop her. One hand grabs my ass, the other one lifts my dick and she pulls me forwards until her lips hit the root of my cock and the tip hits deep inside her throat, gagging her.

"Jesus Christ, woman!" I steady myself, grabbing the edges of the bench, right under her armpits.

She holds me there, sunk deep in the warmth of her hot fucking mouth and I swear I must be dead because I can see Valhalla.

I can feel myself getting harder in her mouth, and when the small hand holding my ass releases me, I know she wants me to pull out. I do until she squeezes my ass again—that's my cue. Sinking into that mouth as she holds onto my hips, I hit the back of her throat again, wrap her hair around my fist and hold her there. In that gorgeous position, with her throat stretched nice and straight, it takes everything in my power not to rip through her.

But then she moans and all my restraints go out the fucking window.

With her hair wrapped around my fist and her hands on my hips holding on for dear life, I fuck her mouth fast, feeling her throat constrict around my dick, saliva dripping everywhere. It's sloppy and violent, but her strained moans vibrate through my fucking dick and as she gags on the tip of my cock, pushing deeper into her throat, my balls get tighter. This feels too fucking good.

I fuck her mouth with a smile on my face, and I feed on the tears dripping out of her eyes, but I don't miss the lustful gaze she throws at me. She's fucking loving it, and from how she grinds her hips on the edge of the bench, I could bet my fucking money that she's pushing herself over the edge.

I steady and stop moving when the tip of my dick hits the back of her throat, swallowing me like a goddamn pro. Her eyes turn a shade darker, her eyebrows morph in a sinful curve, and I feel her tongue sticking out, pressing hard on my cock. I have to force myself not to spill in her mouth right now.

Pulling out, I smile at her, because... fuck... I was certainly not expecting that. She wipes her mouth with the back of her hand, a smile in those devilish eyes, yet she keeps silent. She's fucking challenging me because she is perfectly aware that I brought her into this room for a little punishment and now she's wondering if I'm sticking to the plan.

"Hold on, little siren."

She cocks one eyebrow and grabs onto the handles, her sweet, thick ass wiggling at the edge of the bench, seemingly getting herself comfortable, yet we both know her true intentions. I move behind her, running two fingers between her swollen lips.

Dripping. Fucking. Wet.

I never quite understood this, how women get turned on by sucking a man's dick. Then again, my dick could have fucking done somersaults when I tasted that sweet cunt of hers.

She twitches and moans the moment my fingers touch her, and I know what she wants. Not yet, though. My hand runs from between her lips, on her puckered hole, up between her ass cheeks, on the small of her back, pressing hard on her tense muscles. The moment my hand wraps around her neck, I smack her pussy with my other palm and the delicious yelp that leaves her mouth fills the room and fuels my fucking demons.

"That's it, baby."

I rub one finger between her drenched lips before smacking her clit and repeat this delicious assault until her yelps turn into full-on moans. I slap her right ass cheek hard at the same time I fist her hair, pulling her head back, and the siren sings again, filling me with her sharp song. Sinking two fingers into her cunt as the song continues, the soundwaves fill the room while I pump inside of her, before pulling out and smacking her ass so hard my handprint is painted in red on her skin.

"Fuuuuuuck!" she yells, and I can't help but smile.

"Do you want me to stop, little siren?" A grin paints my lips because I know that even if she says yes, I still won't stop.

Yet, she says nothing.

I smack her on that sensitive piece of flesh where the ass cheek meets the thigh and her body attempts to jerk forward, but I hold her by the hair.

"Noooooo!" she yells as I sink three fingers in her drenched pussy.

"No what, little one?"

"Please... don't stop..." she cries.

"Don't stop what? This?" My fingers pump inside of her as her muscles strangle them. "Or this?" I pull them out, tug her hair, and smack her pussy just as she screams her pleasure.

"Yessss," she hisses, and I smile.

"Hold on." I grab the edges of the high bench and rotate it until she is facing the mirror and a little gasp escapes her lips.

"Don't take your eyes off!"

Her shocked little face nods, and I don't miss the slither of fear in her eyes, but I smile and smack her ass cheek again, before I walk over to where the toys hang. I can see her watching me in the mirror. She smiles when I reach for the leather riding crop, but as I touch the wooden cane her eyes go wide with fear. It's just over an inch thick, not the biggest cane out there, but when the wood hits the flesh, it leaves pretty red marks all over.

I can't help it, the beautiful fear that paints her features makes me lick my lips, and I grab the cane without hesitation, stalking over to her as she swallows hard. I bring the cane down to her calves, gently touching her bent legs and when I stop on the middle of her thighs, I look at her in the mirror and I'm fairly sure she's holding her breath. The demons in her eyes are still, breathing hard and fast, waiting for the cane to hit, like it's something they've been craving their whole life.

The moment the cane hits her thigh, not too hard, but hard enough that it leaves a red mark, her whole body bursts into a shiver, her skin covered in goosebumps, her eyes close and her head bends back. I hit her other thigh and she swallows a moan before her eyes shoot open, looking straight into mine.

I feel like a target, eyes filled with a fire that burns hot and bright, at the brink of an explosion.

"Mooore," she moans at me between her heaving breaths. *Fuck.*

I bring the cane to her ass and hit both her cheeks at once, close enough to her pussy that I know she will feel the shock there as well. She yells in pain, yet never moves away and when I push two fingers onto her clit, rubbing gently, she pushes herself onto my hand, moaning explicit words at me.

I pull away and hit her again and again and again, until

her ass bears crisscross marks all over, her pussy is drenched and her skin damp from the strain. Her moans are full on screams now and tears run down her cheeks, mixing with the lustful smile that paints her face. She's fucking beautiful in this journey of self-discovery, and I'm so happy I was the one to show her how fucking delicious pain can be. Especially after what she's been through.

I almost drop the cane when she speaks.

"One more... please... but..." she looks into my eyes and before she speaks again her demons already tell me what she wants.

I look at her pretty ass and I wonder if she could really take what she's asking of me. Yet before I can debate it, I feel the monster inside of me taking over and after I rub two fingers between her wet lips, I bring the cane down so hard on her ass cheeks, her throaty scream rubs my fucking soul. It takes me a split second to drop the cane and sink myself, balls fucking deep into her pussy.

Her scream turns into moans as she pushes herself into me, her pain strained face morphing into something I've never seen on her. A strange sort of satisfaction, laced with pain, lust and evil... there's no other way I can explain it, it looks evil.

I fist one hand into her hair and the other one I sink into her hip so hard I know she'll be bruised before the end of the night. She smiles at me in the mirror just as I gently pull out of her, and she squeezes my dick with her tight cunt so hard it's fucking impossible not to cum inside of her right now. The little minx knows exactly what she's doing, with that devious smile on her face, she's fucking milking me.

So I grin back, the same fucking grin I give to every single person just before I end them and her mouth falls open. I've seen that expression on all my victims, yet she twists it in a way that makes my fucking heart jump. Her eyes flicker with a vicious depravity, her demons challenging and there... behind the fire that burns too close to an explosion, there's something, something I can't quite distinguish just yet.

"Miiine", I growl and slam so hard into her, she yelps in pain and lust.

She holds on to the bench as I thrust over and over again, rubbing her clit on the soft leather, moaning sick swear words at me.

"Niklas..."

"You're mine, Suki." I pull her hair, forcing her body to bend painfully, her hands propped on the handles and her eyes watching us in the mirror. "Mine!"

She bites her bottom lip, her eyes strained, and she shakes her head gently.

"No?" I ask as I pull out and slam back into her with a force that makes my fucking balls hurt.

She shakes her head again, but no sound leaves her lips. I rip into her cunt again and she swallows a moan.

"Say it, then. Tell me you're not mine, Suki!" I slam in again, and her pussy strangles me so hard I fucking swear my dick is gonna fall off from the lack of blood reaching the tip. I release her hair, but quickly wrap my hand around her throat, holding her there, leaning over her until my lips touch her ear. "Speak Suki, tell me you're not mine..."

Her eyes burn with emotions I don't understand, a strange sadness mixed with lust and evil.

"You are, little Siren, you're imprinted on my fucking skin in blood and no matter what, you will always be mine."

I continue the assault on her drenched cunt, and she slams back into me, in violent movements, the bench creaking under her as she fills the room with lust-fueled moans and screams. She watches me in the mirror, and when she can't hold her eyes open anymore, and I feel her pussy twitching around my dick, I release her throat, pull my dick out, wrap my arms around her and flip her over on the bench as she yelps in surprise.

On her back, she's trying to balance herself on the narrow bench, but I grab her legs and prop them against my chest as she wraps her tiny feet around my neck and I grab her wrists, holding her steady as I continue my assault.

I fuck her until my grunts match her moans, our ragged breaths melting into one as her back arches, her ass grinding onto me. When her head falls back and sees us in the mirror, suddenly her whole body vibrates with her orgasm. It rips from her body through mine, and I come so fucking hard, it seeps out from her pussy as she grinds herself against me, screaming as she rides those waves. Her legs shake as she comes down from that high and I bring them down, wrapping them around my waist as I pull her spent body up to me, holding her tight.

She's fucking beautiful. In these moments, even more so because she's vulnerable and she can't hide—what she is, what she wants, or what she craves. I want her like this, I only want to see her like this, without the mask that she puts on for everyone... even for herself.

SUKI

He holds me here, in the aftermath of potentially the best sex of my life, he holds me. The leather of the bench hot on my ass cheeks, his skin damp against mine, his arms wrapped tight around my body.

I learned something that I never expected, I learned that the loss of control in these moments of dominance is illusory. I did not lose anything; on the contrary, I gained a different type of control. I allowed him to do all those things to me, because the man I was looking at in that mirror was following me along the way. *Following me.*

It was trust. A strange type of trust as he took over my body and temporarily owned it. I never expected this and it might just be the thing that breaks me.

It is not a game anymore, not mine or his, this is us... this is the real danger, because we own each other now.

He pulls me from my train of thought as he lifts me in his arms, carrying me out of the room. I know he is taking me to the bathroom and not the one from his master bedroom... no, to the one he knows I love. The one he knows calms me...

soothes me.

I give in to these thoughts because he proved himself to me and as much as that scares the shit out of me, I enjoy it as well. For now, I am going to allow myself to enjoy it all, even the aftermath of it all.

We are taking our time, soaking our spent bodies under the stream of the shower, allowing them to recover slowly from the abuse, especially mine.

He is careful with me, in a way that surprises me, yet does not shock me anymore. He stands behind me, his hand loosely resting on my hip bone, just in case he needs to steady me, hold me... care for me. There are too many faces to this man, and I know for a fact that what I've been seeing lately, especially now, is his real one.

Yet I am certain that I am the only one to have ever had the privilege.

* * *

As we walk out of the shower and wrap our bodies in Niklas' fluffy navy-blue towels, I hear something outside, in the distance. I turn to the window, but I cannot see anything just yet. I turn back to him and he gives me a quick glance before walking out and to his bedroom as I follow. Standing in front of his massive bedroom windows, I watch the beautiful scenery, and there, against the burnished sky of the afternoon sunset, I can see a helicopter making its way to us.

"Connor?" I ask as I look up to the Viking standing tall behind me.

He looks down, nods and does something so goddamn shocking that it makes me weak in the damn knees—he kisses my forehead, and I am not sure if it is me that is melting, my soul... or my heart.

It better not be my heart. It cannot be my damn heart because this... him... our past... I do not know if I can stand a future that doesn't guarantee me permanence.

I look back into the distance, more at Niklas' reflection than at the helicopter and I run his words through my head— *mine... tell me you're not mine, Suki*—I could not tell him, because deep down, I know I am his. But for how long... for how long am I his?

CHAPTER 26

SUKI

We're both dressed and I am getting strangely attached to his clothes, his hoodies in particular. His smell follows me everywhere. Niklas looks annoyingly handsome in his brown leather boots, blue jeans, and the green checkered fleece he threw on top of a simple white t-shirt. He does not even try...

We are both walking out of the house, towards the plain where Connor's helicopter landed. Of course Niklas told me I did not have to come, especially since it is cold out and I do not have any bottoms, but I insisted. I have to do something, be useful, after all, the supplies are for me as well.

The helicopter landed a few minutes ago, and the snow is just settling on the ground after being disturbed by the waves the propeller made. I spot Connor as he moves around some boxes in the back of the helicopter, and he stops when he sees us, jumping off and walking our way.

I must admit, the closer he gets the more stunned I am. Connor is quite a man, medium length raven black hair, wavy and wild, a short salt and pepper beard covers his face, and eyes so dark that I cannot figure out if they're black or just hollow. He looks haunting, absolutely haunting, like he belongs in a James Wan horror movie, not on a damn snowy mountain.

Yet he is a beautiful man, almost as gorgeous as Niklas—almost. As he gets closer, I get a feel of his stature and he is probably only a couple of inches shorter than Niklas, shoulders not as wide under the thick winter jacket, yet he is still a well-built man.

This mountain seems to be good on its men.

"Hi, you must be Suki." He extends his hand to me and when he smiles, I am done for. Absolutely melted into a puddle, and I know I am grinning like a lunatic. I extend my hand, and when I hear Niklas clearing his throat next to me, I shake myself mentally and learn how to speak again.

"Umm... yes... hi. Yes, Suki. Hi, Connor." I want to slap myself, but then I will just admit to both these men that I was freaking taken aback by this man's smile.

I look at Niklas and he is holding back a smile and rolling his eyes at me.

Well... fuck.

"Hey, man. Thanks for doing this. Come on, let me give you a hand." Niklas walks past us to the helicopter.

At his words, I realize that Connor and I are still holding hands, and I release him awkwardly.

"Sorry..." I mumble.

"Don't worry, sweetheart. I tend to have that effect on people," his voice sounds like sin, laced with a subtle southern accent and his eyes along with the slight quirk of his lips have lust painted all over them.

My mouth drops open, my eyebrows shoot up and I cannot hold in the laughter that bursts out of me.

"Cocky, much?"

"Always, sweetheart, always." That sinful grin falters for just a second before it comes back in full-force and results me into a puddle for the second time in less than a minute. Christ, this man is hot.

I raise an eyebrow and give him the sexiest smile I can muster as I lick the corner of my lips and just like that, it is his turn to laugh.

"Finally, some competition," he jokes as he comes beside me and with a gentle hand between my shoulder blades, he guides me to the helicopter.

The air around this man is light and I thought I would be tense, yet... I feel good. Another damn reason to like this mountain. Another damn reason to keep me here. I catch Niklas' scrutinizing gaze on Connor, and I wonder what goes through his head. He does not say anything, he just watches us under his dark blond eyebrows, looking like he is mentally taking notes.

"I put Suki's things in those two suitcases, in the back. The two boxes are the supplies you asked for, and the big one in the back has the parts for the snow mobile." Connor gestures at the load. "I'll grab the big suitcase then come back for more. Suki, do you want to grab the smaller one?"

I nod as Niklas jumps up in the helicopter, passing the suitcases to us before jumping down and grabbing the biggest box.

"So, how are you feeling?" Connor asks as we walk back to the house. The sun is low in the sky, and we try to move fast so we don't have to rely on flashlights for the next trip.

"Good, I guess. Looking forward to some decent clothes... and jeans."

He gives me an inquisitive look and I can feel his police instincts jumping into gear, holding themselves back from asking deeper questions. I expect them, obviously, he is the sheriff in town, yet I am not sure how he is going to navigate around Niklas.

We walk into the house and they both insist for me to stay inside as they bring the rest of the stuff in. I reluctantly agree and grab the big suitcase, hauling it up the stairs and into our bedroom.

Our bedroom.

I stop in the middle of the room, looking at the sun burnishing itself in the evening sky and I wonder... when did I start seeing his bedroom as *ours*...

I look at *our* bed...

I look at *our* sheets...

I look at *our* space...

And I wonder... is he making the same mistakes I am making? Does he see it as ours as well?

I sigh and turn on my heels to go grab the other suitcase from downstairs. I am practically running back up, excited to open both suitcases like they are Christmas presents. I never thought that simple clothes and tampons could excite a girl quite like this, but I guess having low standards keeps you happy.

I laugh out loud at the crazy shit that goes through my head as I sit on the floor and unzip the big suitcase and marvel at the military-like organization of its contents. Everything perfectly folded and every corner and nook perfectly filled.

Wow! I start pulling out each item—long sleeves, sweaters, joggers and leggings, two of each, then one pair of jeans, knitted pullover, and thick waterproof trousers. A pair of pajamas, like I haven't been sleeping almost naked with Niklas every night, slippers I did not ask for and fluffy indoor socks. I also have a pair of good mountain boots that look strangely stylish and I have to admit Connor has some taste.

I didn't ask for specifics, I just gave him general items and sizes and that was it. He did go off script though with the slippers, fluffy socks, and some other items I can see in here, but I have to admit they are good ideas.

Looking in the pockets of the suitcase, I pull out two packs of five cotton panties and the same of thick white socks, along with two sports bras that look like they could potentially fit me. I must admit, giving a man I never met my bra size so they can buy sports bras for me was a bit weird. Funny how that thought crosses my mind just as I rip the clothes off my body and pull on the fluffy socks, a pair of panties, sports bra, joggers and sweatshirt.

"Clothes my size... finally!" I hug myself, ready to jump up in excitement, yet somehow they feel off against my skin. I thought I got used to clothes again, but I guess not. I turn to the smaller suitcase and the thick navy blue puffer jacket looks so inviting. I pull it out and before I can unfold it my mouth falls open and my breath hitches in my throat.

Right there, under this thick jacket, lie two sketchbooks, a set of charcoal, various pencils, a few ink pens, watercolor pencils, a few brushes, and an eraser.

This was not Connor, this was Niklas.

In this moment, this crucial moment, I am fully aware of the weight of my heart in my chest. It is heavy and I am not sure it is weighing me down, holding me still, or grounding me just as my soul demands. He got me drawing supplies...

because I mentioned how much I love it, how much I miss it. My head falls in my hands as my elbows rest on my thighs and I try to come to terms with the significance of this gesture. *He cares...*

The air shifts, suddenly charged with an electrifying energy. I turn and see him standing in the doorway, the look on his face as passive as ever, and I do not wait for him to say anything. I get up, walk to him, and wrap my arms around his body, burying my head in his chest. He stays silent as he wraps his strong arms around me, engulfing me in his warm body and holding me tight and safe there.

I breathe in the smell of musk and cedar that burns like an aura around him, and it finally hits me... he is not my captor, not anymore. I do not think he has been for a while. I just made him to be one in my head. Yes, he does not want to let me go... Yes, he did say that Connor will not interfere. Yet, I am beginning to believe his purpose for wanting to keep me here has nothing to do with my captivity... at least not anymore.

He may be a monster, but a totally different kind from the one I escaped and even from the one he was when he saved me.

Somehow, my heart gets even heavier, and it is not me that is holding it anymore...

NIKLAS

"So?" Connor pulls me out of my daze.

"Sorry, what were you saying?" I rip my gaze from the calming, hypnotic, simple image of Suki, curled up in front of the fire, sketching in her new book. She's so content, like she's finally in her element.

"Shit, man... I've never seen you like this. This girl..."

"What were you saying before, Connor?" I don't plan on talking about this, so I push the subject back to whatever the fuck he was saying before.

"What the hell happened to her man? I saw her legs out there... she's full of scars." He shakes his head, trying to wrap his mind around it all.

I sigh as I carry on chopping vegetables for the salad while he stirs a pot of pasta sauce. "You're a cop... what do you think happened?!" I look him in his black eyes that freak even me out sometimes.

He shakes his head, and I know that look in his eyes. It's the look he gets when he wants to kill, yet knows he can't because of what he is. It's the look of regret towards

351

the chosen career that he loves so much, yet hates in times like this.

"For how long, Nik?" He's seething.

"About six months..."

"Fuck! On my fucking territory, Nik! My fucking domain, and I had no clue?!"

"It's actually my domain. This is why I don't want you to get involved. The motherfucker attacked her, attacked me, he fucking shot me." I pause as Connor drops the spoon with a thud, startling Suki, and she looks up at us inquisitively. "He already did all this and he's on my motherfucking territory. You know very well that I have every right to kill him."

"If he fucking attacks you!"

I grin at him and his head pulls back, his eyes grow wide. I could bet money that he can see the demons staring back at him right now.

"He might not even attack me, he might just... go back from where he came from." He knows I mean it in the fucking biblical sense. Ashes to ashes, dust to motherfucking dust.

Connor drops his gaze and shakes his head.

"She's not the first, Con... she's just one that survived." His head shoots up, gaze straight into mine and sometimes I swear he mirrors me. "He made her dig up one of the two buried outside the cabin... made Suki look at her, at what she could become, before he forced her to throw the dirt right back on top of the body."

"Jesus fucking Christ." That's all he can say... I can tell the wheels are spinning, coming to terms with what needs to happen. Con knows my extracurricular activities, at least one of them, and although he does not agree, he's turned a blind eye and even dropped some information in my lap once. He knows some of these people deserve to die, and he knows I will stop at nothing to get my fix of blood and violence. It's a dangerous combination, yet it is one that sometimes benefits us both.

"I'm not going to tell her story, not unless she wants me to," I try to keep my tone down so Suki doesn't hear me. "Or if she tells you herself... but the shit she told me, Con, I can guarantee you that whatever will come his way is fully deserved."

He looks at her, peacefully drawing in the light of the fire, then turns to me. "You did your homework, I presume?"

I nod and tell him everything I found out about the guy as we finish making dinner.

"I want in on this." And with those words, Connor manages to shock me, probably for the third time since we've known each other. "Damn the fucking consequences, Nik! I want in! You can make the fucking plan, I don't give a shit, but I'm in."

"You're in what?" Suki startles us both, standing on the other side of the kitchen island, watching us with innocent eyes that we both know are just a little game.

"Nothing." I shoot Connor a warning look. "He's not in on anything."

He shakes his head and grabs two plates of food, walking away from us to the dining table that I never use on the other side of the room. I turn to Suki, and the innocent look in her eyes is gone, demons staring back at me.

"Come on, let's eat." I push the cutlery her way before grabbing the salad bowl and the pasta, walking away.

For the next hour, we sit at the table talking about nothing. All of us aware that we can't quite share everything with the other person around. It's like fucking high school all over again.

"So how long are you staying here?" Suki asks Connor and suddenly my body tenses.

He chews his food, looking at me intensely before turning to her. "A couple of days. I'm giving Nik a hand with the snowmobile, see if we can get it fixed tomorrow and probably leave the day after or the morning after that. It all depends on this snowstorm that was announced."

"Oh, okay." She subtly avoids eye contact with me. I can practically see the wheels spinning in that pretty little head of hers. "So, how did you two meet?"

Connor chokes on his food as his eyes shoot up to me. *Subtle man, real fucking subtle.*

"I used to be a detective in San Francisco." He finally swallows and turns to Suki. It's amusing, watching this situation unfold. "We met when I was working a case, he was a... witness."

Nice save.

"Oh, interesting!" Suki turns to me, head cocked and a fake- surprised smile painted all over her devious face. "So, what was the case about, what did Niklas witness?" She turns back to Connor, and I notice immediately the slight shift in his stance. This has nothing to do with the question, but with the look in her eyes—her demons are demanding a touch of chaos and her light green eyes look unnaturally bright.

"Someone in his company got murdered, we were looking for information from everyone," he speaks slowly, nodding his head before filling his mouth with more food.

"Oh, wow, Niklas, I am sorry. Who was it? You must have been close if, from all those employees you actually knew them." Her attention turns to me, and the amusement in her eyes is endearing.

"No, no, I was not close at all. However, since I was the CEO, it was standard practice for the police to ask me, since I'm technically supposed to know everyone."

"Such a shame. So how did the person die?" She doesn't

ask anyone in particular as her gaze switches between the two of us a few times.

"Shot," Connor speaks.

"Stabbed," I say right at the same time and the little siren grins under her nose, her eyes gleaming with victory.

Connor turns to me, eyebrows raised in an expression that screams *"Really?!"* and I hide my smile by shoving some food in my mouth. "Oh yes, that's it. Shot." I say, finally.

Suki rolls her eyes, and I can't help but be strangely proud of her. Not long ago, she was curled up in the corner of this very room—dirty, bloody and bruised, clutching a blanket to her body like it was her lifeline, shaking like a leaf, afraid to look into my eyes and now... now she challenges a killer with her daring sarcasm. Unbeknownst to her, she's challenging two.

Connor changes the subject, and the two of them begin talking about nothing, but either way I'm not really listening. I'm trapped in this train of thought, trapped by her, her beauty, her talented mind, her vulnerability, the strength that keeps developing within her day by day. And as she grows stronger, her demons are closer to the surface, yet I don't think she realizes this. I don't think she knows that sometimes she sits there, lost in thought, daydreaming about something and her demons rage, her eyes gleam with chaos and darkness. I always want to ask her what she's conjuring in her mind, but I never do because I know she would lie.

Her demons are so close to the surface now, yet she's still fighting them, maybe harder than ever. All her life, since her parents were killed, she's been pretty much on her own in a world she doesn't belong in and I wonder if it was easier for her then to hide her chaos, push her cravings away. I wonder if it's harder now, around me... I have no shame in what I do, on the contrary, I fucking revel in it, my soul feeds on the blood and pain I pull from others and I didn't hide this from her. Is it harder for her to push back her demons when mine are making hers so comfortable?

I look at how her body moves when she speaks, how her smile only occasionally reaches her eyes, how her beautifully defined lips quirk in a corner in amusement, yet never form a full smile, how her hands always find a curl in her hair and she rolls it between her fingers, even when she's eating. There's a strange innocence to her, one I can't put my finger on. I obviously already know it's not sexual, there's nothing innocent about that when it comes to this little siren, yet there's something about her, something pure, something untouched, and it's fucking calling to me.

This woman did a number on me, even more than I thought, considering our revelation from only a few days ago. I know that eventually I will have to tell her the rest of the story about that night in the alley... and she's not going to fucking like it. Yet I can't hide it from her.

There's something about her that constantly urges me to fucking talk, like my mind can't process keeping things away from her and no matter how much it pisses me off, I enjoy it. She's different, so fucking different, she's mine, quite literally the woman of my dreams, and no matter how much I rejected it, no matter how much I fought it, I've changed since she came here.

"Okay, boys." She grabs her plate and gets up from the table. "I'm going to grab a book and head into bed. Dinner was delicious, thank you for cooking." We both nod at her in response and Con wishes her good night.

"I'll be there soon, okay?" I say, ignoring Con's stare that punches a hole through me as she turns her head and gives me her cheekiest smile.

"What the fuck is going on, Nik?!" He rubs his face in

frustration before raking his fingers through his hair. "You're fucking her?! I thought she's been through hell... what the fuck is going on?!"

"You know better than to ask me questions you don't want to know the answer to. You know better than to ask me anything at all." My demons are seething, and I know for a fact they're giving him a warning glare.

"Fuck it! She's a nice, innocent woman, man, what are you doing to her?!"

I can't help but smirk. There is almost nothing innocent about that woman, at least not in the same sense he's referring to.

"Are you keeping her here against her will?!" This particular question hits differently. I was... I think I still am, but for different reasons now. However, technically, I am keeping her here against her will. I'm not entirely sure how to answer this question. Connor rubs the back of his neck with both hands, letting out a long sigh. "You are... fuck... you are!"

"It's not what you think, calm the fuck down." Isn't it? It's exactly what he thinks... only small details are different. "The reasons I am holding her here for are valid; however, if you are worried about me hurting her, you can calm down. Nothing and I mean nothing will touch a fucking hair on that woman ever again!" I'm firm as I point a finger in the direction of the bedroom upstairs. "IF anyone manages to, I will fucking decimate them. And me? I will not hurt her." Not outside the bedroom of course, but that's a detail Connor does not need to know.

His expression shifts, eyebrows gathered in confusion and suspicion and he's rubbing the back of his head, trying to say something, yet all his ideas seem to get stuck every time he opens his mouth. Suddenly, his unnaturally dark eyes soften as he swallows a lump in his throat.

"You're in love…"

His words hit me like fucking bullets aimed at my heart, breaking an invisible shield that surrounded it without me even knowing. It releases an explosion of sensations I never quite understood. Love… an emotion… the strongest one of them all and apparently this is how it feels.

I look at Connor, and I'm not sure what's painted on my face because he surprises me again.

"You didn't know…"

Chapter 27

Suki

When Niklas came into bed last night, I was already asleep. I'm not sure how late him and the sheriff stayed up, but I did hear bits and pieces of a conversation about Adrien. The only reason I heard anything was because the conversation got a bit heated. As much as I wanted to hear more, unfortunately my body let me down, and after the emotional day I had, I fell asleep before I understood exactly what was happening.

I felt him come into bed, though, and there was something different in his touch. As soon as the bed dipped behind me, his long, strong arm wrapped around me and rolled me over until I was buried in his pecks. I wasn't quite awake, but aware enough that I felt something in him, in the way he held me, even his breathing felt different with his face buried in my hair.

Now I'm flipping pancakes as I struggle to take my eyes away from the contrast the sunrise makes with the snow-covered mountains, and I'm trying to make sense of what happened last night. The shift in him made me drop my guard, his hold of me was heavy with meaning, one that I'm not sure I'm ready to accept, one that I felt within myself when I circled his waist and held him to me as I fell back asleep.

I know my heart feels something my brain is not ready to believe just yet. I know my body craves his touch more than it craves the air that keeps me alive. I know my mind wants the answer to millions of questions that are straining to burst out because I want to know everything about him.

I know all this... but I am also having trouble identifying if this is an illusion created by the forced proximity. Is what I feel for him the result of our circumstances? Things I felt even before our earth-shattering revelation... Would I feel the same out there in the real world?

Away from this mountain?

Away from this house?

Away from him?

How would I ever know if all I experience is this? My chest feels heavy with emotions I cannot soothe right now...

"Good morning, sweetheart," Connor startles me, pulling me out of my emotional rollercoaster.

"Good morning. I hope you like pancakes." I smile at him, and even bathed in the morning light, his features look haunting. I swear his black eyes are darker in the sunlight. Niklas was right... there is something about him.

"My god, you cooked up a feast." He sniffs the air in appreciation, most likely identifying the smell of bacon mixed with the fresh pancakes.

"I figured you two will need the calories since you are going to work on that snowmobile and whatever else you have planned." I am still thinking of their discussion last night. Are they planning to go after Adrien? Even so, they would not go today, would they?

"Thank you." He tenses slightly, looking between me and the stairs, and I frown.

"I need to ask you something, Suki."

Here we go... I have not even finished my coffee yet. I turn my attention to the pan, pouring more pancake batter in it, and he takes my silence as a cue.

"Do you know who Niklas is?" Well, that is not quite the question I was expecting. I thought he would ask about what I have been through, something personal, but this... no, I was not expecting this. I turn around and catch his strange gaze. Worry does not look good in those hollow eyes.

"Yes."

"And you're okay knowing what you know about him... you're okay with the person he is?"

I never gave it much thought actually, it never even phased me beyond the fact that he makes my demons a bit too comfortable, always approving of my depravity, of my thirst for goddamn blood.

I nod. "I am more worried about the person I am, yet he has embraced it with open arms."

Is it surprise or shock that I am seeing in the hollows? He wants to know more, but we hear Niklas' footsteps down the stairs and we both stand there, looking at each other, the confusion in his eyes seeping into suspicion and intrigue, while I just feel... lost.

Before Niklas reaches the bottom of the stairs, I turn my attention back to the pancakes, flipping them over. He greets

Connor, before brushing past me, his hand holding my waist in a purely affectionate gesture that makes every cell that forms me melt while simultaneously begging me to scream in confusion. He is not the one confusing me, though—I am.

I look up at him when I am finished taking the pancakes out of the pan, and he looks down at me with an expression that, to the outside world, looks placid, almost devoid of any emotion. Yet that expression bears the subtlest smile, one that is mine and mine alone, the monster in his eyes watching me intensely. He holds me in his stare and even though my expression does not falter and my body does not move, an atomic bomb has been detonated inside of me, shivers replacing the blood in my veins. My chest burns. My demons smile. I want to sink into this feeling, into this comfort, this acceptance... this... affection. And when his monster gives me his cruel grin, my mouth feels instantly parched and I know that the only thing that could sate this thirst is blood.

I need to get away...

The men are sitting at the kitchen island, but I am standing on the opposite side, munching on a piece of bacon, watching the dynamic between the two. I am not particularly hungry and my mind is too busy to even process food. It is interesting though, watching them interact. Of course Niklas is the quiet one, calculated, a man of few words, yet all of them are important. Connor is the extrovert, he does not shy away from the risky questions, not even the dangerous ones, gaining some murderous expressions from Niklas. Yet, he is unphased... interesting. It is almost like a brotherly interaction.

"How long have you known each other?" I hear myself asking. I want to slap my mouth shut, urge myself to actually think before I speak, but it is too late now. They both look at me at once, before turning on each other, their expressions mirrored in a strange way.

"About six years," Connor finally speaks. Strange, almost like Niklas silently approved of him answering me. Makes me wonder what their conversations were about last night. It also makes me wonder how much Connor actually knows of Niklas. I know he is aware of what he does, yet... I am not sure *how* much he knows exactly.

"Mhm... when you were working on a case." I put the piece of bacon in mouth, slowly biting off a chunk as I try to suppress a smile. My eyes betray me though, because Niklas chokes on his food as he tries to suppress his own laughter. Connor shakes his head, but his dark, hollow eyes sparkle with amusement.

"Cheeky woman..." He licks the corner of his mouth, and damn... the man is hot.

Niklas clears his throat, and I realize I have been caught staring, with a piece of bacon held in my hungry mouth. I shift my gaze to him, and I am surprised by the dark look in his eyes. If I did not know any better I would think there is jealousy in there.

I bite another piece of bacon and smile at him while I chew, and he gives me his sexiest goddamn grin behind that gorgeous beard of his. His eyes promising sin while quirking one eyebrow and I feel like I need to leave the room before I soak my damn panties.

"So, what is your plan for the day." I try to change the subject, even if that smile is still on my face and Connor watches me with amusement.

"We're going to try and fix that snowmobile and we have a couple more jobs. One of them is checking the roof, I have a feeling there's a leak." Niklas finishes his food and brings the plate to the sink.

"Seems safe... climbing on the roof in the middle of

winter." I shake my head as I go to the sink after him and wash my hands.

"I know, right?!" I hear Connor behind me. "We'll be okay though, sweetcheeks." At those words, I hear a thump and a loud grunt. When I turn, he is clutching his middle, groaning in pain and laughing at the same time.

"What the hell?" I look at both of them, unable to believe that Niklas actually punched him in the gut.

"My apologies, sweetheart," Connor finally speaks and Niklas grins, one eyebrow quirked in victory.

What the hell is going on?

"I'm probably going to stay in, but please, let me know if you need me for anything. You know I do not like feeling useless." I carry on talking, ignoring whatever is happening between the two of them, as amusing as it is.

"Sure, we'll let you know." Niklas nods as he tops off his and Connor's coffee cups, before heading into the garage.

"See you later... sweetcheeks." Connor grins, taking advantage of Niklas almost being out of the room as I roll my eyes at him and start laughing.

I could get used to this, this banter, this comfort. Yet I know I should not. As Connor closes the door to the garage behind him, I grab my coffee and head upstairs to what used to be my room. I need to think, and I realize that the habit that I used to have as a teenager has not left me yet, as I sit on the floor, at the foot of the bed, looking at myself in the full height mirror sitting in front of me.

You know what you need to do, Suki... No matter how hard it will be... No matter if your heart will break... No matter how scary it will be... No matter if your soul comes with you or stays here. You know what you need to do.

Sitting here, on the floor, for more than half an hour, I am devising some sort of plan for my... escape. But even thinking of this word, *escape,* it goddamn hurts me, because deep down, I know this is not what I need to do. My demons are howling at me, crying and yelling, hurting me from the inside out, but I cannot listen to them.

Not if it means that I will obtain the permanence I am looking for.

I need to know this is not an illusion. I need to regain control. I need to find out what I want and there is no way I can do it here, like this.

NIKLAS

"Shit, man... it's lunch time. Should we head in, have something to eat, then carry on?" Connor wipes his damp forehead, leaving a grease stain all over it. We've been disassembling this piece of crap all morning, trying to replace some parts that I was convinced were broken. Some of them were... but not all.

"Fuck me... I knew I should have bought another one before the winter started." I drop the wrench on the seat of the snowmobile and sigh as I look at the broken-down piece of crap.

"Yeah, man... you have spares for everything, I must admit it kind of surprises me you don't have two of these." The motherfucker laughs, and I feel a strong need to punch him in the gut again. He's right though... "Don't worry, we'll fix it. We know what the issue is, I reckon by the end of the day, or tomorrow by lunch time at the latest it will be done."

"Yes, it will. Hopefully tonight, though." I roll my eyes as I turn to head inside the house, but the door opens before I can grab the handle.

"Hey." Suki stands there in all her glory, dressed in tight leggings, showing off her curves and a sweatshirt that barely covers her lush hips, with waves of her tamed wavy hair framing her face, and she looks fucking fantastic. Her next words get trapped in her throat, her mouth slightly open, looking like she's trying to figure me out.

Jesus Christ... I have it painted all over my fucking face, don't I?!

"Hey, Suki."

"I wanted to ask what you guys want for lunch."

"How do you feel about some sandwiches? Connor brought some bread yesterday. I froze some of it, but left a few loafs out," I say as we all start walking back into the house.

"Sure, sounds good to me. I'll make them now." She goes straight for the fridge, but I catch her soft, small hand and stop her.

"Don't worry. I'll go for a shower and do them myself when I'm back. You're not here to cook for us." I say to her as I give her hand a slight squeeze.

"I know, Niklas. I just need to feel useful."

I know what she means. She needs to feel like she's not a prisoner in this house, she needs some sort of control and since there's not much she can do around here... she makes herself useful in the kitchen. Christ... is it bad that she kind of reminds me of my mother? That woman always has to do something, dad has to force her to relax most of the time.

"Okay. If that's what you want to do, go for it. I just wanna make sure you know you don't have to."

She smiles at me, a sweet smile that makes me feel more than I should from just one small quirk in the corner of her lips. She's fucking gorgeous, her old-world beauty takes me by surprise even now... when I've seen her every single day for... how long has it been? It certainly feels like months... I let go of her hand as she goes to the fridge and head after Connor up the stairs.

Years... it's definitely been years since she's been haunting my dreams.

"You know..." I turn around to see Connor stopped in the doorway to the bathroom. "She reminds me of someone."

I don't say anything, instead I stand before my bedroom door, waiting to hear more.

"Strange... not always though, but sometimes she just reminds of something... Oh, never mind."

I know what he's thinking, and the grin I give him startles him, and his brows furrow as he cocks his head.

"No, never mind. See you in a bit."

I can't help but laugh to myself. It didn't take him long to see similarities that somehow both me and her missed. In all fairness, we had other things to focus on, like the electrifying lust that somehow engulfs both of us. Not to mention that the banshee doesn't really look like her, it does... but it doesn't. However, it is her, it represents her and it's all that matters.

When I'm done with the shower and come back downstairs, Suki is getting a salad ready, the sandwiches already portioned on three different plates. I start walking towards her, but something catches my eye. I head to the coffee table and stare in awe at the multitude of sketches spread all over it. Sketches of my house... the bathroom with the bathtub and the view... the shower and the view... the porch and the view... the bedroom and the view. She loves this house... and she definitely loves this view.

And they're beautiful... not soft, not polished, not finished drawings... rough and sketchy, but beautiful. It makes me smile because no matter how much she tells me of herself... this here offers me a different view. Every stroke is chaotic, yet deliberate and strong, some strokes feel angry, while still calculated. Like handwriting, every stroke, every indent, the leaning direction, every curve, it all means something.

I look at them and I know for sure that there will always be something new to discover of her. Always. I'm glad, as much as I want to know every single piece of this woman, every nook and cranny, every secret, everything... I crave the hunt, the discovery, I want to enjoy peeling the layers.

"So, how is the snowmobile going?" her low-toned voice pulls me out of my train of thought.

"Not quite done yet. We took it apart and of course it threw a curveball at us. Hopefully it will be done soon." I sit at the island as she pushes a plate of sandwiches and the salad bowl towards me.

"So, how come you need it fixed? Do you ride it for fun?" she asks as she sits down beside me.

"Yeah, a lot of the times. Sometimes it's useful when I go hunting. However, when it's like this, the snow so fresh, it's almost impossible to take it out. The snow needs to be a bit more compacted."

"Makes sense." She puts a salad leaf in her mouth and nods.

"Do you really want to leave, Suki?" My question startles her. Her mouth falls open, her eyes grow wide, and I swear to god her heart stops because she's so fucking still, she could be a statue.

"Ohhh, that looks good! Thank you, Suki." Connor walks in, sits beside Suki on the third chair and pulls the last plate of sandwiches. "Suki... are you okay?" He furrows his brows as he taps her shoulder.

"Yes, sorry. No problem, I hope you enjoy." She turns to face her plate, but not before giving me one last confused look. "So, compared to San Francisco, how are you finding small town life?" Suki talks to Connor, and I can tell she is comfortable with him. There's an ease in her speech and I can't help but feel jealous of it. Beyond her lusting over this damn man, she feels comfortable with him. I'm fairly sure that in the last fifteen minutes she asked him more questions than she's ever asked me. I can't help but roll my eyes.

"What?!" Connor asks.

"I didn't say anything." I put my hands up and smile.

"Mhm, like anyone could have fucking missed that eyeroll. I love small town life." He turns his attention back to Suki. "I craved it after everything that happened."

"What do you mean?"

"Justice is not always on our side, and unfortunately, no matter how hard we try... some motherfuckers slip through the cracks."

At his words, her head snaps to me. She knows what happens with some of the ones that slip through. I grin and her head quirks ever so slightly and there's a noticeable spark in her eyes. Her efforts are growing, she's trying harder and harder to fight her nature.

"So, it was frustration that brought you here?" Suki turns her attention back to him, yet her eyes flicker towards me once in a while.

"Among others, yes. I needed the quiet... I didn't belong there anymore."

"Hmm..." she looks to the side, her thoughts drifting and I know for sure they're drifting to one of the conversations we had.

"Did I mention that Suki lived in San Francisco for a while?" I say to Connor, and he shakes his head, his expression somewhere between surprise, confusion, and laughter.

"No fucking way?! How long did you live there?"

"About seven years, moved back to South Dakota three years ago," Suki responds to him, and he quirks his head.

"Oh, so you left pretty much at the same time as Nik here. Huh..." He turns to me and raises his eyebrows in disbelief. "What made you leave San Francisco?" He turns back to Suki.

"It didn't feel right anymore... I didn't belong there anymore."

Connor looks down, lost in thought and all of a sudden we're all just staring at each other. Somehow... we all found each other and our common denominator is a city none of us belonged to.

"I came here about a year before Nik," Connor adds. "I told him about the mountain."

"Yeah, he did... thank god. This fucking mountain is so hard to get to during the winter, otherwise, I wouldn't have come here if I knew that this motherfucker would have constant access to me," I say as I put our empty plates in the dishwasher.

"Sure asshole, keep fucking telling yourself that. You fell ass over fucking heels when you saw that view from upstairs," Connor laughs, I flip him off and Suki shakes her head.

"I think we need to get back to work. All this sitting seems to be affecting you," I laugh as I head towards Suki and kiss the top of her head before I go back to the garage.

The rest of the day goes by in a blur. We actually managed to fix the snowmobile. We tested it as well and even Suki got to test it a bit outside. It was something else, seeing her actually enjoy herself, trying something she has never done before in her life. Not to mention that she had appropriate clothes on for the first time, so she was letting loose, finally not caring about freezing to death.

I must say... I preferred her naked in the snow.

Just thinking of her, bare, running away from me through the thick snow, her wild hair flowing all over the place, brushing her pale flesh... her fine fucking ass, her gorgeous

tits that she always has to hold with one arm as she runs... shit. My dick gets hard, now sporting a semi, and I have to shift uncomfortably to make sure I hide it.

If only Connor wasn't here...

CHAPTER 28

SUKI

I find myself sitting on the steps of the porch, under the moonlight this time around, and with proper clothes and shoes on I am quite comfortable in the cold. The snowy mountain peaks are lit by the moon and the view is probably even better now than it is in the daylight.

I hear the door open behind me and even without looking, I know it is not Niklas. Connor takes a seat beside me, and I look up at him and smile.

"I can't figure you out, Suki." My smile falls. "Niklas is an interesting character, different, emotionless... quiet. Yet, after these two days I can see you have him beat."

"Where are you going with this?" My expression is stern, lips thin and straight, the demons shining in my eyes.

"You confuse me. You're fighting a battle, a battle you look like you could be losing, and Niklas is not your opponent... is he?"

"He is a pawn in this. He wants something from me, something I cannot give him, not without becoming..." I trail off. This is dangerous territory.

"Becoming what, Suki?"

"It does not matter." I shake my head and smile at him.

"Of course it does. What are you scared of?"

I look into his hollow eyes, darker than the night's sky, and I feel like he sucks me into this void, this cold, yet comfortable void.

"Becoming my mother." Fuck. It's that hypnotic stare and I cannot stop myself.

"Ah. Lydia Knoxx... yes, I read all about her." His words startle me, yet he is the sheriff, they should not surprise me. "She was sick, Suki, you know this. You are not her."

"I am more like her than you think, Connor. Too much like her." Another smile, a sarcastic one, hits my lips as I slowly shake my head. "How about you? What are you afraid of?" My question makes him twitch, and there is a flicker in those dark, haunting eyes. Something far in the distance, hidden behind countless walls, tucked away real well.

He turns his gaze to the moon.

"There is something about you, Connor. Something I cannot quite place, yet it feels familiar." His gaze shoots back to me and hours seem to pass as we look at each other. It feels so familiar. I am not the only one fighting my demons, I am not the only one running. Only his race is mental... mine is about to be physical.

"I like you, Suki." His face devoid of emotion could fool

me.

"I like you too." And I do. There is something about him that makes me feel at ease, no matter how much his hollow eyes make me feel like I am about to be buried alive. He feels like the kind of person that could be there for you... for a long time.

A friend.

* * *

When I walk into the bedroom, I find Niklas looking out the window, bathed in the bright moonlight, rubbing a towel through his wet hair, another wrapped low on his hips. His movements are slow, lazy, and there is something so utterly masculine about this image. His muscles ripple one by one beneath his damp skin and no matter how much I try, I cannot seem to tire of seeing him naked—and I cannot suppress my attraction to him. It is an all-consuming hunger. He turns just as I shut the door behind me, my eyes fixed on him.

His body never ceases to amaze me. I never thought myself to be a shallow person, not when I am plump in all the wrong places, but Niklas' body makes me as shallow as one could be. He looks like goddamn sin—strong and thick, strained with muscles built by sheer force. Not perfectly defined, not built in the gym, but here, on this mountain. I watch his wide pecks, dusted with fine hair, rise and fall with every slow, deep breath, his abs tighten as he starts moving towards me and his thick, strong legs ripple with muscles.

He stalks towards me with strong, deliberate movements, as my gaze travels back up his body, and I realize he is watching me just as I am him. The look in his eyes is positively ravenous and fire spreads on my skin wherever his gaze hits.

He is a few steps away, yet I can already smell him, and

as I breathe in that strong cedar and musk scent, I feel the heaviness of the air. It touches my skin, charging it with heat, fueling a fire inside of me that needs to burn.

When our eyes meet, a storm is unleashed. He rips the towel off his body before he even reaches me and as we pull every piece of fabric off mine, for the first time in a long time, I curse the fact that I am wearing anything at all. We cannot take our hands off each other, pulled into the eye of a storm, it's like a tornado caught on fire and swallowed us in its core.

Before the last piece of fabric hits the floor, he lifts me with one arm under my ass, my legs wrap around his waist and as his free hand curls high around my throat, my hands grab onto him, nails digging in his ribs.

Suddenly the storm quiets, like the calm before it somehow found its way in the midst instead. I can feel my pulse against his large hand, his thumb and forefinger pushing my head up by my jaw, but his intense, predatory gaze would be enough to hold me still. A shallow breath escapes my lips when his grip tightens, but he swallows it as his lips crash onto mine and the storm explodes around us yet again.

His lips push on mine, hard and forceful, kissing me with an all-consuming hunger. He licks, I bite, he sucks, I whimper. His cock is underneath me, pushing between my ass cheeks as he grinds on me, my back rubbing roughly on the hardwood door behind me.

Suddenly, he lets go of my throat, reaches between us and when he bites my bottom lip, a sharp pain rips through my left nipple, his fingers pinching hard. I moan in pain, and a shiver vibrates from his body into mine.

"Suki..." I can taste my name on his lips. He rips me away from the door, my nails sinking into his flesh, and I'm too dizzy with lust to understand what is happening as he throws me on the bed. In a split second, he's above me, one hand gripping the headboard above, veins pulsing against the strong, rippling muscles. He strangles his cock with his free hand, rubbing up and down as he moves between my open legs.

His ocean eyes drown me just as his cock rips through my pussy with a harsh buck of his hips, and every nerve ending inside of me sings in ecstasy. His body hovers above mine, dominating every inch of my soul, and his ravenous gaze is eating me alive. I slam my palms against the headboard and push against it, steadying myself as he slams violently inside of me, the harsh slapping of skins making me go wild with lust as his left hand digs into my hip.

I never used to keep my eyes open during sex, it was an involuntary reaction, yet Niklas silently demands it, and I could not take my eyes off his even if I wanted to. It is a delicious intrusion into my mind and soul, almost like with every different, harsh buck of his hips he learns something new about me, and I feel vulnerable. Keeping my eyes on him as he repeatedly slams into my raw pussy is the most intense feeling I have ever felt.

A fire grows inside of me and I need more. I plant my feet on the bed, knees bent, and when I lift my hips, pushing onto him, his cock touches a part of me no other man has touched before, and he looks just as surprised as I am. The orgasm hits us like a goddamn tsunami, ravaging through our bodies as we shake and moan curse words entangled with our names.

His knees slide under my thighs, my ass in his lap, his cock still inside of me as he crashes on top of me, both of us breathing like we ran a marathon in ten minutes.

"Niklas..." I whisper as my eyes close and breathe in his delicious scent.

This was not quite what I expected when I walked into the bedroom.

NIKLAS

All day I've been mulling over one thing in particular, one thing I have to tell her. But when she walked into the bedroom, all bets were off. Her gaze like fire seared my skin, and when I turned around and saw the look in her eyes, the way she was eating me up, inch by fucking inch, it made my dick hard instantly.

I was never a narcissistic guy, but her greedy eyes made me feel thankful for keeping up with my body. At that particular moment in time, I wasn't very thankful that she finally has clothes of her own, yet somehow, even under the gray sweatshirt and tight leggings she still looked like fucking sin.

We're now lying in bed, both on our backs, her head resting on my arm and I can't help but think that this was different. Not just how responsive her body was, but her reaction to me... like she was finally seizing the moment. I shake the thoughts away as I look at her profile brightened by the moonlight, softening her skin even more, and I trace every curve with my eyes, imprinting each and every one into my mind. There's nothing typical about her. She's perfect... absolutely fucking perfect.

"Tell me about your dreams." I'm not quite sure where that question came from, but I have been curious since she first mentioned she's had pretty much the same dream her whole life. She stiffens, her gaze twitching in confusion. "Before Adrien. You told me of them, but... I'm curious, what exactly happened in the dreams?" Her muscles soften, and I can't help but be suspicious of her reaction. There's something going on with her. It makes me uneasy, a strange feeling swirls in the pit of my stomach. Even the demons stir...

She turns her head to me, her gaze catches mine for a couple of seconds, before she turns again, but it's enough. There's definitely something going on with her, there's chaos in her eyes, painful chaos and I feel it my heart. A deep sense of foreboding takes over, and for the first time I feel something, something utterly unfamiliar.

Need.

I need her... need her to ground me. I need her to calm me. I need her to assure me that... I'm just imagining it all, the pain in her eyes... the sense that I'm losing her.

"It's the first dream I ever remember having." She speaks as she looks up at nothing in particular, and I'm forcing myself to listen.

I swallow the lump in my throat and take a slow, deep breath as she continues.

"Since I was a child. So... so young. Maybe four years old. It's the first conscious memory I have. I was alone, standing at the shore of a lake surrounded by a dense forest, and I was looking at the water. So calm, so peaceful, the blue sky reflecting on the soft ripples, and when I felt it, fear like no other invaded my body to the point that I felt pain from my tense muscles." She takes a deep, strained breath.

"Felt... It? Like a monster?" I coax her on, remembering what she told me the other day about her dreams.

She exhales slowly, her bright green eyes looking unnatural, penetrating through me until they hit the bottom of my soul.

"It... it was not a monster yet, it was... something." She holds my gaze, and I suddenly feel cold inside. "Foreboding. Pain. Evil. I felt it in my bones. My skin prickled, my muscles hurt, my lungs weren't taking enough air. Yet I forced a breath in, turned and ran. I ran into the forest as fast as I could, as fast as my little legs managed, and with every step, the fear filled more and more of my body until I felt like I was running in slow motion. I cried and I yelled and I could feel it behind me, but the closer it got, the slower I was, until I felt like I was running through gelatin, and I knew it... I could not escape it. And then it touched me—not a hand, not a physical thing, yet when it touched me it felt like ice was burning me and it flooded my mind. Pain, so much pain and darkness, crimson rivers and death, and so much more I could not explain at that age. My father woke me up, and my throat was raw from screaming, my muscles hurt, even my feet..."

Empathy is not my strongest trait, it barely exists within me, yet it must be traumatizing and confusing, dreaming of such things as a child. And the pain... the death? I wonder if this was the way her young mind was unconsciously dealing with the demons.

"I did not dream every night, yet when I did, this was the only dream I had. I do not quite remember when it changed, but it did, and even though it was the same dream, it looked different every time. A forest, a deserted street, a marsh, a suburbia, a desert... winter, summer, fall... always different, yet the same plot every time." She closes her eyes and sighs.

"The dreams evolved as I grew up and by the time I was in

my teenage years, they were something else... a need, a desire, a longing. And one day I felt *it* behind me and... I smiled. I waited until the last moment to start running, waited until I could breathe in its scent. Until I could feel its body heat against mine, its breath close enough to hit my skin. Then I ran. The more I ran, the more I wanted to get caught and one night, out of the blue, when it caught me, the touch was not ice anymore, it was fire. And I burned... an implosion seeped out and when I woke up, I cried. I cried because it was just a dream..." She opens her eyes and I still, because I know this was after we met. I know it in my bones, because it all changed for me that night as well.

"When did the dreams stop being nightmares?" I ask, remembering what she said before.

"I do not know." Her answer is short, and I can see the pulse in her throat speeding up. She's lying.

"What are you afraid of?" Her head whips at me in a split second, and the look in her eyes is murderous. *What the fuck?* I frown and push. "When did the dreams stop being nightmares?"

"I do not remember," she warns, yet her eyes betray her. She shifts uncomfortably and starts turning away from me, but I stop her with a hand on her chest. A breath hitches in her lungs, and the heartbeats beneath my palm vibrate through me.

"Just because you don't speak it, Suki, it doesn't mean it's not real. Just because you hide it, it doesn't mean it's not there." She's like a walking, talking, ticking time bomb.

She only speaks until she's at the edge of acknowledging the darkness, and I know it's the same darkness she's pushing back now, but it doesn't work like that. The chaos doesn't dissipate just because you don't acknowledge it. It builds and builds until it wreaks havoc and it's better to harness it, release it slowly, sate the fucking hunger, because if it implodes, it will take you with it.

"It's not, Niklas, it is not real! It does not matter when they stopped being nightmares because they were just dreams, only dreams!" her tone grows louder, angrier and there's a thread of fear weaved through it.

"Then why are you afraid of saying it out loud?! If you don't think it's real, Suki, what the fuck are you scared of?! If they're just dreams..." but I don't get to finish the sentence before she rasps at me.

"After I killed my mother! Okay?!" She slaps her mouth shut and looks towards the door.

There it is.

"Don't worry about Connor, he probably put his headphones in when he heard us earlier." Her other hand goes over her eyes and even in the moonlight I can see her cheeks grow red, but I don't give a fuck about her embarrassment right now. "What happened to the dreams after you killed your mother?"

She turns back to me, Connor suddenly forgotten. Sighing, she shakes her head.

"Even before that, they weren't necessarily nightmares anymore. There was only one thing that made them feel like nightmares, one element that terrified me. Darkness, torture, pain, madness, all wrapped up in this all-consuming bloodlust chasing me... always." She pauses for a few seconds. "The night after I killed her and the dream came again it felt like... an awakening. A revelation."

I can see it in her eyes, the hurt when she acknowledges this, a strange, pointless fear that I don't quite understand.

"The bloodlust was mine... The dream I had that night was explosive. I cannot explain it, everything around me caught fire as I was running away. Yet I ran as hard as I could away from the flames, but one touched me before I woke up, and it felt..." She takes a deep breath, exhaling loudly as her eyes close and a subtle moan vibrates through her. "Decadent. It felt decadent. A delicious depravity bursting out from my soul. A primordial need for violence."

"So, the dreams simply showed you who you are, what your soul needs," I acknowledge. Initially I thought that the dreams were about this need, this primal desire to be consumed, dominated. Yet they are about much more... a need for bloodshed at her own hands.

"No. This is where you are wrong, Niklas. I do not need it, and I certainly do not want it."

"Yes, you do. And whatever ridiculous concept stops you from fully embracing it, will eventually crash and burn and you will finally be free. Now all that matters is whether you wish to control the burn or not."

"I've seen it in my mother, Niklas. She crashed hard and burned even harder and unfortunately the flames didn't just touch her. It decimated everything around her and it destroyed her the moment they licked her soul. I have seen with my own eyes what happens when you let the crazy in and you are finally free." Suki shakes her head violently, tears streak her cheeks, yet her eyes hold anger.

"Don't you think that if you were your mother it would have happened by now?! What lies inside of you, Suki... it's not the same monster. Don't insult your demons by comparing them to the sick woman she was. We both know your mother was mentally ill. You must see you are different."

"The only reason I have not seen it is because I have not surrendered to it."

"That's not how mental illness works. Stop lying to yourself."

Actions speak louder than words and soon she will learn

to accept the truth. Soon...

* * *

We've been lying here in silence, calming our spirits, both aware that neither of us will back off.

"What happened to you that night? After we met?"

Her question startles me. All day I have been preparing myself for this specific moment, yet I was not expecting her to ask and it throws me off.

"I put my hands in my pockets, my hood up, and went home," I sigh and look straight into her eyes, penetrating her with a stare I know she won't be able to break. I already ran through all the possible outcomes of this conversation and I think I anticipate which one will prevail. "And the next evening I broke up with my girlfriend."

The weight of those words crashes down on her with a force that physically shakes her body. I can see the threads knotting in her mind until the thought is complete and the conclusion is reached. Her eyes try to break away from mine, she blinks fast, her breathing becomes erratic, and I see the panic settling in. In one quick move I'm on top, straddling her and I trap her wrists on the pillow on either side of her head.

"Breathe, Suki." I lean over and whisper in her ear.

A sharp breath hitches, swallowing a sob as I hold her beneath me and her body tremors. I lift my head and look at her, but her eyes are cloudy as she looks through me, her mind somewhere else.

"Suki, look at me!" my tone is rough and stern, yet she's too far away, trapped in thoughts that I need to pull her out of. "Look at me now!" I let go of one her wrists and wrap my hand around her throat, squeezing the sides until I can see her eyes losing life, yet she is fully numb.

"SUKI!" I rasp, my voice rough, bouncing from every wall in the room, my big hand squeezing her fragile little throat. As the life threatens to leave her body, as the pain takes over her mind and her lungs are crying for life, she comes back to me. She opens her mouth, forcing herself to take a breath, her eyes grow wide and the bright green I learned to crave fills her irises again.

Then I let go.

"My...." she mumbles something between strained breaths. "My fault," she repeats and looks at me with so much pain and guilt in her eyes I truly feel the need to fucking slap it out of her.

"What the fuck are you talking about?" I predicted this, I did and she is wrong.

"You know what I am talking about, Niklas!"

"You think it's your fault she died?! Seriously? I know you're more rational than that, little siren, don't disappoint me."

She frowns and shakes her head. "You." My brows furrow. "You are my fault." Now this I did not predict. "I'm the reason why this happened inside of you that day..."

"Don't fucking kid yourself."

"Stop it!" she bellows. "You said yourself. That night... I was the trigger, I was the reason why."

"You think you're responsible for me?! I'm fucking happy, sweet little siren. I'm happy you're the reason my demons finally found bliss. If it wasn't for you... The path I was on was a destructive one, a turmoil made its home inside of me, fought never-ending battles, and people that didn't deserve it were in the front line." I sigh and continue, "I know you will deny it, yet I also know that your soul recognizes my words. I know that battle is consuming you too. You were my liberation, Suki, my demons revel in their freedom and I... I found you."

"I..." She lays beneath me, her eyes wide, her mouth hanging open.

"I see it in your eyes, Suki. Your demons cry for mine, they want what I have, what they saw that night, what you did to your mother... they crave it all. You are in self-destruct mode, your soul will implode, pulling everything you are in a fucking dark hole, and when the fire is done consuming you, it will move on to the people that care for you."

"Who?!" she rasps. "I'm alone, Niklas. If it implodes, the world will go on like nothing happened. There is no one waiting for me, no one missing me, no one cares!"

"You silly little siren. I thought you've seen it by now." I shake my head and smirk. "I have made many violent threats against you, yet none of them taken to completion." I pause, observing her, but there's no realization in her eyes. "You were perfect, perfect material for my demons to finally let loose—to demand, take, hurt, destroy. You were perfect. But my demons recognized you, recognized your demons. We dance to the same song because we are legion and there aren't many like us."

There's a faint shake of her head as her body bursts into goosebumps.

"It didn't take me long to realize that the only reason I craved that destruction, doing all those things to women is because my demons were searching for you. The one that sang the song that triggered them all those years ago. They were starved and they wanted to devour everything and anything just to sate that hunger. Until you came back to me..."

Tears pool in her eyes and her chest shivers, but she swallows it all back. She knows that she will have to give in to her demons if she stays with me, if she accepts my words. Eventually she will, there's no escape but death, because the hunger will get so strong, she'll end up eating herself up.

I let go of her hands and guide her body to the right side of the bed, *her* side, as I know she enjoys falling asleep looking at the view. I lie down behind her and spoon her short, plump body that fits perfectly alongside mine. Her breaths slow down, the thumps of her heart ease.

"I care, Suki," I whisper and feel the most subtle twitch in her body in response.

I'm almost certain I more than care, yet how could I admit something like that to me or her, when it just means that I will be throwing my fucking heart into the pit, unknowing if it's going be burned or devoured.

I care...

CHAPTER 29

SUKI

The men spent most of the morning on the roof, fixing some loose shingles and some other things I wasn't particularly interested in. I, on the other hand, spent the morning finalizing my plan. It turned out that the snowstorm missed us completely and after lunch Connor is going back home to Bear Creek. He plans on coming back, most likely to help Niklas with Adrien, but I do not plan on being here then.

The small carry on suitcase is ready, hidden under the bed of what used to be my bedroom, yet my plan depends on Connor's need to take two trips to the helicopter. I'm not sure how I'm going to do it, but I will.

I could have told him about this, maybe he would have helped me, but somehow... I doubt he would. Not because he does not want to, but because he trusts his friend and for some reason they both seem to be on the same page. It scares me that there are two people now that seem to anticipate my future, yet I am not one of them.

This mountain feels like a sanctuary for forsaken souls and I can't give in and be one of them. I hear my mother's words in my head every time I think of Adrien, every time I see the monster within Niklas grinning at me in approval.

Yes, I told Niklas about the nightmares, about how much that man scares me, but he is not the thing that scares me the most. Oh, no... what scares me the most is me. I dream of slicing pieces of his skin and burning them as he watches. I dream of peeling off his flesh, his fat, his muscles, until I uncover bones, then I break them. One by one. Slowly. I dream of cutting his balls, gagging him with them and slicing his dick like just like you butterfly a chicken breast. I dream of so much more—violence, blood, and so much pleasure. I dream of crimson waters surrounded by beautiful white mountains and my naked body emerging from them, leaving bloody footprints through the snow as I take my rightful place on Niklas' side on a throne of mangled dead bodies.

I dream of death, chaos, and destruction. All at my hand.

And when I wake up smiling, nearing an orgasm created by the lustful blood lust of these dreams, I hear my mother's voice in my head. *One day you will understand, Suki. One day the demons will sing for you too*. The demons sang the day her blood pooled at my feet from wounds of my own creation, yet I am afraid I cannot distinguish her demons from mine. How can I know for sure that mine are not the same as hers?

I do my best to keep calm for the rest of the time I am here with Niklas. It's not easy acting normal when my demons are wailing inside of me, mourning a loss that is not gone yet, but is about to be. At lunch, every time my eyes catch Niklas', slithers of my soul are being ripped away from me and pain replaces the void left behind. I am swallowing more screams than I am food.

Over and over, I turn my gaze to the view, hoping it will soothe me and make the pain subside, but it does not help. This view, this goddamn beautiful view makes me swallow tears that have not reached my eyes yet. I am pushing back waves upon waves of pain, and the burn in my heart is torture enough to convince me to stay. I charge through it all, because I need to find out if all of this is an illusion. Most of all, his monster watches me and with every quirk of his lips, I can feel my demons giving in. I have to get away, because I am not ready to find out this way whether my demons are hereditary or not.

Connor is upstairs, getting ready to leave, and I am standing in front of the kitchen window, leaning onto my hands that are resting on the sink. The air shifts, charged with fire that heats whatever is left of my soul. I see his reflection in the window, growing larger and larger, until he towers over me, a foot taller than my short frame. His hands go to my waist, he turns me around and two fingers grab my chin, bringing my eyes to his.

The ocean, the dark blue depths of the ocean pull me in. My breath hitches in my lungs. My skin breaks out in goosebumps. A cold shiver runs down my spine and stops where his hand is splayed on my lower back, but from there it spreads like wildfire into my core as he pushes me into his body. I allow myself to sink into this feeling, sink into his touch, sink into the eyes of the monster that makes me feel alive, that makes me feel like I belong, the one that urges me on.

Because this will be the last time.

* * *

I know this was my choice, I know I decided that the best thing for me was to leave. So how come it hurts so much? Why does my heart ache? Why does my soul feel like it is being pulled apart? This is what I wanted. This is what I planned for since the moment I decided not to run away when he found me in the forest.

The distance between the helicopter and the mountain is getting bigger and the pain in my chest stronger. My lungs refuse to take in air and tears fill my eyes.

No. No! This is just in my head—paranoia. It is fear of the unknown.

"Suki, what the fuck are you doing?!" I hear Connor scream over the deafening sound of the helicopter.

Shit.

I peek from behind the cargo he carries in the back and he is staring right at me. Well, that was short lived. And here I was thinking I was being sneaky.

"Move your damn ass in here and strap in! Jesus Christ."

I can barely hear what he is saying, but I walk towards the front, jump over the back of the seat, and sit down. I look at him, biting my lip like I used to do as a little girl when my dad caught me doing something bad.

"Under the seat!" he yells, pointing down under me. I reach under and touch something stashed there. Headphones. After figuring them out, the deafening sound of the helicopter is muted and I do not like it. All I can hear now is the demons in my mind bellowing, yelling, the brutal sound of my soul being ripped out of me.

"I didn't know if you actually made it in or not." I hear

Connor's voice in the headphones.

"You knew?!"

"I'm a cop, Suki... and you hid your suitcase under the bed I was sleeping in."

Well... fuck. I did, I just didn't think he would have any business looking there. I shake my head at myself.

"What? When you stay over somewhere you never check under the bed to make sure you didn't drop something?" He smiles at me, that cheeky grin that must melt all the women in Bear Creek.

"If you knew, how come you did not say anything to me or Niklas?"

His grin falters, his dark eyes pinning me down in my seat, and I'm suddenly cold.

"I didn't actively seek to take you out of there because it's none of my damn business, but at the same time, if you had your own plans to escape... I can't stop you. There were no rules about that. Plus, to be honest I wasn't sure what choice you were going to make. You could have taken the snowmobile for all I knew."

"It's none of your business or... Niklas threatened you not to?" The look in his eyes as I ask that question tells me I might have made a mistake.

"Threatened me? No Suki, he doesn't need to threaten me."

"So... he asked you to leave the kidnapped woman alone and you, as the sheriff, said... you betcha!" I regret the sarcasm immediately. The self-preservation instinct doesn't seem to run through me.

Seconds pass, and his eyes are still on me—cold and emotionless. "Yes." There's a hint of amusement staring back at me, a sinister amusement and as much as it freaks me out, it intrigues me. This man is a peculiar paradox that I cannot quite figure out. Cheeky, yet stern at times, easygoing, yet terrifying. Somehow, he seems like the kind of man that you want on your side in a fight.

"Yes..." I repeat his word.

"I trust him, Suki."

"This dynamic between the two of you, I do not understand it. You are the sheriff, you know what he does..."

"Let me stop you right there." He interrupts me before I can finish. "I'm the sheriff, yes, but me and him... we have a past." He turns his attention back to the glorious view in front of us. "A past that forced me to put my fucking life in his hands and that shit builds trust. I'm not going to deny that he's a crazy motherfucker; however, I don't ever get involved in what he does. This means that I don't know when, who, or how he kills. Or *if* for that matter. I know one thing for sure. The people he kills..." He turns his eyes to me yet again and I swallow a lump that I didn't know was stuck in my throat.

"Each and every one of them deserve it."

It's a strange dynamic between the two, two sides of justice—one is law and the other you would never want to be on the receiving end of.

I turn my attention to the view, and I find myself breathing harder. I see a tiny town beneath me as we descend, and the closer we get, the more detached I am from my soul. There is a peculiar sense of emptiness inside me.

A harrowing emptiness.

NIKLAS

The moment I enter *our* bedroom I know something is wrong. It's a strange feeling, like a severed connection. The sound of silence in this room is deafening and the air feels light, too easy to breathe, and scentless. I hear the running shower in the bathroom and I know, even before I push the door open... I know the only thing that water stream is hitting is the tiled floor.

"She's gone..."

Red, I'm seeing red. Too many thoughts run through my head at the same time and panic fills me, thoughts of Adrien coming for her, taking her from under my nose. I'm running through the house, checking every room, every nook and cranny for signs of her.

"She's gone!"

I never thought that I could feel this, this all-consuming rage. My mind is chaos, and I will burn this mountain to the ground until I find her.

I rush back upstairs, into *our* bedroom, and as I hear the faint noise of Connor's helicopter in the distance, I head straight for the dressers and wardrobes.

Adrien didn't take her.

Most of the clothes Connor brought her are gone. She left voluntarily... she left me. I don't know whether Connor helped her or she sneaked in, but one thing's for sure—she's on that helicopter heading to Bear Creek and I'm snowed in on this mountain.

For a long time, until her, fear has been the only emotion I could identify on other people. I assimilated, turned it over and over again, analyzing is effects on others, yet never fully grasping how it would feel my own skin. Until now. Gut wrenching fear tears through my body.

Fear for her safety.

Fear for her soul.

Fear for my own.

My body aches, my eyes burn, my lungs constrict and my heart... for the first time ever, feels the loss tearing it apart with sharp slashes, spilling its blood within me.

I want to run, I want to scream, yet on the outside I'm as calm as ever as I take a slow, deep breath and walk through the glass doors onto the terrace. My hands rest on the rail on either side of me, and I look into the distance, at nothing in particular. My body calms, my pulse steadies, yet the demons are busy, my mind filling with possibilities—an idea is forming—a love letter to her.

My skin is cold as ice, and I realize I've been standing here for a long time. My favorite time of day has come. The sky burns and the sun dies behind the mountains—the most beautiful view of all.

Inside of me, the monster grins, and I wonder what the outcome of my plan will be. I have thought of many possibilities and most of them are good, but a few are less than desirable. However, I can't control it. I won't, because no matter what, no matter what the demons want or what the monster craves, no matter how much I suffer, no matter how much she does, I will have to accept the outcome. Accept her decision.

I turn and go back inside, locking the door behind me. I walk through the house checking all the doors and windows, making sure it's all secure and retire into my office. Before I can even think about the outcome and the effects it will have on us, I need to do more research.

But first.

"Is she safe?" Connor answers the phone after the fourth ring, and I don't give a shit if he helped her leave or she sneaked in. Talking about that is a waste of time.

"She is. I'm sorry man... I..."

"I don't blame you," I interrupt him. "I had a feeling this would happen, maybe not with you, but I had a feeling." Last night she was acting strange, but I chose to ignore it.

"I don't think this is about you, Nik." Even he can see the effects of her turmoil, and he's only known her for a few days.

"Some of it is. I want to make sure she's safe, because I can't guarantee that the motherfucker is still on this mountain or not. If something happens to her, Connor..."

"I'm keeping an eye on her until..."

"Until, what?!" I rasp, clutching the phone in my hand too firmly.

He sighs, "I can't tell you where she is, not yet anyway. She wants a head start." I hear his words on the other line and my heart fucking breaks. I don't know how I know this... but I do, I can feel it.

"I need her back, Connor. I have to have her back."

"I know..." there's a long pause, a silence that speaks volumes. He knows what I need to do, and unfortunately, I also understand what I have to do. I have to let her go. For now.

"She'll have her head start and, in the meantime, we have work to do."

* * *

It fucking hurts. I can't lie, it hurts. It's a strange, unfamiliar feeling that I can only identify because it's the sense of betrayal that clues me in.

I told her I fucking cared... and the next day she ran away from me. Fair enough, her right to reject me, but I can't let her go until she faces her demons, truly faces them. Only then can she decide if leaving is the best decision for herself. And I can't wait to see her beautiful soul devour the darkness.

After going through my next steps with Connor, I turn on all the cameras on one of my screens and fill the others with information I am pulling from various sources. I have to assume that the motherfucker will anticipate my next move. I have to assume that he will try to come for me. This is a different situation than all the others I have been in before because my current prey is perfectly aware that he is prey, and he might even become a hunter.

I have to assume that everything that could go wrong, will.

The longer I sit here hacking into servers I have no business being on, looking up satellite images, doing this investigation work, I feel the adrenaline spiking. A strange sense of lustful satisfaction floods my body, shivers run through my veins, and I realize how much I miss this. Not the research work itself, because I've done this with Suki here as well, but the buildup, the anticipation of death.

I miss the kill.

That depraved, exquisite feeling when they realize life is slowly leaving their body. Always slow... That empty look in their eyes when panic hits and at that moment they know they would sacrifice their mother, father, brother, or even their own fucking children in order for their life to be spared.

That fear of death that floods their eyes is addictive, and I will never stop being hungry for it.

I shake away the distracting feelings, keeping to the idea that formed in my head earlier as I start opening satellite images of the cabin where Suki was kept. I go through more and more from the last few days and a pattern emerges. One that I'm not particularly happy with. There's nothing changed in these images, nothing at all. Everything looks the same from one photo to the other, no matter the time of day. The snow is untouched... the area empty. The son of a bitch is gone.

From all the research I have done on him, I know that when he leaves, it means he is hunting. Now the question is... is he hunting for a new victim? Or for Suki?

Suddenly, adrenaline floods me, a sense of dread takes over, and I know I need to find him now or at least make sure he is nowhere near Bear Creek. Nowhere near her.

CHAPTER 30

SUKI

Three days have passed since I sneaked into Connor's helicopter and left the peak that quickly felt more like home than the place I'm fighting to get back to now. Connor knew I wanted to escape, he also knew he should have told Niklas about it, yet he decided not to. He made up some half-assed excuse that he didn't know if I would sneak in or choose the snowmobile, but we both know now that he was perfectly aware I was going to choose the helicopter.

Once it set off the ground, slithers of regret started wrapping themselves around my soul, growing larger and larger the higher we flew, and they ripped it away from me.

There was no turning back though, I had to leave, even if my soul did not come with me. I knew this would happen, weeks ago when we sat in front of the fire and I shared with him what I did to my mother, I knew since then that my soul would not leave with me. Not when my demons danced freely on heathen songs sung by his, not when even I could not deny how well I fitted into this world... *his* world. Isolated on that beautiful peak in the company of the dangerous valleys and the looming mountains.

And Niklas... the quiet stranger that saved me, captured me, and threatened to rip me open and make me bare myself not only to him, but to myself as well. I am still fighting myself, but fighting him was getting harder and harder each day, and I had to leave before I gave in. Because how could I not oblige him when he was the one that helped me put my soul back together?

Only now, I have lost it again, for different reasons though, a sacrifice I made knowing that staying there would have cost me my heart. He would have pried it out of my body and fed it to the monster lurking inside of him, and no matter how deeply I would have reveled in that decadent devourment... I could not risk it. Not when I cannot trust myself, my instincts, my heart, while it was cooped up on that mountain, in that beautiful world that seemed to be built for us.

When I met Adrien, I thought that was it, I finally found the man that I could trust with everything—my soul, my body... my depravity. He took them all and broke them, but I managed to save my heart when I saw what type of monster he was. Yet, that does not mean that it did not break at all. It broke, it definitely broke... not for the man that he was, but for the man he appeared to be for all that time we talked online.

Yet Niklas, I crave him in a way I cannot rationalize. I crave his body, his voice, his fucking heart, and that beautifully psychotic mind. He is a ruthless murderer with no remorse or empathy, and I crave the destruction he brings. I crave the chaos, but he craves the fear. My fear. What happens to me when he gets bored with the lack of it in my voice? The only thing I truly fear now is what I feel for him, and that does not translate into any song.

What happens to the siren when she stops singing?

I cannot help but wonder if I will be enough after that. I do not want to be there the day his monster stops smiling at me and the demons halt their efforts to break me open and watch me burn as I finally accept my own. I know that is what he wants from me, maybe even more than he wants to devour my heart and make it his. He wants me to succumb, to revel in my heinous cravings, to accept this gruesome calling. And I had to leave, because more and more I wanted that too.

Now, three days after I left, in this small hotel room in Bear Creek, I find myself looking at this little suitcase that holds the clothes and shoes Connor brought me at the cabin. I turn to look at the old clock sitting on the bedside table, and I realize I have been staring at my packed suitcase for almost forty-five minutes. I am about to leave, go *home*, back to my sad little apartment, back to a life that was never truly mine, and more and more I am questioning my actions.

I am free, yet I feel no joy. I am trying to fool my brain into thinking that it is only because I am still too close to the two people that captured me. Yet the slithers of my soul that still cling to me and the heart that bleeds inside my chest, are screaming otherwise. They know... I will never feel the happiness they crave, not away from him.

Home.

What a sweet term for a place I never had a real connection to. A space inside a shitty apartment building, with shitty neighbors I do not even know, in the middle of a city that means nothing to me. Yet I am fighting my ass off to go back there. I roll my eyes at myself, at the ridiculousness of this situation, making a mental note to open my laptop when I get home and look for a different place to live. New town, new home, new everything.

After spending these few days in Bear Creek, I am more certain that what I am looking for is a small town like this one— charming, yet rough around the edges. Most locals are friendly, and the ones that aren't, tend to keep to themselves. Only three days have passed, yet I already know that when I'm gone I will miss the local cafe, the bakery, the owner of the small hotel I'm staying at... and that view of the peak from down here. If it's even possible, it's even more beautiful... this ethereal aura about it. A home up in the clouds. It could have been my home.

I violently shake the thought away. I have a plan and I need to stick to it.

I grab the suitcase and leave the room that kept me safe for the last three days. I miss being up on the mountain, constantly sheltered by Niklas, because here, alone in this hotel room, alone in general, I barely slept, constantly scared that Adrien would get me. I chose this though, no matter how much Connor insisted I stay with him, I needed to be alone. Even scared.

Now, I feel like I am running, running from my troubles, running from him, hiding, when actually I should find him and finish him as I promised myself. I wanted to, I really did, but at this point Adrien is not the only thing I need to run from.

It is too much, too many things plaguing me—the heart that breaks for Niklas, my demons demanding blood, and the guilt at the thought of his ex—if it wasn't for me, she might have been alive today. An innocent soul caught in the crossfire of these disturbing desires. Yet no matter how much I want to truly feel guilty about it, the only guilt I have is for the lack of it. More and more, I see in myself the same darkness that most likely drove my mother to her demise and I am not going to take the same path.

Connor took time off work to drive me home. It is a long way, and I am thankful he is taking me, because when Adrien kidnapped me, my wallet disappeared as well. Most likely burned to eliminate any trace that I ever existed in his life. Without a driver's license, I cannot rent a car myself or fly or pay for any of it for that matter.

Luckily, the birth certificate I have at home will help me get them back—my license, access to my bank accounts, and my bank cards. Funny how the practicalities of life are forgotten when you get kidnapped. Connor will have to help me break into my apartment since I do not have a key anymore. You do not think about how thankful you are that your bills are on a direct debit and there is money left in your account, until you realize that without it, you might have not come back to a home at all.

"Are you ready to go?" Connor waits for me, leaning on his car on the quiet street of Bear Creek. The sun isn't fully up yet, but since driving back home is going to take at least twelve hours, most likely split in two days, we want to set off early.

"Ready." I hand him the small suitcase that actually belongs to him, and as I open the door to his truck, I stop to look around. The sleepy town slowly comes to life as the bird song fills the snowy streets. Lights turn on in the apartments above the small shops, the sun creeps from behind the low buildings, and the peak stands proud in the distance.

I take a deep breath and will my demons to end their useless fight as I climb in. I knew it was going to hurt, yet the agony taking over my heart in this moment is nothing like I expected.

I blink once, twice, and by the third time, the peak is getting further away from me in the rearview mirror of the car.

Agony...

NIKLAS

I never thought that being alone, trapped on my mountain, would be torturous. I never thought I would ever resent the remoteness, the silence. Yet here I am, standing on the porch, looking down the hill that holds the road covered in an impossibly thick blanket of snow.

Too much time has passed since the house has fallen into an unnatural silence. I spent too many days trying to convince myself that I don't need Suki, that it was the proximity, the attraction, or our past that made me want to break her open, feed on her beautiful mind, her depraved soul and that fucked up lust that matches mine. It was futile, and the more I thought about how hard she rejected her nature, how she rejected me, the easier it was for me to realize why it bothers me so much.

In these last two weeks alone on this mountain, I wished that caring was the only feeling that could describe what I felt about her. It isn't. It's an unnatural addiction, a sweet destruction of my soul, a burning mark on my heart which that meek four-letter word that starts with an L doesn't quite do justice.

I promised her the day we found out who we were for each other, I promised her that no matter what, I will split the fucking earth open to find her. And I will. I should be a good man, I should let her go, I should give her the freedom she ran towards. However, I'm not a good man, I'm a fucking monster, *her* monster. I will hunt her, catch her again, and bring her *home*. Yes, I should give her a choice, but now, now is not the fucking time. She ran out of goddamn fear and that fear needs to be abolished. Burnt to the fucking ground.

And there is only one way that can be done.

Her darkness will explode when vengeance clouds her fear.

And her darkness needs to explode. Only then can she decide if she really needs to be away from me.

The phone rings in my pocket and when I see Connor's name on the screen, I know the plan is in motion. I cock an eyebrow and answer with a grin on my lips.

"Is it happening?"

"Good morning to you too, motherfucker," his deep, lazy voice sounds on the other line, but he takes my exasperated sigh as a sign that I will not bother with pleasantries. "Yes, they're starting today, actually in about half an hour. The gossip is gonna hit the town, so I made up a story about you visiting your family."

"Fair enough. How long will they take?"

"Two days at most. It hasn't snowed in a while, so hopefully it won't be too hard for them to clear the road. I'll be up as soon as they come back. Do you have eyes on him?"

"I do. He hasn't noticed the trail cameras yet and he's been staying in the cabin since he came back a week ago. I'm not sure if he thinks that I just gave up on him, if he does, this will be so much easier." I tracked that son of a bitch, found him, his mobile phone, his laptop, everything. That paranoid motherfucker covered his online footprint so well, used cash, and every move he made was off the grid. But I got him a few days after Suki left. Thankfully he was nowhere near her, but in a completely different state, driving back here according to his phone. The road to that cabin passes through another town, on the other side of the mountain and because it's right at the edge of my property, almost at the base of the mountain, he still has road access and to be honest, I was grateful for that. I need him here. Close to me. He's been cooped up in the hunting cabin ever since he came back.

"And Suki?" His voice lacks the confidence he had ten seconds ago.

"Safe. Googling apartments for sale away from there." I've been tracking her laptop and her phone, keeping tabs on her. I have to, I need to know she is safe and as far as possible from Adrien. I'm bringing her back, and I would feel worse about what I am about to do, but her search history proves she misses me. Quite amusing though that she thinks if she searches for my name or this peak in incognito mode on her internet browser that I won't be able to see it. And she googled me quite a bit, images mostly. She misses me and I her. When she left, a piece of my fucking soul left as well, and until I hacked into her laptop, I wasn't sure if that piece simply disappeared or she took it with her. Now I know.

"How are you going to bring her back?"

"A part of me foolishly believes I will be able to strap her in the car and she won't put up much of a fight." At those words, Connor snorts on the other line. "Yet the realistic side of me knows that a sleeping pill will probably be the best solution."

"I can't fucking believe I'm condoning this." I can practically hear Connor shaking his head in disappointment.

"You're not. What you are actually condoning is coming

here and helping me catch this son of a bitch."

"Just... take care of her."

"You know I will." There's silence. He does, he knew even before me what I felt for her. "And Connor..."

"Yeah..." his tone weary now.

"He's been going in the cellar a lot."

"Fuck." A loud thud sounds on the other line, along with more explicit curse words. If he didn't punch a hole through a wall, then he definitely broke some piece of furniture. We both know what it means—we need to hurry.

The conversation ends with newfound motivation instilled in both of us. I have two days to prepare myself, two days to get the room ready, two days in which that motherfucker needs to stay in that hunting cabin. Before the week ends, our lives will be changed. The trees are hit by the crimson hues of the sun rising behind the house, and I can already feel the change in the atmosphere. The world knows it's about to shift.

A new dawn, painted in crimson hues. As if the sun knows what awaits this mountain.

SUKI

Home.

That warm cozy place you crave after a long day of running errands. The place you feel most comfortable in. Safe. Happy.

Home.

This is not it. This small apartment in this sad city, in a shitty part of town, in this god forsaken building. I have been spending almost every waking hour on the internet looking for a new house, a new apartment, a new town... a new home. Yet nothing feels right, not when in the back of my mind I know I already found it. I fucking know, and nothing will ever live up to that. Nothing. Because every single sleepless night, every single goddamn tear I shed, every single bump in the night, every heartbroken wail that leaves my throat, every single one of them is for one reason and one reason only—*he* is my home. Not the house, not the mountain. Niklas is my home.

Seventeen days have passed. Seventeen sorrowful days, each worse than the one before. Seventeen long days where my demons have thrown in my face one revelation after another. Yes, I wanted and needed the space away from him, away from the mountain. Many nights as I laid in bed, I told myself that I will never go back, yet I knew I was lying to myself. All I wanted was the space to figure out if what I felt for him was real and not a mirage created by the environment, by the proximity, the isolation, and... the lust.

I could have dealt with the lust, I could have fed on the pleasure he gave, on the fulfillment of my fantasies, on how he fed the cravings that took over me since my dreams turned into something else. Yet, when everything shifted, when the monster in his eyes smiled at me, when his hold on me was more protective than possessive and his lips became softer against mine, I could not deal with it anymore. I needed to find out if it was my imagination or my broken mind adjusting to a new imprisonment.

It was not.

It is not.

We are bound together, him and I. Bound by lust and blood. Bound by forces we do not even understand, cravings most people cannot fathom. Bound by fear and pain. Bound by death.

Our story started a decade ago and fate threw us back in each other's path for a reason. He was right—I am his. Another reason I fled is because I wondered if the lack of fear in my song would make him tire of me. I feared that his and Adrien's monsters were cut from the same cloth and he would eventually dispose of me, just as Adrien did with the ones before. Yet I failed to listen to all the words he spoke to me. Fear was the only emotion he could truly feel in other people... until me.

Yet alongside the revelation concerning my feelings, something else brewed. Regret. Anger. Madness. Vengeance. Blood lust.

Niklas craved to break me open, he wanted to see me burn and wanted to be the one to light the fire and push me into the flames. I thought it was for destruction's sake, but rebirth was the purpose. A cleansing of my old soul, the birth of my hidden one. He wanted me to embrace my demons, accept the fact that I am like him, that I crave the bloodshed, the taste of fear, the smell of death. My mother's words ringing in my ears were the only thing holding me back. My disgust for that foul creature held me in place. The horrifying idea that my demons mirror hers. This has haunted me my entire life, even before I sunk a knife in her flesh.

The regret I hold towards leaving the mountain before I took my vengeance on Adrien is what made me understand that the only things that haunt me are ghosts of my own creation. My inability to see that my own insecurities, the self-doubt, is the only thing making me believe that I could be my mother.

Most people live with that gnawing *what if* question and I do too now. It is what made me realize I am a coward. What if I succumb to my demons on that mountain? What if I cut Adrien open and spill his guts at my feet? What if I slit his throat? What if burn him? What if I stop thinking I will become my mother and give my soul the gift of death that it oh so craves?

I know now that I am not her. I hate her enough not to be her. I'm done. Done holding back, done living by the rules of a world I do not belong to.

I step out of the shower, wrap my head in a towel and wipe my body with another before I cover myself with it. By the time I finish drying my hair it is late, past midnight and after the day I had, planning and organizing my next steps, all I want is sleep. I need all the energy I can get for what awaits me tomorrow.

I walk through the dark living room, into the bedroom lit only by moonlight and change into the pajamas I left on the bed. I down half the bottle of water sitting on my bedside table and crawl into bed under the covers.

I'm not sure how much time has passed, yet the world around me feels strange, my vision blurred and the air is heavy. I try to blink a few times to focus my vision, yet my eyelids are not cooperating. Suddenly, the hairs on the back of my neck stand up. My body bursts into goosebumps. A burning shiver spreads from my spine all over my body. A sharp breath catches in my throat and I am all too aware of the reason why.

The last thing I saw before sleep involuntarily took me was a monster grinning at me, yet I did not know whether it was a dream or reality.

Do not let this be a dream...

CHAPTER 31

SUKI

I do not know how much time has passed since Niklas tied me to this chair. He did not bother gagging me since I am in the basement below his house, and even if there was someone around on this mountain, no one could hear my screams anyway. I contemplate how I ended up in this situation and somehow I am not surprised. I hoped... damn it, how I hoped he would come for me. Fight for me. Every single day I was away from him, my heart hurt and I knew—I cared too. I more than cared.

It is the reason why I gave up on finding an apartment, the reason why I changed my plans last minute.

I knew I would come back here, I just never thought it would be under these circumstances. Forced. Tied to a chair like a prisoner waiting for torture. Like one of his victims. I have no clue what his plans are for me. This room is covered in plastic, even the metal table that sits in the middle is covered, ready for whatever sadistic, bloody plan he has, and I cannot help but mourn the connection I thought we had. The feelings I thought he held for me.

I know what he does in this room, he told me himself of some of his methods and the instruments sitting on the metal cart are making my overactive imagination run wild with crimson images of flayed flesh and exposed organs.

I take a deep breath and urge my body to relax, but my efforts falter when I look to my left—a St. Andrews cross sits there against the wall. It is not the same as the one upstairs, but my mind still wanders to the first time he put a knife in me and I wonder if today I will finally feel the blade end of it. This cross is metallic, though, and it takes me a second to understand why. Metal does not absorb blood. My body shakes and my fear of him is slowly filling my veins again.

This cannot be. He cares! He cannot do this!

I can feel the cracks in my heart, the slithers of pain that are pulling it apart. Yet my demons howl at me, they howl their opposing thoughts, they howl their disagreement, urging me to hold on. But how can I hold on when I am tied up to a chair in the room he uses to sate his thirst for blood? The room where his demons feast.

Tears fill my eyes, my chest heavy, my breathing strained, my skin prickly, and I want to scream. But I don't, because that is exactly what he craves and I refuse to give it to him. My heart bleeds, my lungs heave, and my eyes... my eyes burn with tears I am holding back.

Many times before, I have contemplated this moment, I

imagined it, turned the picture over and over in my head. I counted all possibilities and calculated all outcomes. I guess, in the end, it had to be him. Niklas had to be the one to end me. And I am not surprised it came to this.

I wanted freedom; this will be the ultimate form.

* * *

The sound of a door creaking in the distance startles me.

I hear heavy, strained footsteps coming down the stairs, along with a strange, muffled noise I cannot quite place. My anxiety grows, my eyes widen, and I can hear my heartbeat. My back straightens against the chair and I promise myself I will be strong for this. I will take what he gives me, because the ultimate goal is my freedom. And I am done, done fighting a losing battle with myself.

I want to be free, no matter what that freedom entails.

I look ahead towards the corridor that leads to this room and I feel the air charging with an electricity that fuels my senses. And just like that, Niklas appears through the doorway, filling it completely, the air getting thicker with his presence in the room.

I almost forgot what impact he has on me. His ocean eyes, his delicious grin, those broad shoulders and strong arms that could break a man's neck in a second, his thick chest and those long, strong legs. The look in his eyes is feral, but there is something disturbing in his features—a smile—a terrible, frightening smile filled with anticipation and a strange sense of triumph.

What the hell?

And then I see it. The object of his triumphant amusement as he drags it with one hand behind him while he stalks towards me. He stops in the middle of the room and, like he weighs nothing at all, he swings him forwards, his body sliding on the plastic covered floor, until I stop it with my feet.

Adrien.

I look at him, then raise my gaze to Niklas.

The tears that sat in my eyes fall, slowly running down my cheeks, my breathing calms, my muscles relax, my demons howl in victory. They were right, I should have trusted them, I should have trusted him. I should have trusted my instincts, not my insecurities.

I look down at Adrien, his clothes stained with fresh blood, and I am not even sure where it is coming from. He is alive, but unconscious. He looks good like this, hurt and mangled, one wrist most likely broken, considering the strange angle it is bent in. I study him, study the bruises forming on some of the exposed flesh, and as I wonder what Niklas did to him, I completely miss that he is standing behind me, untying me. My body jerks in surprise, but strong hands settle on my shoulders, holding me steady in place.

There is so much uncertainty in this moment, in my soul, in my future, in ours... yet when I feel him, this eerie sense of calm takes over, my body involuntarily relinquishing all control to him, and it feels... liberating. My eyes close, his hands squeeze my muscles and all I can hear are the strained breaths of the unconscious asshole laying at my feet. *A gift.*

Niklas' breath on my ear warms me, and I finally feel at home again.

"I will kill him for you, Suki." I still, and feel my brain looking for quick resolve. A choice is presented, yet I feel like something is being taken away from me.

He moves in front of me, Adrien now laid between us and pulls a gun, aiming it at that sack-of-shits head.

No, no, no!

My mouth falls open, but no words spill. I want to stop

him, yet my mind views this as an escape, an escape from the carnage that threatens my soul if I am the one that takes his pathetic life away. Oh, no, no, this is not how it is going to go down! *That son of a bitch is mine!* My plan to return here included my vengeance.

"No!" I yell, and there is a slight flicker in Niklas' eyes that I could have missed if I blinked.

"He needs to die, Suki." The gun is still pointed at his head.

I am on my feet before I realize it. "No!"

"What the fuck do you mean?! He deserves to die!" The safety of the gun clicks.

"He deserves to suffer and only when his flesh has bled enough will he deserve to die. And his death is mine," my voice echoes through the cold room and silence falls upon us. Niklas' eyes glisten with victory and a grin paints his lips as he lowers the gun and clicks back the safety.

Confident, arrogant bastard. This was his plan all along. To push me.

"Table or cross?" The calm, warm, rough voice of the monster before me fills the sterile room. I look to the right at the metal table, then to the left at the St. Andrews cross, weighing in my options.

"Cross."

Ten minutes, this is all the time it took for him to secure Adrien on the cross, but not before we stripped him, his naked body stretched hard against the metal. Niklas places a metal tub on the floor, pretty much between his legs and I wonder if it is there to contain the spilled blood. He steps back and I am too mesmerized by the view in front of me to look back and see where he went. Something is happening, not in the room, but within me. Something strange. Sweet. Beautiful. Something breaks. The demons howl in excitement and delicious shivers take over my flesh, filling me with a macabre anticipation.

There is a knot in my chest, a knot that has been there for years, one that is loosening up and I feel charged, my back straighter, my shoulders pulled back, my cheeks flushed, and my lips twitch—just on cue, Adrien opens his eyes. I smile.

His lids heavy, they slowly lift, uncovering his brown irises and I can taste the various stages his mind is going through. His eyes squint—confusion; his brows furrow—annoyance; his limbs twitch—anger; his eyes go wide—realization.

I am here, in this room with my nightmare, in this room with what will be my second victim, yet a rapture has taken over me, a beautiful, delightful haze. He starts talking, but I cannot hear him, his expression goes wild, a mix of fear and anger, his tone grows louder. He is shouting now, music to my fucking ears, slithers of fear run down my spine, but it is not my fear. My smile grows bigger and through the song playing in my head, I hear explicit lyrics he is singing and the knot in my chest unravels. And I laugh, tears running down my face as I finally understand what is happening to me.

My mother saw the demons in my eyes my whole life, she knew who I truly was and who I pretended to be and in that brief moment before her soul left her body, I saw it in her eyes—pride. And it disgusted me, because it meant that I was like her. Yet I could not deny it, that decadent pleasure I felt when the blade sliced her flesh, that morbidly satisfying feeling as her blood was pooling at her feet and in that moment, I could feel something. Something I rejected the second it exploded inside of me—an awakening.

I screamed, I bellowed, I cried. Cried for days because I unleashed the demons that lurked in my mind my whole life. That gnawing feeling that I was not who I was supposed to be. I unleashed them and I had to put them back, but how could I, how could I when I knew that by acknowledging them, acknowledging the pleasure her blood gave me, meant that I could never go back. Ever. Yet I sealed that awakening inside me, like a boulder sitting on my chest my whole life. I tied it up, knotting it so tightly because I knew I could never allow myself to be like her, like my mother. I could not lose myself to my unorthodox cravings. I was normal, I was going to live a normal life, have a normal job, a normal boyfriend. I was normal. I repeated that to myself like a mantra for years, until it felt real. And for a second there, maybe it was.

But I was wrong, I am *not* normal.

And I am also, most definitely *not* like my mother.

However, I fear that I am worse. She did what she did her whole life because she was mentally ill. I, however, I am about to finally embrace this awakening because it gives me pleasure. A morbid, sweet pleasure amplified by satisfying vengeance.

The song ends, my smile fades into a subtle grin and I know for a fact—I am ready. No more hiding who I am. No more pretending. No more torturing myself. Especially not here, where I can unleash the demons, not around Niklas. I turn my head around, enough to see him leaning against the far wall, his strong arms crossed in front of his chest, tattoos glistening in the soft, dim light, and he is grinning at me. A knowing grin, a victorious one. This is what he wanted all along, my awakening. He can see it now and I do not know what I appreciate more; the fact that he continuously pushed me to get here or that he gave me this gift, Adrien, for me to unleash it upon.

I return his grin and bring my attention back to Adrien. I have been quiet for a long time. During his angry, fear-filled song, I smiled, I laughed, I cried, and from the outside I probably looked like a crazy person. Inside... well, inside it felt positively insane, deliciously so.

"You stupid fucking bitch, what do you think you will do now? Take revenge? Kill me? Go ahead! Kill me then." He has a disturbing grin on his face, one laced with fear and challenge.

I cock my head and watch his naked body, studying from head to toe. He is not a bad looking man. Tall, pretty nicely built, more of a swimmer's body, really, fairly large cock dangling limp between his spread legs. There was a time when I was attracted to him, but now I loathe him. And in this moment, I am thankful because he is my gift and I cannot wait to unwrap him, one strip of flesh at a time.

"Kill me! It doesn't change the fact that I broke you. I ruined you and even after you kill me, I will stay imprinted in your mind, between your fucking legs in that tight cunt of yours, and on your flesh. The memory of me will stay with you." He looks towards my branded thigh and gives me his signature disgusting smile that used to make me cower in anticipation for what was to come, yet it does not affect me anymore, so I return the smile and his falters.

"Then, how about we make this memory better." I smile and take a couple of steps forward. He is challenging me to kill him, because he knows he would not be able to withstand the torture he put me through, or the others before me. I see a slight shiver in his body and he spits at my feet.

"It's already better," I laugh at the fear emanating from him. I laugh at the fact that he has only known me as a scared, broken woman. I laugh at the satisfying thought that he is not aware of what secret my past holds and we are about to discover together what else I am capable of.

"I will not kill you, Adrien, not yet." I turn around and head to the table that holds a few interesting instruments. There aren't many, Niklas tends to be a simple man when it comes to his tools because his imagination prevails. He enjoys the manual labor and I could not agree more with him in this particular moment. He stands a couple of feet behind the table, still leaning against the wall and he does not interrupt me. Just watches me intently. I pick up each instrument, one by one, turning them over on both sides, analyzing them, seeking inspiration. I see three saws of assorted sizes and inspiration hits me and my smile goes wide. I made a vow to myself on the porch of this house with Niklas kneeling at my feet. I made a vow and I intend to keep it.

There are more on the table: a few knives, small, large, serrated, some quite dainty, lighter fluid, a lighter, pliers, forceps, gags, and a long, narrow piece of fabric. I smile, pick it up and hand it to Niklas.

"Would you mind?"

He does not respond, just keeps that sexy devious grin on his lips as he pushes away from the wall and takes the fabric from me. I would have done it myself, but I am short and Niklas can reach better.

"Mouth open, please. I want to hear him scream, but I would prefer him not spitting on me." He nods as he obliges.

I hear Adrien shouting at Niklas in the background, but I do not listen to what he has to say. I pick some instruments and put them on a large metal tray sitting on the table. I carry it with me and walk slowly towards the St. Andrews cross, and as he catches the glistening shine of the instruments I have laid out for him, he almost pisses himself. Drips fall into the metal tub beneath his feet and now I understand its purpose. People shit themselves when fear takes over, people shit themselves when they die as well.

There is practicality in murder and it makes me laugh.

I lay the tray down next to the cross and I wonder how fast I want to finish this. I feel like I did the first time I had sex. I just wanted to get it over with and move on to the next time, when I would actually get to enjoy myself without the stinging pain, yet I had that romantic notion that I needed to make it last and enjoy it. I did not enjoy it and it did not last either. Maybe this can. I lift my eyes to Adrien, my head cocked to the side, and I feel a surge of pleasure wreaking havoc through my body, reaching my lips through a smile. Must be a devious one, because Adrien's eyes go wide, a tremor in his lids.

I pick up one of the knives from the tray and turn it around in my hand. I have seen this before, a flaying knife. As I step towards him splayed open for me on the cross, I see his body twitch and somewhere in the distance I hear muffled sounds, screams, I do not know what they are, too far away for me to understand and my demons sing the closer the shiny blade gets to his flesh. I touch it to the front of his thigh, close to his hip, pressing slowly until I see drops of blood flowing. I drag the blade down his thigh and the resistance the skin opposes silently cheers me on. I reach right above his knee and he must acknowledge that if he moves too much I will cut too deep because I can see the strain of his muscles as he forces himself to keep still. As I remove the blade, I watch the strands of blood dripping slowly down his leg, painting the plastic sheet beneath us in drops of crimson.

Beautiful.

I bring the knife to the middle of the thigh, towards the inside and press it in, dragging it horizontally, painting a pretty cross on his olive skin. When I take the blade out I look up at him and he's drooling around his restrained lips, his eyes slightly wet and a murderous look in them.

"I know, I know, I could move quicker. I promise, I will begin in a minute." Goosebumps fill his flesh as he weighs in my words. "I'm just reminding myself how it feels when the flesh splits open under the blade, testing to see how deep I can go without killing you too fast."

His head moves in a frenzy, spouting muffled bullshit at

me, but I am gone already, focused on my exploration. The thin blade travels to the inside of the bicep, on the pale, thin flesh that starts on the armpit and goes up towards the elbow. Different type of skin, different sensation, right?

His whole arm tenses up instantly, the muscles contracting one by one, his flesh twitching. I sink the blade into the thin skin, dragging it towards his elbow as I watch in fascination how the skin splits like a tight seam, revealing yellow fat and deep pink muscles.

Delightful...

NIKLAS

She's not *on* fire, she *is* fire.

The look in her eyes, the hunger, the rapture, it's as disturbing as it is beautiful. Yet somehow, beautiful doesn't cover it. There's a surge of animalistic, ravenous power emanating from her. This is how I imagine the great renaissance painters looked when inspiration struck and they picked up the paintbrush. Only Suki's paintbrush is a flaying knife, her canvas is flesh, and her paint is crimson.

Beautiful vivid crimson.

I can't wait to see her masterpiece. Observe that beautiful mind of hers as it breaks open and reveals itself to me.

I take a seat on the chair she occupied minutes before, and I can't help but wonder how easy her transition has been. When she left me, she quite literally ran from this, from herself, from me. Something must have happened while she was away, something inside of her must have cracked because she looks so incredibly eager to sink that little knife into that motherfucker's flesh.

I'm not complaining, it's a beautiful surprise. A

pleasant one.

She's taking her time and the more I watch her small hand wrapped around the handle of the knife, the more I want to bury it into her pussy. I definitely did not get to play with her enough. There are so many more things that I can do to her. So many ways I can break her body. I can just see it, strapped on that St. Andrews cross, naked, spread eagle for me, her pussy dripping on her inner thighs, her skin flushed, her nipples hard with anticipation. So many games left to play.

I catch her seductive gaze focused on me, and I have to shift my legs to make more room for the semi growing between them, as all those thoughts pass through my head.

She's mine. Forever.

She turns her attention back to that sack of shit hanging on that cold metal cross and she meticulously runs the knife on his untouched thigh, drawing what could be a rectangle if it wasn't missing the bottom line. I'm confused at first, but when she slides the blade under the cut at the top I understand. It's a little doorway, a painful one revealing Adrien's thigh muscle as she flays the skin and fat away from it. He's screaming against the piece of fabric covering his gaping mouth, bellowing and crying and it's fucking music to my ears. When she finishes, that rectangle of skin just hangs there, like a thick piece of fabric that hasn't been cut completely, and Suki looks so fucking proud of herself. Giddy as she claps her hands and jumps a few times in excitement. I can't help but smile and wait patiently for her masterpiece to take shape. At this point, I realize that I don't actually know what to expect from her. She's already surprised me. I thought she would stab him a few times... maybe torture him a little bit, yet as she flays a third piece of skin, much bigger this time, in the center of his chest almost from nipple to nipple, I realize that this is most definitely not what I expected.

She's ruthless, in a trance, completely oblivious to the excruciating screams coming from Adrien, and I wonder if she can even hear them. From time to time, I swear I can see her sway, like she hears music in her ears. She understands... fear sings to her as well and her demons dance to the notes painted in blood. She's more like me than even I expected and the monster inside of me roars his triumph. Adrien's body looks like something pulled out of a cannibalistic ritual, covered in blood that now pools in the metal tub beneath him. Suki didn't stop her torture even when he was pissing himself from pain. She is absolutely relentless.

He's starting to lose consciousness from the pain and Suki looks a tad annoyed with that, so I give her a hand. Even though I was not expecting anything quite like this, I still prepared. She slaps him a few times to bring him back, and his eyes grow wide as he sees me walking towards him with a syringe in my hand. Half is enough to pump enough adrenaline in order for him to stay awake through the next round.

Yet when I am done and sit down again, watching where Suki is aiming her knife, I realize I might have been wrong. I've seen this done to animals before. She splits the skin of his ball sack and quite literally castrates him, cutting his testicles out. I can't lie, that was hard to watch, and no matter how many inventive methods of torture I have applied to my victims in the past, this one makes even me cross my legs. She shoves them in his mouth, before she covers it back up with the fabric, gagging him with his own balls. This is retribution, payback for the violation of her own body.

The drugs pumping through his system are keeping him fully aware and awake, gagging on every slice of torture splitting his body open. My fingers are twitching to hold a knife and sink it into his foul flesh, but this is not my show. It's Suki's. And what a show it is indeed.

What happens next has me on my feet in an instant, the syringes heavy in my pocket. She makes a cut on his chest, through flesh, through muscle, pushes through his cries, through his pleading wails and exposes part of his ribcage. She takes a second to admire the beautiful anatomy of the human body, and with the saw in hand she proceeds to cut the cartilage that connects the ribs to the sternum. It takes her a while, but she takes her time, slow delicate movements cutting deeper and deeper into his bone, eventually revealing that beautiful muscle that pumps blood at a dangerous speed through his body.

She turns her beautiful face to me and smiles.

"Thank you," her sweet voice sneaks through the wails of the man strapped before her. I return her smile, and with a calm look in her eyes she grabs the lighter fluid, soaking his beating heart with it before she grabs the lighter.

Adrien watches in horror, his eyes bulging, painted red with burst veins from the strain and before any of us have time to take it all in, she slides her small hand inside his chest cavity, wraps it carefully around his heart and pulls it out gently, close enough to his body that it's still attached to the major blood vessels, but far enough that Adrien stops yelling at the sight of it. Shock and disbelief paint his features. Even my breathing is heavier at the sight with anticipation.

I'm close to them now, standing only three feet away on Suki's side and the view of Adrien's heart pumping in her small hand is mesmerizing. They look into each other's eyes, and I can almost see the strands of life leaving him and a strange peace entering her as her thumb flicks the lighter. It all happens in a split second. The flame touches the beating heart and before they touch Suki's hand, she drops it, the burning heart ripping itself from the veins that tie it to his body, blood gushing everywhere, painting all of us in crimson.

It's beautiful, fucking beautiful and morbidly poetic how life still inhabits him, even as his heart burns in the tub filled with his blood and piss, which slowly extinguishes it. His eyes lose their light and after a few seconds, pure silence fills the room.

An eerie silence.

I turn my gaze to her and what I see in her eyes fills me with hope.

Freedom.

SUKI

It is over. Truly over.

As I look at his limp, lifeless, butchered body strapped to the metal cross, I cannot help but be thankful, as disturbing as that sounds. The moment he found me online set off a chain of events that brought me to this place, brought me true freedom to indulge, not only in my filthy desires, but in my bloody ones as well. A chain of events that brought me back to the man that became my monster all those years ago.

I turn to Niklas and his greedy eyes on me unleash a storm inside my body. A split second is all it takes for me to jump into his arms, wrap my legs around his waist, my hands fisting in his dirty blond hair stained with the blood of our enemy, my lips crashing on his with a force that threatens to bruise us both.

We kiss for what feels like hours, my lips sore from the harshness of his beard and when I break away and breathe in the air he breaths out, sinking into the dark ocean of his eyes, I finally understand what this feeling truly is. I feel alive. For the first time in an awfully long time, if not ever, I feel truly and utterly alive. In movies, this moment right here would be the conclusion at the end of it. The resolution. For me though, this feels like the beginning. This is the moment of rebirth, of acceptance. The start of an unholy union, a decadent destruction of everything that held us back.

"You are mine, Miss Knoxx." Niklas breaks the silence. "You belong to me forever, and I will imprint on your heart, like a branding iron burning myself in it, and it will be the end of you. There will be no running anymore." The intensity of his gaze imprints on my soul, sending shivers through my spine.

"You demand my body, you demand my soul, you demand my heart. That hardly seems fair, Mr. Bergman. I will carry you forever, burnished on my heart while you walk free."

"Free? That's where you are mistaken, little siren. You failed miserably. Failed to see how you crawled into my soul the day your broken gaze found mine on the floor of my house. Your demons grabbed me by the throat, demanded my devotion and I fought it... oh, how I fought it thinking it's not my nature." He squeezes my body tight and I sink into the way it feels. "I was yours long before you became mine, you just failed to see it."

I did fail to see it. More than that, I rejected it, blinded by the haze that made me believe that even my instincts were playing tricks on me.

Not anymore.

My bloody fingers leave strokes of crimson on his cheeks as my hands cup his face and I know... he is already imprinted on my heart, already burnished in it so deeply that the scars healed over it, making him part of me. I am home, finally home.

"You are mine," I whisper. "Until the day we die, you are mine and I am yours."

"Even in death, Suki."
I smile.
"Even in death."
My kind of monster...

Epilogue

NIKLAS

J found something. Falbridge, Nevada. I can't guarantee it, but there is a trace in the route of the IP."

"Please, Nik, don't explain it. You know that tech jargon bores the fuck out of me." Connor rubs his temple as he takes in my words. He's stressed, this situation is getting to him, but at the same time, I can see there's something else clouding his mind.

"So how's it going with... her?" He exhales, a heavy breath filling the silence of my office as he takes a seat on the sofa, elbows resting on his thighs, his hands rubbing together.

"I don't know." He looks at me and his hollow eyes hold a

darkness I've never seen in them before.

"There's no progress?"

"None... the hit she took to her head was bad. Really bad. She's obviously okay physically, thank fuck, but her mind... She still can't remember her name, Nik, her fucking name. I look at her some days and I don't know how to start a conversation because all I can think about is... I don't know the most basic thing about her and I have no fucking clue how to help."

"She still refuses to go to that psychologist?"

"Yeah. She went... what, three times maybe? She said they mostly spoke about her trauma, about what Adrien put her through and she just stopped going. Refused to after that. It's strange, she is starting to remember irrelevant stuff, like foods she doesn't like or the ones she loves, smells, she remembered how she broke her arm as a kid. Shit like that."

"That's something. That means her mind is not completely broken then."

"No..." he trails off, and his eyes travel somewhere else. There's something there, something going on with him and I don't know whether it's about him or the woman he rescued from Adrien the day we stormed his place and brought him as a gift for Suki. The woman was broken, bloody, tortured, and raped, tied up in his cellar—the dungeon—and it took everything in me not kill the motherfucker then and there. Unfortunately, before we were able to get to Adrien, he managed to hurt this woman, smacked her head so hard against the stone wall that she went into a three-day coma. When she woke up, she had no idea who she was.

We tried so fucking hard to trace her, yet somehow even the skills I have online weren't successful. I found her and Adrien's conversations online, found her IP and whatever details they held; however, that was it. It was a dead end then and there, and it fucking baffled me. They led nowhere, only phantom pings on various servers across the web. All intentional.

All three of us, Connor, Suki and I, have been on a mission for over a month to find out more about her. This is the first lead I got—Falbridge—potentially the most remote place in Nevada, less than 100 people live there, and so many other remote residences spread around the wilderness.

There's something about this woman though, something Suki noticed first, a strange vibe, and through her broken memory, we're not sure she understands or is aware of it. Connor might be though, if the look he carries in his eyes right now is anything to go on.

"So, how are the two of you getting along then?" I ask him, and his black bushy eyebrows scrunch together.

"Just fine. Peachy."

I can't help the grin that lifts the corner of my lips. Connor refused to let her go, not that she has anywhere to go. He feels guilty for her, guilty that he didn't manage to get Adrien before he smashed her head against that wall. Either way, the woman doesn't remember who she is or where she came from, she can't function on her own, doesn't quite know if she has any skills. She has nowhere to go, so Connor kept her in his house.

Going on his current reaction, I could say that he's regretting his decision, but I see the way he looks at her, the way his eyes follow her around the room even when he's talking to someone else, the way he tenses when she's not around and how he breaths easier when she comes back.

I would bet my money on this, Connor found his match in a woman without a name.

"Hey, guys?" A soft knock sounds on the door before it cracks open and Suki's beautiful face pops through.

Some days I still can't believe I wake up next to her in my bed, in my house, in my world. This beautiful creature that ran into my fucking lap. My little siren, my little monster, the one that cracked me open, broke me apart, and took the pieces for herself.

"Yes, Suki," I reply, and I can't help the smile that I feel in my eyes before it falls on my lips.

"Lunch is ready." She smiles and suddenly I wish we would be alone.

"Thank you, sweetcheeks." Connor gives her his devious smile that make women melt at his fucking feet.

I still feel the need to punch him in the gut when he calls my woman that, but her fucking face lights up with amusement every time and I can't take it away from her. She's been through more than most people can endure in a fucking lifetime, and she deserves every single bit of happiness she can get.

We all sit down at the dining table, Suki next to me with Connor and the nameless woman across from us. She's doing better, I can see it, even completely clueless about who she is, she smiles, laughs, jokes around... she's more relaxed than most people would be in her situation. Maybe too relaxed.

We go through two courses of food cooked by Suki and her, and by the time we reach dessert, we're all too full and start drinking instead.

"We got a lead." I look at both of them.

A subtle twitch ripples through her muscles. She's a beautiful woman, tall—about five-foot-seven, strong to the point that she looks like she enjoyed the gym at least three to four times a week. She has curly black hair and her eyes are probably her most distinguishable feature, a blueish light gray with a dark thick ring around them. She and Connor fit together with their black hair, yet their eyes are complete contrasts in color... not in feel though. They both seem to have darkness lurking deep beneath the surface.

"What? Where?!" She places her glass on the table a bit too hard.

"Falbridge, Nevada," Connor takes over. "We're going to go there, see if we can find something, if we can jog your memory." She looks at him, an uneasy look in her eyes, and Suki and I exchange subtle glances. One would jump in ecstasy in this situation, yet she looks weary of what she could find there.

"Thank you." She smiles at Connor and suddenly I feel like a third wheel. Yet as I gaze at Suki, I realize she feels like the fourth one. She gives me a knowing cheeky grin, and I know that, yet again, her and I have mirroring thoughts. "So, Suki, did you sell your apartment? Is it all done now?" She turns her attention to the gorgeous woman sitting beside me.

"It is, yes. Signed the contract last week and I thought it would be strange, but somehow... I felt relief. Breaking all ties with that place, that city, felt good." Connor is still unaware of the extents of her past, of what her mother did to her... or vice versa. He is unaware of what Suki did to Adrien, for that matter, and it will stay that way. All he knows is that Adrien got what he deserved and that was enough information for him.

By the time evening comes, we are all spent, the alcohol is almost finished, and Connor decides it's time for the two of them to retire.

"Thanks for coming." Suki hugs both of them as they're about to go out the door. "It was a great birthday... it's been a long time since I got to celebrate with anyone." She gives her small innocent smile and all I want to do is gather her in my arms and promise her that it will never ever happen again. But this is not the time.

"We'll see you soon, okay?" Connor smiles, and they both walk out the door. We watch the headlights of the truck disappear down the dark mountain road.

"I wonder how long until they start fucking their brains out." Suki asks as she heads to the dining table, cleaning up our mess.

I can't help but laugh as I watch her sweet, domesticated ass clean up after a dinner party we hosted. Perfectly fucking ordinary. Yet we both know that this is a contrast to most of our favorite activities. Two weeks ago, after we finished sorting out and packing up her old apartment, we killed a man. Together. Like a celebration. Then we got rid of him in the Black Hills. I revel in this. Seeing the transformation, the way her eyes brighten up more and more every single day... she's happy. And I with her.

"Not sure." I finally reply as I help her carry plates to the kitchen. "Wouldn't be surprised if they have started already."

"Seriously?!" She smirks. "You could cut the pent-up sexual tension with a knife. No way they have already done it, and I could bet that Connor is the one with the high moral compass." She laughs as she rinses all the dishes and slides them in the dishwasher.

"Yeah, I think you're right with that," I agree.

"Can you please go to the bedroom and bring me your hoodie? The brown one please? Should be in the wardrobe," she asks as she finishes up the perfectly mundane task.

Almost ten minutes later, I'm still searching our bedroom for this goddamn hoodie, yet it's nowhere to be found. I open the door to the terrace to check the lounge chairs. Nothing. Yet the smell of the looming spring hits my nostrils and I linger for a few more seconds. It's a mild night, the moon high on the starry sky and the snow is melting, the crowns of the trees, the green of the pines, visible now.

I'm just about to go in when the night fills with the sirens song.

Her sharp screams invade my senses and I can feel them on my tongue. There's no fear in them anymore, only challenge and anticipation. My dick springs to fucking attention. Months ago fear was my ecstasy, now... Suki is.

I run through the house and out the door and as a second scream echoes through the forest, I follow it and run.

I run for my fucking siren, and she better wish she is fast enough.

SUKI

I do not know what got into me. Maybe the looks Niklas kept giving me today, maybe the fact that with company around I could not do what I craved every single time he gave me his sinful grin, but all of a sudden that primordial need overtook me.

I needed my monster. I needed the chase, the anticipation, the feel of danger on my heels. I needed the hunt.

I run through the forest, the snow thin and easy to navigate, yet I know I am still leaving a trail through it, far too easy for Niklas to follow. I push myself harder, jumping over the dips and mounds of the uneven terrain, struggling to find the right path through the dark, eerie forest. I stumble several times, yet the chase fills my soul with a delicious sense of dread.

I do not fear Niklas anymore, not even close, yet the fact that I ran out into the night, ran away from him, fills me with enough anticipation. I know he thrives on this, on the hunt, and he is not the only thing chasing me right now, his demons and the monster are eager to get their greedy hands on me. All bets are off and my own demons howl.

Niklas threatened me... there are games still left to play, and I have a feeling the rest of our life is not enough for all he has in store for me.

My calves burn, my feet start hurting, and each cold breath starts to feel like barbed wire on my lungs. Yet I push, each step is another rush of adrenaline through my veins and my core tightens with need. There's a surge of anticipation wreaking havoc through my body, starting from my pussy and spreading like wildfire until it reaches my skin, bursting into goosebumps that feel electrified.

And I scream again, unable to contain the rush.

I feel him on my heels before I can even hear him. His eyes on the back of my neck spread a heat through me, fire on my damp skin and I smile. Oh, how I fucking smile. Before I can revel in this feeling, my foot catches on something and I stumble forwards, but a strong arm catches my waist, before I hit the cold forest floor. I yelp and try to break free, my hands grabbing anything in sight, but he flips me over before I get any traction. My back slams on the rough ground and before I can make sense of his intentions, he crashes over me, his teeth sinking into the nape of my neck and a rush of pain spreads fast through my body. My pain-filled scream morphs when he forces his hand into my jeans and two thick fingers rip through my pussy sinking so goddamn deep, ecstasy mixing with the pain in my neck.

I thought I knew enough to be blissfully unafraid of him; however, the moment he releases my neck, pulls his hand from my core, and rips my jeans in half, my soul trembles. Involuntarily, I scramble backwards, but he is here, straddling my thighs, his thick erection straining against his jeans and a second later the t-shirt I am wearing turns into scraps of fabric hanging around my naked body.

He grabs my throat, squeezing the sides, my lungs fighting for air, and his lips crash down on mine. This is not a kiss, this a possessive storm wreaking havoc on me, yet it ends too soon. He shifts, bracing himself on one hand, his thighs nudging my legs and sliding under, spreading me open for him. His eyes bore into mine, and I am suddenly still, the hunger in his seeping out through heaving breaths.

"Touch yourself, little siren. Sink those fingers in your tight cunt until you feel it twitch around them." His words vibrate through me, and I know my pussy is twitching already. I do as I am told, dragging it out, circling my hard nipples first, slowly dragging my fingers between my breasts, down my belly, around my belly button, and I know, even though his eyes do not move from mine, he can see what I am doing. The hunger in his eyes turns feral and I know I am playing with that fire.

And goddamn it, how badly I want to burn.

I sink two fingers between my wet folds and my back arches, a strained breath catches in my throat, against his constricting hand. My eyes close involuntarily as I fuck myself with my own fingers, and I can feel his cock pulsing against the back of my hand, behind the thick fabric of his jeans.

"Don't fucking close your eyes, little siren. Look at me!" he spits out that order, and when I do as told, pure fire rips through me. He forces me to hold his gaze as I slam my fingers harder and faster into my pussy and it all feels so much more intense. I do not even realize he released my throat until I catch him licking his lips before he gives me a menacing grin.

"Fingers out."

I cry out in protest, but do as I'm told.

"Show them to me."

In an instant my fingers are in his mouth and his are buried so deep inside my pussy, I swear he reached the end of me. I scream at the delicious intrusion, but he does not give me time to breathe. He starts finger fucking me, so hard and fast, pain and pleasure mixing together, forcefully ripping out of me an orgasm that makes my throat raw from screaming. He drags out every last bit of pleasure and I am heaving so hard, the cold of the snow beneath me doing wonders to my hot, damp body.

He flips me over, my front slamming on the forest floor before he lifts my ass up with one arm. He slips one finger in my drenched pussy, swirling it around, and I almost want to move away from him, the intrusion too much on my sensitive flesh. He pulls it out, and my eyes go wide instantly when he wets the puckered entrance of my ass with it. My nipples harden against the melting snow beneath me and when that finger pushes against me, slipping into my ass at the same time his impossibly thick cock rips through my pussy, I am convinced I am being split in half.

He is not waiting for me to adjust to the intrusions, he does not take it slow, he fucks me like he hates me, slamming his cock inside of me so hard I have to brace myself against a tree root. He forces a second thick finger inside my tight ass, and I cannot help but scream, yet the pleasure it brings is so much more than the pain, and the fullness of it is making my eyes roll. He grabs my hair and pulls my head back so hard my skull hurts and the sound of our damp skins slapping against each other fill the quiet forest, mixing with my screams and his ragged breaths. The orgasm hits me out of nowhere, ripping through me with a force that leaves my limp, shaky body at Niklas' mercy and the feel of his cock spilling inside of me feels like fire filling my core. His fingers come out of my ass, his cock pulling out of my sore pussy, and before my body falls on the forest floor, he shifts me, turns me, and pulls me against him.

I am straddling his thighs as he sits on his heels and his warm body feels like a furnace against my damp skin. I bring my legs around him and gather my arms on his chest, resting my head on the crook of his neck as he wraps me tightly in his strong arms, and we wait patiently for our sated bodies to come down from this incredible high.

I do not know how much time has passed... Seconds? Minutes? Hours? His hand wraps around the back of my neck, guiding my head to look at him, the other one gently brushing the side of my face and the hair away from it. The ocean blue eyes staring back at me are softer, the same possessiveness as always, but so calm now, satisfied.

"You're mine, Suki, do you understand?" His words are soft, yet possessive. "Your mind, your soul, and your fucking heart are all mine, little siren, and nothing and no one will hurt you ever again."

I feel the truth in his words, they seep into my soul, burning their way into my heart, and I know love is not a strong enough word for what was bred between us. Love does not do us justice. We would kill for each other, burn for each other, die for each other, and we would follow each other anywhere. Even in hell, because being apart is not an option anymore.

I watch him reach into a pocket of his discarded jeans, clueless about when he managed to take them off, and he pulls out a small wooden box, most definitely made by him. Before I can look to see what he carved into the wood, he flips the lid open and my heart stops.

I look at him in disbelief, then back at the yellow gold filigree band holding an emerald cut blood red ruby. I would cry if I was not so utterly shocked.

I turn my gaze back to him, and the smile painted on his gorgeous face breaks me. I smile back, unable to hold in the overwhelming happiness bursting inside of me, and I know one thing for sure...

Even death will not be the end of us.

* * *

Thank you for reading Niklas and Suki's story.
Continue the dive into Lilith's world with **Dangerous Strokes, a dark mafia romance where a black market deal brings two people in a world of passion and danger.**

scan the QR code

ACKNOWLEDGEMENTS

Too many people come in mind as I write these words, however it would be unfair to begin with anyone but *my husband*. My sweet man, the only person that has told me for months that he will most definitely not read this book, scared of what he would find out about me. Then, just as I finished writing these acknowledgements, including two quite funny jokes that I now had to delete, he proceeded to announce that he will indeed be reading it. Well... husband, I love you, don't leave me after reading this.

To the *Bookstagram community*, the gorgeous people that made this journey so amazing... I know how to navigate this world because of you. I love you all.

To *Duchess*, you were the first... you hype me up like no one else, you push me, encourage me and constantly remind me to stop giving a fuck, but most of all, you understand me. You'll cringe when you'll see your name here, because you don't do sweet, and that makes me smile. Messing with you will never get old. I adore you.

To *Vani* and *Alex*, you two have been amazing, putting up with me through the various stages I've gone through in this book publishing journey, all the indecisions and confusion. Thank you!

To *K Webster*, *Charity B*, *V Domino*, *Ami Van* and *Runyx*... I had this preconceived notion that the popular, successful authors are well out of reach, like movie stars, you can never truly connect with them outside of their work. I was wrong. Not only did I exasperate you with dozens of questions about how to do this author thing and you answered every single time, but we went further than that and actually connected beyond writing. This book, this experience, these past few months... I can't imagine how it would have been without you. Thank you!

To *Kenzie*, the one I'm proud to call my Editor. You are amazing! I am so thankful to have met you and so happy I chose you. I've never had any other editors before you yet I am convinced you are one of the best. Not just because of your skills, but because of how funny, helpful and amazing you are. Thank you!

And *Amy*, my soulmate. One day I will come to the other side of the world and thank you properly for your friendship and support, for putting up with me and my rants, for making me laugh with your perverted humor that matches mine, for being there for me every single day since I joined this community. I adore you, I really do!

And to *you*, the one that gave this book a chance... Thank you.

Love,
Lilith

ABOUT THE AUTHOR

Lilith Roman is a romance author who lives with her husband and fluffy bear-dog in the UK, where she writes stories laced with a little danger, intense passion, and dark themes, always ending in a Happily Ever After.

She's an introvert with an addiction for pretty hardbacks she never reads. A lover of anything with chocolate, cursing, and steamy books. And her love for horror movies convinced her without a shadow of a doubt that... even the monster under the bed needs a love story.

For exclusive insights, join her Newsletter, or
Lilith Roman's Corrupted Souls Facebook group.

scan the QR code

ALSO BY THE AUTHOR